UP CLOSE AND PERSONAL

Carla Cassidy

A SIGNET ECLIPSE BOOK

SIGNET ECLIPSE
Published by New American Library, a division of
Penguin Group (USA) Inc., 375 Hudson Street,
New York, New York 10014, USA
Penguin Group (Canada), 90 Eglinton Avenue East, Suite 700, Toronto,
Ontario M4P 2Y3, Canada (a division of Pearson Penguin Canada Inc.)
Penguin Books Ltd., 80 Strand, London WC2R 0RL, England
Penguin Ireland, 25 St. Stephen's Green, Dublin 2,
Ireland (a division of Penguin Books Ltd.)
Penguin Group (Australia), 250 Camberwell Road, Camberwell, Victoria 3124,
Australia (a division of Pearson Australia Group Pty. Ltd.)
Penguin Books India Pvt. Ltd., 11 Community Centre, Panchsheel Park,
New Delhi - 110 017, India
Penguin Group (NZ), 67 Apollo Drive, Rosedale, North Shore 0632,
New Zealand (a division of Pearson New Zealand Ltd.)
Penguin Books (South Africa) (Pty.) Ltd., 24 Sturdee Avenue,
Rosebank, Johannesburg 2196, South Africa

Penguin Books Ltd., Registered Offices:
80 Strand, London WC2R 0RL, England

First published by Signet Eclipse, an imprint of New American Library,
a division of Penguin Group (USA) Inc.

First Printing, October 2009
10 9 8 7 6 5 4 3 2 1

Printed in the United States of America

Acknowledgments

I've never written an acknowledgment page before, but feel compelled to do so with this particular book. First and foremost I'd like to thank retired sergeant Cheryl Rabin from the Kansas City, Missouri, Police Department. Cheryl answered dozens of questions about the workings of a homicide case and the police department. Of course, as a fiction writer I have taken much of what she said and twisted it to serve my creative purpose, so all mistakes in this respect are my own.

Second, I'd like to thank my seven-year-old granddaughter, Carlee, who wanted me to write a book about cheerleaders. Carlee, I'm sure this isn't exactly what you had in mind, but thanks for planting a germ of an idea in my head.

To John and Marie Cook, great fans and greater parents. A special thanks to you for all the hours you spend reading my works in progress, brainstorming new ideas, and promoting me wherever you go.

Finally, a special thanks to my husband, Frank, who never complains about fast food and crummy dinners when I'm under deadline. I find it amazing that after all these years you're still my favorite hero.

Chapter 1

"What do you mean, she can't come this weekend?" Jordan Sampson pressed her cell phone more tightly against her ear as she walked out of the downtown Kansas City municipal courthouse. "I was just on my way to pick her up."

"She doesn't want to come," Dane replied in his irritatingly cool, calm voice.

"Why not?" Jordan's heels clicked against the concrete of the sidewalk in time with the racing beat of her heart as she headed for her car in a nearby parking lot. Autumn leaves skittered out of her path as if afraid of being crushed beneath her fast-moving feet.

"There's a birthday party tomorrow evening at the skating rink. Mandy doesn't want to miss it."

"She doesn't have to. I can take her," Jordan protested.

"She doesn't want you to take her. She wants me to. Face it, Jordan: Mandy is twelve years old and you need to think about her needs instead of your own." Her ex-husband's voice sounded like nails on a chalkboard to Jordan, especially when he criticized her parenting skills.

Tears burned Jordan's eyes as she reached her car and hit the button to unlock it. "If I weren't a homicide cop, I'd seriously consider putting a hit out on you, Dane." She disconnected, jerked open her car door and threw the cell phone onto the passenger seat.

She dived into the car and started the engine, then dropped her forehead to the steering wheel as she fought back tears. Damn him. She knew he was slowly poisoning their daughter against her. Mandy and she had been so close before the divorce, but now their relationship was strained at best. Mandy was growing more and more distant with her.

Jordan knew her first mistake had been marrying Dane, but the biggest mistake had been trusting him through their divorce. He'd blindsided her and managed to gain custody of Mandy, giving Jordan only weekend visitation, and lately she wasn't seeing her daughter even then.

As the vents began to blow warm air, she raised her head and drew a deep breath to calm herself. She would call Mandy later this evening and see whether she could change her mind about the weekend. In the meantime, she'd see whether Della was around to do a little guy bashing and general cheer-up work.

She grabbed her cell and punched the number two on her speed dial. The line rang once, then was picked up by an answering machine. "You've reached Designs by Della. Great designs that will blow your mind. Leave a message."

"Della, I've had a shitty day and I'm heading for Iggy's. If you can get away, meet me there." Jordan hung up, pulled out of her parking space and headed for the bar, where she knew her fellow off-duty cops would be hanging out.

For a brief moment she wished she were driving to her parents' house, that she could sit on their blue-flowered sofa and talk to them about Dane and Mandy, about her work—her life. She could go over there; she could even sit on their sofa, but there would be little conversation. There would be nothing but the thick silence of old grief and the faint whisper of the tragedy that had changed the Walker family forever.

She would find no comfort in her parents' home, for they had lost the ability to comfort even themselves fourteen years ago when they had buried their youngest daughter. Jordan shook her head to dispel these thoughts. She couldn't think about Julie now. Jordan was already in a foul mood, and if she dwelled on thoughts of Julie, she'd go from foul to maudlin in no time.

The day had begun with great promise. She'd been looking forward to Mandy's weekend visit and had checked the movie selections, thinking it would be nice for mother and daughter to see one of the new releases.

Her good mood had continued when she'd found the pair of black Ferragamo heels she'd thought she'd lost in the move. She'd passed the morning with paperwork, which, unlike her fellow officers, she really didn't mind. Then she'd been due in court at two for what she'd thought would be a simple fifteen minutes of testimony in a murder case.

The fifteen minutes had become two grueling hours as the defense attorney had homed in on her as if she'd personally strangled and beaten young, beautiful Rebecca Sinclair, then arrested poor Parker Sinclair simply because she hadn't liked the way he dressed.

Meanwhile, the defendant, Parker Sinclair, an unusually handsome man, had stared at Jordan with a knowing smile curving his lips, as if the two of them shared a secret. It had been damned disconcerting. The news that Mandy didn't want to come to spend her weekend with Jordan was just the icing on the cake of crap she called Friday.

Within minutes she had arrived at Iggy's. As always, the parking lot was full despite the fact that it was just after five o'clock. She shut off her car and stepped out, the cool mid-October air holding a hint of woodsmoke as she headed toward the front door.

Iggy's was a cop cliché, a bar owned and operated by retired sergeant Ignatius Cortez, who had taken a bullet in the spine and now served up strong drinks and old stories from his wheelchair. His wife, a bleached blonde named Heidi, worked as head waitress.

Located five blocks from the courthouse and the downtown police station, Iggy's was a favorite place for cops to chew over cases and blow off some steam. That was exactly what Jordan needed, to blow off some steam before heading north to her rental house in the suburbs.

If you wanted elegance, you didn't come to Iggy's. As Jordan opened the door, she was greeted with a haze of thick blue smoke that appeared to rush toward the open door for a breath of fresh air. Peanut shells and bottle caps crunched underfoot as Jordan made her way toward a table in the back where she knew her coworkers would be gathered.

"There she is." Her partner, Anthony Garelli, gestured toward a tall pink drink with an umbrella floating on top. "Got one waiting for you. Figured you'd be in to lick your wounds."

"Yeah, we heard Rabinowiz ripped you a new one on the stand today." Adam Kent kicked out the chair for her with one of his massive feet.

"Don't even mention his name." Jordan scowled at the thought of the defense attorney. She plucked the umbrella from her daiquiri and took a sip, then leaned back in her chair and looked around the table.

There were four of them. She liked to refer to them as her urban family. Her partner, Anthony, was a thirty-six-year-old Italian whose flirting was legendary but harmless. His wife had divorced him three years ago and he had yet to move on.

Adam Kent was a big, burly black man who always smelled of expensive cologne and had the fashion sense of a male model. He was smart and street savvy and had recently moved his father, who was suffering from Alzheimer's, into his home with his family.

The eldest of the group was John Lindsay. His wife was dying of cancer and Jordan suspected that John had developed a drinking problem. And the youngest and newest member of the bunch was Ricky Copeland, a hotshot twenty-four-year-old, whose younger sister had committed suicide two years ago, when she'd been a senior in high school.

They were an eclectic group, each suffering from hard kicks in the ass by fate, but they shared one thing in common—they were all members of the "murder squad," an elite team of detectives whose sole job was to solve homicides in Kansas City.

For the next thirty minutes they talked about the Sinclair trial, second-guessing the prosecutor and speculating on the outcome. It wasn't a slam dunk. The case against Parker Sinclair was strictly circumstantial.

The marriage was troubled. There had been two previous reports of domestic disturbances and Parker Sinclair's whereabouts at the time of his wife's murder hadn't been fully established. Still, there had been no physical evidence left at the scene to tie him to the murder.

"It's in the jury's hands now," Adam said. "I hear they're working through tonight and into the weekend."

"On another subject, I saw that Dane's latest book debuted on the *New York Times* best-seller list in the number two spot." John motioned the waitress for another drink. "Pretty impressive the way he manages to get into devious criminal minds."

Jordan bit her lip. What she wanted to say was that it takes one to know one, but she'd promised herself at the time of their divorce that she would never speak ill of Dane. Not because she cared for him, but for Mandy's sake. Unfortunately she didn't think her ex-husband adhered to the same code of honor.

What she found most impressive about Dane's latest was that he'd received a million-dollar contract two months after the divorce had been final. She suspected the offer had been on the table before the marriage ended, but he'd stalled making the deal until the time when he would legally be under no obligation to share the spoils.

Water under the bridge, she thought. He could have all the money in the world. She just wanted her daughter.

At that moment the door to Iggy's opened and Della Broadbent walked in. She beelined toward the table where Jordan and her friends were seated. As usual, several pairs of male eyes watched her as she moved with a sinuous grace across the floor.

In her bright yellow tank and slacks with a multicolored tunic swirling around her slender legs, she looked as out of place as a tigress on the monkey bars.

A husband who adored her and a career as a successful interior designer had transformed mousy, overweight Della into a sleek, self-confident powerhouse. "Hello, boys," she said in her throaty contralto. She smiled at Jordan. "Got your message and got here as quick as I could."

As the men continued their discussion of the latest murder case that had them all stymied, Della leaned closer to Jordan. "Let me guess. Dane is being an asshole."

"Mandy isn't coming over this weekend. She has a birthday party at the skating rink tomorrow night and wants her father to take her instead of me." Jordan tried to keep the surge of emotion out of her voice. "Why doesn't she want me to take her, Della?"

"You know the answer to that question. Dane is using Mandy to hurt you. There should be a law against it, but there isn't. It's a moral issue. I'm sorry about your weekend, but this means you can come tomorrow night."

Jordan grimaced. "I really don't want to go, Della."

"You have to go," Della exclaimed. "We can go together. Ben is going to be out of town for the weekend. I've already bought two tickets to attend, so it's all taken care of."

"Go where?" Adam asked.

"Our fifteen-year high school class reunion," Della replied. "We didn't have a five-year gathering and some idiot scheduled our ten-year in January and it got snowed out, so this will be the first time since graduation that we're all getting together again." Her dark eyes flashed as they gazed back at Jordan. "You know everyone is going to want to see you. As a cheerleader and homecoming queen, everyone is going to want to see if you got fat and ugly."

"Wait, you were a cheerleader?" Anthony hooted with laughter. "Oh my God, I'm partnered with a rah-rah girl."

"Not just a cheerleader, the head cheerleader," Della replied.

Anthony laughed again and Jordan threw the little umbrella from her drink at him. "What's so funny?" she demanded.

"Nothing. You've just never struck me as the cheerleader type," Anthony replied.

Jordan leaned over the table toward him. "And what exactly is the cheerleader type?"

"Stuck-up, in a clique of other stuck-up girls," Della replied with a belligerent gaze at Jordan. "Well, it's true," she exclaimed. "Cheerleaders are girls behaving badly to girls who aren't cheerleaders—mean girls who rule the world of high school." Della shrugged. "That's a fact."

"I gather you weren't a cheerleader?" Ricky asked Della.

She shook her head. "Not me. I was the school-council and French-club type."

"I once dated a French-club type," Adam said as a smile curved his lips. "She loved talking French whenever we did it, and she liked to do it a lot."

"Ha, Jordan's other claim to fame was that she didn't do it in high school. She was the proverbial ice princess," Della replied.

"Are you done now?" Jordan asked her friend.

Della grinned. "Only if you agree to come with me tomorrow night. If you don't agree, I'm going to tell these fine lawmen about that football game where you—"

"Okay, I'll go." Jordan laughed. "And they talk about cheerleaders being mean girls."

"I'm not mean. I'm just determined," Della replied.

For the next hour they all laughed and joked, telling high school stories, some of which couldn't possibly be true. By the time Jordan had finished her drink, some of the stresses of the day had vanished.

It was almost seven when she pushed back from the table. "I've got to get home."

"Yeah, me, too," Della said. "I've got to help get Ben packed for his trip out of town tomorrow. That man is helpless without me."

They said good-bye to the men; then the two women headed for the front door. "You realize you blackmailed me into agreeing to go to the reunion," Jordan said as they stepped out into the chilly evening air.

"And your point is?" Della raised a perfectly plucked dark eyebrow. The eyebrow dropped and Della grabbed Jordan's arm. "Don't look so miserable. We're going to have such fun."

"I'd rather take Mandy to a movie," Jordan replied.

"But that isn't possible tomorrow night, so you might as well come with me rather than sitting at home and brooding. Besides, wouldn't you like to visit with old friends? The other girls who were on the cheerleading squad? Haven't you ever been curious about what they're doing and what they look like now?"

A faint whisper of anticipation swept through Jordan. "It might be fun," she admitted.

Della laughed and squeezed her arm. "Well, of course it's going to be fun. You're going to be with me."

Minutes later Jordan was in her car and headed north toward the small suburban house she'd rented three months ago. Initially following the divorce, she'd moved into an apartment. For several months after Dane's maneuver to gain custody of Mandy, Jordan had been almost too depressed to move.

She'd tried everything she knew to get the judge to change his mind. She'd said she'd quit her job, she'd move to a bigger place, she'd twist herself inside out, but the judge had remained unmoved. Dane had more money, he worked from home and Jordan suspected the judge had been more than a little starstruck. Dane had won the battle, but the war wasn't over yet.

But no matter how much she told herself that everyone had conspired against her, the truth was that when the judge had asked Mandy where she'd wanted to live, she'd indicated she wanted to stay with her father. It had been an indescribably painful blow.

Della was right. The worst thing Jordan could do was sit at home tomorrow night and brood. Unlike many kids, Jordan had reveled in her high school days. Those four years of life had been near perfect for her.

Her younger sister hadn't yet been murdered, her parents had laughed often and Jordan had dreamed of being a professional dancer. The world had revolved around football games, dance class, cheerleading practices and boys.

The vision of one particular boy filled her head. Clint Cooper. God, she hadn't thought about him in years, but there had been a time when he'd made her heart race, when the sound of his deep voice over the telephone could weaken her knees.

Theirs had been a tumultuous relationship. They'd dated on and off for three years. If she had been the girl who'd had it all in high school, then Clint had been the boy. Football quarterback, handsome as sin, he'd also understood the power of his sexual magnetism. He'd broken her heart over and over again because she refused to sleep with him. He'd break up with her to go with a girl that would, and eventually he'd come back to her only to repeat the cycle.

She smiled and shook her head as she pulled into the driveway of her cozy three-bedroom ranch house. It was a rental, but she was hoping to convince the owners to sell it to her. The huge house where she'd lived with Dane for the years of their marriage had never really felt like home. This place was beginning to—all it lacked was Mandy.

Her smile fell and she got out of the car and hurried to the front door, wanting to call her daughter before it got any later. Maybe she could still talk her into coming for the weekend after all.

She dropped her purse on the table in the small entry hall and went directly for the phone on the end table by the sofa. Thankfully Mandy answered. "Hi, honey, it's me."

"Mom, I'm on the other line," Mandy exclaimed, as if Jordan has just committed a cardinal sin.

"I'll make it fast. I just wanted to see if I could change your mind about coming tomorrow. You know I'd be happy to take you to your party and I thought maybe Sunday we could see a movie."

"I've already made plans," she said with a touch of impatience. "After the skating party some of us are going over to Emily's to spend the night. I gotta go."

She clicked off, leaving Jordan to press the phone against her heart. Part of the problem was Jordan didn't know what was normal twelve-year-old attitude and independence and what was Dane's manipulation to slowly push Jordan out of Mandy's life.

There's always next weekend, she told herself as she finally hung up the phone. Missing a weekend wasn't the end of the world. But it felt like it. She pulled herself off the sofa and walked back to the front door, where she retrieved her purse and locked up for the night.

She headed down the hallway, and stopped in the first bedroom and stepped inside. Pink. The room was an explosion of pink. The curtains and the bedspread were a hot pink and the walls were a rose-petal hue. A television sat on the dresser with a PlayStation system hooked up, just waiting for somebody to play. Toys and stuffed animals sat on shelves.

Jordan had spent every spare dime she'd had when she'd moved in here making the room a place where Mandy would want to be. Of course, she couldn't begin to compete with Dane in the material department, but she'd given it her best shot. A lot of good it had done her.

She left the room with a knot pressing hard against her heart. She went into the master bedroom, where the bedcovers were still rumpled from the night before and a half dozen blouses and skirts were tossed across a chair.

She'd deal with the mess in the morning. The drink at Iggy's coupled with the stressful day had her exhausted and ready for an early night. As she walked toward the adjoining bathroom, she stripped, and by the time she reached the bathroom mirror she was naked.

Staring at her reflection, she decided she didn't look much different than she had in high school. Although she'd cut her long mane of blond hair and now wore it short and spiky and there were some character lines beginning to show on her face, at least nobody at the reunion would be able to whisper that she'd gotten fat and ugly.

She was just about to drift off to sleep when her cell phone rang. She fumbled on her nightstand, grabbed it and answered.

"Hey, partner, it's me," Anthony said. "Just thought you might want to know that the verdict is in on the Sinclair case."

She sat up. "Already?"

"You aren't going to like it."

"Don't tell me—a hung jury?"

"Nope, they found him not guilty. As we speak, Parker Sinclair is a free man."

"Jesus, were they all smoking crack?"

"Apparently. They deliberated for under two hours. Anyway, just thought you'd want to know."

"Thanks, Anthony. I appreciate it." She clicked off, set the phone back on the nightstand, then lay back once again and thought about Parker Sinclair. The minute she'd taken the stand, he'd sat up straighter in his chair, as if she intrigued him, as if he knew all the secrets she might possess.

A sudden chill raised goose bumps on her arms. She'd faced many defendants in the courtroom over the years, but something about Parker Sinclair had creeped her out like never before.

And tonight he was a free man.

Sleep was elusive that night. It had been a busy day.

He sat at the kitchen table peeling an apple with a paring knife and reading the little local free paper that was thrown on his doorstep once a week.

The paper mostly held local human-interest stories and sales flyers. He made a mental note that Tide laundry detergent was on sale, as were the Slim Jim sausage sticks he liked to eat between meals.

Mr. and Mrs. Bob Fyack were celebrating their fifty-year wedding anniversary. Mrs. Fyack had held up well over the years, but Bob looked as if he'd lived hard and every mile of life had dug a line into his round face.

Of course he didn't know the couple, but he always found it heartening when a couple managed to stay together for that particular milestone.

He turned the page and then paused to cut a bite off the apple. As he chewed, he heard the crying. Low and mournful, the noise filled his head and tugged into his heart a sickening sense of distress.

He focused on the paper in front of him. A little girl had saved her family by waking them when a fire had broken out in their house. She'd been given an award by the local fire department.

Still the cries continued.

It wasn't the first time he'd heard it and he knew it wouldn't be the last. He'd become adept at ignoring it most of the time, but tonight the wails seemed louder, more persistent than usual.

Narrowing his eyes, he turned the page once again and tried to focus on anything but the sound in his head. The article he turned to froze him in place.

AWARD-WINNING ARTIST TO DONATE TO HER ALMA MATER.

The headline caught his attention and he quickly scanned the two paragraphs that accompanied two pictures.

Artist Joann Hathoway was donating one of her award-winning pastorals to Oak Ridge High School, where on Saturday night she would be joining other schoolmates for their fifteen-year reunion.

The weeping grew in volume as if begging for his attention. He rubbed the front of his forehead as he gazed at the two pictures. One showed the artist at work in her studio and the other was a photo of her and her fellow cheerleaders years ago.

The weeping became deep, gulping sobs as he continued to stare at the picture of the six girls in their light blue and dark blue uniforms. The sense of distress that had nagged at him exploded into a need to act, to do whatever it took to finally silence the noise of those pitiful, heartrending cries.

Rage swelled up inside him, a white-hot rage that cast all rational thought from his mind. He stared at the photo of Joann Hathoway. "Two, four, six, eight, who do we appreciate?" He whispered the words with a monotone rhythm. "Two, four, six, eight, who do we eliminate?" He stabbed the paring knife into the photo of the smiling artist. "You."

She would be the first. But she wouldn't be the last. He knew now what he had to do and for a sweet, blessed moment, the crying voice in his head was silent.

Chapter 2

Warm lips slid up Della's bare back, pulling her from the unconsciousness of sleep. She cracked open an eyelid to the early-morning light drifting into the nearby window. A glance at the clock on the nightstand indicated it was just after seven. She knew her husband had to leave the house in the next twenty minutes in order to get to the airport for his flight out of town.

As his mouth found a sensitive spot in the center of her slender back, she moaned. "Hmm, don't start something you can't finish."

He chuckled, his breath warm on her bare skin before he straightened and moved away from the bed. Della rolled over on her back and smiled at the man who had forever changed her life.

Ben Broadbent wasn't a particularly handsome man. His ears looked as if they belonged on a bigger head, and his nose sported a lump on the bridge. He was a stocky man with a belly paunch that spoke of his love of all things sugar. But he carried himself with a strength and poise that demanded attention, that inspired confidence. Besides, he had the nicest blue eyes Della had ever seen.

And he loved her. Mindlessly. Passionately. And he'd loved her that way when she'd been pudgy, insecure Della Hightower.

She sat up and pushed her hair away from her face as

she watched him straighten his tie in the dresser mirror. "When will you be home?" she asked.

"If all goes well, then I should be home Tuesday morning or early afternoon." He turned from the mirror and looked at her. "I'm sorry I can't go with you tonight to your reunion."

"It's all right. I know how important this merger is for you." Ben was CEO of a company that had developed software equipment for businesses and for the handicapped, a business that had made him a wealthy man. The merger with a computer company would make him even wealthier.

"So, you're going with Jordan tonight?" He turned away from the mirror.

"Yeah. Don't worry about me. Jordan and I will have a blast together. We always do."

Ben looked at his wristwatch and grimaced. "I've got to get out of here." He walked over to the side of the bed and leaned down and kissed her on the forehead, then touched her cheek with his warm, thick fingers. "Are you nervous about tonight?"

"Not at all."

"Don't let those mean bitches get to you."

She laughed. "Don't worry. I'll be fine. I can handle whatever those mean bitches dish out."

"Then I'll see you sometime Tuesday." Once again he pressed his lips against her forehead. "Take care of yourself, doll face."

As he left the bedroom, Della fought the need to call him back, to tell him not to leave her. Instead she turned over on her side and stared out the window where the sky was becoming the blowtorch-flame blue of a beautiful autumn day.

Only Ben knew the true torment of those high school days so long ago. Funny how four years of your life could be so important in a lifetime. Maybe it wasn't the same for boys. Perhaps the male species didn't feel that throat-clenching need to belong, to be a part of the in crowd.

There was nothing Della had wanted more during those years than to be a cheerleader. She'd desperately yearned to be one of those slender girls who backflipped at school assemblies, who owned the hallways during the days and the football field on the weekends. She wanted to be one of those popular girls whom the boys looked at longingly and who seemed to glide through their days with an enviable ease.

Della had tried out for the squad three times, her sophomore, junior and senior years. Not only had she not been chosen, but she'd also heard some of the other girls' snickers, the catty comments about how they didn't want a fat girl with bad skin representing their school.

"She's a nobody," they'd whispered. "She's nothing."

It's in the past, she told herself. Tonight she would return to face those mean girls as an attractive, successful businesswoman, as the best friend of the girl who had been the most golden during those tumultuous years.

She and Jordan hadn't been friends in high school. Jordan's friends had been girls like her, popular and pretty. But at least Jordan had always smiled at Della whenever they'd passed in the hall or when they were in the classes they shared. They'd become friends six years ago when Dane had hired Della to redecorate his home.

It made Della sad that the gilt had definitely slid off Jordan the golden girl. A murdered sister, a failed marriage, a thankless career and the loss of custody of Mandy all just proved that being popular in high school didn't automatically give you a pass through life.

Della released a sleepy sigh and closed her eyes once again. Nervous? Hell, no. She couldn't wait to show those bitches what fat, dorky Della Hightower had become.

Chapter 3

The reunion was being held in the ballroom of the Windsor Hotel, a stately brick building in downtown Kansas City. The hotel had stood on the corner of Thirteenth and Main for years and had recently been renovated to compete with the new Marriott that had gone up on the opposite corner.

Ben had surprised Della with the use of a limousine service for the night. As the stretch limo pulled up in front of the hotel, Jordan felt ridiculously pretentious. If it hadn't been for Della's sheer delight, Jordan would have insisted that she bring her own car.

Della was a skinny Fourth of July sparkler in a glittery gold dress that Jordan thought was just a bit over-the-top. Jordan had opted for a simple black dress that she'd worn to Dane's last book signing before their divorce.

A mix of curiosity and dread filled her as she stepped out of the limo. She hadn't seen many of these people for fifteen years and suspected that after tonight it would probably be another fifteen years before she saw them again.

She'd left high school with such an excitement for real life, eager to pursue a career in dancing. She'd gone to the prestigious Stephens College in Columbia, Missouri, on a scholarship and entered their rigorous dance training.

It was Julie's murder that had arrested her life, and it

had been that crime that had forced her away from the few high school relationships she'd maintained.

The kind of grief that came with the murder of a loved one changed people in the most profound ways. The shallowness, the self-absorption, of her twentysomething friends had seemed alien as Jordan grieved deep and hard for her only sibling. And none of her friends had wanted to be around somebody in mourning.

Tonight she was looking forward to shallow. She needed meaningless conversation and laughter with people who in the big scheme of things no longer mattered to her. She wanted anything that would take her mind off the emptiness of what her life had become and the fact that a jury had let a man she believed was a killer walk free.

"Ready?" Della asked as she looped her skinny arm with Jordan's.

"Sure, let's do it."

The lobby of the hotel was lush with huge vases of fresh-cut flowers in the autumn colors of red, orange and gold. The marble floor of the entry gave way to thick carpeting that threatened to swallow Jordan's heels.

"We're in the Grand Ballroom," Della said, and pointed to a discreet sign that marked the way. "We go up. It's on the top floor."

"Terrific," Jordan muttered beneath her breath. She was one of those people who didn't even like to stand on a stepladder. Heights terrified her. Of course the elevator going up to the twenty-fifth floor had to be one of those glass-encased cubicles on the outside of the building that gave heart attacks to even the mildest sufferers of acrophobia.

Jordan stepped into the torture chamber and stood just inside the door and stared at the elevator control panel, while Della walked directly to the windows to peer outside at the city lights. "I'm so excited I can hardly stand it," she said.

"Della, these people don't mean anything to you,"

Jordan replied. "They were just a blip on your radar for a short period of time. You have Ben and your business and friends. You certainly don't need the approval of anybody at this reunion."

"Well, of course I don't," Della exclaimed indignantly. "But I can't help but want them all to see how I turned out." She moved to stand next to Jordan in front of the elevator door. "Is my lipstick still okay?"

"You look gorgeous, Della. Everyone is going to be talking about you for weeks after this is all over."

"God, I hope so." She gave Jordan a cheeky grin, then grabbed her arm as the doors whooshed open and they stepped out into a long hallway.

Music and laughter guided them toward the ballroom, and despite her initial reluctance to attend, an edge of excitement fluttered through Jordan. The two women entered the room, which was bedecked with glittering chandeliers and a huge bank of windows that overlooked the downtown area. A DJ was set up on a small stage with party lights spinning a multitude of colors across the polished dance floor.

"Ladies, get a name tag," an attractive brunette that Jordan didn't recognize said from behind a small table that held fancy tags and a felt-tip pen. "Maiden names, please, and write your married name underneath," she instructed as Della handed her the tickets she'd purchased.

Della wrote her name with a flourish and Jordan carefully printed her own. They slapped the tags on, then headed for the cash bar in the corner. As they made their way across the floor, Jordan saw familiar faces and struggled to find names to match them.

The name that came to her lips most easily when she reached the bar was Tom Collins. It was only when she had a drink in hand that she and Della found a table at the edge of the empty dance floor to sit and really look at the other people around the room.

"See that redhead?" Della gestured across the room

at a tall, reed-thin woman who was surrounded by a small crowd of people. "Isn't that one of your cheerleader friends?"

"Joann Hathoway. Did you see the article in the paper about her donating a piece of her artwork to the school?" Jordan asked.

"No." Della looked slightly depressed. "So, what, she's some kind of famous artist?"

Jordan grinned. "Don't look so depressed, Della. Maybe she has a dysfunctional husband."

"Oh my God. Jordan Walker, what have you done to your hair?" Betsy Collier, now Betsy Baker, yanked Jordan up off her chair and into her arms for a hug. Of all the cheerleaders that had been on the squad with Jordan, Betsy had been the one Jordan had found most irritating.

Petite, with curly blond hair, she looked like a Kewpie doll who'd accidentally wandered off from a carnival game. She'd always been pukingly perky and it took only two minutes of conversation with her to realize that hadn't changed.

"Do you remember Della? Della Hightower? She was in English class with us senior year," Jordan said as Della rose to join them.

Betsy stared at Della and shrugged. "Sorry, I don't remember you. Nice to see you, though." Her gaze went just over Della's shoulder and she squealed and clapped her hands together. "Oh, look, there's Hank Terrell. I heard he and his wife have six kids. No wonder she looks so mousy and exhausted." She squeezed Jordan's shoulder. "We'll catch up more later." She hurried off in the direction of Hank and his wife.

"I knew she wouldn't remember me," Della said as she and Jordan once again sat at the table. "She had her head so far up her ass in high school, the only thing she could recognize was her own colon."

Jordan nearly spit her drink across the table as she laughed. She was glad she'd come. She had a feeling the entertainment value alone of the reunion would definitely beat a night at home in front of the television in her lonely house.

For the next hour she and Della mingled among their old classmates. Joann and Betsy weren't the only cheerleaders who had returned for the reunion. All six of them were there, Joann and Betsy, Pamela Albright, Jennifer Taylor, Sally Kincaid and Jordan. As the six of them gathered to visit, Della wandered off to talk to some of her old friends.

It didn't take long for Jordan to realize that as an adult she had nothing in common with these women. Her life was filled with the aftermath of violence, with murder and mayhem. They talked of fashion and soccer games, of exotic vacations and charity work.

Betsy hadn't outgrown her high school catty bitchiness and Jennifer Taylor still possessed that aloof, condescending air that subtly said she was far better than anyone else in the room.

Funny, for those years in school Jordan had considered all of them her best friends. They'd shared slumber parties and cheer practices; they'd gossiped and clung together like a tiny army who feared any alien force that might try to work into their inner circle.

It was Sally who grabbed Jordan by the arm and pulled her away from the group. "You looked like you could use a rescue."

"I just don't have much in common with them anymore," Jordan said.

Sally smiled. "That's because you grew up. Some girls stay cheerleaders for the rest of their lives," she said with a touch of humor.

"You live in Chicago now, right?" Jordan asked.

Sally nodded. "I moved there ten years ago after college. I work with disabled kids. I don't have much time to shop or do lunch. I'm not married and I don't consider being a cheerleader at Oak Ridge High on the same level as being a Nobel Peace Prize winner. I definitely don't belong in the in crowd anymore. More than that, I don't care."

Jordan laughed. "Poor you, imagine being so well-adjusted to adult life."

"That's me," Sally replied.

"How long are you in town for?"

"Just until tomorrow morning. I'm not even sure why I came. To be perfectly honest, I haven't thought about high school for a very long time." She took a sip of her drink and looked back at the cluster of cheerleaders still standing together. "Unfortunately there are some people who really never leave high school behind." She looked back at Jordan. "I heard about Julie's murder while I was in college. It must have been terrible for you."

Even after all the years, a stab of pain shot through Jordan at the mere mention of Julie's name. "Yeah, it was tough."

"She was a sweet kid. Has the murderer ever been caught?"

Jordan shook her head. "No, it's a cold case now and remains unsolved."

"Is that why you decided to become a cop?"

"Yes." Jordan smiled. "I went from ballerina to ballbuster."

Sally laughed, but sobered quickly. "Must be tough. The way I hear it, that's one career where it's still a man's world."

"There can be days when the testosterone in the squad room is pretty stifling, but for the most part I like what I do."

"You don't miss the dancing? You were always so talented."

"I still dance. I just do it in my basement instead of professionally like I once thought I would. And now I think I'm going to get another drink. You want something?"

"No, thanks. It was good seeing you again, Jordan."

As Jordan headed toward the bar, she noticed that

the dance floor was filled with couples. Della was there, dancing with a lanky red-haired man whom Jordan thought she remembered from one of the school plays.

She got her drink, then turned around, and that was when she saw him. He stood in the entrance, obviously having just arrived, and for a moment it was like a flashback. Her heartbeat revved and butterflies took wing in her tummy.

Clint Cooper. As a high school boy he'd been hot. As an adult man he was even hotter. And after all these years, it seemed he still had the ability to make her breath catch.

Then his gaze met hers and he smiled. She watched as he made his way across the crowded room toward her. He looked handsome in his dark suit. Though he'd broken her heart more times than she could count, she couldn't ignore the flush of pleasure that washed over her at the sight of him.

She took a big swallow of her drink to ease the dryness of her mouth and reminded herself that by now he was probably married with a couple of kids.

"Jordan," he said as he reached her. He took her hand in his, his eyes just as blue as they'd been in high school. "I was hoping you'd be here."

"Hi, Clint. It's nice to see you again," she replied, pleased that her voice didn't reflect the foolish rush of emotion that swept through her at his simple touch.

She didn't know him. She didn't know what kind of a man he'd become. She pulled her hand from his. "You cut your hair. I like it," he said, half yelling to be heard above the din of the music and laughter. He grabbed her by the arm. "Let's go someplace a little quieter where we can catch up."

She allowed him to lead her out of the ballroom and down the hallway to a tufted bench where it would be easier to carry on a conversation. They sat side by side and warmth filled her cheeks as he studied her. "You look great," he finally said.

"You don't look like life has beaten you up too badly," she replied.

"So, let's get some of the basics out of the way. Are you married?"

"Divorced, with a twelve-year-old daughter," she replied. "What about you?"

"Divorced, no kids."

Somehow she wasn't surprised that he was divorced. He'd been a crappy boyfriend. He'd probably been an even crappier husband. Still, there was a flirtatiousness in his eyes that she found just a little bit exciting. It had been a long time since a man had looked at her like that.

"I heard you're a cop," he continued.

"Homicide detective," she replied.

"I was sorry to hear about Julie. How are your parents doing?"

"They're well. What about you? What are you doing these days?"

"I'm trying to redeem myself for my behavior in high school."

"Oh, you've become a monk?" she asked dryly.

He laughed and the deep, warm sound filled her mind with a hundred wonderful memories. "Oh, Jordan, it's nice to know some things don't change. You still shoot from the hip with a directness few people possess. And no, I haven't become a monk. It's worse than that—I'm the football coach at our alma mater."

"I hate football," she said. It was perverse and untrue, but that laughter and the warmth of his gaze had her heart pitter-pattering in an uncomfortable way.

"Really? That's downright un-American."

"It's worse than that," she said, echoing his words. "I also think George Washington was an ugly man and I'm not too fond of apple pie."

He leaned closer to her, close enough that she could smell his cologne, a pleasant, fresh scent. "I've thought about you often over the years, Jordan."

"I'll confess that you've crossed my mind a time or two," she admitted.

"I hope when you thought of me, it wasn't all bad."

Had his eyes always been that amazing shade of blue? And why, after all these years, did she feel that old crazy chemistry where he was concerned? "Of course it wasn't all bad," she replied. "We had some good times, Clint."

"And we had some bad."

She nodded and smiled, but before she could reply, several men stepped out of the ballroom and began to talk to Clint about the current football team. Jordan excused herself as Clint shot her a look of obvious frustration. "We'll catch up more later?" he asked, an unmistakable longing in his voice.

"Sure," she replied as the butterflies began to dance in her stomach once again. She turned and hurried back into the ballroom.

When Clint gazed at her, she felt a rush of teenage emotion that had nothing to do with the woman she'd become, that had no place in her present life.

"Jordan!" She found herself grabbed up in an embrace with a bear of a man. She laughed in delight and looked up into the warmest brown eyes on the planet.

"Danny McCall. You're a sight for sore eyes. Now, let go of me before you break a rib."

Danny had been a fullback on the football team, but more important, he'd been one of Jordan's best friends in high school. He hadn't been a handsome boy and he hadn't grown any more so in the years since.

His nose was broad and flat, his forehead as wide as a billboard. He had a weak chin and a protruding belly and he'd never been the brightest crayon in the box. But Danny had possessed an innocence of spirit that had made him everyone's best friend. He'd been the boy who could always be depended on to keep a secret or to take you home if you'd had a fight with your boyfriend.

They chatted for a few minutes and were joined by more people who remembered Danny fondly. Although the reunion was supposed to end at midnight, it was just before eleven when Della came up to Jordan and grabbed her by the arm. It was obvious she was more than a little drunk and upset.

"Let's go," she said, the words slurring into four syllables. "I called for the car."

"What's wrong? What happened?" Jordan asked as Della yanked her toward the door.

"Nothing. I just want to get out of here."

"Okay, we're going." She cast a fleeting glance over her shoulder in an effort to see Clint one last time, but she didn't see him as Della pulled her from the ballroom.

Della didn't say another word as they rode down the elevator and left the hotel. The car was waiting in front and she fell into the backseat and burst into tears.

"Della, what's wrong? What happened?" Jordan asked, bewildered as she sat next to the weeping woman.

"I hate those bitches, all of them." She dug into her tiny sequined purse for a tissue. "They're still as mean and hateful as they were in school."

Jordan didn't have to ask what girls she was talking about. She placed her arm around Della's shoulder. She had a feeling that the booze Della had consumed had more to do with this breakdown than anything else. "You'll feel better in the morning."

"Betsy and I were having a nice conversation," Della said as if she hadn't heard Jordan. "I was telling her about my business and she said she and her husband had been thinking about hiring a decorator. I gave her one of my cards and she looked at it, then looked at me. 'Oh my God, now I remember you,'" Della said in a squeaky parody of Betsy's voice. "'Didn't you try out for cheerleader every year? We used to call you Thunder Thighs.' Then she laughed."

"Della, it's been fifteen years," Jordan exclaimed. "Why do you care what Betsy thought about you then? Why do you care what she thinks about you now? Get over it. Move on."

"That's easy for you to say," Della replied. She scooted away from Jordan and nearly fell over sideways in the seat. "You were one of them." She glared at Jordan as if she were personally responsible for the angst of every unpopular teenage girl in the world. "I hated you. Oh God, I hated you because I wanted to be you."

"Della, maybe we should talk about all this tomorrow when you're sober," Jordan said uneasily.

"No, because I won't talk about it when I'm sober," she replied. "You don't know what it's like to have the heart of a performer and be stuck backstage because you're too fat or don't have the right friends. You don't know what it's like to stand on the sidelines and watch girls like you glide through life being adored and revered."

Jordan said nothing. She just let Della spew old insecurities that should have been put to rest years ago. "It was just high school," she finally said when Della fell silent.

"You just don't get it, do you? Some people never get past the pain of alienation, the ache of wanting to belong so badly. It writes on their hearts in indelible ink," she said dramatically, then slumped against the seat in abject misery.

Jordan tapped on the window between the back and the driver. When the window opened, she instructed him to take Della home first. She didn't like the idea of Della trying to get into her house alone.

When they reached the Broadbent residence, Jordan helped Della out of the car and into her house. It was as if her outburst had drained every ounce of energy. She sagged against Jordan as Jordan led her up the massive staircase to the master bedroom.

"You need me to help you undress?" she asked as Della collapsed on the king-size bed.

"No, just go home. I'll be fine." Della turned her head aside into a pillow and by the time Jordan walked back to the bedroom doorway, she was snoring.

Within half an hour Jordan was home. It took her only minutes to get out of her dress and into bed. She was stunned by Della's vitriol about things that had happened more than a decade ago.

Had Jordan been unkind to other girls when she'd been in high school? Probably, although she had certainly tried to be nice to everyone. She'd never consciously snubbed or made fun of anyone.

What Della neglected to remember was that as gracefully as Jordan had skated through high school, the bad times had been awaiting her. Della wept because she hadn't made the cheerleading squad. If Jordan was going to cry, she would release tears for the loss of her sister to a murderer who had never been brought to justice.

But, Jordan didn't look back. She didn't want to dwell on the fact that when her parents had buried their youngest child, they'd mentally buried their eldest along with her. She didn't want to examine the painful path that had led her to divorcing her unfaithful husband and losing physical custody of Mandy.

Still, despite her penchant for focusing on the future, as she closed her eyes, her mind drifted back in time, back to Clint Cooper. . . .

They'd started dating their sophomore year and Jordan had been completely besotted with the dark-haired, handsome young man, who had exuded a simmering sexuality even then.

Whenever Clint broke up with Jordan, she'd focus on her schoolwork, hang out with her girlfriends and casually date other guys while she waited for Clint to come back to her.

Until graduation day. On that day Clint had come to her with his heart in his hands, begging her to once again forgive him and take him back, and even though she still loved him, she'd told him no. That had been the last time she'd seen him.

Until tonight.

For just a moment as she'd gazed into his eyes, she'd

felt that familiar flush of heat, of excitement, that he'd always stirred inside her. She punched her pillow and turned over. Mean-girl taunts were nothing more than a piece of Della's past, just like Clint Cooper was nothing more than a bit of hers.

Chapter 4

Lying in wait. He'd heard the term before but never really understood the subtle nuances of it until now, as he stood behind a large tree and gazed at the house in the distance. He'd been lying in wait for the last two hours.

The moon overhead was a mere sliver of silver and the October night air held a hint of frost. A faint breeze stirred the leaves that had begun to die, creating a rattle that would hide any noise of his approach.

She'd arrived home twenty minutes ago from the class reunion. He'd watched her get out of her car and go into the house. All he was waiting for was the lights to go out, for her to fall into the vulnerable state of sleep.

He'd already checked and discovered there was no alarm system. She also didn't have a dog to bark and warn her of a potential intruder. Foolish woman. Living alone and so arrogant as to believe she was above any danger.

Gripping the handle of his knife, he tried to tamp down the excitement that filled him. He'd come prepared with all the tools he would need. Duct tape, rope, the knife and a gun if absolutely necessary.

It wouldn't be murder.

He wasn't a murderer.

She might have fooled everyone into believing she was a philanthropist, giving her artwork to the school, but he knew the truth. She was diseased. She might have managed to hide the ravages of her illness from those around her, but he recognized the mean-girl heart that beat inside her chest. He was simply a shepherd, culling the diseased from the rest of the flock.

It had been the announcement of the reunion, the picture in the paper, that had crystallized what he had to do. Six girls in their matching uniforms, a united force against the unpopular, the less pleasing of humanity.

Some things never changed, and the power of the cheerleaders in every school each and every year was one of those things. They were mean girls, heartbreakers who wielded their power carelessly.

It was amazing the kinds of things that went through your head when you were waiting to take a life. The stocking cap he wore should assure that no hairs were left behind, and the latex gloves would leave no fingerprints. He'd gone over and over the plan in his head and he could find no flaws.

He'd even begun to wonder whether he should paint his living room, whether he'd like to have a puppy or whether it was a good time to make some stock investments.

He hissed in surprise and melded deeper into the shadow of the tree trunk as the front door flew open and she stepped outside. Clad in a rainbow-colored caftan that swirled around her long legs, she headed directly to the large shed in the distance.

What in the hell was she doing? It was almost two in the morning. He waited until she disappeared into the building; then he crept forward. There were two windows in the front and as he reached one of them, he peered inside.

Bright lights filled the interior and she stood with her back to him. She stared at a large canvas in front of her. It was the beginning of one of her famous pastoral scenes. Apparently the artist intended to work for a while before calling it a night.

That didn't change his plans. She would die tonight for her sins. He would rid the world of a nasty germ. He slid away from the window and leaned with his back against the shed.

Could he do it?

His hands sweat beneath the thin latex gloves.

But it's not murder, he reminded himself. It's the right thing to do.

He burst through the door with his gun drawn. Joann Hathoway's eyes widened. "Who the hell are you and what do you want?" she demanded.

Amazing. Even with the barrel of a gun pointed at her chest, her eyes flashed with annoyance and her voice was rich with arrogance.

"I'm the man with the gun and right now I want you to sit down and shut up." He motioned her into a nearby chair.

Her initial bravado oozed out of her as she eyed the gun in his hand. "If it's money you're after, I have some in the house." She sat in the chair as he pulled the rope from his pocket, and for the first time her eyes radiated fear. "Please, if you'll just tell me what you want."

He didn't reply. She was surprisingly docile as he bound her to the chair and slapped a piece of duct tape over her mouth. A rush of heat filled him as he saw the terror that darkened her eyes, and smelled the acrid scent of her fear.

It was only then, when she was utterly helpless, that he allowed himself to feel the first real flush of success. He looked around the shed. It smelled of turpentine and paint, of burnt coffee and scented candles.

Her studio. The place where she created her works of art. He'd done enough research to know that she'd never married. Probably thought herself too good for mortal men. He'd read an article, an interview she'd given to the local paper. She'd said her paintings were her children.

How many girls had gone to bed each night and cried

themselves to sleep because of her callous words or actions in high school? How many teenage girls had she hurt during those four long years?

He eyed the large canvas in front of him. It was a winter scene. He hated winter. It had been when the leaves had left the trees and snow had covered the ground that his world had fallen apart. Death. Winter was the time of death.

Shoving the gun in his waistband, he turned back to look at Joann. "Feel like doing a cheer? Can you still backflip across a gym floor?"

She searched his face and shook her head, obviously not understanding what this was all about. He pulled the knife from his pocket and approached her canvas. "Is this what you care about? Is this what you care about most?"

His anger whirled inside him and he heard the weeping inside his head. He began to slash the canvas. Again and again, in a frenzy of rage that momentarily stole his breath from him.

Red-hot flames filled his head, obscuring his vision, as the crying grew louder and louder. The sound of ripping, of tearing, filled the air and still he slashed until the red faded in his head.

When he was finished, the canvas was in shreds. The only sound was Joann's wheezing sobs into the duct tape.

Justice, he thought with a sense of euphoria he'd never felt before. He approached her and her eyes widened once again. "You were a mean bitch in high school. Did you really think that you could get away with it? All the boys you rejected? All the girls you laughed at? Did you never think about who you and your cheerleader buddies hurt with your gossip and inner-circle mentality?" He spit the words at her as the cries inside his head grew louder.

He yanked the tape from her mouth and she gasped in a deep breath. "Who are you?" she sobbed wildly. "Do I know you?"

"I'm all those little people you ignored in high school. I'm all of those nerds you made fun of, those pathetic losers you had nothing to do with. I hear them all crying in my head."

She cringed with each of his words, any arrogance she might have possessed swallowed up by the force of her terror. "Please," she whispered as he placed the blade of the knife against her neck.

Once again his rage swept a red curtain in front of his eyes and swelled inside his chest. "You were so proud to be a cheerleader, flitting down the halls in your short skirts with your nose in the air." He pressed his mouth against the side of her face. "Give me a cheer now, Joann."

She sobbed again, deep, wrenching gasps that shook her body. "Come on, give me a cheer," he yelled. "Two, four, six, eight. Who do we appreciate?"

She was weeping uncontrollably now and he could no longer hear the cries in his head. He could hear only her—her misery, her terror—and it filled him with a new burst of righteous rage. "Say it," he screamed. "Two, four, six, eight."

"Who do we appreciate?" The words ripped from her throat.

He leaned close to her, so close that if he wanted, he could touch her lips with his. "Two, four, six, eight, who do we eliminate?" he whispered. "You."

He plunged the knife into her chest. She stopped screaming with the third thrust and still he kept stabbing until she was like the canvas, ripped beyond repair.

He fell to the floor, covered in her blood and yet so euphoric that laughter bubbled to his lips. He hadn't been sure he could do it, but it had been so easy—so incredibly easy.

Drawing deep, cleansing breaths, he remained still for a long moment. Inside his head was silence—sweet, blessed silence. He leaned forward and dipped his finger into the blood that had seeped out of her and pooled on the floor next to the chair leg.

Using the still-warm gelatinous liquid, he wrote *2468* in front of the chair, then pulled himself to his feet. He stared down at the numbers that he knew would mean nothing to law enforcement, but they were the final cheer, the death chant for Joann Hathoway.

He got to his feet and left the shed. He barely noticed the chilly night air that wrapped around him as he headed toward the nearby woods, where he'd parked his car.

When he reached the vehicle, he peeled off his bloody clothes and stuffed them in a plastic garbage bag. Then he opened a container of Clorox wipes and washed himself down. The bloody tissues joined the clothes in the bag.

He stood naked in the sliver of moonlight that filtered through the trees. Her death had empowered him. Slashing the canvas had hurt her almost as much as the knife that had stolen her life. It had been good, destroying what she loved most before killing her.

It was fitting. It was right. And now that he knew exactly what he was capable of, it was just the beginning. His work had only just begun. There was still Betsy and Pamela, Jennifer and Sally and, of course, the queen of them all, head cheerleader Jordan.

He dressed quickly, then went home, and that night he slept more peacefully than he had in years.

Chapter 5

It was one of those perfect fall days with the temperature hovering right around sixty and the sun a beautiful ball in an azure sky. The trees that lined the residential street were clothed in autumn finery, leaves of burnt orange, deep red and lush gold.

Jordan's morning had begun with an apologetic call from Della, who was suffering a massive hangover and was spending the day in bed. Jordan had spent the afternoon reading over notes and case files and had made the requisite Sunday phone call to her mother and she'd spent far too much time thinking about Clint Cooper.

In fact, he'd been her first thought when she'd awakened that morning. Her head had filled with a vision of him, not the way he'd been in her teenage memories, but rather a picture of the man he'd become. He'd definitely aged well, at least physically, and she had to admit she wouldn't mind finding out what kind of a man he'd become over the years.

He'd said something about them catching up later, but she'd scooted out of the reunion with the distressed Della before being able to tell him good-bye. He'll call if he really wants to catch up, she thought as she got into her car and pulled out of her driveway.

The best part of the day was about to occur. Jordan was now on her way to Dane's to pick up Mandy for dinner. They were going to Mandy's favorite pizza place, but more important, Jordan was going to get to spend a couple of hours with her daughter.

The Northland neighborhood where Dane lived was composed of stately homes that had been built the year before Dane and Jordan had been married. The million-dollar homes came with membership to the golf course and the athletic club, and the schools were the best in the city. Jordan had made sure her rental house was not only relatively close to Dane's but also in the same school district.

Dane had been wealthy when Jordan had married him. His parents had come from money and had died in a tragic car accident when Dane had been twenty-two. They'd left him with enough money to live exceedingly well and the ability to stay home and focus on his desire to be a writer.

Jordan and Dane had met when she'd been a rookie cop and he'd been writing the crime beat for the local newspaper. He'd pursued her with a single-mindedness that had overwhelmed her. Not only had she found him handsome, but she'd admired his drive to succeed as a writer, the aura of maturity and command that clung to him.

It was only in retrospect that she wondered if he'd married her for love or because she might provide a valuable inside source to crime in Kansas City. They'd been married for four years when Dane had his first affair with a young assistant he'd hired. When Jordan had confronted him about it, he'd promised it would never happen again, pleaded that he'd been weak and foolish. She'd been the fool for believing him.

She'd been desperate to keep her marriage intact for Mandy's sake and she'd tried to put it behind her and learn to trust him again.

In the end it had been Dane's continued infidelity that had driven her to seek a divorce, which had been finalized a little more than a year ago. She'd wanted more for herself, felt she deserved better than what he gave her. She'd decided she'd rather be alone than be with a man who cheated on her.

History, she thought as she pulled into the circular driveway of the house where she used to live. It was a three-story brick with columns across a wide sweeping porch. Bright orange and yellow mums lined the sidewalk, and a sweet gum tree had laid a thin layer of red leaves across the fading green grass.

Jordan nearly skipped up the sidewalk in anticipation of spending a couple of hours with Mandy.

She tried to understand Mandy's desire to remain living in the home where she'd been born. There was a sense of security here for her, and even though it killed Jordan not to have Mandy with her, first and foremost she wanted what was best for Mandy.

There was never any question of Jordan getting the house in the divorce. Dane had owned it before their marriage, so it wasn't considered a marital asset. Dane had given her a monetary settlement to help her get into a house of her own, a house where she'd hoped Mandy would live with her. The money was now in a savings account. If the people who owned her rental would sell, then she had enough money to put down and keep the mortgage manageable.

Dane opened the door before she'd raised a hand to knock. "Mandy will be down in just a few minutes," he said as he ushered Jordan into the entry. "You'll have her back by seven? She still has some homework to take care of tonight."

"No problem," Jordan replied, although a faint edge of irritation whispered through her. Why couldn't he have seen to it that Mandy had already done her homework so they wouldn't have had to worry about hurrying back after dinner? There were several moments of awkward silence. "You working on a new project?" she finally asked.

Dane wasn't a traditionally handsome man. His face was a bit too lean and his mouth too thin. But he had luxurious dark hair that had begun to gray when he'd been thirty and piercing eyes that radiated an intense intelligence. He looked smart and sophisticated on the dust jackets of his books.

"Crime in Kansas City has been fairly boring lately," he said.

She smiled. "That's the way we like it."

"I need another Berdella or Radar."

"Please, I shudder at the thought," she replied.

Bob Berdella had been Kansas City's most notorious serial killer. He'd raped, tortured and killed six men before finally being arrested. Dennis Radar was the BTK killer from Wichita, Kansas. "BTK" stood for "bind, torture and kill." Radar had killed at least ten people before his arrest. Both cases had been before Jordan's time on the force and both had been the subjects of best-selling books for Dane.

"I heard Sinclair got off."

She shrugged. "The jury got it wrong. It happens." It felt good to be talking civilly, without the tension that often marked their conversations. She didn't want to fight with Dane. She harbored no ill will toward him except when it came to Mandy.

At that moment Mandy came down the stairs. The sight of her, clad in a pink Windbreaker and jeans, with her blond hair loose and flowing around her shoulders, made Jordan want to reach out and grab her to her breast. She wanted to smell the scent of her hair, that wonderful blend of strawberry and innocence.

Instead she smiled. "Hi, girlfriend."

"Hi, Mom." Mandy grabbed a small, sparkly pink purse from the table in the entry. "I'm starving."

Dane rolled his eyes. "She's always starving these days."

Jordan looped an arm around Mandy's shoulder. "That's because she's a growing girl. Let's go fill that empty tank with some pizza."

Minutes later as Jordan backed out of the driveway,

she saw Dane standing in the doorway and for a moment she had the impression of a lonely man. She dismissed her ex-husband from her mind as she focused on enjoying the company of her daughter.

Mandy chattered about the slumber party she'd attended the night before as they drove to the pizza place. Jordan was pleased that Mandy appeared to be in an exceptionally good mood. Lately she never knew what she was going to get with her daughter—either a bright, fun girl or a sullen, prickly preteen. She was pleased that at least for this evening it was the nice girl with the bright smile who had shown up.

By the time they reached the restaurant, the conversation had moved on from the slumber party to school activities. "There's an autumn festival in two weeks," Mandy said as they waited for their pizza and salad. "It's really a Halloween party, but they aren't supposed to call it that anymore."

"Are you going to go trick-or-treating this year?" Jordan asked.

Mandy nodded, her blue eyes sparkling with excitement. "I'm going as Sabrina the Cheetah Girl."

"Cheetah Girl?" Jordan looked at her blankly.

"Oh, Mom, you're so out of it," she exclaimed with disgust. "The Cheetah Girls are an awesome all-girl band. Sabrina is, like, totally gorgeous and Dad bought me a sparkly outfit to wear and I'm going to carry my pink microphone. Dad said I can't go by myself, so I'm going with Megan and her mom. You want to come with us?"

It was absolutely pathetic how much the invitation meant to Jordan. "I can't think of anything I'd rather do on a Halloween night."

"Cool. I'll let you know what time we're going." The waitress arrived with their salads and the conversation lagged as they focused on eating. By the time they'd finished the salads, their pizza had arrived.

"Megan and I have been talking and we've both decided we want to try out for cheerleader next year," Mandy said as she pulled another piece of the cheesy pizza onto her plate.

Jordan was beginning to feel as though the topic of cheerleading was everywhere in the past couple of days. "I could help you, if you want me to."

Mandy eyed her suspiciously. "What do you mean? How could you help?"

"Well, I was a cheerleader in high school."

Mandy's eyes widened. "For real? Why didn't you ever tell me that before?"

Jordan laughed. "I guess the subject never came up before. Actually, I was head cheerleader for three years."

"And you could teach me cheers and how to do backflips and stuff? And maybe you could help Megan, too?"

"Anytime, honey," Jordan replied. Finally there was something that could bring mother and daughter together. "If you're interested, I have a bunch of pictures from high school that I can show you."

"Maybe next weekend when I come over?"

"Okay, that would be fun," Jordan agreed. It was the first time in a long time that Mandy had acted excited about spending the weekend with her.

The rest of the meal passed pleasantly with Mandy chattering about her friends and her favorite teacher at school and the drama club she wanted to join. All too quickly it was time for Jordan to get her back home, and that was when the sickness began in the pit of her stomach.

It was always the same. No matter how much time they spent together, when it was time to part, Jordan felt the kind of sick bereavement that came with death. It was an actual physical pain that cramped her stomach and stole part of her breath away.

When she pulled into Dane's driveway, she reached out and stopped Mandy before she could exit the car.

She twined her fingers with her daughter's. Mandy had not gotten only Jordan's blond hair and pouty bottom lip; she'd also gotten Jordan's hands—long-fingered and slender.

"Mandy, you know how much I love you and you know that anytime you want to come and live with me, you can."

"I know, Mom." Mandy pulled her hand from Jordan's. "And you know I love you, too. But I like the way things are right now." She offered Jordan a tentative smile.

Jordan forced a smile in return. "I just wanted you to know that my door's always open."

Mandy leaned over the seat and kissed her on the cheek. "I'll talk to you tomorrow, okay?"

And then she was gone, leaving behind the bittersweet scent of strawberries and failure.

As Jordan drove home, a weight of depression fell onto her shoulders. She'd love to blame Dane for her strained relationship with Mandy, for the fact that Mandy didn't want to live with her, but the truth was from the moment Dane and Jordan had sat down with Mandy to talk to her about the divorce, she had indicated that she might want to stay where she was with Dane.

Rational thinking aside, Jordan felt as though she hadn't been a good enough wife to keep Dane faithful. She'd apparently failed as a mother and she'd even failed at being a daughter who could bring comfort to her grieving parents. And to add insult to injury, she hadn't heard from Clint.

It was little consolation that she was a good cop and that she'd once been one hell of a cheerleader.

Chapter 6

The Kansas City Police Department was headquartered in an eight-story brick building downtown at 1125 Locust Street. Often when an officer was bringing in a perpetrator, he'd radio in "Hocus-pocus, Twelfth and Locust."

On Monday morning Jordan parked in the municipal lot across the street from headquarters. All the detectives worked four ten-hour days. Jordan was the only one who consistently had her weekends off, thanks to her coworkers, who rotated the weekends so she could have the time to spend with her daughter.

There were only two places where Jordan felt completely in control. One was on the dance floor and the other was in this building. "Good morning, Joe," she said to the security guard who stood next to the metal detector that all visitors to the building had to walk through.

"Morning, Jordan," he said as he motioned her around the machine. "Did you have a good weekend?"

"Not bad," she replied. "How about you?"

"Can't complain."

She headed toward the elevator bank. The first floor of the building was research and dispatch offices. The investigative units worked on the second floor. Third floor was accounting and more investigation units. From the fourth floor to the seventh were offices, computer control, the chief's office, the media center and personnel. The eighth floor was the holding cell where prisoners went before being transferred to the county jail.

The murder squad had their little squad and interrogation rooms on the second floor. The minute she stepped into the investigation-unit squad room, she knew something was up. There was an air of expectancy, an unusual hush, in the room. As she passed the officers already at their desks, none of them met her gaze.

She headed toward the back of the room, where the entrance to the murder-squad room was located. The powers that be had decided several years ago that keeping these officers separated from the other crime units would increase their productivity.

A wave of apprehension swept through Jordan as she headed for the murder room. Had she screwed up something? Was that why nobody was looking at her? Was she in trouble for something?

Her footsteps slowed as she eyed the closed door ahead of her. Why was the door closed? Was the chief in there waiting to fire her? Her heart thumped as she turned the knob and a snicker of laughter sounded from someplace in the room behind her. What the hell? She opened the door and gasped.

Pom-poms in all colors decorated the top of her desk. A megaphone with her name stenciled down the side rose up from the center. "Give us a cheer, partner," Anthony said.

"Yeah, give us a cheer," several of the men from the outer squad room yelled.

They all began to clap and cheer. "Jordan, Jordan, she's the one. Instead of poms she's got a gun. Jordan, Jordan, high school dream. She now works for the murder team."

"Give us a backflip, Jordan," Ricky said.

"How about the splits?" Anthony added.

"How about I split your head?" she countered with a laugh.

"Okay, okay, fun's over," Sergeant Benny Wendt's deep voice rang out above the din. "Everyone back to work." He handed Jordan a large black trash bag, his eyes twinkling with merriment. "Clean off your desk, Sampson. What do you think this is, a high school party?"

"Right away, sir," she replied. Even though she knew they were all making fun of her, her heart was warm as she piled the pom-poms into the bag. She knew the teasing had come with a lot of affection from her fellow officers.

It was ten o'clock when the call came in, a homicide at the northern edges of the city. "Sampson, you're up," Wendt said as both Jordan and Anthony stood. She'd be lead detective and Anthony would be second.

Wendt gave her the address. "Blues are on the scene and have it secured and the crime-scene boys are on their way. Copeland, go with them. Despite her rah-rah background, you could learn a lot from Detective Sampson."

The young detective jumped to his feet. "Yes, sir." He radiated excitement, a sure sign of just how green he was when it came to murder investigations. It wouldn't take too many dead bodies to change that excitement to dread, the eagerness to weary acceptance.

Minutes later the three of them were in a car and headed to the address they had been given. "How was your reunion?" Anthony asked as they left the downtown area.

"It was all right. Saw a lot of people I hadn't seen in years and probably won't see again," Jordan replied. "Della got stinking drunk and had a major meltdown."

"A meltdown about what?" Ricky asked from the backseat.

"Mean-girl cheerleaders and old wounds," Jordan replied. "I guess it's a girl thing."

"Must be," Anthony replied. "You know, Stacy was a pom-pom girl in high school. She was the sweetest girl in the world. She only turned into a mean girl when we divorced." He sighed. "I can't figure out how a woman I loved so much turned into somebody I hate so much."

"Divorce can definitely be a nasty business," Jordan replied.

As they got closer to the location, the partners fell silent.

Jordan turned onto a narrow two-lane highway, then again on a dusty road that led them to a farmhouse with a large flat-roofed shed. "Definitely out in the middle of nowhere," she said.

"Tough for anyone to have seen anything," Anthony replied.

Two police cruisers were parked in the driveway, their lights flashing red and blue flames in the air. A gold Ford Taurus was also in the driveway. "Looks like we beat the crime-scene boys," Anthony said as Jordan parked the car next to one of the cruisers.

"Looks like," she agreed.

The three detectives got out of the car and approached the two uniforms standing in front of the shed. Another patrolman stood off to one side with a sobbing dark-haired woman.

"What have we got?" Jordan asked one of the officers. His badge read JOHNSON.

"Obvious homicide. Victim is inside," Officer Johnson replied.

"Who's the woman?"

"Apparently the victim's lover. According to her, she arrived here approximately forty-five minutes ago and found the victim. She immediately called 911."

Jordan nodded. She didn't like to ask too many questions before seeing the scene. She didn't want any information in her head that might prejudice her. "Let's see what we've got."

"It's not pretty," Officer Johnson said.

"Murder never is," Anthony replied dryly.

The three of them pulled on gloves and booties; then

Jordan opened the shed door. It was impossible not to see the victim instantly. Jordan gasped and stumbled back against Anthony.

"What's wrong?" he asked.

"I know her." Jordan drew a deep, steadying breath as she stared at the lifeless body of Joann Hathoway. Jordan had seen a lot of dead bodies over the course of her time as a homicide detective, but she realized this was the first time in her career that she personally knew the victim.

Officer Johnson was right. It wasn't pretty. Jordan had no idea what the original color of the caftan Joann wore had been, but now it was the rusty brown of dried blood. There was so much blood it was impossible to discern whether she'd been shot, stabbed or both. Certainly the ragged tears in the caftan indicated knife wounds.

The scent of blood, of violent death, hung in the air. It had been a long time since Jordan had gotten physically ill at a murder scene, but her stomach rolled and kicked as she stared at the face of the woman who had smiled and chatted at the reunion.

Anthony had worked with her on enough cases to know that for the first few minutes Jordan liked silence. She needed to assess the scene with all her senses before beginning the actual physical work involved in such a scene.

"Aren't we going to do something?" Ricky asked, obviously chomping at the bit for any kind of activity.

Jordan held up a hand to still him. "Please, just a moment." She tried to still the thundering of her heart as she continued to stare at the woman who had been so vibrant and self-assured on Saturday night.

Her mind processed several things at once—the slashed painting on the easel near the body, the numbers drawn in blood on the floor at Joann's feet and the aching human frailty of chipped pink toenail polish on Joann's toes.

What had happened here? There didn't appear to

be any defense wounds on Joann. Had she known her killer? Had she been lured out here to her workplace or had she come willingly? And finally the question that burned inside her—what had the killer left behind that would allow him or her to be found?

"She was at the reunion on Saturday night," she finally said, breaking the silence. "Her name is Joann Hathoway."

"Right, I read an article about her giving a painting to the school," Anthony replied.

"It looks like somebody doesn't like her work," Ricky observed as he gazed at the ripped canvas.

"Crime-scene boys have arrived and the coroner's ETA is five minutes," Officer Johnson said from the doorway.

And so it begins, Jordan thought as she prepared herself to lead the investigation.

It was almost one when she left the shed and walked toward the farmhouse, where Officer Johnson had taken the woman who claimed to be Joann's lover. Somehow Jordan wasn't surprised to discover that Joann was gay. Despite the fact that she'd been pretty and popular in high school, Jordan couldn't remember her ever dating anyone.

She was grateful to leave Anthony and Ricky in the shed to oversee the evidence gathering. Ricky's enthusiasm had gotten under her skin. Maybe she'd just been doing this long enough that she didn't remember the flush of excitement that came with the first murder investigation. She was light-years away from her rookie days, not only in physical time, but in her mentality as well.

More than once over the last couple of hours she'd had to bite her tongue to keep from yelling at him to slow down, pay more attention and spend less time chattering.

She already had a bad feeling about this whole thing. The coroner had fixed time of death between midnight and seven Sunday morning. That meant Joann had been killed mere hours after leaving the reunion.

Jordan didn't bother to knock on the door of the house. She entered into a living room that screamed chaos and she wondered if the perp had tossed the place looking for valuables. On second look she realized it was a controlled chaos. Joann Hathoway might have been a talented artist, but it appeared that she sucked at housework.

She heard voices coming from the kitchen, but instead of going in to face the bereaved lover, their first potential suspect, she instead walked down the hallway to check out the other rooms in the house.

The guest bath was neat and tidy, as was the first bedroom. The second bedroom was an office and the third was the master suite. Here, once again, was chaos. Clothes littered the floor and were tossed haphazardly over a chair. The bed was unmade, but there were no signs of a struggle in the room. The red dress she'd worn to the reunion was slung carelessly across the bottom of the bed.

The adjoining bathroom was also a mess, containing the evidence of a woman getting ready for a night out. Makeup and hair products littered the top of the counter as if Joann had been running late on the night of the reunion and hadn't bothered to re-cap anything she'd used.

Jordan didn't touch anything. She'd have the crime-scene unit go over the room, but in the meantime she had a woman to interview. She went back into the kitchen, where Officer Johnson and the woman sat at the table.

The woman was beautiful. She had delicate features and her fine dark hair was cut short to emphasize pretty brown eyes and high cheekbones. She was clad in a pair of jeans and a red plaid flannel shirt. She stared into an empty coffee cup, her face splotchy and her eyes red-rimmed.

Officer Johnson got up and left the room as Jordan sat

down across from the woman. "I'm Detective Sampson. I know this is a terrible time, but may I ask you a few questions?"

She wrapped her fingers around the coffee cup and gave a curt nod.

Jordan pulled a notepad from her pocket. "What's your name?"

"Linda. Linda Thorpe." Her features twisted and a choked sob escaped her. "I can't believe this is happening. I feel like I'm in a nightmare and I can't wake up."

"Can you tell me what your relationship is to Joann?"

"For the last two years we've been lovers. I told her she shouldn't be living out here all alone. I told her it wasn't safe, but she didn't listen to me, and now look what's happened." Once again a sob choked from her. Then she sucked it up and released a tremulous sigh.

"When was the last time you saw Joann?"

"Saturday night before her reunion."

"And you didn't come by here yesterday?" Jordan asked.

Linda shook her head. "I never come by on Sundays. Sundays were workdays for Joann and she didn't like to be bothered." Linda pulled a tissue from her shirt pocket. "Who did this to her?" She began to cry, deep, wrenching sobs that shook her body.

Before continuing, Jordan waited for her to gain control. "I'm sorry, I know this is difficult. Do you know anyone that Joann was having problems with? Somebody who might be capable of this?"

Linda shook her head vehemently and then lowered the tissue from her eyes. "Oh, sure, Joann could be difficult sometimes, the artistic temperament and all that. But I can't imagine anyone doing something like that." She frowned and her fingers tightened around the tissue. "Was she . . . Did he rape her?"

"Our initial finding is that there was no sexual assault," Jordan said gently. "Where were you on Saturday night?" Jordan certainly couldn't discount the possibility that a woman had committed the murder, especially in the absence of any sexual assault.

Linda's eyes widened. "Oh God, you think I had something to do with this? I loved her. I could never hurt her. I would never hurt anyone."

"Linda, I know how hard this is for you, but we need to know your whereabouts so we can discount you as a suspect. It's the way these investigations work."

She dabbed her eyes with the tissue once again. "I went home. As Joann left for the reunion, I just went home."

"You didn't want to go to the reunion with Joann?"

"It was never an issue," Linda replied. "In the art world people are a lot more open about alternative lifestyles, but Joann didn't want the people she went to school with to know about her personal life."

"Did that bother you?" Jordan asked.

"Not at all. I don't invite Joann to my family functions. We had clear boundaries in the relationship. It was what we both agreed to when we got together."

"Do you live with anyone? Is there somebody who can corroborate the fact that you were home the night of the reunion?"

"No, but my neighbor stopped by around nine. She stayed for about a half an hour and then I went to bed."

"And what about yesterday?"

"I worked. I work for a cable company and I was laying lines from nine yesterday morning to five last night."

The questions continued for another fifteen minutes, and then Linda's features twisted with grief once again. "Can I go now? I feel sick. Please, I need to go home."

Jordan nodded and closed her notepad. She'd gotten what she needed for the moment. She got up from the table and Linda stood as well. "Linda, I know it sounds very Hollywoodish, but please don't leave town without letting me know."

Her words caused a fresh wail of tears at the same time Anthony appeared in the doorway. "Could you escort Linda to her car?"

"No problem," he agreed. As they left the house, Jordan went back to the master bedroom. She stood in the doorway and thought about the Joann she'd known in high school and the woman she'd spent a little time with on Saturday night.

At first glance, it appeared to be a rage killing. Somebody had hated Joann so much they'd wanted to destroy not only her but also the work that she loved.

"Did Linda leave?" she asked.

"Yeah," Anthony said from behind her. "How did you know I was behind you? I didn't make a sound."

She turned and smiled. "You have this little throat-clearing thing you do that you probably aren't aware of. I know you by that sound and Adam by the smell of his cologne. Ricky has a shoe that makes a small squeaking noise and John cracks his knuckles incessantly."

Anthony looked at her in surprise. "I've never noticed that stuff before."

"That's what makes you a good detective and me a great one," she replied. Her smile dropped as she turned back to stare at the room. "I keep thinking about how she looked at the reunion, so alive and successful."

"You going to be okay with this?" Anthony's brow puckered with concern. "I mean, with you knowing her and all?"

"It's not going to be a problem. I knew her when we were both teenagers, but until Saturday night I hadn't seen her in years. Get Ricky in here and the crime-scene unit. We need to treat the house as if it's part of the murder scene. We don't know if somebody came in here and pulled her out of bed or what. We also need to get some officers out there in the woods and see if they find anything that might be linked to the crime."

"You know she was something of a town darling.

There's probably going to be some pressure on this one," Anthony said.

"You trying to cheer me up?" Jordan replied.

"No, just warning you that I've got a bad feeling about this one."

"The real problem, as I see it, is that there were about a hundred people who showed up at that reunion and right now each and every one of them is a potential suspect."

"What about the lover?"

Jordan shrugged. "I don't know, maybe. She seemed genuinely grief-stricken, but so did Parker Sinclair when he heard that his wife had been strangled. Her alibi isn't very strong." She released a weary sigh as Anthony left to get the crime-unit boys.

At three forty-five the alarm on Jordan's wristwatch sounded. No matter where she was, no matter what she was doing, she tried to make a call to Mandy when she got home from school.

She stepped outside the farmhouse and used her cell to call her daughter. As she talked to Mandy, she frowned at the news vans parked in the driveway. Several uniform cops kept the reporters back behind crime-scene tape that had been strung around the area.

Mandy was in one of her moods and the call lasted only a few minutes. Jordan stuck the cell phone back in her pocket and thought about the people she had spent time with on Saturday night.

Had Joann been murdered by somebody who had attended the reunion? Or was the murderer somebody who had been in her life more recently?

It was after six by the time the team of detectives returned to their squad room. "Ricky, you can start researching the numbers twenty-four, sixty-eight. See if they have any literary meaning or what they might refer to," Jordan instructed. "Anthony, see if you can get hold of Marisa Delaney. She's head of the alumni committee and should have a master list of everyone who attended the reunion. I'm going to give Joann's agent a call and see what he can tell me about what was going on in her life in the last weeks or months."

Linda had told Jordan that Joann's parents were deceased and that Joann had been an only child, leaving the next-of-kin issue up in the air. Jordan was hoping to get some valuable information from the man who had represented her as an artist.

They all worked until almost midnight, when it was decided that nothing more could be done until morning. Ricky left first, followed closely by Anthony. "You calling it a night, too?" Adam Kent said to Jordan from his desk.

"Yeah. We can hit it hard again tomorrow. You're burning the midnight oil."

"Working the Miller case." He reared back in his chair and stifled a yawn with the back of his hand. "Hey, you know that thing this morning, all the pom-poms and stuff. You know we were all just having a good time."

"I know, but I'm still contemplating the sexual harassment suit," she said with a straight face.

Adam's eyes grew so big she thought they might pop out of his head. "For real?"

Jordan laughed. "Honestly, Adam, I could have filed sexual harassment suits every day working with you boneheads. A few pom-poms aren't going to push me over the edge. Don't work too late and I'll see you in the morning."

As she left the station, the chilly night air penetrated through her lightweight jacket and chilled her to the bone. Or maybe it wasn't so much the autumn air that iced through her but rather thoughts of Joann roped to that chair and stabbed over and over again.

Thoughts of the murder continued to haunt her as she drove the twenty minutes it took to get to her house. She'd been unable to get ahold of Joann's agent, but she'd left a message for him with his answering service.

At this point it was impossible to know whether the

murder had anything to do with the reunion. Jordan desperately hoped it didn't. She'd prefer not to believe that any of the people she went to high school with might be capable of such a crime.

She yawned with exhaustion as she pulled into her driveway, wishing she'd used some of the weekend to empty a few of the boxes that were still stacked in the garage.

"Before winter," she muttered to herself as she turned off her engine. She definitely needed to get the garage cleaned out so she could park inside for the Kansas City winter ahead.

She grabbed her purse and the file folder she'd brought home and got out of the car. She'd gone only a couple of steps when she felt it, that faint tingle at the nape of her neck that pulled forth the crazy edge of paranoia.

Was somebody nearby? Watching her? She shot a glance first to the left, then to the right, but didn't see anyone on the darkened street. Of course, it was an old neighborhood with mature trees lining the street and bordering the side of her property.

Dead leaves danced across the sidewalk. The moon was partially obscured by clouds and in the distance a dog howled. Halloween was still two weeks away, but it was a witchy night and Jordan couldn't shake the creepy sensation that followed her in through the front door.

Once inside she moved to her front window and pulled the curtain aside a mere inch and peered out. Nothing. Absolutely no reason for her to feel like she did. Maybe her jumpiness came from the fact that for the first time in her career she was investigating the murder of somebody she had known. It was the first time a murder had come so close to her since her own sister's death.

She was about to let the curtain fall back into place when she saw it—the shadow of a tree trunk across the street that suddenly split into two shadows. Every muscle in her body tensed as the smaller shadow darted away and disappeared down the street.

Somebody had been there. She thought about pulling her gun and chasing down the street after him—or her. Instead she told herself to breathe and calm down.

The family across the street included a teenage son who apparently was a popular hunk. It was quite possible the shadow she'd seen had belonged to some lovelorn teenage girl hoping to catch a glimpse of her one true love.

"It's not all about you," she reminded herself as she allowed the curtain to fall back in place. Still, before she got into bed, she double-checked to make sure all the doors were locked, and placed her Glock on the nightstand instead of in the drawer where she usually kept it.

Chapter 7

"Sampson, what have you and your team got for me this morning?" Sergeant Wendt asked as he reached for another of the fresh doughnuts that Ricky Copeland had brought with him when he'd arrived at work that morning.

"I'm waiting for a call back from Joann's agent to see if he knows of any problems she might have been having in her personal or professional life. We're checking out the lover's alibi and today we're going to start the interviews of people who were at the reunion Saturday night."

"What about those numbers? Anything on that?"

Ricky cleared his throat with self-importance and stood. "I did a search to see what I could find for twenty-four sixty-eight. It's a model number for everything from electric drills to sunglasses."

Jordan had already gone over the information with Ricky and Anthony before the briefing had begun. It was going to be a long day as they began talking to all the people who had attended the reunion. It was probably going to take them all week to get to everyone. Hopefully something would pop with the agent that would point them in a different direction.

"I found one more reference to the numbers that I thought everyone might be interested in," Ricky said. "It's a short sermon by a Reverend Jacob Nightsong."

Jordan frowned. He hadn't mentioned anything about a sermon when she'd spoken with him earlier. Hot dog, she thought with irritation.

"I took the liberty of printing off the sermon for everyone." Ricky stood and began to pass out copies to the others in the room.

"Nice work, Copeland," Sergeant Wendt said.

"Suddenly he thinks he's the Lone Ranger?" Anthony muttered beneath his breath to Jordan.

Jordan took the copy Ricky handed her and scanned it quickly. Apparently Reverend Jacob Nightsong was a preacher who wasn't a stranger to the fire-and-brimstone form of communication. The sermon was one damning same-sex marriages and the liberal political powers attempting to twist the morals of the innocent.

"Terrific." Sergeant Wendt frowned. "Looks like we have a potential hate crime here."

"And Reverend Jacob Nightsong just moved up to the top of our suspect list," Jordan said.

"Okay, that's it. Get to work and let me know if anything breaks." Wendt left the squad room and Jordan turned in her chair to face Ricky. "Copeland, you don't want to be a team player, then get off my team."

He flushed with obvious embarrassment. "I just wanted to surprise you." It was a lame excuse and they all knew it.

"Wipe the brown spot off the end of your nose and let's get to work," Jordan said. "See if you can find us an address for this Reverend Nightsong. We need to have a little chat to see what else the good reverend does besides write inflammatory sermons."

By ten o'clock they had Jacob Nightsong's home and church addresses. Jordan left Ricky to wait for the call from Joann's agent and any early lab reports that might come in and to field the crank calls that would surely begin to burn up the phone lines. She was still irritated with the young cop for his grandstanding.

"If I could put him in time-out, I would," Jordan groused as she and Anthony got into the car.

Anthony laughed. "Ah, cut him some slack. He's young."

"I don't mind young if it involves drinking too much at a football game or mud wrestling in the backyard, but I don't like it if it involves trying to showboat for Benny."

"Copeland is just trying to make a name for himself."

"Yeah, well, he isn't going to like the name he's making if he doesn't play well with others." She started the car and they took off in the direction of Jacob Nightsong's home.

"Speaking of drinking too much, I think John is developing a real problem."

Jordan nodded. "I know it's been tough on him with his wife so sick. I heard hospice volunteers are pretty much managing her care during the day now."

"I know the chief has told him to take some time off, to stay at home with her, but John told me he made a promise to Mary that he'd keep his life as normal as possible."

"That's not normal," Jordan replied.

Anthony grinned. "Yeah, like we're the barometers for normal. I can't get over the wife that left me three years ago and you pretend like you've got it all together and we both know you're just a heartbeat away from murdering your ex, kidnapping your daughter and moving to a little town in Mexico where you can imbibe in umbrella drinks all day long."

Jordan laughed. "I don't want Dane dead, but I do want Mandy with me and I definitely love umbrella drinks."

"Did you see the paper this morning?"

"No, I didn't have time before getting to work."

Anthony cracked his window to allow some of the fresh cool air into the car. "Joann would have probably been disappointed that she didn't make the front page, but she made the third page. The article didn't mention the numbers written in her blood, so at least we didn't have any leaks about that."

"Keeping that information away from the public will make it easier to sift through the calls that come in," Jordan replied.

It always amazed her how many people called in to confess to a high-profile murder. The mentally ill, the morally corrupt, attention seekers, lonely souls, they all seemed to crawl out of the woodwork to call the tip line and confess to murders they hadn't committed.

"Have you heard from Della?" Anthony asked.

Jordan shot him a quick glance. "Not since Sunday. Why?"

"Just wondering. You mentioned she had a meltdown at the reunion. It didn't have anything to do with Joann, did it?"

"Surely you don't think Della had anything to do with Joann's murder," Jordan exclaimed. "She was too drunk to swat a fly when I left her Saturday night."

Wasn't she? Jordan tightened her hands on the steering wheel as she thought of the bitterness Della had spewed on the way home. But it hadn't been directed at Joann, she reminded herself. It had been Betsy that had set Della off, not Joann.

Surely it was crazy to even consider that Della might have had anything to do with Joann's death. Still, Jordan recognized that her friend was as much a suspect as anyone who had been at the reunion. Of course, they hadn't discerned yet if Joann's murder had anything at all to do with the reunion.

"Maybe we'll find something on Joann's cell phone," she said.

"You mean like somebody who bought a painting and called her to tell her he was going to kill her because she used too much red in the tree leaves?"

"It could happen," Jordan replied.

The Reverend Jacob Nightsong lived in a small bungalow-type house just north of the river. The yard was neat, although the house itself desperately needed a fresh coat of paint.

By the tenor of the sermon, Jordan expected an older man with white hair and beard and the fear of hell burning in his eyes. The man who answered their knock on the door was a nice-looking thirtysomething clad in jeans and a sweatshirt, and he sported a pleasant smile.

"Jacob Nightsong?" Jordan asked.

"That's me," he replied.

"Reverend Jacob Nightsong?"

He nodded. "That's right. Can I help you?"

Jordan introduced herself and Anthony. "Could we come in and speak with you?"

His pleasant smile fell away as he opened the door to allow them inside. "Has something happened? Is one of my parishioners in trouble?" He gestured them toward the shabby sofa and he sat opposite in a straight-backed chair.

"Actually, what we'd like to talk about with you is your sermon numbered twenty-four sixty-eight," Anthony said.

Jacob frowned. "I'm sorry, you're going to have to refresh my memory. I'm now working on number twenty-six twenty-eight."

Jordan pulled out her copy that Ricky had given her and handed it to the reverend. He quickly scanned it and then returned it to Jordan. "Ah yes, now I remember. So, what's this about?"

"You have a problem with gays?" Anthony asked.

"I have several friends who are gay," he replied.

"That really doesn't answer the question. You have friends who are gay yet you wrote that sermon," Anthony said.

Jacob leaned forward in his chair. "I'm the head of a small, fundamentalist church that follows the Bible in the strictest sense. I've also preached sermons on the topic of gluttony and gambling, but I have several friends who are overeating gambling addicts. Now, you want to tell me why you're here? I'm sure it isn't just to have a discussion about my sermons."

"Do you know Joann Hathoway?" Jordan asked.

Jacob's face paled. "You mean the artist woman who was murdered? I read about it in this morning's paper. No, I don't know her. I'd never heard of her before reading the paper this morning."

"Can you tell us what you were doing late Saturday night?" Anthony pulled out his notepad and pen.

"That's easy. I was painting the church with a handful of congregation members. We started around five that afternoon and worked until almost three in the morning. We wanted it ready for services on Sunday."

As Anthony took down the names of the people who had helped with the painting, Jordan felt the disappointment of a bust. She didn't believe the good preacher had anything to do with Joann's murder, despite the inflammatory nature of his sermon, a sermon that had originally been written well over a year before.

"It will only take a few phone calls to check out his alibi," Anthony said as they left the house.

"Let's hope Ricky has learned something from Joann's agent. Otherwise we need to start interviewing the people who attended the reunion." Jordan slid into the car and started the engine.

"It's going to be a long week," Anthony said.

"Lately it seems like they're all long," Jordan replied with a sigh.

"Come on, boys. You can run faster than that," Clint shouted to the members of his football team who were running the track around the ball field. "What's up with Chandler?" he asked his assistant coach. "He looks like he's got rocks in his pants."

"He told me he had a bellyache before we started practice," Jim Pettison replied.

Jim was one of the physical education teachers, like Clint. Jim was also Clint's right-hand man when it came to getting the team into the shape that might take them once again to the state championships.

"Have them do one more lap. Then they can hit the showers," Clint replied. "I'll be in my office."

He walked back inside the school building and into the glass-enclosed office inside the boys' locker room. He sat in the leather chair and thought about Chandler Stewart, his star quarterback.

The kid reminded Clint a lot of himself when he'd been that age. Too handsome for his own good, cocky and with a chip on his shoulder, Chandler thought he could solve any problem that came his way by screwing his brains out with any willing girl.

Clint remembered that mentality all too well.

Like Chandler, Clint had come from a broken home. His parents had divorced when he was eight. It had been a bitter divorce, with Clint as a pawn being pushed and pulled by the two people he cared about most. Ultimately it had left him boldly arrogant on the outside and an insecure mess on the inside.

It had taken years for him to achieve the kind of maturity to look inward and see his own flaws and then consciously make an effort to correct them. Just about the time he'd believed he'd gotten it right, he'd married Holly.

Holly, with the red gold hair and leaf green eyes. She'd driven him half-mad during their three-year marriage. She'd had big dreams for him, for them, but quickly became disenchanted with him and with the marriage.

It had been wild, hot sex that had brought them together and it had been the same thing that had ended the marriage.

He shuffled some papers into a file and spied the blue Post-it note that had been sitting on his desk since early the day before. Jordan's cell phone number. He'd called Marisa Delaney and she'd talked to somebody who had talked to somebody and had gotten him the number. Seeing her again had stirred all kinds of crazy emotions inside him.

There had been moments over the years that he'd thought about her, wondered about her. She had been his first real love, but unfortunately most of the decisions he'd made in high school had been made with his dick and not with his head.

He hadn't gotten enough time with her at the reunion. He would have liked to have had a chance to visit with her longer. For the last three days he'd toyed with the idea of calling and asking her out for a drink or maybe a meal and still he hadn't made the call.

Clint had done his homework and learned that her ex-husband was a wealthy best-selling author. After living that kind of a lifestyle, why would she want to have drinks or dinner with a high school coach?

Besides, he'd been such a jerk to her in high school. Maybe she'd never forgiven him for that.

He shoved the Post-it note aside and got up as the football team members filled the locker room with their chaos. Maybe tomorrow he'd work up the nerve to give her a call.

John Lindsay sat next to the hospital bed that stood in the center of his living room. The beautiful woman he'd married almost thirty years ago was no longer evident in the emaciated shell of a body that lay in the bed.

Cancer was a pitiless bastard that didn't care if it struck the good, the bad or the ugly. In the case of Mary, the beast was taking away the very best of John.

It had always just been the two of them. There had been no children and that had never mattered to John because Mary was all he'd ever wanted, all he'd ever needed to be happy.

The hospice people had told him it was just a matter of days now, but for all intents and purposes Mary was already gone. For the past couple of days she'd been unconscious more than she'd been conscious.

He'd never realized before how much she'd filled the house with her sounds, how she'd colored his entire world in bright and happy tones. Now the world was nothing but painful silence and shades of gray.

He glanced at the coffee table where dozens of slick travel brochures stared back at him. "I'm going to beat this, Johnny," Mary had said time and time again. "I'm going to beat this and you're going to retire and we're going to have the most wonderful golden years a couple could ever have. We'll travel the world, just you and me."

Grief ripped through him with a stabbing pain that stole his breath. If he hadn't already been sitting, it would have thrown him to his knees. There would be no island retreats, no mountain resorts, for the two of them; there would be no two of them at all.

Already the house held the signs of her absence. The kitchen no longer smelled of lemon wax and cinnamon. The scent of her gardenia perfume no longer wafted in the air. Her makeup didn't litter the bathroom countertop, and her side of the bed remained achingly cold whenever he reached for her warmth in the middle of the night.

He didn't know why she was still here. The cancer had ravaged her from the inside out and yet she clung to life by a tenuous thread. He knew somehow that she stayed for him, because she knew how utterly empty his life would be without her.

Tears burned at his eyes and he raised his glass of scotch to his lips. He took a deep swallow, welcoming the burn in the back of his throat, the blossoming warmth in the pit of his stomach.

He knew he was drinking too much, but it was the only way he could sit here night after night with her; it was the only way to ease some of the agony of losing Mary.

He leaned forward and took her thin, cool hand in his. He knew he should tell her that it was okay to let go, that it was past time for her to leave, but he couldn't release her. He simply wasn't ready to tell her good-bye forever and that filled him with a self-loathing as he recognized his own selfishness.

"I got a couple of new brochures in the mail today, honey," he said. "What do you think about one of those little grass huts in Tahiti? You can sun topless on the beach and I'll climb trees for fresh coconuts and at night we'll make love with the sound of the ocean crashing to the shore. Or there's a little lodge in Aspen where we could spend the days learning to ski and sip hot cocoa and snuggle in the evenings."

A sob raced up the back of his throat and he washed it down with another deep gulp of the scotch. The next couple of hours passed like most of the late-evening hours had in the last couple of weeks, with John talking about vacation spots until he was hoarse, and him drinking enough that finally he passed out in the chair.

Chapter 8

Jordan's cell phone rang the next morning as she left her desk to get a cup of the coffee that had just been brewed in the squad room. She'd already had three cups, trying to wake up after a late-night phone session with Della, who had learned of Joann's murder and was having one of her dramatic breakdowns.

Della had wailed like a baby, insisting that even though she'd hated Joann in high school, she wouldn't have wished this on her. The cool, confident Della that Jordan knew had vanished. It was almost one in the morning when Jordan had finally managed to get off the phone.

She now pulled her cell phone from the pocket of her blazer and answered.

"Jordan."

The sound of her name spoken in that deep, familiar voice sent a rush of heat through her. "Clint," she replied, and ducked into the ladies' restroom, where she could be alone.

"How are you?"

"Crazy busy. What about you?"

"I'm okay. I was disappointed that we didn't get more time together at the reunion and I was wondering if maybe some night you'd like to meet me for drinks or dinner."

"How about this evening?" Jordan replied. She told herself it would be strictly business. She had to interview him sooner or later. She might as well make it this evening. "Just coffee," she continued. "I've been working long hours, but if you'd like to meet me at the Coffee Shop, across the street from the courthouse downtown, then I could take a few minutes."

"Just tell me what time and I'll be there," he replied.

"How about seven?" she asked.

"Sounds perfect. And, Jordan, I'm really looking forward to it."

She leaned against the cool tile wall when the call ended. She'd told herself it would be strictly business, but no business she'd ever conducted before had sent a flame of heat raging through her veins.

At the sink she sluiced cool water over her face, wondering how it was that after all these years Clint still affected her on a level that no other man ever had.

Maybe it was because he'd been the young man in her life as she'd begun to experience her own sexuality. He'd been her first real kiss, her first make-out session. The sexual attraction she'd felt for him had been more powerful than anything she'd experienced before or since him. She'd spent many restless nights in high school wondering what it would be like to make love with him.

What she felt at the moment where he was concerned was a sense of unfinished business, a lack of closure. "The only closure you need is to find out where he was on the night of the murder," she told her reflection in the mirror. She dried off her face and then left the restroom.

The rest of the morning was spent dividing up the list of reunion attendees between herself, Anthony and Ricky; then the three of them went their separate ways to begin the arduous task of interviewing everyone.

It was just after noon when she drove to Danny McCall's apartment. She'd called him minutes earlier to make sure he was home, so he was expecting her. As she drove north, her mind kept racing back to Clint.

If it had been about just sex in high school, Clint would have broken up with her and they would have never gotten back together again, but their attraction to each other had been about more than sex.

He'd made her laugh and they'd had so many things in common. Many nights after a movie or going out to eat, they'd end up at Englewood Park in front of the pond, where during the day neighborhood kids came to fish for bluegill or swing on the swings and play on the other playground equipment.

When the weather was nice enough, they'd sit on the hood of his Thunderbird and talk about anything and everything that popped into their heads. When the weather wasn't so nice, they'd snuggle in the backseat and listen to the radio, content just to be together.

She had no idea what kind of man he'd become, but she knew who she was at the moment. The last thing she wanted was any kind of meaningful relationship with anyone. She had enough on her hands trying to maneuver through the status quo; she hardly needed to add a man into the mix.

It had been well over a year since she'd had sex. If she was perfectly honest with herself, finally knowing what he'd be like as a lover wasn't completely out of the question.

The thought brought a smile to her lips and the smile was still there when she knocked on Danny McCall's apartment door.

He answered on the second knock, a smile on his blunt features. "Jordan, I sure didn't expect to see you again so soon. Come on in," he said.

He ushered her into a tiny living room with furniture that looked as if it had come from the local thrift shops. A card table was set up in one corner and on top was an intricate puzzle that was partially put together. The walls were lined with puzzles that had been glued and framed.

"Wow," she said. "Looks like you're terrific at puzzles."

He shoved his hands in his jeans pocket and grinned in pride. "I like puzzles," he replied. "So, why'd you want to see me?"

Jordan sat on the edge of the sofa. "I need to ask you a few questions, Danny. Do you read the paper?"

"Nah, don't watch the news either. All that stuff depresses me. Why?"

"Joann Hathoway was murdered the night of the reunion."

His brown eyes widened in what appeared to be genuine shock. "No way." He sank down into the chair opposite the sofa and dropped his head in his hands. When he raised his head to look at Jordan, she was stunned by the wealth of despair she saw in his eyes.

"I always had a crush on her, all through school. She never paid any attention to me, but I thought she was one of the prettiest girls I'd ever seen. I even saved up some money and a couple of years ago I bought one of her paintings from an art gallery. I got it hanging in my bedroom."

Jordan was stunned, not so much by the fact that he'd had a crush on Joann in high school, but because as recently as a couple of years before, she'd apparently still been on his mind. And it was obvious he had no idea that the information he'd just given her might be incriminating.

"Danny, we're talking to everyone who attended the reunion to find out where you went afterward."

Once again his eyes grew wider. "You think somebody from the reunion killed her?"

"We don't know. We're just trying to cover all the bases," she replied. "So, what time did you leave the reunion?"

"Right at midnight when it was over."

"And did you go anywhere afterward?" she asked.

He shook his head. "I just came home. I'd worked all day. I work at General Mills. I pack flour, and by the time the reunion was over, I was pooped."

"Do you always work on Saturdays?"

"Usually. It's a shift nobody much likes to work if they have family. Why would somebody want to hurt her?" He looked at her with the wide-eyed innocence she remembered from high school. "She was beautiful and she created beauty. Why would somebody want to take that away?"

"I don't know, but we'll find whoever is responsible. Now, did you talk to anyone after you got home that night? Did any of your neighbors see you coming in?"

He frowned. "Not that I know of. My neighbors are all senior citizens. They're usually in bed pretty early in the evening. They always tell me I'm a good neighbor because I'm so quiet."

"You haven't married?"

"No, just hasn't been in the cards for me," he replied. "You know me, good old Danny, everybody's friend."

"Have you kept up with anyone from high school?"

Danny shrugged. "A couple of the guys. Fred Martin works with me down at the plant. He and I occasionally go out for a beer or watch a football game together. Mike Walburn lives not far from here and sometimes he and his wife have me over for dinner."

They talked for a few more minutes; then Jordan left to head to her next interview. It was only as she was driving away that she realized Danny hadn't asked exactly how Joann had died.

It was five o'clock by the time she returned to the station in order to check in with Anthony and Ricky.

"I'm about to open up a can of whoop ass on you," Anthony said as she walked through the door of the small interrogation room they'd commandeered to coordinate their efforts.

"Why, what did I do?" Jordan flopped down at her desk and released a weary sigh.

"You put that crazy Betsy on my list. That woman is like a windup doll on crack," Anthony replied. Jordan grinned at the description.

"Did you know she's got these glassed-in bookcases in her living room and they're filled with some kind of collector dolls? There must be a hundred of them and she thought it was important for me to look at each and every one of them."

"Blakely dolls," Jordan replied. "She was collecting them back when we were in high school."

"Apparently she never stopped, and she never stops talking." He opened his desk drawer and pulled out a bottle of aspirin. He shook two into his hand and dry swallowed them. "So, what have we got?"

For the next hour and a half the three of them went over the list of interviews they'd done, and by the time they were finished, they had broken down the original list into three: one of people who had solid alibis, one for people who had shaky alibis and one of people who had yet to be contacted.

Joann's agent had called and Ricky had spoken with him. He'd been stunned by the news of the murder and had no information to add to help them with their investigation. He'd explained that he'd had a professional relationship with Joann, that there were certainly no problems in her professional life and he didn't know anything about her personal life.

The list of suspects was pathetically small and the initial urgency that marked a fresh murder case was already waning. The preliminary reports from the evidence collection were dismal. The killer had left no forensic evidence on the body or in the general area.

All they knew for sure was that Joann Hathoway, along with her latest painting, had been stabbed to death with a knife that had a six- to eight-inch blade. The coroner had confirmed that there had been no sexual assault.

The three detectives once again split the list of people who still needed to be interviewed. As Anthony and Ricky left, Jordan went into the restroom to prepare for her interview with Clint.

The good thing about her short hairstyle was that a little bit of gel in the morning kept it in place all day long. She dabbed on a bit of lip gloss, then spritzed herself with the purse-size bottle of her favorite perfume.

It was only as she turned away from the mirror that she thought of her earlier idea of finally having sex with him. What made her think that wasn't exactly what he had in mind? She was probably one of the few women in his life who had told him no. Maybe his whole reason for wanting to see her again was to finally nail the one who had gotten away.

Of course, the real question she needed Clint to answer was where he'd gone after the reunion and whether he had any reason to want Joann Hathoway dead.

The sun was sinking as Jordan left the station. The pinks and oranges of sunset painted the buildings and pavement in lush, warm tones.

The Coffee Shop had opened in 1935, a year after the Jackson County Courthouse had been built and two years before the twenty-nine-story City Hall had been completed. It was a no-frill place that didn't offer fancy lattes or mochas. The coffee was either regular or decaf, the food packaged sandwiches and a variety of muffins and sweet rolls. The clientele was mostly lawyers and cops in a hurry or people cooling their heels before facing a judge.

The place was now empty except for Sam, who stood behind the sandwich counter when Jordan entered. Sam was as much a fixture of downtown as the famous Savoy Hotel that had stood on the corner of Ninth and Central since 1888.

"Hey, Sam," she greeted him as she approached the counter.

"Ah, lovely Jordan. Working late again tonight?" He poured coffee into a tall foam cup and set it on top of the counter, his wizen face wreathed in a broad smile.

"You know how it is, Sam. As long as folks are mostly crazy, I work late."

They visited for a moment and then she took the cup of coffee and sat at a table near the window to wait for Clint as Sam disappeared into a back room. Besides the interviewing of the last two days, Jordan had been trying to reconstruct the last week of Joann's life.

She pulled her notepad from her pocket and read over the notes she'd made when she'd interviewed Linda. Was it possible that Linda had wanted to attend the reunion with Joann, but Joann hadn't wanted any of her old friends to know her sexual preference?

Despite the fact that being gay no longer had the same stigma attached to it that it once had, there were still plenty of people reluctant to come out of the closet. Maybe Linda had lied about the boundaries the two had put into place when they'd begun dating.

Had Joann and Linda fought before the reunion, and then had Linda been there waiting for Joann to return home afterward? She could have killed Joann, then gone home and pretended to find the body Monday morning.

There was no question that it had been a rage killing. Joann had been stabbed fourteen times. Definitely an overkill that implied enormous passion and hatred. Had it been Linda waiting for Joann or had somebody followed Joann home from the reunion that night, somebody who hated her so much that he or she had been unable to control the rage?

The whoosh of the door opening pulled her from her thoughts and she looked up to see Clint. Clad in a pair of worn, tight-fitting jeans and an Oak Ridge High School sweatshirt, he looked ridiculously handsome.

"Hi." He sat across from her, his gaze warm and open. "I hope you haven't been waiting long."

She smiled and shook her head. "I've only been here a few minutes. But as I recall, you were always late for dates."

"Ouch," he said with a mock wince. He glanced over at the counter. "You need anything?" She shook her head. "I'll be right back." He went to the counter, where

Sam poured him a cup of coffee, and then he returned and once again sat at the table. "I looked for you later in the evening at the reunion, but you were nowhere to be found."

"I left early," she replied, not feeling any need to elaborate about Della's breakdown. "What about you? How late did you stay?"

"Until the bitter end. There were ten of us on a cleanup committee. It was well after two when we left the hotel, and then we all gathered at Denny's and ate breakfast. I didn't get home until after four."

Jordan hadn't realized how much she'd hoped he had a good alibi until the moment she heard it. Tension she hadn't recognized was there but that weighed heavy on her shoulders suddenly lifted.

For the next few minutes they talked about the people they'd seen at the reunion, laughing about who had lost their hair, who had come into their own and the fact that the boy who had been voted most likely to succeed was now serving time in prison for white-collar crimes.

Clint still had the amazing ability to make the woman he was speaking to feel as if she were the most important person in the world. He had a direct gaze that never wavered as he spoke.

It was both evocative and just a tad bit disconcerting.

"So, tell me, are you seeing somebody? Do you have a significant other in your life?" he asked.

"Shouldn't you have asked me that before you invited me for drinks or dinner?" she countered.

"I was hoping the fact you agreed to meet me here now was my answer."

"No, I'm not seeing anyone at the moment. My life is too complicated right now to be interested in any kind of a relationship."

"Complicated how?"

She could tell that it wasn't just an empty question, that he was truly curious to know. She leaned back in the chair and frowned thoughtfully, trying to decide how much or how little to tell him.

"Aside from my job, which requires a great deal of time and energy, I'm also working hard to maintain a relationship with my twelve-year-old daughter, Mandy, who lives with my ex-husband. I have her most weekends and she's the most important person in my world."

He nodded, his dark hair gleaming beneath the artificial light overhead. "As it should be. But having a daughter who is important in your life shouldn't prevent you from having a relationship. I mean, you're here now with me."

His words reminded her why she was there. "Have you heard about Joann Hathoway?" she asked in an abrupt change of subject.

"What about her?" His light tone indicated that he definitely hadn't heard.

"She was murdered."

Clint's eyes flared slightly and a small gasp escaped him. "When?"

"Saturday night after the reunion."

"At the hotel? Was she mugged or what?"

"She was killed at her home north of the river. Clint, I need the names of the people who you went to breakfast with early Sunday morning." She pulled her pad and pen from her pocket.

It was his turn to lean back in the chair and his eyes narrowed slightly. "So, you agreed to meet me tonight because you needed to interview me. It had nothing to do with an interest to connect on a more personal level."

"It was a little bit of both," she admitted sheepishly.

"Then let's get the business out of the way." He named the people he'd been with after the reunion. "I'm really sorry about Joann, but if she was killed in the hours after the reunion, none of those people can be responsible." He leaned forward once again. "Now, tell me when you and I can have a real date."

It was a rush, no doubt about it, that he wanted to go out with her after all these years. If he were a viable suspect in the murder case, she wouldn't consider seeing him on a social basis. But it would take only a couple of phone calls to confirm that he couldn't possibly have anything to do with Joann's death.

She had a sudden memory of how his lips had felt sliding slowly down her neck, how his hands had warmed her breasts even through whatever blouse she'd been wearing at the time. It had been so long since she'd felt the sheer pleasure of sexual excitement. That had been one of the first emotions to leave her marriage when she'd discovered Dane's infidelity.

"Like I said, I spend most of my weekends with Mandy, but maybe we could have a late dinner on Sunday evening?" She hadn't intended to agree to anything, somehow knew that this was probably a big mistake.

"Great, what time would be good for you?"

"I take my daughter back to the house at six. Why don't we say around seven?" She wrote her address on her notepad and tore it off and pushed it across the table to him. "I have to get back to work," she said. She stood and he rose as well. She started for the door, then turned back to face him. "You know, Clint, we aren't the same people we were in high school."

He grinned, that sexy smile that had always had the capacity to weaken her knees. "I'm betting there's still just a little bit of that girl who drove me half-crazy inside you."

"We'll see about that," she replied, and then walked out the door and into the chilly night air.

At eight o'clock in the evening the streets were mainly deserted. Jordan had never been afraid to walk in this area after dark. Having a Glock in her holster definitely gave her a confidence she wouldn't have felt without it.

Still, tonight as she crossed the street and headed toward police headquarters, she once again got that tingly feeling at the nape of her neck, as though somebody was watching her. She whirled around to see if maybe Clint had come out of the restaurant, but she did not see him.

She narrowed her gaze and checked the shadows that clung to the buildings where the streetlight illumination didn't reach. Was somebody hiding there? She scanned the area, seeking a source for her uneasiness, but saw nothing, saw nobody.

Putting her hand on the butt of her gun, she picked up her pace and didn't breathe easily until she was in the building.

He watched her disappear through the front door of police headquarters and then he hurried toward a nearby parking lot where his car was located. He raised his collar against the chilly night air and smiled to himself.

He was pleased that she was lead detective on the Hathoway case. She had the reputation for being tough and smart. But he was smarter. She had a terrific solve rate on the homicides she worked, but this one wasn't going to be solved.

He'd been careful. He'd been clean and they would have been left with no real leads to follow.

He now had the addresses for all of them—the five remaining girls who had broken fragile hearts and made high school miserable for so many. Sally Kincaid would be difficult, as she was now living in Chicago, but the rest of them had remained in Kansas City.

All day today an urgency had filled him. The need to strike again, to take another one of them out of this world, had burned in his gut since the moment he'd opened his eyes that morning.

He wasn't a murderer, but there was no question that he'd enjoyed killing Joann. He'd relished the fear in her eyes, the sobs of terror that had ripped from her throat.

He'd liked the feel of her blood on his hands, so warm and slick.

Justice, that was what it had been.

Mentally he was ready to act again, but there were two things holding him back. He needed to do some more research into the women. He needed to discover what they cared about most and when they were most vulnerable. He'd gotten lucky the first time. Joann had been easy because she'd lived alone out in the middle of nowhere. The others wouldn't be so easy.

He reached his car and slid in behind the steering wheel. Instead of starting the engine, he leaned his head back and thought of Jordan Sampson. Head cheerleader. Lead detective.

She wasn't going to solve the Hathoway case, and when the next one happened, she'd probably be able to put the pieces together and realize she was on the killer's hit list. He'd save her for last, though. He wanted the big bad detective to look over her shoulder, to sleep with one eye open. He wanted her afraid. He was going to take particular pleasure in her death.

"Eenie meanie miney mo—who will be the next to go?" He grinned as he started the engine and pulled out of the parking lot. He might not be a murderer, but he was definitely starting to enjoy the game.

Chapter 9

"Wow, I can't believe you had such long hair," Mandy exclaimed as she looked at an old picture of her mother she'd dug out of the box in front of her.

Both Mandy and Jordan were seated on the floor in Jordan's living room, a carton of take-out pizza in front of them along with the box of old photos.

"Why did you cut it?" Mandy asked.

Jordan couldn't tell her that she'd cut her hair so she didn't look so much like her dead sister, that she'd hoped that by doing so she would enable her parents to look at her again without pain darkening their eyes. "It just got to be too much work."

Mandy dug into the box and came up with another picture, this one of Jordan and her fellow cheerleaders. They were all in their uniforms and had their arms around one another, mugging for the camera with laughter in their eyes.

"Your uniforms were dorky," Mandy announced.

Jordan laughed. "Styles have definitely changed since I was in high school."

It had been a good day. She'd picked up Mandy just after ten and they had gone to see the latest teen movie. It had set a lighthearted tone for the rest of the afternoon, which was exactly what Jordan had needed after a week of dealing with murder.

They'd followed the movie with a trip to the mall,

where they'd eaten fat salty pretzels and ice-cream cones, then bought new blouses for each of them. It had been a perfect mother-daughter day and the pleasantness continued as they riffled through the old pictures.

"Don't forget you promised that you'd show me some cheers in the morning," Mandy said.

"I won't forget," Jordan replied. "I just hope I can make these old bones and muscles move the way they used to."

"You aren't old," Mandy protested. "You're prettier than all my friends' moms."

"I'm glad you think so." Jordan plucked a photo out of the box. "Look, here's one of you when you were two."

Looking at old pictures always evoked a touch of melancholy in Jordan. Seeing the pictures of Mandy as a toddler made her realize how quickly childhood passed. She wanted to lock Mandy in the bedroom and never let her go; she wanted to talk and talk and talk until she'd convinced Mandy to move in here with her. But she did neither of those things. Instead she embraced each and every moment she had to share with her daughter.

She was just about to put the box of pictures away when Mandy grabbed one and frowned. "Who is this?" She held out the picture toward Jordan. "She almost looks like you."

Jordan's heart squeezed as she took the picture of Julie. She'd never discussed her sister with her daughter. It was a subject, like cheerleading, that had never come up. "Her name was Julie. She was my younger sister."

Mandy's eyes widened. "You had a sister? What happened to her?"

"She died."

"How? How did she die? What happened to her?" Mandy asked.

Jordan thought of all the stories she could tell her daughter, stories about mysterious illnesses or tragic accidents. In the end she opted for the truth, deciding that

Mandy was both old enough and mature enough to hear it.

"She was murdered." Jordan stared down at the photo and her heart ached with the familiar sense of loss and a faint whisper of guilt. She looked at Mandy and laid the picture back in the box. "She was a senior in high school and one night she sneaked out of the house and somebody strangled her to death."

"Oh, Mom." Mandy moved closer and leaned against Jordan. "That's so sad."

"It was sad," Jordan replied, and placed an arm around Mandy's shoulders. "She was a year younger than me and she was my best friend. I still miss her." She stroked Mandy's hair. "I wish you could have met her. She was funny and she would have adored you."

"Is that why Grandma and Granddad are sad all the time?"

"I guess so. Losing Julie changed our family and they've never been able to find a way to move forward." It was so rare that Mandy allowed herself to be hugged or kissed anymore. Jordan wished this moment with her daughter in her arms could last forever, but all too quickly Mandy pushed away and sat up.

"Maybe I shouldn't have told you about Julie," Jordan said, suddenly second-guessing herself. "Maybe I should have waited until you were older."

"Mom, I'm not a baby," Mandy exclaimed with a huff of exasperation. "Daddy says if I ever sneak out of the house, he'll ground me until I'm thirty."

Jordan laughed. "I'll help him board up your windows and doors."

Mandy reached for a piece of the pizza. "I'm glad you and Dad don't fight anymore. I get that you didn't love each other anymore and needed to get a divorce, but Susan Willoughby's parents got a divorce and they scream and yell at each other all the time."

"Your dad and I just want what's best for you," Jordan

replied. "We agree on most things, so we don't have to scream or yell at each other."

"When are you gonna get a boyfriend?"

Jordan sat back in surprise. "Why? Do you want me to get a boyfriend?"

"Maybe. I mean, Daddy has Claire, and you don't have anyone."

Jordan knew that Claire was Dane's newest research assistant and the current woman sharing his bed. "Right now I'm happy just being your mom and doing my job. I really don't need a boyfriend."

Mandy looked at her somberly. "I'd feel better if you had one. You know, so you wouldn't be all alone here all the time."

"I'm not alone here all the time. On the weekends I have you here," Jordan protested.

"But maybe I can't come on all the weekends. I mean, there's other stuff like slumber parties and stuff on the weekends and I can't always be here for you." Stress made Mandy's voice rise an octave.

"Honey, it's not your job to be here for me. I want you here when you want to be here. I don't want to keep you from having fun with your friends and I don't want you coming over here because you're afraid I might be lonely. I love it when you're here, Mandy. I wish you were here all the time, but I'm fine when you aren't here."

Mandy eyed her dubiously. "Promise?"

"I promise. Now, maybe we should think about getting to sleep. I'm planning a cheerleader boot camp in the morning for you and you'd better be ready." Jordan got up from the floor and held out a hand to help Mandy up.

As Mandy went into her bedroom, Jordan went to hers and dressed for bed. Jordan wished things were different. At times like these she wished she and Dane could have made the marriage work. But it had been impossible to maintain a marriage that she believed Dane didn't want and wasn't willing to work for.

When she was finished, she went back into Mandy's room, where Mandy was already in bed. She sat on the edge of the mattress and smiled at her daughter and her heart filled with such love she could scarcely talk.

She leaned down and kissed Mandy on the forehead. "Sweet dreams, cupcake."

"Back at ya," Mandy replied, her eyes already droopy with sleep.

By the time Jordan got up and walked back to the door, Mandy was sound asleep. Jordan leaned against the door and watched the rise and fall of Mandy's chest. Mandy had always been the kind of child who could fall asleep in the middle of a party or any noisy event. When she was tired, sleep came remarkably easy for her.

As Jordan walked down the hallway to her bedroom, a deep weariness descended on her shoulders. It had been the week from hell. The detectives had spent all day Thursday and Friday interviewing reunion attendees.

Although they had a growing list of people who had no solid alibi for the time of the murder, they also didn't have any real viable suspect jumping out from the pack. Nobody had noticed Joann arguing with anyone on the night of the reunion. There had been no indication of tension between her and anyone.

They had no idea if the numbers found written in Joann's blood at her feet pointed to Jacob Nightsong's sermon or something else altogether. The sermon had been on the Internet for more than a year and it was impossible to trace who might have seen it and whether it had incited somebody to kill Joann.

A sense of failure had followed her home from work late on Friday night, and as she climbed into bed, that same feeling weighed heavy in her heart. She felt an intense responsibility to the victims and their families. She wanted to find justice for them, to give the families closure. Of course that was the goal of all homicide detectives, to solve and close each case, but for Jordan it was more than a job; it was an obsession.

It didn't take a psychiatrist to understand what drove her. Julie's murderer had never been found, and Jordan knew what it was like to lie in bed at night and wonder where Julie's killer was now, whom else he might be hurting. She knew what it was like to suffer nightmares, ones where her sister cried out to her for help, ones where the killer came back to murder Jordan as well. She wouldn't wish that kind of hell on anyone.

Still, no matter how much she wanted to solve Joann's murder, they had nothing to grab on to, no leads to take them in a specific direction. They were shooting in the dark and hoping to hit someone, but Jordan was beginning to lose hope that they'd ever solve the case.

Even with everything she had on her mind, she slept like a baby and the next morning after a breakfast of pancakes she and Mandy went down to the basement to work on cheerleading moves.

One of the things that had sold Jordan on this particular rental house was that the basement wasn't finished. She'd installed several floor-to-ceiling mirrors and a ballet barre and this was where she came when she felt as if she needed a good physical workout. It was a daylight basement with two windows that allowed in the morning sun.

She and Mandy worked together until noon. There was plenty of laughter and Jordan was shocked when Mandy announced she was ready to go home. She had the closed-in look on her face that Jordan had come to dread. She'd disconnected, pulled into herself, and Jordan knew from past experience there was nothing she could do to change Mandy's mind and get her to stay until six, when she was usually taken home.

It was just after one when she pulled into Dane's driveway. Together she and Mandy got out of the car and walked to the front door. "You going to practice those moves I showed you?" Jordan asked.

"Every day," Mandy agreed. "And I'm going to show them to Megan so we can practice together." She started to open the front door, but instead it opened and Dane greeted them.

"I thought I heard a car pull up," he said. "Did you have a good time?" he asked Mandy.

"Yeah, it was fun." She reached up and kissed Jordan on the cheek. "Thanks, Mom. I'll talk to you tomorrow." She disappeared through the door as Dane stepped out on the porch with Jordan.

"Everything all right?" he asked.

"Fine. She was just ready to come back. I told her about Julie last night," she said. He raised an eyebrow and she continued. "We were going through old pictures and she found one of Julie. She seemed to take it all okay."

Dane reached out and placed a hand on Jordan's shoulder. "That must have been tough on you."

His gaze was warm and supportive and she momentarily remembered why she'd fallen in love with him in the first place. "It was all right." She took a step away, forcing him to drop his hand from her shoulder.

"I hear you're lead on the Hathoway case."

She nodded. "And at the moment I'm leading the team nowhere."

"Tough case?"

"We can't figure out if maybe it was somebody who attended the reunion with her the night of her murder, which means we have far too many suspects."

"Oh yeah, I forgot about your reunion. Did you go?"

"With Della. It was fun until Della got drunk and had a meltdown about the cheerleaders being mean to her in high school."

Dane rolled his eyes. "Della is always having a meltdown about something. I don't know how Ben puts up with her."

Jordan smiled. "That man would walk across fire for her. How's Claire?"

"She's good. I'm thinking of asking her to move in." Dane studied Jordan's features carefully. "Would that bother you?"

"Only if you intend to break her heart. She seems like a nice woman and Mandy likes her."

"That's certainly not my intention," he replied.

Jordan gave him a wry smile. "That's never your intention, but somehow it just happens. I've got to get going. I'll see you next Friday night unless Mandy has something come up."

"Good luck on the case," he said as she turned and walked back to her car.

They needed more than luck, she thought as she headed back toward her neighborhood. As she drove, her mind shifted gears to the night ahead and her date with Clint.

One thing she had managed to do between the night she'd met him at the Coffee Shop and tonight was check out his alibi with the people he had gone to breakfast with the morning of the murder. All of them had been cleared as potential suspects.

On the way home she stopped at the supermarket and fleetingly wished she was one of those women who shopped off-hours, clipped coupons, studied the circulars, made grocery lists and remembered the reusable grocery bags. Instead she was parking in the last row of the crowded lot and planning an impromptu trip that would take twice as long as it needed to and still she'd get home and realize she'd forgotten something.

Once she was inside, the few things turned into a basketful. Besides the necessities of milk and bread, she also picked up some cheese and crackers and a nice bottle of wine in case she decided to invite Clint into her home after their date.

An hour later she was pushing the basket filled with her purchases across the parking lot toward her car when she once again got that crazy self-conscious feeling of somebody watching her. There were shoppers everywhere, loading car trunks with bags, pushing baskets to and from the store, and nobody seemed to be paying any attention to her.

She'd taken only a couple more steps when she saw him—Parker Sinclair. He slid into a car two aisles over from where Jordan had parked, and slammed his car door.

"Hey!" she yelled. Was the bastard stalking her?

All the frustration of the Hathoway case, the disappointment of Mandy wanting to go home early and the pure misery of an hour wasted in the grocery store culminated in a white-hot rage that ripped through her. She felt reckless, wild with anger. She left her cart and ran toward his car, but he'd already started the engine and pulled away in the opposite direction.

She ran back to her cart, threw her groceries in the backseat and then roared out of the parking lot. She knew he still lived in the house he'd shared with his wife, the home she had gone through painstakingly, trying to prove that he'd killed her.

Had he tailed her yesterday when she'd gone shopping with Mandy? Had he watched them driving home from the mall? Peeked in through the windows to watch them practicing cheers that morning?

The thought terrified her. The idea of a man like Parker Sinclair even looking at Mandy made her physically ill. What did he think he was doing?

Whatever it was, she intended to put a stop to it here and now. She thought of the times in the last week she'd felt as if she was being watched. Had it been him all along? By the time she pulled into the Sinclair driveway, his car was there, but he had apparently already gone into the house.

She got out of her car, drew her gun and advanced on the house. As she passed his car, she laid a hand on his hood. Still warm. It had definitely been this car she'd seen with that bastard behind the wheel. She walked to the front door and rapped on it with the butt of her gun.

He opened the door and looked at her in surprise. "Detective Sampson. To what do I owe this honor?"

"Listen, you bastard, I don't know what you think you're doing, but I'm here to warn you to stay away from me." Although she didn't point her weapon at him, she kept it ready by her side.

"I have no idea what you're talking about," he replied.

"That innocent face of yours might have worked for the jury, but it doesn't do a damn thing for me. I'm only going to tell you this once. Stay away from me or I'll see to it that you're back behind bars."

"I still don't know what you're talking about. You've obviously been working too hard, Detective Sampson. Maybe you should consider a vacation." He gave her a smug smile that she would have loved to wipe off his face.

"Consider yourself warned, Sinclair. Stay away from me." She didn't give him an opportunity to reply, but whirled on her heels and walked back to her car. It was only when she was on her way home that she breathed a sigh of relief.

Men like Parker Sinclair were cowards at heart. He was a wife beater who had escalated into a violence that had seen his wife dead. She doubted if he was accustomed to a woman standing up to him. She hoped this was the end of it. She hoped he was smart enough to take her warning seriously.

She also hoped she wasn't underestimating how dangerous he might be.

Chapter 10

At six forty-five that evening Jordan stood in front of her bedroom mirror and gave herself a final look. She'd braved the grocery store on a busy Sunday afternoon, confronted a suspected killer and warned him off, and she hadn't felt the kind of nervous tension that now tightened the back of her throat as she contemplated an evening with Clint.

Her last date had been thirteen years ago with Dane and she didn't remember being this nervous then. She'd already called Mandy and told her good night. The house was cleaner than it had been in weeks and she'd obsessed over what to wear. She'd studied her reflection in her mirror until she was sick of herself.

She left her bedroom and went into the living room, where she plumped the throw pillows on the sofa and wished she'd had Della help her with some decorating ideas. She'd spent so much time and attention decorating Mandy's bedroom and she had yet to even hang pictures on the living room walls.

Della had been nagging her to let her loose in the room, but while Della's over-the-top decor had worked in the mansion Jordan had lived in with Dane, the idea of Della's designs in the small living room made her heart race, and not in a good way.

At precisely seven o'clock the doorbell rang, announcing Clint's surprisingly punctual arrival. She opened the door to his warm, sexy smile. "I'm on time," he said.

"Yes, you are," she replied. And he looked amazingly hot in a pair of dress slacks and a gray sweater that clung to his broad shoulders.

"Are you ready?"

"I am," she replied, and pulled her coat around her shoulders.

"As I recall, Mexican food was always your favorite. I hope that hasn't changed," he said as he walked her to his car parked behind hers in the driveway.

"No, it's still my favorite," she replied, touched that he'd remembered after all these years.

"There's a great new place on Oak Street, Miguel's. Have you been there?"

"Not yet. I've been meaning to go but haven't gotten a chance," she replied as he opened the passenger door.

She slid inside and was instantly engulfed with the scent of his cologne. Fresh and clean, it smelled much like the scent he had worn in high school and reminded her of stolen kisses in school hallways and seductive caresses in the back of his old Thunderbird.

He got in behind the wheel and started the engine. "Good day?" he asked.

"Crazy day. I spent the morning teaching Mandy cheers and the afternoon chasing down a creep who I think is stalking me."

He flashed her a dark look. "Stalking you? That doesn't sound good."

"I have it under control," she replied. "What about you? How was your day?"

"Lazy. We won a football game last night and some of the team members and the coaches went out for pizza afterward. I didn't get home until almost one. I slept late this morning, spent an hour sitting at the table drinking coffee and reading the paper, then at noon watched the Kansas City Chiefs beat the tar out of the Oakland Raiders." He glanced at her once again.

"But I shouldn't be talking about that because you hate football."

She remembered telling him that at the reunion, when she felt herself being drawn in by his charm, by his sexy smile. "I might have exaggerated a bit when I told you that," she confessed.

"Maybe one night you could bring your daughter to one of our games. If she's interested in cheerleading, then she could watch this year's squad perform. They were champions last year."

"Maybe," Jordan replied. It was impossible for her to guess whether Mandy might be interested in doing that.

He pulled into the parking lot of the restaurant. At this time of the evening on Sunday he practically had his pick of parking spaces. Together they got out of the car and as they walked toward the front door, he placed his hand lightly on the small of her back. It was a casual touch, but it felt surprisingly intimate to Jordan, who hadn't been touched by a male in a very long time.

Miguel's was an upscale restaurant with low lighting, green plants and lush painted screens set up to provide an intimate dining experience. They were led to a table toward the back in a small alcove with a candle burning in the center of the table.

"Pretty romantic for a Mexican restaurant," Jordan observed.

Clint smiled and took her by the arm. "Exactly what I had in mind."

Within seconds a waitress was there to serve them water and hand them each a menu. Jordan gave it a quick look and then set it aside. She took a drink of her ice water, hoping it would cool down her temperature. She needed to get a grip, but it was hard to pull herself together when he smiled that lazy, sexy grin.

The waitress returned and they ordered. "We have fifteen years to catch up on. I'm not even sure where to start," he said when the waitress had departed. "I know you went to college at Stephens and were majoring in dance, but something must have changed, since you're now a detective."

"I didn't even finish out my first year. Julie's murder changed everything. I came home from school to be with my parents, and after we'd buried Julie and it was time for me to go back to school, I just couldn't. Dancing seemed so ridiculous, so utterly frivolous. It ate at me, that her murderer hadn't been found."

"And so you became a cop."

She smiled ruefully. "I thought I was the only person in the world who could solve her murder and the best way to do that was to become a police officer. I worked her case for months, along with my other duties, but ultimately there just wasn't enough evidence against anyone to make an arrest."

"Is that when you cut your hair? When you went into the police academy?"

She reached up and touched the short hair at the nape of her neck. "Actually, I cut it before I entered the police academy." She paused as the waitress returned to bring their margaritas, and then continued.

"It was about three weeks after we'd buried Julie that I realized my parents weren't able to look at me without pain. Everyone always said how much Julie and I looked alike, and I realized that every time they looked at me, they were seeing their loss. So I cut my hair, hoping it would help."

"Did it?"

"No." She fought against the surge of pain that welled up inside her. "They still can't look at me. I only see them about once a month and on the holidays. It's easier that way for them and for me."

He reached across the table and covered her hand with his, the warmth of his touch seeping up her arm. "I'm sorry for you and for them."

"Thanks, but it's okay. It has to be okay." She pulled her hand from beneath his and reached for her drink.

The waitress arrived with their orders and Jordan was grateful for the interruption. She quickly changed the subject.

"So, tell me about you. I know you went to KU on a football scholarship. I always thought someday I'd see your name on a pro football team."

"I never really wanted to play pro. I always wanted to teach, to coach."

"And your wife, was she from this area?"

"Actually she's from a little town in western Kansas. We met at college, but we didn't get married until a year after graduation."

"And how long were you married?"

"Three years. Holly was ambitious. She'd come from nothing and was looking for a lifestyle she thought I'd be able to give her. Two years into the marriage I got two offers, one to coach at the University of Missouri and the other to coach at Oak Ridge High School. Holly encouraged me to take the college job. She was hoping eventually I'd be coaching a pro team, but that's not what I wanted. I took the job at Oak Ridge and for all intents and purposes that ended the marriage."

"That's sad," she said.

He smiled and shrugged. "That's life. But I've been single a long time now."

"I doubt if you lack opportunity," she replied. "You haven't exactly gotten gross as you've gotten older."

He laughed. "You aren't too gross yourself. Actually, it's harder than you'd think to date at our age, but you should know that. You've been single for a while, right?"

"Yeah, for a little over a year, but I wouldn't know about the dating scene. This is the first date I've been on since my divorce."

He looked at her in surprise. "Then I feel honored."

"You just caught me in a weak moment," she replied with a teasing smile. "Do you miss it? Being married?" she asked.

"Some days I do and some days I don't." He leaned forward, his features animated. "I liked being married. I liked waking up to the same woman beside me each morning and going to bed with her that night. Unfortunately in that last year of our marriage Holly enjoyed waking up in the morning in somebody else's bed instead of ours."

"She cheated on you?" Jordan asked in surprise.

He grinned. "Yeah, imagine that. I was the monogamous one."

"I think Dane started having affairs about an hour after we got married," Jordan replied. "I caught him cheating several times before I finally decided I'd rather be alone than continue in a charade called our marriage."

Their conversation turned to high school days and Jordan was cast back in time to when life was far less complicated. They laughed about school assemblies and talked about teachers they'd liked and not liked. They talked about friends and football games and everything except their own crazy relationship.

The conversation continued as they left the restaurant and drove back to Jordan's house. "Would you like to come in for a glass of wine or some coffee?" she asked.

"Coffee sounds good," he agreed.

Minutes later they were in her kitchen. As the coffee started to brew, she excused herself and went back to the bedroom that served as her office. She wanted to check her messages and make sure nothing important had come up while she'd been out.

Even though she'd had her cell phone with her, most of her coworkers and friends would have assumed she was home on a Sunday night. Besides, she needed a moment to breathe. Being with Clint again was like being in a room where there wasn't quite enough oxygen.

She'd felt half-breathless all evening, on edge in a delicious kind of way. It was amazing that after all these years he still affected her that way, that he still made her heart beat just a little too fast, that he still made her wonder how things might have been different if she'd agreed to sleep with him in high school.

The message light was blinking, indicating she had one message. She pushed the play button and Mandy's voice filled the room. "Mom, plans have sort of changed for Halloween. Megan's mom is taking all of us to a mall and she's already invited Brittney's mom to go with her, so there's really not room for you to go. So . . . umm . . . I'll talk to you tomorrow, okay?"

Not room for you to go. The words reverberated around in her head as she leaned weakly against the desk, a new ache ripping through her heart. She'd been so looking forward to spending Halloween night with her daughter and her little friends.

Not room for you to go.

Somehow she felt as though she was missing something, that she was doing something dreadfully wrong as a mother. But she couldn't fix it because she didn't know what it was. She knew only the yawning black sense of failure that threatened to swallow her whole.

She wasn't enough as a daughter; she wasn't the right kind of mother. She wasn't getting anything right in her life.

She thought of the man waiting for her in her kitchen. Suddenly she didn't want him here. She wanted to be alone to wallow in the self-pity that had taken hold. She left the office with a sense of reckless abandon, pain simmering deep inside her. Clint sat at the table and smiled as she came into the room.

"I've changed my mind. I hope you don't mind, but I think it's best if we call it a night," she said.

His smile fell away, but he made no move to get up from the table. "What's wrong? What happened?"

"Nothing is wrong. I'm just tired and ready to call an end to the evening." She tried not to be affected by the look of disappointment on his face.

He stood. "Did I do something to offend you?"

"Of course not." She raised a hand to her temple where a headache suddenly pounded. "I have a headache and didn't realize how tired I was until just now." Someplace in the back of her mind she knew she was being rude, that she was in self-destruct mode. But she wanted—she needed—to cry and she didn't want to do it in front of him.

He stepped closer to her and placed a hand on her arm. "Is there something I can do? Get you a hot compress or some aspirin?"

She shook her head and stepped back so that his hand fell away from her. "Please, I just think it would be best if you'd go now." She couldn't meet his gaze and instead looked at the coffeepot filled with dark brew.

"Okay," he said after a long moment of hesitation. "I hope you feel better soon. I'll just see myself out." With that, he walked out of the kitchen and a minute later she heard the sound of the front door closing and knew he was gone.

Terrific. She shut off the coffeepot, then left the kitchen as she fought against a wave of tears. "Nice going, Jordan," she muttered as she flopped down on the sofa. She sure knew how to screw up the ending of what had been a pretty terrific date.

She'd allowed the phone message from Mandy to ruin the night. She'd overreacted to the disappointment and she now felt like a fool.

He wouldn't be calling her again; that was for sure. He probably thought she was some kind of nut, inviting him in, then promptly tossing him out without any real explanation. Well, she'd lived the last fifteen years of her life without him. She could live the next fifteen years without him as well.

Chapter 11

The knock on the door pulled Jordan from her nap on the sofa. She'd gotten up early, but been so depressed she hadn't even dressed for the day. Outside the weather seemed to reflect her mood. It was a gray day with a mist of cold, fine rain falling.

She'd taken one look out the window, then wrapped herself in a fuzzy warm stadium blanket and gone directly to the sofa for a day of self-pity. She'd even called in sick, something she absolutely never did.

Over and over again the scene from the night before with Clint had played in her head, and each time it played she was disgusted with herself, that she'd allowed a phone message to screw up her entire evening.

She frowned with irritation at the front door, willing whoever was on the other side to go away. The phone had rung twice and she hadn't answered. She didn't want to talk to anyone. She didn't want to see anyone. She wasn't ready to give up her pity party yet.

The knocking sounded again, this time more forcefully. "Jordan, I know you're in there. Your car is in the driveway and somebody at the police station told me you'd called in sick."

Jordan was shocked at the sound of Clint's voice. She'd figured it would be a cold day in hell before she heard from him again.

And just that quickly, her pity party was over. Jeez, she

should kick her own ass for being such a pathetic whining loser. That wasn't who she was. She was an optimist at heart, a fighter, and she owed Clint a huge apology for the way she'd ended their date the night before.

She jumped up off the sofa and pulled her robe belt more tightly around her, wishing she were dressed, sorry she hadn't at least put on a dab of makeup when she'd gotten out of bed that morning.

She opened the door and as always felt a wave of heat sweep through her at the sight of him. "Are you all right?" he asked, his expression worried.

"I'm fine." She gestured him inside. "No, actually, I'm not fine. I'm embarrassed by the way I acted last night."

"Embarrassed?" He frowned. "You had a headache. That's nothing to be embarrassed about. When I called you at the police station this morning and they told me you'd called in sick, I was afraid that maybe it was more than a headache."

"No. What I suffered last night was a self-indulgent pity party. Why don't you come into the kitchen and drink some of that coffee that you didn't have last night and I'll explain?" she said.

He followed her into the kitchen, where he sat at the table and she made the coffee. He waited expectantly until it began to brew, then asked, "Explain what?"

"Why I kicked you out of here so abruptly. I had a message from my daughter on the phone and that's what set me off." She explained to him about what Mandy had said and by that time the coffee was ready for her to pour.

She poured them each a cup, then joined him at the table. "I was disappointed and hurt and I was afraid I might cry and I didn't want to do that in front of you, so it was easier just to kick you out."

"I'm just glad it wasn't something I had done," he replied. He took a sip of the coffee and eyed her over the rim of the cup. "I'm sorry you're having problems with your daughter."

"It breaks my heart. Initially I was going to fight tooth and nail for custody, but when Mandy told the judge she wanted to remain with her father, I focused my efforts on renting this house and creating a place that could be home for her when she decided she wanted it to be. But, at least for now, Mandy doesn't want to live here. She doesn't want to live with me." Jordan swallowed a mouthful of coffee to stanch the unexpected sob that threatened to erupt.

"Has she told you why?" Clint's gaze was warm, empathetic, and for just a moment it helped to feel as if somebody was on her side.

She couldn't very well bare her soul to her parents or to Dane where Mandy was concerned. Della didn't have children and couldn't possibly understand the heartache of Jordan's situation. At the moment Clint seemed a safe sounding board.

"She won't tell me." Jordan wrapped her fingers around the warmth of the coffee mug. "There are times I feel like there's something she wants to say to me, that there's something I'm not doing or not saying that she needs, but for the life of me I can't figure it out."

"Aren't girls that age a little difficult anyway?" he asked. "You know, hormones and all that."

Jordan smiled. "Girls at any age are difficult when it comes to hormones and all that."

"Have you talked to your ex about it? Is he doing or saying something to her to make her not want to be around you?"

"No, I haven't really sat down and talked with him about it." She raised the coffee cup and took a sip, and then continued. "I've tried to tell myself that Dane has to be putting stuff into her head, that he has to be trying to alienate her from me. But even though Dane had major flaws as a husband, he was always a terrific father. Deep in my heart I can't imagine him really doing something so awful to her and to me."

"Maybe you should sit down with him and see if he knows what's going on with her," Clint suggested.

She looked into her coffee cup and thought about Dane and her daughter. "I guess that's what I need to do." She gazed back at Clint. "I'm sorry about last night. That wasn't me. I don't usually act that way. And I definitely didn't mean to dump all this on you."

"No need to apologize," he replied. "I just needed to come over here and check to make sure you were okay. I've got to tell you, last night I felt a little bit like a teenage boy again and you were the girl I wanted to be with more than anyone else in the world. We cared about each other a lot in high school and I wanted to see if those feelings were still there between us."

"And are they?" she asked as her heart raced just a little bit faster.

He smiled. "I can only speak for myself, but I enjoyed being with you last night. I want to see you again."

"You must be a glutton for punishment," she replied. "My life is definitely a mess right now."

"And mine has been too boring lately," he countered with that charming twinkle in his eyes. He reached across the table and covered her hand with his. "When I look at you, I still see some of that young girl who drove me crazy, but I'm more interested in getting to know the woman you've become." He pulled his hand away and sat back. "So, when do I get a second date?"

Maybe he was just what she needed in her life at the moment, she thought. She didn't need him as a bed buddy, but rather as a friend. "I'm not sure. I'm in the middle of Joann's murder investigation."

"How's it going?"

"Terrible. Right now our only real potential suspect is Joann's lover." Frustration burned in her gut as she thought of the case.

"He doesn't have an alibi?"

"She. She doesn't have a solid alibi. Joann was gay. You don't look surprised."

He picked up his cup and took a drink of coffee. "I am and yet I'm not. There was a lot of speculation about her in high school. She never dated. We all just thought she was too stuck-up to want to date any of us. But, back to my original question, when can I see you again?"

"Why don't I call you if I get a free night?" she finally replied.

"This isn't a kiss-off, is it?" he asked.

She smiled. "No kiss-off."

"Good." He pulled a piece of paper from his wallet and handed it to her. "My cell phone number. I wrote it down earlier hoping I'd get a chance to give it to you." He got up from the table, as if he'd accomplished what he'd set out to do. "So, we try it again?"

"Definitely," she replied as a wealth of warmth swept through her. "And I promise you that the next time I won't kick you out before you're ready to leave."

He smiled, that wicked sexy grin that deepened the hue of his eyes and made her knees feel just a little bit wobbly. "That's a pretty open-ended kind of promise."

She laughed and got up to walk with him to the door.

"Then I'll wait for your call," he said when they reached the door. He turned back to face her. "Oh, and just one more thing." Before she knew what he intended, he leaned down and touched his lips to hers in a feather-soft kiss that electrified her. It lasted only a moment; then he stepped back. "I didn't get a chance to do that last night and I look forward to doing it even longer, better, on our next date ." He didn't wait for her reply, but instead turned on his heels and left. She remained standing in the doorway, that same crazy breathlessness possessing her.

Her very own personal pity party was definitely over. All it had taken was the warmth of Clint's gaze on her and a calm, rational discussion, not only about what had happened the night before, but also about Mandy.

She was going to set up a meeting with Dane. She should have done it months ago when she first started feeling Mandy distancing herself. She might not be able to solve Joann's murder in the next couple of days, but maybe she could solve the mystery of Mandy in that time.

Betsy Baker liked to tell everyone she had a wonderful life, and to outward appearances it was a wonderful life. Married to a doctor and with two children, Betsy lived in a luxurious home on three acres in a gated neighborhood of equally lavish homes.

The truth of the matter was Betsy and her husband were in debt up to their necks and the two kids were spoiled and unruly and often gave her headaches that drove her to her bed.

Her husband, Ralph, had become a boring middle-aged man who worried about their credit card debt and preferred parking himself in front of the television instead of socializing with other prominent members of Kansas City society.

None of that mattered this evening. She was meeting Jenny Taylor for dinner in a chic restaurant on the Plaza and she would be on, lit like a lightbulb and brimming with the wonder of her life.

Her mother had taught her that appearances were everything and it was a lesson Betsy had embraced in her heart. No matter how bored or unhappy she might be with the way things had turned out in her life, nobody would ever know.

Some of the best days of her life had been in high school when she'd been a cheerleader. She'd loved the way other girls had looked at her, with such envy and longing. It had been like a drug, intoxicating her, and she'd spent most of her adult life chasing that same adulation.

She now stood in front of her bedroom dresser mirror, checking her appearance one last time before leaving the house to meet Jenny. The Michael Kors mock-neck sheath dress was perfect for an evening out and it fit her body as if it had specially been designed for her.

Thanks to hours of workouts and denying herself, she still had a slamming body, and she smiled at her reflection as she remembered that at the reunion she'd noticed that Jenny had put on a bit of weight.

Checking her watch, she saw that it was almost seven. She was meeting Jenny at seven thirty, so she needed to get on her way. She left the bedroom and walked down the hallway to the living room, where her collection of dolls smiled at her from their glass display cases.

She loved her dolls, but Ralph always complained that their living room looked more like a toy store than a place where he could relax. She didn't want him relaxing in this room. That was why they had a basement. She headed for the stairs to go down to the family room.

As usual Ralph was sprawled on the sofa in front of the television. Nine-year-old Danny was on the computer and six-year-old Ellie had half the floor covered with Barbie paraphernalia.

"I'm off. Danny still has homework to finish and Ellie needs to get into the bathtub," she said.

Ralph sat up with a befuddled frown. "Where are you going?"

Betsy stifled a sigh of irritation. "I told you I was meeting Jenny for a late dinner." He never remembered anything she told him about her schedule.

"Jenny?"

"Jennifer Taylor. Remember, you met her at the reunion. I was a cheerleader with her?"

"Oh, right," he replied, although Betsy could tell he didn't have any idea whom she was talking about.

"I've got to get going. I shouldn't be too late. Goodbye, kids. Mind your father." They ignored her as they usually did.

Betsy hated fall. The grass went brown, the flowers all died and the trees went bare. As far as she was concerned, it was an ugly time of year, and Betsy hated ugly.

Only seven o'clock in the evening and it was already

dark. She'd pulled her car out of the garage earlier in the day and now she stepped outside. At least the rain had stopped, although a layer of fog had descended in its place.

She'd taken only three steps toward the car when she heard a noise, the sound of a foot crunching in the pile of dead leaves just around the side of the house. She froze.

"Hello? Is somebody there?"

Her voice sounded reedy and thin as a cold breeze gusted to brush her face. She wondered for a moment if it was a dog or another animal. She'd definitely heard something that didn't belong and she sensed somebody or something standing in the darkness, hiding in the fog. She sure as hell wasn't like those silly girls in those slasher flicks.

She wasn't stupid enough to open a basement door to see what was on the other side. She wouldn't be stupid enough to run out on the porch to check out the sound of somebody screaming, and she definitely wasn't going to wander around in the foggy dark night to find out who or what was crunching leaves near the house.

With a fear that felt too big for the situation, she ran to her car and didn't breathe easily until she was inside with the doors locked and the engine running. It was only then she laughed at herself and checked in the rearview mirror to make sure her lipstick still looked fresh.

Chapter 12

"Sarge is looking for you," Anthony said to Jordan when she arrived in the squad room Tuesday morning. "And I gotta tell you, he looked like he'd been chewing rusty nails. What did you do?"

"Nothing that I know of," she replied in surprise. Maybe it had something to do with her calling in sick.

After Clint had left the day before, she'd called Dane and set up a meeting with him for this evening at the Coffee Shop. Then she'd spent the rest of the afternoon reading over the Hathoway files, hoping she might find something that they'd missed. But she hadn't found anything.

"Maybe I should get a cup of coffee first," she said, and eyed Sergeant Wendt's closed office door.

As if by the magic of her quick glance at the door, it burst open and Wendt glared at her. "Sampson, I've been waiting for you. Get your ass in here." He disappeared from the doorway and Jordan exchanged a worried look with Anthony.

"Good luck," Anthony breathed as she walked by him.

One of Benny's strengths as a sergeant was that he rarely got flustered or angry. One of his weaknesses was that when he did get angry, it was a scary thing to experience.

Jordan could practically smell the anger in the room

as she entered. He stood behind his desk and thumbed her into the chair before him. Florid streaks of red crept up his thick neck, always a bad sign.

She sank down in the chair in front of him. "What's going on, Sarge?" she asked.

The red streaks on his neck were bad enough, but the fact that he didn't sit at his desk was another sign that he was highly agitated. And then she knew why he'd called her in. "I can explain," she began.

He held up a beefy hand to stop her from speaking. "We got a phone call this morning. A complaint call—no, scratch that—a threatening call. Parker Sinclair is threatening a lawsuit because one of my detectives apparently went to his house half-cocked, brandishing her weapon and making all kinds of threats." He slammed his hands down on the desk and glared at her. "What in the hell were you thinking, Jordan?"

"I think he's stalking me."

"What do you mean, you think? We don't think around here." His face flushed as he realized what he'd said. "We don't act on supposition," he amended. "We act on facts." He drew a deep breath and sat at his desk. "What makes you think he might be stalking you?"

"Lately I've just sensed somebody watching me, following me. Then Sunday afternoon I was at the grocery store and got that same feeling. I looked around and there he was, driving out of the parking lot. I admit I lost it. I drove right to his house and warned him to stay away from me. I'm sorry. I know I was way out of line."

Benny's neck began to pale to a more natural color. "Why on earth would Parker Sinclair be stalking you?"

"I don't know." She leaned back in the chair and relaxed a bit. "All I can tell you is when I was on the stand at his trial, the way he looked at me, smiled at me, it gave me the creeps."

"He's a creep, but right now he's faced his accusers and was found not guilty and that makes him an ordinary citizen with his rights intact. Any appearance that the police are targeting him because of the lack of conviction in the murder case will only reflect poorly on the department. You're on notice, Jordan. Stay away from him. Come to me if you have more problems and we'll go through appropriate channels to keep him away from you. I think I managed to soothe his feathers this time, but if you bother him again, we're going to have big problems. *You're* going to have big problems."

"I screwed up, Sarge. It won't happen again." She knew what she'd done was wrong, but in the heat of the moment it had seemed perfectly logical.

"Now, tell me what's new on the Hathoway case."

"Not much," she admitted. "We're finishing up the interviews of people who attended the reunion with her on the night of the murder, but so far nobody is jumping out. The preliminary lab reports are coming in, but so far there's been nothing helpful. We've gone over her phone records, checked her cell phone and e-mail, but there was nothing there to indicate any threat from anyone. We still have the lover in our radar as the best suspect. Unfortunately we've got to get some real solid evidence in order to make an arrest."

"We don't want another Sinclair. We need to nail this bastard with enough evidence that he or she won't walk."

"Trust me, none of us want another Sinclair," she replied.

"Okay, we're done here. Get out of here and get back to work."

Jordan didn't wait for him to tell her twice. She jumped out of the chair and hurried out of the office before he had time to ruminate on her visit with Sinclair and decide to tear into her more thoroughly.

"Everything cool?" Anthony asked worriedly as she returned to the desk they shared. Ricky sat next to Anthony and eyed her with an equal amount of concern.

"I did a stupid thing and Benny got wind of it and chewed my ass," she replied. She told the two men about her visit to Sinclair. "As far as I'm concerned, he's not just a murderer who got away with his crime, but he's also devious as hell. He didn't call to complain right after it happened. He waited until I was back at work to make the call."

"It's no fun to tattle on somebody who isn't immediately available to face the consequences," Ricky replied.

"The show is over, my butt is just mildly chewed and we all need to get to work," she said.

The morning passed with all of them on the phone. Most people didn't realize how much of an investigation took place in the squad room, at the desks and on the phones.

Grunt work. That was what solved most murder cases. Sifting through reports, analyzing details, with the hope of finding that one little element that would eventually lead to an arrest.

The Hathoway case wasn't the only one they were working on. They each had other cases sitting on their desks waiting for attention. Still, it was Joann's murder that haunted Jordan more than any other.

One name kept popping up in her mind. Danny McCall. It bothered her that he'd bought one of Joann's paintings, which she knew didn't go cheap. His furniture looked as though it had come from garage sales, and the apartment building he lived in was relatively cheap, mostly catering to the social security crowd.

Why would a man who didn't appear to be rolling in extra dough pay for a piece of artwork to hang in his bedroom? Danny didn't strike her as the art-collecting type of guy.

Was it just the remnant emotion of an old high school crush or was it something deeper, something darker—an obsession that might have led to murder?

One thing they had learned. Joann had led a solitary life. There were few friends to interview and no family. She'd lived in the same farmhouse for the last ten years, yet her nearest neighbors knew her only well enough to nod and say hello.

Which led Jordan to believe that either one of the people she'd gone to high school with had committed the murder or Linda the lover was guilty as hell.

It was just after six when Jordan walked across the street to the Coffee Shop. Dane was already there seated at a table near the window. She nodded to him and went to the counter, where Sam poured her a cup of coffee and offered her a sly grin.

"Jordan is a busy girl—two men in one week," he said as she paid him.

She grinned at him. "One's an ex and the other is not."

"And both take their coffee black," Sam replied.

Jordan laughed and carried her cup to where Dane waited. "Thanks for meeting me here," she said as she sat across from him at the small table.

"Not a problem. I know how busy your schedule is when you're in the middle of an investigation, and it sounded like you wanted to meet me on neutral ground." He gazed out the window at the police headquarters building, then looked back at her. "Although I'm not so sure how neutral this is with all your buddies with guns right across the street."

"You're safe," she replied. "I have no intention of calling the SWAT team." She frowned at the man who had been her husband for twelve tumultuous years. "I want to talk to you about Mandy." He nodded, obviously not surprised. "Where is she tonight?"

"At home. When I left, she was in her bedroom on the phone, where she usually is these days. Naomi said she'd hang around and keep an eye on her until I got home." Naomi was the housekeeper that had worked for Dane and Jordan since Mandy's birth.

Jordan took a drink of her coffee, needing the warmth of the drink to chase away the cold knot that had jumped into her stomach at thoughts of her daughter. "I feel like

I'm losing her, Dane, and I don't know why." She swallowed hard against the unexpected sob that threatened to erupt. The last thing she wanted to do was cry.

"I know you've been frustrated because she makes plans with her friends for the weekend, and to be honest with you, I don't know how to fix that. It's only going to get worse as she gets older."

"I know, but it's more than that. Even when she's with me, I don't feel like she's with me. She's becoming more and more distant. I guess I was just wondering if maybe she'd said something to you about it, about me. Maybe she told you something I'm doing wrong or not doing at all?"

Dane leaned back in his chair and frowned thoughtfully. "No, she hasn't said anything to me. She hasn't indicated that there are any problems. But you know she's not exactly the type of kid to talk about her feelings. If it's the attitude that worries you, let me assure you that she doesn't reserve it just for you. There are times she looks at me as if I'm the dumbest male on the face of the planet."

His words didn't make Jordan feel any better. "It's not the attitude," she replied. "It's that I feel her pulling away from me. She'll let me get so close—then she puts up a wall I can't get through. It's like she doesn't love me anymore." Jordan blinked to dispel the hot burn of tears.

"Ah, Jordan." He grabbed a napkin from the container on the table and handed it to her. "I know this has all been really difficult for you and I know you probably think I have something to do with this, but I don't. I don't talk bad about you. You weren't the screwup in our marriage. I was, and I'd never do anything to sabotage your relationship with Mandy."

Jordan took another sip of her coffee and held his gaze above the rim of the cup.

"I was a lot of things in our marriage," Dane continued. "I was a cheating husband. I was thoughtless and self-involved, but I never stopped loving you, Jordan, and I've never wanted to hurt you in any way. More than that, I would never hurt Mandy by talking bad about you or trying to alienate you from her."

Jordan had desperately wanted to believe that it was all Dane's fault, that he was intentionally poisoning Mandy against her. But she'd been with Dane for a lot of years. In many ways she felt she knew him better than anyone else on the face of the planet.

He'd been a lousy, unfaithful husband, but she'd never known him to be intentionally mean or hurtful. He was also smart enough, secure enough, not to be threatened by Mandy loving Jordan.

"I wanted to blame you," she confessed. "It would be so much easier to understand if you were filling her head with negative stuff about me."

He leaned forward and reached across the table and took her hand in his. "I would never do that. You've always been a terrific mother and I would never do that to you or to her. She needs you, Jordan. Maybe it's her age and some sort of stupid rebellion thing." He pulled his hand away and leaned back once again. "You and I agreed when we divorced that we would never bad-mouth each other, that we would never make the kind of mistakes other people make by using their kids to hurt one another. I haven't broken that agreement in any way."

Jordan sighed. "It would be so much easier for me if you were a total asshole instead of just half of one."

He laughed and for a moment she felt a warmth of affection for him. She didn't love him romantically, hadn't felt that way about him for a very long time. But the divorce hadn't suddenly erased the years they had shared together, both the good and the bad.

"I'll talk to her, Jordan. I'll see if I can get her to open up to me and see if there's something really wrong or if it's just preteen crap," he said.

"I'd appreciate it. She's the most important thing in the world to me."

"We'll figure it out. Whatever's going on, maybe she'll outgrow it."

"I don't think so," Jordan replied. "I think it's something more serious than just normal attitude and growing pains." She glanced at her watch. "I need to get back to the station. Thanks, Dane, for meeting me and for listening to me whine."

He smiled. "You were never a whiner, Jordan. I'll call you, okay?"

"Thanks again," she said as she got up from the table. She left him there seated at the table and she made her way back across the street to work for another couple of hours before calling it a night.

She might have made a mistake in going to Sinclair's house, but she hadn't felt that creepy-crawly sensation since she'd warned him off, she thought as she crossed the darkened streets and went into the building.

In the squad room she found that Ricky had called it a night and left, but Anthony was at the desk shoving papers back and forth in front of him. "Anything exciting shaking?" she asked as she flung herself into the chair next to him.

"Not a damn thing. I think it's possible we'll never be able to make an arrest in the Hathoway case."

"Don't say that," she replied. "It's too early to give up."

He pulled out a photo of the bloody numbers that had been found at Joann's feet. "I'm seeing these in my sleep at night. We know the perp left them for a reason and I feel like if we could just figure it out, we'd have our first real lead."

"I agree, but Ricky used every search engine known to man and nothing hit that meant anything except that sermon." She frowned. "Maybe we need to get the list of members from Reverend Nightsong's congregation and see if any of them also attended the reunion that night. It's a long shot, but I'm out of ideas."

"Yeah, I hear you." Anthony shoved the photo back into a manila folder and got up and stretched with his arms overhead. "I'm outta here. You should go home, too. Brass has been bitching about overtime and there's nothing going to pop on this case tonight."

"I think I will head home," she replied, and grabbed her purse and jacket. Together she and Anthony rode the elevator down and then left the building.

"You got plans for Halloween?" he asked as they walked together toward the parking lot.

"No. I thought I was going to go out with Mandy, but she made plans with a bunch of her friends. I guess I'll stay at home and hand out candy to little ghosts and goblins. What about you?"

"I don't know. I'll probably hang out at Iggy's."

"Why don't you find a nice girl and take her out to dinner, maybe see a movie or go to a club? You're a good-looking guy, Anthony. It's not normal that you aren't dating."

They stopped by the driver's-side door of her car and he cast her a crooked grin. "Unfortunately the only woman I'd be interested in taking out doesn't believe in dating her partner."

Jordan looked at him in surprised dismay. "Oh, Anthony, you'd really hate dating me. You hate the way I eat. You think I can be a total bitch sometimes."

"But that would be the beauty of it," he replied. "I already know all your faults. I wouldn't have to go through the whole getting-to-know-you kind of thing. We could just go right to the sex part."

She laughed. "That's just plain lazy."

He grinned again. "Yeah, I know."

"Besides, think how awful it would be to have to work together after we broke up, and we would break up, because we'd drive each other insane."

"You're kind of making me nuts right now," he admitted.

"Get out of here," she laughed.

"I'm gone," he replied. "See you tomorrow." As he ambled off in the direction of his car, she got into hers.

Within minutes she was headed home. Although she was surprised by Anthony's impulsive idea that they might date, she wasn't worried about it. They'd been partners for the last four years and seen each other through some of the best and the worst that life had to offer. Never had there been any sparks between them.

The thought of sparks brought Clint to her mind. Maybe she should invite him over for Halloween night. He could help her hand out candy and they could get to know each other better.

And he could kiss her again. Longer. Harder. That little kiss he'd given her the day before had simply whetted her appetite for more. She had a feeling that had been his wicked intention.

She had no desire to allow her heart to get involved with him. She still felt as if her life was far too complicated for her to invite anyone in, but she also couldn't ignore the fact that the idea of making love with Clint Cooper was definitely more than a little appealing.

By the time she got home, she'd decided she would welcome Clint's company on Halloween night. Maybe it would keep her mind off the fact that Mandy was spending her Halloween with somebody else's mother.

The piece of paper with his phone number on it was in her room on the nightstand by her bed. She went into the bedroom, took off her holster and placed her gun in the drawer, then picked up the phone and dialed his number.

He answered on the second ring. "I've been hoping you'd call."

"It's been a busy couple of days," she replied. "I was wondering if you'd like to come over here Halloween night, maybe have some supper and help me pass out treats to the trick-or-treaters. It's a Thursday, so it wouldn't be a late night because I know we both have to work the next morning."

"Sounds good to me," he replied. "But instead of you cooking, why don't I just bring a pizza and some beer?"

"I don't mind cooking, but pizza and beer sounds perfect," she agreed.

"Just tell me a time and I'll be there."

They agreed on six o'clock, and then ended the call. Jordan sat for a long few minutes on the edge of her bed and waited for the ridiculous rivulet of warmth the sound of his voice had evoked to leave her.

She was aware of the fact that it wasn't Clint the man who made her feel flustered and warm, but rather memories of what had once been, thoughts of what might have been. She couldn't allow those powerful memories to be the foundation of a relationship with him now. She still wasn't even sure she'd like the man he'd become. Time would tell.

Getting up from the bed, she glanced at the clock. It was just after eight, but she was still wound up with enough energy to know that sleep would be impossible. She changed into a leotard and leggings, deciding that an hour's workout in the basement would wear her out and make her sleep better.

She headed downstairs and turned on the stereo to a station that played classical music, and then got to work at the ballet barre, stretching tight muscles and warming up.

Her mind filled with the music and the movement, making thoughts of heinous murders and troubled relationships impossible. She needed this time to just be . . . to not stress about Mandy and murders, to not wonder about Clint and what the future might hold.

When she was sufficiently warmed up, she moved across the floor, working each and every muscle group as she accomplished perfect pirouettes and dozens of other ballet moves in time to the music that filled the air.

There were times she wondered what might have been if Julie hadn't been murdered. Would Jordan have continued to pursue a career in dancing? But then she reminded herself that if that had been the case, there would be no Mandy.

She danced until she was exhausted, until her muscles burned and her mind was completely void of thoughts. Deciding she'd had enough, she walked over to the stereo and turned it off midsong.

In the sudden silence that ensued, a floorboard squeaked overhead.

Her gaze shot upward as every muscle in her body froze.

Was somebody in the house? Her heart banged against her ribs as a lump of fear lodged in the back of her throat. She held her breath and the sound came again—a distinctive creak.

Oh God. There was somebody up there. She released a gasp. Her gun was in her nightstand upstairs. She frantically gazed around the basement, seeking something she could use as a weapon against an intruder. There was nothing.

Who was it?

What did they want?

Her legs felt wobbly as she moved to the foot of the stairs that led up from the basement. She was a police officer, for Christ's sake. Her legs shouldn't feel weak. She shouldn't taste the tang of fear. But as a cop she knew the danger of confronting an intruder.

God, she should have carried her gun down here with her. She should have made sure her doors and windows were locked up tight before she came down here to work out.

She was a virtual prisoner down here. The basement wasn't a walk-out. There was a window she could crawl out, a fire-safety feature necessary for the house to be up to code.

She grabbed hold of the banister with bloodless fingers and stared up the staircase.

Was somebody standing up there? Waiting for her

to come up? Preparing to come down? Time ticked by. Agonizing seconds of indecision. Should she go out the window? Should she stay where she was and wait to see what happened next?

She cocked her head and listened.

Nothing.

No creaks.

No groans.

Nothing.

With her heart still pounding fast and furious, she took two steps up, then paused to listen again. Maybe she'd just imagined the noise. Maybe it had been the natural settling of a house on a chilly late October night. Or the furnace rushing warm air through cold vents.

She took another two steps, taut with fight-or-flight adrenaline, half-afraid that some masked monster would suddenly appear at the top of the stairs. The sweat she'd worked up moments before now clung to her skin like an icy shell.

Another two steps.

She felt as if she were climbing a mountain. Six more stairs to go and she'd be at the top. Still she heard nothing, and some of the sharp edges of her adrenaline began to wane.

Drawing a deep breath, she raced up the last of the stairs and into her living room. There was no maniac with a chain saw, no monster waiting to pounce on her. The living room looked just as it had when she'd gone downstairs. Still, she had the sensation of air displaced, of something alien having passed through.

She went straight down the hallway and to her bedroom, where she pulled her gun from the drawer. With its familiar weight in her hand, she forced her fear away and began to systematically check each and every room of the house.

Nothing seemed out of place and nobody was in the house. Both the front and back doors were locked, but the dead bolt wasn't turned on the front door. Had she twisted the knob when she'd gotten home? She didn't remember. She'd been in a hurry to get inside and call Clint before it got too late.

She clicked it into place, then walked over to the sofa and sank down with an exhausted sigh, her gun still clenched tightly in her hand. She felt as if she were losing her mind, seeing phantoms in shadows and hearing ghosts in the house.

Maybe she'd been working too hard. Maybe if she got a good night's sleep, she'd feel better in the morning. She got up from the sofa and did another pass through the house just to assure herself that she was safe and alone.

Still it was a very long time before she was able to relax enough to sleep.

He could have had her.

He leaned against the side of her house and drew in deep, tremulous breaths. It had been so easy. He'd watched her through the windows as she'd gone downstairs. He'd heard the sound of her music, and a peek in the basement window had shown her working out at a ballet barre.

He hadn't intended to go into the house, but had found the back-door lock easy to pick, and suddenly he was in the middle of her kitchen. His heart had roared with excitement.

The classical music wafting up the basement stairs assured him that she was still dancing and as he stood in the center of the kitchen, he'd been filled with a sense of omnipotent power.

How easy it would be to kill her here and now. She'd never hear him coming down the stairs. She'd be trapped in the basement with no escape. He'd even moved to the top of the stairs, his body trembling with excitement. But instead of going down, he'd backed away from the stairs.

It wasn't time yet. He wasn't ready to take her next.

He wanted her to know what was happening, to know the fear that came with anticipation. Instead he'd walked around her living room, not touching anything, but just breathing in her scent that lingered in the air.

He'd walked down the hallway to her bedroom and stood in the doorway, checking out the room where she slept and dreamed. It was surprisingly bare. No pictures were on the walls; a pink-flowered bedspread lay half on, half off the unmade bed. Several outfits were thrown across the back of a chair and the scent of her lingered in the room.

On the top of the dresser was a single photograph. He gazed at the image of Jordan's daughter. She was a lovely girl, already with the gilt of popularity clinging to her.

At that moment the music from the basement had stopped and his heart had nearly halted with it. As he'd stepped back into the hallway, a creak in the floorboard had sounded as loud as a gunshot. The second step produced the same sound.

Knowing that it was just a matter of minutes before she came upstairs, he raced as quiet as a shadow to the back door. Making sure that it was locked behind him, he went out into the cold night air.

He now pushed himself off the side of the house and ran down the street to where he'd parked his car nearly a block away. It would have been so easy to take her tonight.

But he hadn't been able to because it wasn't right. In those moments in Joann's shed he'd recognized the heady power of destroying something she loved just before he killed her. It had been like symbolically killing her twice.

Joann had loved her art and he'd destroyed that before destroying her. Jordan loved only one thing and that was her daughter, the young girl who had all the potential of growing up to be another mean girl.

No, it hadn't been time tonight.

Soon, he promised himself.

Chapter 13

It was a spooky Halloween night. A cold damp breeze blew from the north and a low-lying fog combined with a mist to make it the perfect atmosphere for mischief.

Jordan stood at her front door and waved at Mandy as she left to rejoin the group of girls and mothers in the van in the driveway. They had stopped by so Mandy could show her mother her costume. Mandy had told her she was going as part of an all-girl singing group, but with her hair all curled and sprayed and a touch of makeup, Jordan thought Mandy looked achingly beautiful.

She had oohed and aahed and wished desperately she was getting into the van to go with them all. At least Mandy had looked happy and excited for the night ahead and she'd given Jordan a hug that had lasted longer than the ones Jordan had recently received.

When the van pulled out of the driveway, Jordan closed the door and walked back to the kitchen, where she was in the process of frosting a cake and trying to make it look like a jack-o'-lantern. At the moment it just looked like a bright orange blob.

She had fifteen minutes to transform it before Clint was due to arrive. She figured since he was providing the pizza and beer, the least she could do was make something for dessert.

She'd told Mandy that she had an old friend from high school coming over to spend the evening, but Mandy had been in such a hurry to get on her way with her friends she hadn't even asked if it was a male or a female, which was probably just as well because Jordan wasn't sure where this was going with Clint and she wasn't sure what she was ready to share with her daughter.

Her biggest fear was that somehow Clint was trying to re-create those bittersweet moments of the relationship they'd shared in the past, and Jordan knew that was impossible.

There was no going back to that time of innocence and simplicity. Life had changed her from the girl she'd once been, and she wasn't sure Clint would like those changes. She grabbed the pastry tube with the chocolate frosting and began to make the eyes and mouth on her cake, and as she squeezed the tube, her mind drifted to work.

The last week had yielded no more clues to Joann's murder and the case was getting less and less attention as new cases hit the detectives' desks. It was the nature of the beast in the murder business, that fresh cases took precedence over ones that were going nowhere.

They were hoping that something would come over the tip line concerning the Hathoway case. Joann's agent, who had been as helpful as he could be in the investigation, had set up a ten-thousand-dollar reward. In the meantime nothing more could be done.

Dane had called the night before to tell her that he'd had a talk with Mandy, who had insisted that there was nothing wrong, that she loved her mother and wished everyone would get off her back.

And that was what Jordan intended to do. She was going to get off her daughter's back, allow her space to breathe and grow, and hope that eventually she'd want to talk about whatever was bothering her, whatever was creating the distance Jordan felt.

She'd just finished making the smiling mouth with two big teeth when the doorbell rang. She threw the pastry tube in the sink to soak, then hurried toward the front door.

Clint stood on the doorstep balancing a large pizza box in one hand, with a six-pack of beer in the other. He grinned at her, displaying bloody wax vampire teeth.

She laughed and opened the door. "Please, hurry up and get in here before my neighbors see what kind of dork I hang out with."

"Call me a dork again and I'll bite your neck and bring you over to the dark side," he replied, the words slightly garbled as he entered the house.

She gestured him toward the kitchen and followed behind him, not able to help but to notice that his butt was just as taut in his tight jeans as she remembered. He set the pizza and beer on the table and then turned to face her, the ridiculous teeth still in his mouth.

"If you're nice to me, I'll share my spare set." He pulled a set of wax teeth still in the wrapper out of his pocket. She reached out for it, but he snapped it away and back into his pocket. "Only the head vampire decides when his apprentice gets her teeth."

Jordan opened the box of pizza and cracked open a beer. She took a drink, then eyed him with a lazy grin. "What the head vampire doesn't realize is that if he doesn't knock it off and eat, the pizza is going to be cold."

Clint pulled the wax teeth out of his mouth and set them on a napkin on the table. "Then let's eat."

"I guess you're one of those people who love Halloween," Jordan said minutes later as they sat at the table.

"It's one of my most favorite celebrations," he replied. "I can still remember the excitement that I felt when I was young and walked home from school on Halloween day. I loved dressing up in whatever costume I'd chosen and getting a bagful of candy that I could gorge on until my stomach hurt. But the best part was that it was a night I spent with my father."

"You didn't see him that often when you were young?"

"I was eight when my parents got divorced, and from that time on, my mother made it very difficult for me to see my father. But on Halloween she liked to go to a party at the local bar and so that was always a night I got to spend with Dad."

Jordan studied him in surprise. "You never told me that before."

He gave a small laugh. "Jordan, you should know that high school boys don't talk about stuff that really matters. Mom was so bitter over the divorce she wanted to hurt Dad and the only weapon she had available was me. She made it incredibly difficult for him to get visitation."

"Dane and I swore when we got divorced that we wouldn't use Mandy to hurt each other. Truthfully, I don't want to hurt him. I still like him—I just didn't want to be married to him anymore. And I'm pretty sure he feels the same way about me. We talked about doing the complicated custody thing where Mandy stayed with me four days one week, then three days the next, but it was Mandy who put her foot down and said she didn't want to be shuffled back and forth like that, and to be honest it would have been difficult with my crazy work schedule."

"But you want more," Clint said.

Jordan nodded. "I want her all the time, but she's old enough that I feel like I need to respect her wishes and right now she likes being home during the week and visiting me on the weekends—when her social life doesn't interfere."

"And she's getting to that age where she has a social life," Clint observed.

Jordan laughed. "She has a much better social life than I do. Eventually I'm going to talk to Dane about having her one or two evenings a week, since she makes plans so often for the weekends."

"It's nice if you can still be friends after a divorce, especially when there are kids involved."

"What about your ex-wife? Are you two still friends?" she asked curiously.

"No, I don't even know where she is. I heard that soon after our divorce became final, she moved to California. Without kids we had no real reason to stay in touch." He reached for another slice of the pizza.

"Did you want kids?"

He nodded. "I did, she didn't, and she was in control as far as that was concerned. Now I'm grateful we didn't have any."

"You've been divorced a long time. Why haven't you remarried and had children?"

He paused a moment to take a drink of his beer before answering. "I've dated casually since my divorce, but haven't found that special connection with anyone that would make me want to jump back into a marriage. I've got the boys on the football team. They're kind of like surrogate kids, and for the last couple of years that's pretty much been enough for me, but it doesn't feel like enough anymore."

He leaned forward and dabbed the side of her mouth with his napkin. This close she could see the tiny silver shards in his eyes, felt the heat of his fingers through the thin paper of the napkin. Her breath caught in her chest.

"You had a little stringy cheese," he said as he sat back in his chair.

"Thanks," she replied. "So, are you and your dad close now?" she asked, trying to concentrate more on the conversation and less on his physical presence.

"When my mom was keeping me from seeing him when I was younger, she always told me I'd have plenty of time to spend with my dad when I got older. But by the time I was old enough to make plans to meet Dad without having to get my mother's permission, he'd remarried and had a new family of his own. There wasn't much of a place for a sixteen-year-old boy from a previous marriage. So, the short answer is no, we aren't real close."

"What about your relationship with your mother?" Jordan pushed her plate away before she reached for one last piece of pizza that she really didn't want and her hips didn't need.

"It's a bit strained. She never really got over the divorce and as an adult I recognize how manipulative she was with my father and with me."

"She's never remarried?"

"No, her life is still wrapped around making my father as miserable as possible. She refuses to let go of the past and move on."

Jordan thought of Della, who had never really moved beyond the pain and alienation of her high school years. "There seems to be a lot of that going around." She picked up her beer and took another swallow, then continued. "Maybe that should be the newest rage in mental illness, the inability to let go of the past. We could build hospitals to hold those angry, bitter and hurt people."

He laughed. "We couldn't build the hospitals fast enough."

At that moment the doorbell rang and the trick-or-treaters began to arrive. For the next three hours they answered the door and handed out candy to princesses and ballerinas and Incredible Hulks and monsters. She earned her vampire teeth by serving him cake and they both wore them and had a ridiculous conversation about the pros and cons of being a vampire.

In between doorbell rings they talked, about anything and everything, and not only ate the cake Jordan had baked but also dipped into the candy bowl she'd prepared for the trick-or-treaters.

He told her about the boys he was closest to on his football team and she talked about her partners, including the newest kid on the block, Ricky Copeland. "He's just so eager to make a mark," she said as they sat in the living room waiting for the next knock on the door. "It's a quality that's either going to make him a great detective or get him into big trouble."

"Maybe that's what people were saying about you when you first joined the force," Clint replied.

She laughed and the sound of her laughter reminded him of the girl she'd once been, a girl he still saw each time he looked at her. Over the years there had been changes in her, but in a lot of ways she hadn't changed at all.

She still had that golden shine about her, a shine that drew people to her. And despite everything that had gone on in her life, she hadn't lost her sense of humor. She'd always been easy to spend time with and that was something that hadn't changed either.

As a knock sounded at the door, he watched her get up from the sofa with a sinuous grace. Maybe he was one of those people who should be hospitalized for being unable to let go of the past, because each time he looked at her, he remembered loving her.

There was no question that he was still intensely physically drawn to her. At least a half a dozen times tonight he'd wanted to grab her by the hand and make a run for her bedroom. He would have liked to ignore the trick-or-treaters and instead treat himself to making love to Jordan.

They would be good together. He'd always known she'd be great in bed. He remembered the way she moved against him in the back of his Thunderbird when they would park and make out. He still remembered her whispered moans as he stroked beneath her blouse, under her bra.

But he didn't want to move too quickly. That had always been his mistake. He got the sex right but failed in the after-sex department. He didn't want to make that error with Jordan. He wanted to build something first, then sleep with her.

"Want another beer?" she asked as she returned from the door.

"No, thanks. I'm good," he replied, although what he needed was a cold shower.

She gave him a teasing smile. "That's what you always told me in high school."

He laughed. "I think I also told you that not having sex as a teenage boy could lead to instant death."

Her gray eyes twinkled. "And as I recall, I promised to cry at your funeral."

"You did," he replied as he laughed again, and then sobered. "You were so strong in high school, so sure of yourself and your own convictions. And I was such a mess," he admitted.

"You were the mess all the girls wanted to be with and I refused to be just another one of the gang who gave in to you. But it's all water under the bridge now. It was a different time and we were different people."

"Not so different," he countered. "We've just grown up."

It was nearly ten when Clint decided to call it a night. The doorbell had been silent for nearly an hour and they both had to go to work the next morning. "I'm going to get out of here," he said as he got up from the sofa. "I can tell you're tired and the last thing I want is for you to be exhausted tomorrow and face bad guys."

"I am tired," she admitted. "It's been a long couple of weeks." She got up and walked with him to the front door. "Thanks for dinner," she said.

"Thanks for the cake and the company," he replied.

She opened the door and turned back to face him and he knew he was going to kiss her good night. A simple kiss, he told himself as he leaned toward her, like the brief, light kiss they'd shared before. Her eyes widened slightly as his mouth touched hers.

Soft and sweet, her mouth tasted just as he remembered. A white-hot flare of desire struck him and he wrapped his arms around her and pulled her more closely against him.

As she opened her mouth to him, the simple kiss became something far more complicated. His tongue swirled with hers as she leaned more intimately against him and raised her arms around his neck.

Just one kiss, and he was hard as a rock. He half expected her to pull away from him, but in the end it was he who reluctantly stepped back from her.

"I'll be in touch. Good night, Jordan."

"Night, Clint," she replied, her voice slightly husky.

He stepped out the door before he did something stupid. Relationship first, sex second, he reminded himself as he got into his car.

She'd always loved Halloween. John sat next to his wife's hospital bed in their living room and remembered all the Halloweens past when Mary had dressed up in costume to greet the kids at the door.

Over the years she'd been a lusty barmaid, a gypsy, a witch and an angel. Tonight she was in costume as a woman in a coma still fighting the clutches of death.

John hadn't bought candy to give out at the door. When he'd gotten home from work, he'd turned off all the lights in the house except for a small lamp in the living room. He didn't want to see little trick-or-treaters and remember the delight Mary had always gotten when passing out candy.

"Aren't you just the cutest little angel I've ever seen?" she'd say. Or, "Oh my, you're a scary thing." And the kids would giggle and hold their bags out for a treat.

Tonight was different. Instead they'd passed the evening as they had all the others in the last couple of weeks. John had talked to her about retirement plans and resorts they would visit as he tried to drink himself into oblivion.

Unfortunately, oblivion wasn't happening. In fact tonight it seemed the more he drank, the clearer his thoughts became. There was no miracle waiting for them. Mary wasn't going to get better. She was going to die.

It wasn't fair. This wasn't what they'd planned. For

years they had saved their money, forgoing trips to a restaurant or the movies. Mary had shopped at thrift stores instead of shopping new so they could tuck extra money into their retirement account.

He leaned back in his chair and closed his eyes. The only sound in the room was Mary's breathing. Her breaths weren't deep and even, but rather shallow and gasping, as if each one took a tremendous effort.

Let her go, a little voice whispered inside his head. He'd been hearing that voice a lot lately. He didn't know if it was the booze talking or his conscience. Just let her go, it whispered.

He opened his eyes and looked at the woman in the bed. The woman he'd married was gone. She'd been gone for a long time. He leaned forward and took her hand in his. It was cold, as if death had already claimed her.

"I love you, Mary," he whispered, his voice husky with emotion. "I'll always love you, but it's time for you to go now." A band of grief tightened around his chest, but he tried to ignore it. "Let go, Mary. It's okay to just let go."

As if she heard him, she drew a deep breath and then breathed no more. It was as if the only thing tethering her to this life had been John's inability to release her.

John laid her hand on her bed, then once again leaned back in his chair as the grief pierced through him. It was a pain too deep for tears. There were two things on the end table next to where he sat. One was his drink and the other was his service revolver.

He picked up his drink and took a deep swallow, then set the glass down and grabbed his gun. It felt unusually heavy and unwieldy as he raised it to his mouth.

Mary was dead. He had no reason to continue on with his life. Mary had been his reason to get up in the mornings. She'd been the reason he'd become a cop. They'd spent the past twenty years socking away money so that when he retired, they could travel and enjoy each other's company. It was all dead now . . . the plans, the dreams, everything.

A sob ripped from his throat as he jammed the barrel of the gun into his mouth. He could end it all now. He could be with Mary through eternity. He tightened his lips around the cold metal. All he had to do was pull the trigger. The hospice volunteers who showed up in the morning would find them. There would be no loneliness, no grieving, just sweet peace.

His hand shook violently and beads of perspiration began to track down the side of his face. He bit down on the barrel and told himself to pull the trigger. Just do it, he commanded himself. Just end the misery right now.

But still he hesitated. Finally, with another deep sob he dropped the gun into his lap. He was nothing but a loser, too afraid to go on with his life by himself and yet too much of a coward to take his own life.

He reached for his glass once again and thought about whom he needed to call to tell that Mary was gone.

Chapter 14

"Tell us what you did to Glenda Washburn, and this time tell us the truth. We're all sick of your lies." Jordan slammed her hands down on the table in front of Max Tanner, an ex-con who had been seen running from the scene where his girlfriend, Glenda, had been pushed down to the sidewalk and kicked and beaten to death.

Witnesses at the scene had described Max as the assailant and he'd been picked up at the apartment he shared with Glenda less than an hour after the death occurred

"I tell you, I don't know what you are talking about. I was home all morning watching the tube. Glenda left to do some shopping and that was the last time I saw her. Now back off, bitch."

"That's Detective Bitch to you, asshole," Jordan replied as she took a step back.

"Look, Max," Anthony said, using his good-cop voice. "I know how it is; believe me. I got an ex-wife I'd like to smash in the face sometimes. They get mouthy and they buck your authority. It's enough to make any guy lose his cool."

"What did she do, Max? Get in your face? Tell you to get a damn job or get out?" Jordan stepped closer to him once again, so close she could smell his sweat. "Did she tell you that you suck in bed?"

Max half stood from the chair, then sank back down

and scowled at Jordan. He narrowed his eyes. "Get her out of here and I'll talk to you," he said to Anthony. "But I'm not saying another word with that bitch in the room." He crossed his arms over his chest and stared up at the ceiling.

"I'm not going anywhere," Jordan said.

Anthony stood from the chair where he'd been sitting, and walked to the door of the interrogation room. "Detective Sampson, could I speak with you for a moment?" He opened the door and looked pointedly at her.

"Don't think I'm done with you yet," she said to Max as she left the room.

Anthony stepped out as well and closed the door behind him and then grinned at her. "You make a great bad cop."

She returned his smile. "It was in my job description: must catch criminals and play bad cop in the interrogation room. Go back and close it out. He's ready to confess."

As Anthony went back into the interrogation room, Jordan headed back to her desk, where a month of paperwork awaited her. They'd finished up the interviews of everyone who had attended the reunion, and had narrowed the suspect list down to twenty people. It might as well be a million, for there was no forensic evidence to point to any one of those people's culpability.

At the top of the suspect list were Linda, Danny McCall and Wayne Marcel, a classmate of Jordan's who'd had a fender bender with Joann two weeks before the reunion. Apparently things had gotten ugly between the two at the scene of the accident.

She glanced over at John, who sat at his desk and stared off into space. It had been a week since his wife had died, three days since the funeral. Benny had tried to talk John into taking time off, but John had insisted he needed to work. So for the past three days he'd shown up, but Jordan had a feeling very little was getting done.

Thankfully John had a strong partner in Adam and they were all hoping that Adam would see John through this and get him back on track.

Throughout the past week Jordan had done a lot of thinking about Clint. He'd called on Wednesday just to check in with her and see if they could get together again soon. But she hadn't been able to tell him any night that would work. She'd assumed Mandy would be coming over tonight, since it was Friday, but a call from her daughter that morning had let her know that Mandy had plans with friends, but that Dane would bring her to Jordan's in the morning.

Word had come down from the brass that they were discouraging overtime, so it was just after five that evening when Jordan left the station. With no new leads in the Hathoway murder and most of her paperwork done, there was no point for her to stick around.

With the empty evening hours ahead of her, on impulse she decided to stop and say hello to her parents. Each time she headed to her parents' home, it was always with the hope that somehow they'd connect with her, that they'd love her like they used to before Julie's murder. *But you know why they don't*, a little voice whispered in the back of her brain. She silenced the voice with a shake of her head. She definitely didn't want to go there.

As she pulled into the driveway of her childhood home, she steeled herself for the usual pallor of half life that existed inside. Since Julie's death her parents had grown comfortable in their roles as victims. They refused to throw off the mantle of grief that had shrouded them so many years ago.

She knocked on the front door and then opened it and walked inside. The scent of pot roast and hot rolls set her stomach rumbling and reminded her that she'd had only a stale doughnut for lunch at her desk.

"Mom? Dad?"

"In the kitchen," her mother called out.

The first thing Jordan noticed as she entered the kitchen was that the room was cast in semidarkness. The room faced the south and once the sun began to sink, it got little sunlight. "Something smells good," she said with forced cheerfulness as she flipped on the overhead light. She almost expected them to shrink and screech in protest at the bright light.

"Get a plate if you want. There's plenty," her mother replied without any real invitation in her voice.

Just that easily Jordan's appetite fled. "No thanks, I'm not staying. I just thought I'd swing by on my way home from work and say hi."

"That's nice, dear." Her father forced a smile to his lips, then focused back on the food in front of him.

Jordan stood awkwardly in the doorway. There was a part of her that wanted to scream, a tiny childish piece of her that wanted to cry and throw a temper tantrum to get attention.

But she wasn't a child anymore and she knew the myth of negative attention being better than no attention. After fourteen years she'd be a fool to expect things to change.

Over the years she'd grieved not only the loss of her sister but also the loss of her parents. The killer would never realize how many threads of life he'd pulled undone when he'd strangled Julie.

"So, anything new?" she asked. "Dad, how's work?"

For the next few minutes she tried to keep some small talk flowing; finally the strain was too much and she left. As she headed home, she recognized that nothing would ever change between her and her parents. She wasn't sure why she put herself through the visits. She had a feeling if she stopped going to see them, she wouldn't even be missed.

Julie and Jordan had been inseparable and she knew each time her parents looked at her, they were always somehow seeking the one who was missing. She couldn't fix it. She couldn't fix them. They had grown too comfortable in the state of perpetual grief.

She arrived at home just after six and the moment she stepped into the silence of her house, she knew she didn't want to remain there. Quiet and inactivity were conducive to thinking, and after the dismal visit with her parents she didn't want to give herself a chance to think, was afraid of where those thoughts might take her.

Maybe there was a football game at the high school tonight. It might be fun to go, but she didn't feel like going alone. Clint would be on the field and she'd be alone among strangers.

Although she doubted that Della would be interested in going, she pulled her cell phone from her pocket and called her.

"What's up?" Della answered on the first ring.

"I'm at loose ends tonight and was wondering if you'd want to go with me to a high school football game."

There was a moment of stunned silence. "A football game? Why?"

"I thought it might be fun, but I understand if you aren't interested. I just thought I'd ask."

"Sure, I'll go. Why not?" Della replied. "Ben is out of town again and I'm bored to tears."

"Really, you don't mind?"

"Nah, it might be fun. But I've got a couple of errands to run before I can go, so why don't I meet you at the high school, in front of the gate to the stadium?"

"Sounds perfect," Jordan replied. "How about we meet at around seven?"

"That means I've got to get moving. I'll see you there," Della said.

The two hung up and Jordan drifted into the kitchen to grab something to eat. She was glad Della had agreed to go with her. Since Joann's death, Jordan hadn't seen much of Della and she knew her friend was feeling ignored.

Jordan gulped down a ham and cheese sandwich

and then went into her bedroom to change clothes. She pulled on a navy sweater and a pair of jeans and then did a quick touch-up on her makeup. Just in case, she thought as she applied fresh lipstick, although she really didn't expect Clint to see her in the stands.

It was just before seven when she reached the high school. It took her several minutes of driving around to finally find a parking space in the packed lot. There was nothing better than a winning football team to fill the stands, and Oak Ridge High School had been a winning team for the last five years.

As she got out of the car, she heard the crowd and a voice over the loudspeaker announcing the team players. The scent of popcorn filled the air, along with the smell of grilling hot dogs, and a sliver of excitement sliced through her.

One of the things she'd always loved about football games was the feeling of being part of something bigger than yourself. An entire stadium of people all came together to cheer for their team and enjoy the game. Positive energy sizzled in the air.

It was a beautiful evening, cool but not too chilly. As she reached the gate where she was to meet Della, Jordan felt the weight of her workweek falling away. Tonight she would enjoy the football game and first thing in the morning Dane would be bringing Mandy over to spend the night. She didn't want to think about murder until she went back to work on Monday morning.

It was quarter after seven when Della finally arrived, half-breathless from the walk from her parking space to the gate. "I can't imagine why you decided to come here on a Friday night," she exclaimed. "We could have had a few drinks at Iggy's."

Jordan shook her head as she paid for two tickets. "Too much shop talk there. I needed a night away from my coworkers." She grabbed Della's arm. "Come on, this will be fun."

As they entered the stadium, Jordan spied free space

on the bleacher right behind the Oak Ridge team bench and that was where she led Della. The minute she sat, she saw him. Clint stood with his arm around the quarterback, his head touching the boy's head as they spoke.

He looked energetic and handsome as sin. The cool evening breeze ruffled his dark hair with careless abandon and he looked as if he'd been born to wear the navy dress slacks and light blue sweater that were the school colors.

"Ah, I'm beginning to understand the sudden attraction to football," Della observed.

"I don't know what you're talking about," Jordan exclaimed in mock innocence.

At that moment Clint turned around and gazed into the bleachers. She realized the moment he saw her. His mouth curved into a smile and he raised a hand. She returned the wave, warmth creeping into her cheeks.

"You don't know what I'm talking about, my ass," Della said dryly. "Are you sleeping with him yet?"

"No. We've really only gone out twice."

"So, what are you waiting for?" Della asked.

"I'm waiting for him to make the next move," she replied.

"And he hasn't yet? Wow, that's a bit out of character for the high school stud."

"You can't judge people from their high school days," Jordan said. "I mean, look at the difference in you."

"Mostly superficial," Della replied easily. She grabbed Jordan's hand. "Just go slow. I know how much Dane hurt you and you've told me about your relationship with Clint in high school. I don't want to see you get hurt all over again."

Jordan squeezed Della's hand with affection. "Don't worry about me. He can't hurt me, because I'm not allowing him to get that close to me. I'm not looking for love, just a good time."

Della snorted in disbelief and released Jordan's hand. "You say that now, but I'm just worried about history repeating itself. If he isn't having sex with you, he's probably having it with somebody else."

At that moment the crowd erupted with the opening kickoff.

"Where's Ben?" Jordan asked when there was a lull in the noise level.

"He flew out this morning." Della frowned. "Either for Chicago or Milwaukee or it might have been St. Louis—I can't remember which. Lately it seems like he's gone more than he's home." She offered Jordan a petulant frown. "He's working on some big merger and he's been obsessed with it."

"And you're upset because normally he's obsessed with you," Jordan replied with a laugh.

"But, of course," Della replied with a guilty giggle.

By halftime the game looked like a total blowout. The score was 21–0 with Oak Ridge in the lead. Jordan and Della visited the concession stands and stood to eat decadent chili dogs topped with everything imaginable. The mood of the attendees was exuberant and the sound of the Oak Ridge marching band's halftime performance filled the air.

"This is fun," Della exclaimed as they left the concession stand. "I'm glad you invited me along."

They had just returned to their seats when a young man approached Jordan.

"Mrs. Sampson?" he asked.

She nodded and he handed her a folded piece of paper, then raced back up the bleachers. Jordan opened the paper. *MEET ME AT THE OUTER BOYS' LOCKER ROOM DOOR AFTER THE GAME*, and it was signed with a *C*.

"Love notes being passed—isn't that sweet?" Della said. Jordan elbowed her and tucked the note in her purse. "So, are you going to meet him?"

"I came with you. I'll leave with you," Jordan replied.

"Don't be a dunce. I came by myself and I'll leave by

myself. What you do after that is your business," Della exclaimed.

"You were the one who was just warning me off him a few minutes ago."

Della shrugged. "You told me you have it all under control."

Jordan looked back at the field where the second half of the game was under way. Her gaze found Clint in the middle of a huddle of uniformed players. She told herself all she was doing where he was concerned was easing a bit of her loneliness, using him to fill up empty hours.

But as she thought of the fun she'd had with him on Halloween night, as she remembered how he'd held her in his arms when she'd cried about Mandy, she'd have to admit to herself that he was already more than a little bit in her heart.

She didn't want to fall in love with Clint Cooper. She'd been there, done that, and it hadn't been fun. In fact, loving him had been downright painful. So why was she even contemplating meeting him at the locker room door?

Betsy Baker was in heaven. Ralph had left that morning for a medical conference in St. Louis and she'd farmed out the kids for the weekend with her parents.

She now sank lower in the tub of lavender-and-thyme-scented bubbles, a glass of wine at her fingertips and the stereo playing oldies. She loved it when she had the house all to herself, when she could take a long, leisurely bath without interruption. No kids bursting in wanting their favorite blouse or soccer socks, no husband to wander through asking about dinnertime or something else.

Tomorrow her day would begin with her sleeping in as late as she wanted. She raised a toe and placed it on the edge of the tub to inspect her polish. She might get a pedicure and maybe meet one of her friends for dinner.

It would be a day all about her and her wants—just the way she liked it.

She'd had lunch with Jenny Taylor again that afternoon, but she was a little bit worried about Jenny. Betsy suspected there was violence in the marriage. Jenny had been sporting a large bruise on her wrist and another on the side of her face. She'd told Betsy she'd fallen, but Betsy wasn't sure she believed it. She'd tried to get Jenny to talk about it, even offered to help, but Jenny had insisted there wasn't a problem.

Betsy used her toe to twist the hot-water faucet and settled back once again as steamy hot water flowed into the tub to heat the water that had grown tepid. She was going to be a prune by the time she got out, but she didn't care.

She shut off the faucet and took a drink of her wine. Closing her eyes, she let the warmth of the water lull her as the radio played a song that had been popular when she'd been in college. Of course, she hadn't graduated. Instead she'd met Ralph and seen her future in his degree from medical school.

The sound of the music suddenly stopped, as if somebody had pressed the power button on the stereo. Betsy frowned with irritation. Sometimes the station she liked to listen to just went silent for a minute or two, as if their signal got interrupted for some reason.

Deciding she'd had enough of the bath, she opened her eyes and he stood in front of her, her white terrycloth robe in his hands. She screamed and sank beneath the water in an irrational attempt to escape.

"There's no point in screaming. Nobody can hear you. Get out and put this on." He held the robe out to her.

"What do you want? Why are you here? My husband is going to be home any time." The warm water that had been so inviting now felt icy cold as Betsy stared up at the intruder in her home. He wore a ski mask, making it impossible for her to see his features. She could see nothing but the glitter of his eyes.

"Your husband is in St. Louis and your kids are gone for the night." He smiled, a gesture that didn't reach the cold center of his eyes. "Now get out of there before I lose my temper."

It was then she saw the gun and realized that she was in terrible trouble. Stay calm, she told herself, despite the frantic beating of her heart. Don't make him mad. She half rose from the water and tried to shield her nakedness with one hand as she reached for the robe with the other.

As she stepped out of the tub, she hit her wineglass. It fell to the floor, splattering red wine on the beige carpeting. "That's going to be a bitch to get out," the man said as she quickly wrapped the robe around her.

"Please, what do you want?" Was he here to rob her? To rape her? Her knees knocked together as he gestured with the gun for her to leave the room. "I have money," she said as they walked down the long hallway. "And diamonds. I have a lot of jewelry. You can have it all. Anything you want, just please don't hurt me."

He remained silent, the gun barrel pressed into the center of her back. "Please don't hurt me. I'll do whatever you want, but just don't hurt me." She said the words over and over again as she moved on leaden feet.

When they reached the living room, she saw one of her kitchen chairs sitting in the middle of the room. He led her there and she sat, feeling as if her trembling legs wouldn't hold her up another minute.

It was when he pulled the length of rope from his pocket that the terror that had been building since the moment she'd opened her eyes and seen him exploded. With a cry of terror, she jumped off the chair and headed toward the back door in the kitchen.

She made it only two steps into the room when he tackled her from behind. She hit the floor as she sobbed hysterically. He yanked her up without effort and pinned her arms to her side, then dragged her back to the chair.

"You do that again, I'll shoot you," he said angrily as he shoved her back down.

She was crying too hard to attempt anything. Her sobs increased as he tied her into the chair. Once he was finished, he stepped back from her and his lips, which were barely visible in the slit of the ski mask, moved upward into another smile. It was a cold, empty gesture.

"Now we're going to talk about high school, Betsy."

These words penetrated through her terror and she gazed at him with incomprehension. "What?"

"You were a bad girl in high school, Betsy, and you haven't changed a bit since then and now it's time for you to face your punishment." This time when he smiled, there was glee shining from his eyes.

Chapter 15

Jordan stood outside the door that led to the boys' locker room. She wasn't alone. Half a dozen giggling high school girls stood there as well, waiting for their football-playing boyfriends to exit.

She'd said good-bye to Della minutes after the game had ended. It had been a victory for Oak Ridge High, the final score 31–7. She smiled at two of the girls who stood huddled together, their cheeks pink from either the cool night air or the excitement of what might come after the game.

She remembered that excitement. She had many memories of waiting in this very same place for Clint to come out of the locker room after a game and she couldn't help the faint flutter of excitement that now filled her.

It was another moment of déjà vu. The crisp fall night, the lingering noise from the football fans as they left the stadium, the residual scent of popcorn, all combined to cast her back in time.

At that moment he came out the door, bringing with him the scent of minty soap and that delicious smell of his cologne. "What a great surprise," he said as he took her hand and led her away from the gaggle of giggling girls. "I couldn't believe it when I looked up in the stands and saw you there."

"I found myself at loose ends tonight and decided to

see how the team looks this year," she said, overly conscious of the warmth of his hand surrounding hers.

"We look awesome," he said with exuberance. "It's tradition after a win we all head to Roberto's Pizza and I buy the guys pizza. Come with me."

"Oh, I don't want to intrude on your celebration," she protested.

He squeezed her hand. "Don't be silly. You won't be intruding. The more, the merrier. You can ride with me and when we're finished at the pizza place, I'll bring you back here to your car. Come on, Jordan. I can't think of anyone I'd rather celebrate with."

She wasn't sure she trusted him, wasn't sure she trusted herself to maintain the distance she wanted to from him. But she nodded her agreement and warmed with pleasure as he slung an arm around her shoulder. "Okay, sounds like fun."

"It was a great game," she said moments later when they were in his car and headed to the pizza parlor.

"I've got a great bunch of guys on the team this year. So far it's been a pleasure to coach them."

"You love it, don't you?"

He flashed her a quick look. "I do. But don't you love what you do?"

She started to reply with the automatic answer that of course she loved her job, but instead she thought about it for a long moment. "I'm good at what I do. At the time I joined the department, I felt it was a true calling, but I'm not sure I absolutely love what I do," she finally said.

"What would you rather be doing?"

She smiled. "I can't think of anything, so I must be doing what I'm supposed to be doing."

"I'd better warn you, it's going to be a rowdy crowd at Roberto's. It's always a little crazy after a win."

"And what's it like after a loss?"

He grinned. "I can't remember. It's been a long time since we've lost a game."

"Then you must be a great coach," she replied.

"Not really. I'm a good motivator, but the boys do the real work."

She liked his modesty, although she suspected he was much more than a motivator to the boys on the team. That feeling was justified when they arrived at Roberto's and she saw him interact with the team members.

As they gathered around several tables, with pizzas in front of them, it was obvious the boys liked Clint. There was plenty of good-natured teasing, but beneath it was an underlying respect and real affection.

They were all polite to Jordan, offering her slices of pizza and refilling her soda from the self-serve station. It was hard to believe that she and Clint had ever been this young, this full of bravado and possibilities.

But she did remember that high school mentality of believing that you had it all figured out. She'd felt that way when she'd been in high school, so in control and almost omnipotent. It was only when you left high school that you realized you didn't have any answers and that life would never be that easy again.

It was almost midnight when Clint told his team good-bye and he and Jordan got back in his car. "That was fun," she said. "They all think a lot of you."

"I think a lot of them," he replied. "They liked you."

"I'm just grateful you didn't introduce me as Detective Sampson. That would have definitely changed the way they interacted with me," she replied.

They continued to talk about the players and the girlfriends who had been with some of them. "I know they're the same age we were when we were in high school, but I felt so grown-up, so mature at that age, and they all seemed so young and yet so self-confident," she said.

"Part of the pleasure of being a teenager is being absolutely certain that you know it all. Your teachers, your parents, they all tell you differently, but you are so sure of being invincible and in the illusion that you have all the answers to life in your head."

"I was thinking that very same thing a few minutes ago. So, with age comes both knowledge and vulnerability," she replied as he pulled up next to her car in the empty parking lot.

He shut off his engine and turned to look at her. "Are you feeling vulnerable?"

"Only when I'm with you," she admitted. She unfastened her seat belt and he did the same. "You scare me just a little bit. When I'm with you, I remember a lot of good times, but I also remember the bad."

"That's why it's important to me that you get to know me again as a man before we become lovers," he replied, his blue eyes holding her gaze intently.

Even the word "lovers" shot a thrill through her. "I'd better get home. Dane is dropping Mandy off early in the morning." She got out of the car and he did as well. "Thanks for tonight. This was fun," she said as she reached her driver door.

"I should be thanking you for braving such a night," he returned as he stepped closer to her.

She knew a kiss was coming and she welcomed it. She stood with her back against her car door as he leaned into her, his mouth hungrily taking hers. She raised her arms and wrapped them around his neck as he pressed closer to her.

He gripped her by her hips and she imagined she could feel the warmth of his hands through her jeans. Still the kiss continued, becoming more frantic as she moved her hips against his.

His hands left her hips and snaked up beneath her sweater, warming her bare back. At the same time his lips slid from hers and instead trailed down her jawline, down the length of her neck.

She threw her head back, allowing him access to the sensitive spot behind her ear, the tender skin beneath her chin. The night air chilled her face, but Clint warmed her with his lips, with his hands.

When his mouth sought hers once again, she felt a

wildness growing inside her. He leaned into her, trapping her against the car door. Their hips ground together and he released a faint groan, as if he, too, had the same wildness building inside him.

Jesus, they were standing in the middle of a parking lot and she was more turned on than she'd been in a very long time. What she wanted to do was pull him into the backseat of her car and get naked. But, even as the thought entered her mind, he pulled away from her and took several steps backward.

He shoved his hands in his pockets and for a long moment just stared at her, his eyes hot and hungry.

"Is this some sort of way you're getting back at me for all those nights I refused to give in to you?" she asked half breathlessly.

He gave a half laugh. "No. That was supposed to be just a light and easy good-night kiss. I'll have to remember in the future that when it comes to kissing you, there is no light and easy."

If he touched her one more time, she would definitely pull him into her backseat, but instead he took another step backward. "Drive safe going home. Good night, Jordan."

He turned and walked back to his car. She drew a deep breath and released it on a tremulous sigh as she got into her car.

This thing with Clint was going to make her crazy. She told herself she didn't want a real relationship with anyone, that her life was full enough without her throwing a man into the mix. And yet, when she was with Clint, she forgot that she didn't want anyone in her life.

She rediscovered her femininity whenever she was with him, something it was easy to lose sight of in her line of work. There was no question that he stirred a passion in her that had been missing for a very long time. Equally as important was the fact that he'd brought laughter back into her life.

It was only when she was in bed that night that she realized there was still a big part of her that didn't quite trust Clint Cooper.

Clint couldn't sleep. He lay in bed and tossed and turned, his thoughts filled with Jordan. He was as crazy about her now as he'd been in high school. There was no question that a wild, hot desire existed between them, and it was a desire he had every intention of following through on, but he wanted more.

They'd jokingly called her the ice princess in high school, not just because she refused to sleep with anyone, but also because she'd always held herself just a bit distant from everything and everyone.

He felt that distance now, only it was deeper, greater than it had been when she'd been young. She was easy to be with, easy to talk to, but he had a feeling she never let down her guard, never allowed herself to be totally and utterly vulnerable.

And this time when he gave his heart to a woman, he wanted her open and vulnerable. He wanted to know all the secret places inside her, all the things she'd never confessed to anyone else.

He'd had enough relationships in his life that had been built on superficiality, ones he'd kept on cautious ground. He wasn't willing to settle anymore for something safe and easy.

He just wasn't sure if Jordan was ready to open herself up completely. He wasn't sure if they had a real shot at making it work or if this was just another study in frustration with her.

One thing was certain. If she couldn't, or wouldn't, completely open up to him, put her heart on the line for him, eventually he'd have to walk away from her, and this time there would be no going back.

Chapter 16

The ring of her cell phone on the nightstand pulled Jordan from a deep sleep. She sat up, for a moment disoriented as to day and time. Then she remembered it was Sunday night. She'd gone to bed early, having taken Mandy home after a difficult weekend. Mandy had been in one of her moods, sullen and distant, and had spent most of her time on her cell phone, either texting or talking to her friends and ignoring Jordan.

Jordan rolled over and grabbed the phone from the nightstand. "Sampson," she answered groggily.

"Get dressed. I'm on my way to get you," Anthony said.

"What have we got?" Jordan asked as she turned on her bedside lamp and shook off the last of her sleepiness.

"Don't have any details. I'll see you in ten minutes."

The minute he clicked off, Jordan bounded out of the bed and into the bathroom. It was as she pulled on a pair of navy slacks that she remembered her dream. She'd been dreaming about Julie.

It hadn't been a particularly pleasant dream and it wasn't the first time she'd had it. In many ways the sisters had been alike, but in many ways they'd been very different. Julie had been more carefree, more open to new experiences, and as much as the two sisters had loved each other, they'd occasionally fought with a vengeance. The dream had been a replay of their last phone conversation, a petty fight that had ended with Jordan hanging up on her sister.

The dream always left Jordan with a pall of weighty guilt and stoked the embers of grief back into a blaze. *You should have done more*, a little voice whispered in her head. *You might have been able to change things if you hadn't been so selfish.*

She pulled on a white blouse and quickly buttoned it, shoving thoughts of the dream and Julie aside. She couldn't think about that now. She had work to do, and if she allowed those thoughts to play in her head, she'd lose it.

By the time she grabbed her blazer from the closet, her doorbell rang, announcing Anthony's arrival.

"I've got something to tell you," Anthony said a few minutes later as he backed out of her driveway.

"What's that?" She took a sip out of the foam cup of coffee that Anthony had brought with him.

"The address where we're headed. It's the Bakers' address."

"The Baker address?" She frowned and then gasped. "You mean Betsy Baker?"

He nodded. "Apparently the husband had been out of town to a medical conference. He arrived home and found her dead in the house. It's definitely a homicide."

"Oh my God." Jordan felt half-dizzy as she digested the information.

"That's all I know, but I figured I'd better warn you." He shot her a quick glance. "You okay?"

"Yeah, I guess." She stared out the side window into the darkness of the night, the taste of the coffee now bitter and acrid where it lingered on her tongue.

First Joann and now Betsy. It had to be tied to the reunion. A sickness welled up inside her. That night in the ballroom she might have had drinks with the killer. She might have smiled at him across the room, never knowing that he was planning on killing women who were there.

"It might not be related," Anthony said as if he'd read her thoughts. "I mean, it's possible the husband got home earlier than he's reporting. Maybe he and Betsy had a fight and things got out of control. Or maybe it was a robbery gone bad. Don't jump to any conclusions until we see the scene."

Jordan knew he was right. It was possible this had nothing to do with Joann, nothing to do with the reunion, but telling herself that didn't stop the sickness that rolled in her stomach.

As they drove through the security gate, it was obvious where all the action was happening. The Baker place was a huge two-story home, and when they pulled up, several cop cars, the medical examiner's vehicle and the crime-scene-unit van were already there. The authorities milled around the sweeping front porch, obviously awaiting the arrival of the detectives.

Anthony and Jordan got out of his car and as they walked toward the house, Jordan felt every muscle in her body growing taut as she prepared for what lay inside.

"Where's the husband?" she asked one of the blues.

"We've got an officer with him in an upstairs bedroom. Victim is in the living room. Nobody's been in there except the husband. We're just waiting for you."

"We'll let you know when we're ready for everyone to come in," Anthony said as he and Jordan pulled on a pair of booties and gloves. They entered a large marble-floored entry with a vaulted ceiling and a chandelier that probably cost more than Jordan's house.

"Fancy digs," Anthony said.

"I wouldn't have expected anything less from Betsy," Jordan replied. Neither of them mentioned the scent of death that lay heavy in the air. It was an all-too-familiar odor that was as much a part of their job as their badges.

They took only one step into the living room and stared at the carnage before them. "Holy crap," Anthony breathed softly.

It wasn't difficult to imagine what the room had once looked like with its glass-enclosed display cases holding the collectible dolls that Betsy had loved. Now it looked as if a tornado had whirled through the room. Glass littered the floor and the dolls were everywhere, their porcelain faces shattered and limbs detached from the bodies.

But that wasn't all. The real horror was Betsy, who was tied to a chair in the center of the room, her eyes wide-open and her features frozen in death. The robe she wore was soaked with blood that had dried to rusty stains.

Jordan experienced a fierce déjà vu as she stared at Betsy, left so much like Joann had been left in her studio. She instantly looked at the area around Betsy's bare feet, but there were no numbers written in blood there.

Still, the rage that had taken place in the room was apparent and there was no way not to compare the two crime scenes and suspect that the same perpetrator had done both of the killings.

Jordan hadn't liked Betsy in high school and she hadn't liked her at the reunion, but nobody deserved this kind of death. It was obvious that she'd suffered before she'd died.

"Are you thinking what I'm thinking?" Anthony asked.

"Don't even say it," she replied. They had assumed that Joann's death was an isolated incident, but Betsy's murder put a whole new spin on things, a horrifying spin. Was it possible both Joann and Betsy had pissed off the same person on the night of the reunion? Definitely. Joann had been arrogant and Betsy had been a catty bitch.

Jordan walked around the room, trying not to step on anything that might become evidence. She stepped up next to the dead woman and looked at her hands. The polish was perfect, not a chip or crack on either hand. "We'll bag her hands, but I doubt if we'll find anything. She doesn't look like she fought back."

"Looks like she was stabbed multiple times," Anthony observed.

Jordan glanced toward the entry to the kitchen, where the table was visible. "The chair is one from the table. Make sure the crime-scene guys check the doors and windows for the point of entry."

A new sense of horror swept through her. "Where are her kids? I know she mentioned having a couple at the reunion." God, the last thing Jordan wanted to do was check a bedroom or a bathroom and find two little bodies.

Anthony sighed. "I guess we'd better check out the rest of the house."

By the time they'd checked all the rooms except the one upstairs where Dr. Ralph Baker was with a police officer, Ricky had arrived on the scene and they learned that the two kids had been spending the weekend with their grandparents.

The three detectives stood in the master bath, where they believed that the killer had first approached Betsy. "She was in the bathtub, relaxing with a glass of wine," Jordan said thoughtfully. "And then he appeared and startled her, she dropped her glass and grabbed her robe and he made her walk into the living room and sit on the chair."

She frowned as she tried to reconstruct the scene in her head. "He had to have a weapon other than a knife."

"Why? What makes you think so?" Ricky asked.

"There were no defensive wounds on Joann and at least at first glance there are none on Betsy. Why did these two women allow themselves to go docilely with a man without at least trying to fight back? They allowed themselves to be tied to a chair without any protest?" She shook her head. "It just doesn't make sense. There had to have been a gun."

"It's a theory," Anthony replied.

"And why did he leave numbers at Joann's feet and

not at Betsy's?" she asked, although she knew none of them had an answer.

"Maybe it's not the same killer," Ricky offered.

"It's the same," Jordan replied flatly. She felt it. She knew it and the evidence pointed to the same killer. "Ricky, why don't you check the master bedroom and the desk drawers in the kitchen and see if you can find an address or appointment book that Betsy might have kept."

"It's possible this has nothing to do with your reunion," Anthony said. "Both of them might have gone to the same hairdresser or had their nails done in the same place."

"That's what we'll need to figure out. How the killer ties into both women's lives," she replied, although Jordan felt in her gut that it was the high school reunion that had brought a killer into their lives.

"Hey, anybody home?" John Lindsay's voice called down the hallway. He'd been drinking. Jordan could hear it in his voice before she saw his face.

"Shit," she exclaimed, and hurried out of the bathroom with Anthony and Ricky close at her heels.

She met John and Adam in the hallway. Adam's ebony features were taut with tension as John gave them all a loopy grin. "What are you all looking at me for?" he asked. "Let's catch this mother."

"I met him in the driveway as I was coming in," Adam explained.

The idea of John behind the wheel of his car was appalling. "Take him home, Adam," Jordan said.

"Whaddya mean? I'm working here," John protested. "I don't wanna go home." His words slurred and his eyes were bloodshot. He wasn't just tipsy; he was totally plowed.

"You're drunk, John. I can't let you compromise the scene. Let Adam drive you home. There will be another case another day for you." Although she was angry with him, she couldn't help but feel a deep compassion for the man who had so recently lost his wife.

"Come on, buddy. Let me take you home," Adam said, and grabbed John by the elbow.

John's eyes flared wide and he stiffened with belligerence. As senior detective on the scene, Jordan prepared herself for a battle, but instead of fighting, John seemed to fold into himself. He leaned against Adam as tears filled his eyes. "I screwed up. Sorry."

"I'll take care of him," Adam said, and the two men went down the hallway toward the front door.

"Somebody should talk to the sarge," Ricky said.

Jordan whirled around to look at him. "Don't you dare say anything. I'll handle the situation. For God's sake, he just lost his wife. Cut him some slack."

"It's one thing to cut him some slack. It's another to have a drunk stumbling around at a crime scene," Ricky said, a flash of irritation in his blue eyes.

Jordan felt the rise of her anger and tried to tamp it down, not wanting friction on the team. "Ricky, you have a lot to learn about teamwork. John's one of our own. We don't run to the brass with every problem. We take care of each other. Now, let's get the crime-scene boys in here and get to work."

As she strode back down the hall to the living room, she knew something was going to have to be done about John, but it wasn't going to be done today. Right now they had a scene to process and notes to be taken, and that was just the beginning.

"I'm going to go upstairs and talk to the husband," she said.

"I'll come with you," Anthony replied. "Ricky, you stay down here with the crime-scene boys."

"I'm trying really hard with him," Jordan said as they climbed the stairs. "But that kid gets under my skin more than anyone has in a long time."

"He still has a lot of things to figure out. By nature he doesn't seem to be a team player, but he's exceptionally bright. He'll figure it out. But he's right about one thing. We do need to do something about John."

"I know," she agreed.

She opened the bedroom door and it was obvious Dr. Ralph Baker was a mess. He lay prone across the king-size bed staring up at the ceiling with eyes that were nearly swollen shut from crying.

The officer sat in a chair next to the bed. As Jordan and Anthony walked into the room, he stood and nodded, then left, closing the door behind him. "Dr. Baker, I know this is an extremely difficult time for you, but we need to ask you some questions," Anthony said.

He closed his eyes, as if the very idea was overwhelming.

"Is there somebody we can call for you?" Jordan asked. "A friend or a relative you'd like to be here with you?"

"No, there's nobody." Wearily, as if the effort was far too great, he pulled himself to a sitting position on the edge of the bed. "I need to be with my kids." He gazed at them, torment darkening his eyes. "How am I going to tell them that their mother is gone? Jesus, how do I explain something like this to them, to anyone?" He broke into a torrent of weeping.

Jordan and Anthony waited patiently until he pulled himself together once again. Then they began the arduous task of getting as much information from him as they could.

He'd arrived home after spending the weekend in St. Louis and found Betsy. It was obvious she was dead and he'd immediately called 911. He hadn't touched anything, had sat on the porch to wait for the police to arrive. The last time he'd spoken to Betsy had been late Friday afternoon. He hadn't tried to call her again, as he'd been busy with his conference.

As he gave them this information, he sobbed off and on, appearing to be a bewildered, grief-stricken husband. The only thing worse than interviewing a family member of a victim was having to give notice of death to unsuspecting family members. Both those parts of the job sucked, Jordan thought as Dr. Ralph sobbed so hard he began to retch.

When he returned from the bathroom, he was the color of a bleached sheet and Jordan had a feeling they would get nothing more of substance from him tonight. "We'll have one of the officers take you wherever you need to go for the next couple of days," she said.

He gazed at her blankly, as if he hadn't considered that he wouldn't be able to stay here. Minutes later he left with an officer who would help him make the notification to Betsy's parents.

They would need to talk to him again, but Jordan knew the next couple of days would feel like hell to him. They had plenty of other things to do before they sat down to take a comprehensive statement from Ralph.

"Jordan, Anthony, I've got something to show you," Willie Anderson, one of the crime-scene techs, said as they came down the stairs. He led them into the living room, where Betsy's body had been taken away.

"We didn't notice this until just a few minutes ago." He picked up a large piece of glass that had been broken from one of the display cabinets and held it up for them to see. Numbers written in blood, they were the same numbers that had been written at Joann's feet.

"I guess now we know for sure that we're working with the same perp," Anthony said.

Jordan stared at the numbers.

2468.

2468.

Joann. Betsy. And 2468. Her heart thundered as realization struck her.

"It's not twenty-four sixty-eight," she said.

"What do you mean?"

"It's two, four, six, eight. Who do we appreciate?" She stared at Anthony. "It's a cheer. Joann, Betsy—they were both cheerleaders. Oh God, he's killing cheerleaders."

Anthony stared at her for a long moment. "You were a cheerleader with them."

"Head cheerleader," she replied, her voice sounding as though it came from some distant place. Her mind raced over the past two weeks, all those times when she'd felt somebody watching her.

She'd thought it was that creep Parker Sinclair. But what if it wasn't? What if it had been the killer checking her routine, watching her habits, seeking the time and place where she would be most vulnerable?

Waiting.

Watching.

Two, four, six, eight. The chant resounded in her head to the frantic beat of her heart as she realized she could very well be marked as the next victim.

Chapter 17

"Let's go over things again," Jordan said on Tuesday afternoon. She hadn't been home since the discovery of Betsy's body. She was running strictly on willpower and coffee. Her eyes felt gritty and raw from lack of sleep, but she had a personal stake in finding the killer as soon as possible.

A small task force had been formed with Jordan at the head and they'd commandeered one of the conference rooms to set up their base of operation. There were a total of six detectives assigned to the case: Anthony and Ricky, Adam and John, Jordan and José Torres, a middle-aged man with a good sense of humor and an attention to details.

Jordan had a feeling that she'd been assigned lead detective in an effort to keep her in this room coordinating rather than on the streets. She suspected it was Sergeant Wendt's way of putting her into partial protective custody.

At the moment the only ones present besides her were José, Anthony and Adam. "We know the Bakers were on the verge of bankruptcy and Ralph had a half-a-million-dollar life insurance policy on his wife, but his alibi in St. Louis checks out. According to the ME, at the time Betsy was being murdered, Dr. Ralph was speaking to a hundred conference attendees on medical malpractice and the modern doctor," José said. "But we knew he wasn't a viable suspect anyway. There's absolutely no connection that we've found between him and Joann."

"What about the appointment books? Have we found anything there?" she asked.

"Ricky told me he'd gone over both of them and wasn't able to find anything that would connect the two women. They shopped in different places and had their hair and nails done in different salons. They didn't lunch at the same restaurants." He shrugged. "So the short answer is no, we haven't found anything there."

Jordan closed her eyes and squeezed the bridge of her nose, her exhaustion reaching the critical point where she knew she needed to go home and crash for at least a couple of hours.

She'd requested protection for Pamela Albright, Jennifer Taylor and Sally Kincaid, the three remaining cheerleaders besides herself, but her request had been denied. Impossible with the current budget, not enough evidence to warrant such a move—the reasons for not complying with her request didn't matter. What mattered was that there were three women out there who might be in the killer's sights at this very moment.

Jordan had already called Sally Kincaid in Chicago to tell her what was happening and she was set to meet with Jenny and Pamela in fifteen minutes here at headquarters.

After the meeting she had to go home. She needed a hot meal, a warm bed and a break from the urgency that had gripped them all since Betsy's murder. She whirled in her chair and faced the bulletin board that held not only the murder-scene photos of both women but also a disappointingly short list of potential suspects.

"We need to start reinterviewing the same people that we did in Joann's case. See if we come up with some names of people who don't have an alibi for the nights of both murders," she said. "If it's not the cheerleader connection, then it's probably somehow tied to the reunion. That was the killer's trigger." She frowned, her thoughts getting more and more difficult to process."You need to go home, Jordan," Anthony said. "You've been up for almost forty hours straight. You won't be any good if you don't go home and get some sleep."

"I know, I know. I'm just going to have that talk with Jennifer and Pamela. Then I'm out of here." She checked her wristwatch. Almost three. She could be home by four and in bed by five. "Anthony, check with the lab and see if they have anything new for us. Adam, you coordinate with everyone and start the interviews. José, check our resources and see if anything like this has happened anywhere else. I'll be back here at seven in the morning and I hope you all will have something to report."

She stood and stumbled slightly, half-dizzy from lack of sleep. She left the task force room and went into the break room for one last cup of coffee and tried not to think about the fact that she might be as much at risk as the two women coming in.

Was it the cheerleader thing or was she leading everyone down the wrong path? She'd been so certain when she'd seen those numbers at Betsy's house. But what if they were an address or some sort of code? What if they had nothing to do with cheers, and the fact that both Joann and Betsy had been cheerleaders was just a strange coincidence? The more tired she grew, the more she second-guessed everything.

Even if she was wrong about the cheerleading connection, it wouldn't hurt to tell Jennifer and Pamela to be alert, to take precautions just in case. Right now there just wasn't enough information to be sure about anything.

At least they'd been able to keep the numbers out of the press. They were a key element that only a handful of detectives and crime-scene men and the killer knew. It was information that would be used to counter all the false confessions coming in.

She sat in the break room and drank her coffee until it was time to meet with Jennifer and Pamela. Jennifer arrived first and Jordan led her into one of the interrogation rooms. She wore dark glasses and pulled them off only when the two women were alone in the room. Beneath the glasses she sported a black eye.

"Quite a shiner," Jordan said.

Jenny grimaced. "I feel so stupid. I rolled over in the middle of the night and hit my face on the nightstand. I couldn't believe it when I got up this morning and saw what I'd done."

She was lying. Jordan felt it in every bone in her body, but before she could dig a little deeper, an officer opened the door to admit Pamela and she got down to the matter at hand.

An hour later she left the station to head home. She hoped that Jenny and Pamela understood the situation. She'd told them both not to go out alone, to be aware of their surroundings and to make sure their doors and windows were locked before they went to bed. She hoped she put the fear of God into them, or, rather, the fear of death.

Certainly there was a thrum of anxiety inside her. She checked her rearview mirror as she pulled out of the parking lot and somehow wasn't surprised to see a patrol car fall in line behind her. Apparently she was going to have an escort home.

That was fine with her. She just wanted to get home and fall into bed and start fresh in the morning. She felt drugged and knew in this state of mind nothing would make sense.

The patrol car followed her all the way to her house, where she was surprised to see Clint parked in the driveway. He got out of the car and raised his hands as a cop jumped out of the patrol car with his gun pulled.

Jordan scrambled out of her car. "It's all right," she exclaimed. "Stand down, Officer. It's fine. I know him."

The policeman holstered his weapon and got back into the patrol car.

Clint slowly lowered his arms and gave her a shaky

smile. "I knew there would be drawbacks to dating a detective."

"You're lucky he didn't shoot first and ask questions later," she replied. "What are you doing here?"

"I was worried about you. I stopped by yesterday evening and you weren't home, so I decided to stop on my way home from work and see if I could catch up with you." He gestured toward the front door. "I left a note."

Even though she was beyond exhaustion, his concern touched her. "Come on in. I figure I have about fifteen minutes of conversation left in me before I crash and burn."

As she unlocked her door and opened it, the patrol car pulled away from the curb. She stumbled into the entry and Clint caught her by the elbow. "Whoa. Maybe you overestimated the fifteen minutes you had left. When was the last time you ate?" he asked as he led her into the kitchen.

"You mean something other than a doughnut or a candy bar?" She sank into a chair at the table and frowned. "Sunday night. Mandy and I had burgers and fries."

"What are you doing? Trying to kill yourself?" he asked. He walked over to the refrigerator, opened it and peered inside. "How about I make you a cheese omelet and some toast, then tuck you into bed?"

She smiled at him wryly. "I really hope you mean that literally, although it would be just my luck that today is the day you've decided to forgo your personal issues and screw my brains out."

"Don't worry; starving, exhausted women really aren't my thing," he replied as he pulled a carton of eggs and a package of cheese from the refrigerator. "I prefer my women to be well rested and fed so they can keep up with me."

As he prepared the meal, they talked about Betsy's murder and Jordan's belief that somebody might be eliminating the cheerleaders. "That explains the police escorting you home," he said, and then frowned. "But they left. Aren't you in some sort of protective custody?"

"I'm a cop, Clint. I'm smart and I have a gun. I don't need protective custody. I can take care of myself."

"I'm sure you're right, but as somebody who cares about you, I get to worry," he replied. "Now eat."

She was grateful that he hadn't told her to take a vacation or find a hiding place. He understood what she did and who she was, and he definitely got points for that.

She devoured the slightly overcooked omelet and two pieces of toast along with a tall glass of milk. By the time she was finished, her face was nearly in her plate.

"Come on, Detective Sampson, let's get you into bed."

She was barely conscious of Clint pulling her up and out of her chair. She leaned heavily on him as he helped her down the hallway to her bedroom. Once there she pulled off her blazer, then collapsed on the bed, barely conscious as he removed her shoes, then sat her up enough to take off her gun and holster.

Her last conscious thought was that she found it interesting that she trusted him completely to take care of her gun—to take care of her.

She dreamed of being chased by a faceless man through a dark house that she didn't recognize. Her heart thumped and she tasted terror as she tried to run faster. But no matter how fast she pumped her legs, he gained on her, finally drawing so close she could feel his hot breath on her neck.

She knew what would happen when he caught her. She knew he'd tie her to a chair and he'd stab her. He'd stab her over and over again with all the rage a man could possess. He'd stab her until she'd beg for death.

When his icy hand fell on her shoulder, she screamed and shot straight up in the bed. Gazing around wildly, she recognized that it had been a dream, a nightmare.

"Jordan?" Clint appeared in the doorway, silhouetted against the hall light. "You okay?"

She reached over and turned on the lamp on the nightstand, needing the illumination to chase away the bogeyman. She trembled uncontrollably and shook her head.

In three long strides he stood next to the bed. "Bad dream?"

She nodded and felt the hot press of tears. From the moment of finding Betsy's body, she'd held it together. Even when she realized that the killer possibly had her marked for death, she'd remained cool and collected. But now, in the grip of an exhaustion she'd never known, she didn't have the strength to fight the fear.

Clint sat on the edge of the bed and wrapped her in his arms. He held her until the shivering stopped, until the sharp edges of the dream faded. "You want to talk about it?" he asked softly.

"No. What time is it?" She didn't move from the warmth of his embrace.

"Around midnight."

"What are you doing still here?"

"I was worried about you. I didn't want to leave you here alone."

She was grateful he'd stayed. At the moment she felt fragile and frightened and didn't want to be by herself. "Stay with me, Clint? Sleep with me?"

"Whatever you want, Jordan. Whatever you need."

She pulled away from him and as he stood, she got out of bed. Her slacks were uncomfortable and her blouse was twisted and bunched. "I'm going to get into my nightclothes," she said, and went into the adjoining bathroom.

She pulled off her blouse and slacks and took off her bra and pulled on her nightgown, then brushed her teeth and left the bathroom. Clint's clothes were tossed carelessly on the nearby chair and he was in bed under the covers with the bedside lamp turned off. The only light was the spill of the hall light into the room.

Sliding in beneath the sheets, she was grateful when he pulled her into his arms. There was still a core of icy chilliness inside her left over from the nightmare.

He wore only his briefs, and she welcomed the warmth of his bare skin against her. He spooned around her back, his arm around her waist, and she closed her eyes and tried to go back to sleep.

But the need for something other than sleep began a slow burn in the pit of her stomach. As the scent of him eddied in the air and she thought of their kisses in the parking lot of the school after the football game, she wanted to feel alive, to keep thoughts of a killer and death at bay.

She took his hand that rested at her waist and placed it on her breast. He stiffened, but she also felt his erection against her backside. "Jordan, you're supposed to be sleeping," he murmured against her neck.

"I don't want to sleep. I want you." She turned over to face him, his features barely discernible in the pale light. "I need you, Clint. I need us tonight, right now."

He leaned forward and kissed her, a hungry, grasping kiss that let her know that she was going to get what she needed. His tongue touched her lips and she opened her mouth to him, swirling her tongue with his.

Sharp desire flooded through her, warming her veins, pounding at her temples. It had been so long, so achingly long since she'd felt needed, felt wanted.

His hands skimmed across the silk of her nightgown, across the swell of her breasts and down the flat of her stomach. Each touch fired her want of him higher, hotter.

This was life, this aching need to make love, this burning desire to be one with another. His hand slid lower and he cupped her mound through the material. Sweet sensations cascaded through her as he rubbed her. At the same time his mouth left hers and nipped and kissed down her neck.

She sighed in frustration as he moved his hand from her. He raised his head and looked at her, his eyes glittering. "Slow, Jordan. I feel like I've waited a lifetime for this, for you. I don't want it to be over too quickly."

His words only made her want him more. As their lips met once again, she stroked down the length of his bare back, loving the play of muscles beneath her fingers.

They kissed and caressed, but it wasn't long before Jordan wanted to be naked with him. She sat up and pulled her nightgown over her head, then kicked off her panties as he took off his briefs.

His long, thick erection pressed against her as he took one of her breasts in his open mouth. He sucked on her nipple, creating a maelstrom of fire inside her. She circled his pulsing erection with her fingers and he gasped against her breast.

She stroked him, loving the way he felt in her hand. He allowed the intimate touch only a moment, then pushed her hand away and took her mouth again with his. Urgent. Demanding. He kissed her like no man had ever done before.

As he kissed her, he moved on top of her, his long, lean body fitting perfectly against hers, his erection nudging between her thighs. He rubbed against her, making no effort to enter her, but stimulating her to the point where she was wild with an impending climax.

She moved faster against him, mindlessly seeking her release. When it came, it crashed onto her, over her. She sobbed his name as wave after wave of pleasure shuddered through her. She was still gasping for air when he entered her.

He slid into her slick moistness with a deep, low moan of her name. He gripped her hips and pulled her closer to him as he began to thrust and stroke deep inside her.

Jordan was lost in the act, lost in him. She clung to his shoulders, her nails biting into his skin as she once again felt herself tensing with another climax. Her rapid breaths combined with his as he stroked faster, harder into her.

"Jordan," he whispered against her mouth as he stiffened against her. As he climaxed, she felt the world tilt and she shuddered against him.

There was no talk afterward. He pulled her back against him and almost immediately she fell asleep, safe and secure in his arms.

She awakened just after dawn to find herself alone in the bed. The scent of coffee wafted in the air, letting her know that Clint was still in the house. She rolled over on her back and stared up at the ceiling.

Clint. When she'd been seventeen, she'd tried to imagine what it would be like to make love with him, but nothing in her seventeen-year-old imagination could have come close to the real deal.

He'd been exactly what she'd needed at the moment. Although she considered herself a strong woman, she'd enjoyed the novelty of him taking care of her, cooking her meal and making sure she ate.

His desire had made her feel alive, had chased away all thoughts of nightmares and murders. But Jordan wasn't sure what to think about him. She wasn't sure where he might fit in her life.

Of course, she wasn't sure he wanted to fit into her life in any meaningful way. She got out of bed and went into the bathroom to shower. Standing beneath a hot spray, she admitted to herself that she wasn't at all sure she was willing to put her heart on the line.

Since the night of Julie's murder Jordan had felt as if fate had delivered harsh kicks that were marked indelibly on her soul. *But you know why*, a little voice whispered in her head. *You know what you did, or more precisely what you didn't do.*

Oh, how she wished she could go back in time and do things differently. How desperately she wished she'd done the right thing on that night so long ago.

She shoved her head under the water in an attempt to drown that little inner voice that occasionally whispered in her head to torment her. She couldn't go back in time. She couldn't change things that had already happened. She could just deal with the aftermath of her bad decision on that fateful night.

Once out of the shower she scampered back into the bedroom and pulled out her usual uniform for work, dark slacks, white blouse and a blazer to hide her shoulder holster.

By the time she walked into the kitchen, she smelled not only the inviting fragrance of fresh coffee but also the hearty scent of frying potatoes and onion and bacon.

"Aren't you supposed to be at school?" she asked Clint, who stood at the stove.

"I called in sick."

"You shouldn't have done that," she replied as she moved to the coffeemaker on the cabinet.

"Why not? I have this terrible tickle in the back of my throat and I sure wouldn't want to pass anything on to the football team."

She smiled and carried her coffee to the table. "We sure wouldn't want football players with tickly throats." She took a sip of her coffee. "Seriously, Clint, you didn't have to hang around. I'm headed back to work in just a few minutes."

"After you eat some breakfast. I haven't gone to all this trouble for you to take your coffee and run. Besides, I knew you'd be heading back to work. I wanted to make sure you got off with one good meal because I know you're probably going to subsist on doughnuts and coffee until you crash again. And a simple thank-you would be nice."

"Thank you."

He grinned. "You're welcome. And thank you."

"For what?"

"For last night."

To Jordan's surprise she felt her cheeks warm. "I'm

the one who should be thanking you. I was kind of an emotional mess and you took me away from all of it for a little while. But, Clint, I've told you before, my life is complicated right now. I don't know what you want from me and I don't know how much I can give."

He scooped up the fried potatoes on a plate and then poured scrambled egg mixture into the skillet. "For now I want from you whatever you can give, no more, no less. If that's an impromptu dinner, fine. If it's fifteen minutes in the parking lot of the police station, that's fine, too. I don't want to add any stress in your life, Jordan, but I want to be a part of your life. What do you want from me?"

She eyed him over the rim of her cup. "I'm not sure," she admitted.

"Let me know when you have it figured out," he replied easily. "In the meantime we'll just see where this ride is taking us."

He flashed her that slow, sexy smile of his and she wanted to take it right back to her bed, go right back into his arms. But she had a killer to find, one she hoped to catch before he caught her.

Chapter 18

John had decided to follow through on his plan to kill himself.

He'd made the decision as he'd stood next to Mary's grave on the day after her burial. She'd been gone only a week, but each and every moment since her death, she'd haunted him.

Her ghost invaded the house. He saw it in his peripheral vision, a movement out of the corner of his eye, a shadow in the corner of the room. He'd hear the soft shuffle of her worn slippers down the hallway or the tinkle of the charm bracelet she often wore, and joy would momentarily fill his heart.

Then he'd remember. She was gone.

Even though he knew she wasn't really there, he so desperately wanted her to be there that it ached in his soul. Each morning he sat at the table to drink his coffee and stared at her empty chair and listened to the overwhelming silence of the house.

He slept with her favorite sweater wrapped around his pillow, the scent of her that lingered in it comforting him. If he closed his eyes and just breathed in that floral fragrance, he could imagine that she was in the bed next to him.

Each night he went to sleep believing she was there, curled up on her side with her feet sticking out of the covers. She always hated to have her feet covered up no matter what the temperature of the room. And each morning when he opened his eyes and saw the emptiness next to him, it was the same crashing grief all over again.

It was in these early-morning hours when tears scalded his cheeks and mucus stuffed his nose that he realized he just wanted to die, to stop the pain of loss that was like a chronic horrible toothache.

But before he took his own life, he wanted one last hurrah as a cop. He wanted to find the killer the press had now dubbed with a lack of inspiration "the Butcher." He wanted the man who had murdered Joann Hathoway and Betsy Baker, and now quite possibly intended to kill Jordan, behind bars.

He knew he couldn't do that if he was drinking himself into oblivion. He needed to be sharp and focused, without the haze of alcohol clouding his mind.

So on Wednesday morning instead of reaching for the bottle, he made a pot of coffee and cooked himself a hearty breakfast. The kitchen was where Mary had always been the happiest. As he sat at the table and ate his sausage and eggs, he remembered how much she'd loved baking.

He'd often come home from work to find her face speckled with flour and the scent of a cherry pie or a pineapple upside-down cake in the air. She baked cookies for the neighborhood kids, was the first to take a cake to a bake sale or to a friend celebrating a birthday.

He could tell the time of year by the treats that came out of the kitchen. In the spring and summer it was blueberry cobblers and homemade shortcake. In the fall it was apple dumplings and pumpkin muffins. Winter in the Lindsay home smelled like gingerbread and sugar cookies.

That morning as he ate his breakfast and prepared to go into the station, the grief was less intense. He had a plan. Take down the Butcher and then take his own life.

Instead of spending his retirement years with Mary at some exotic resort, he'd spend his eternity with her and leave this miserable loneliness behind.

As he ate his breakfast, he read the morning paper and the latest on the Baker murder. No new leads in the Butcher cases. He snorted at the stupid name that he'd been dubbed. Of course, they didn't get it. They hadn't made the connection. He liked to think of himself as Mr. Payback.

Mr. Payback. He definitely liked the sound of that.

Jordan had made the cheerleader connection. Maybe instead of leaving the numbers at the scene, he should have signed his new name. It didn't matter now. What did matter was the fact that he hadn't thought about what would happen when the connection was made.

He hadn't thought about the others being warned.

"Stupid, stupid," he said aloud as he picked up a pair of scissors and began to cut out the latest article.

He'd already written off trying to get to Sally Kincaid in Chicago. There was no way he could take time off work and with the new security measures at the airports it was impossible to fly incognito.

She would live simply because she'd moved away from Kansas City. But now the others were going to be an even bigger challenge because they'd been told to be careful.

But he liked challenges. He liked puzzles that had to be worked and reworked until all the pieces fit. Joann had been a job that had to be done, a test to make sure it could be done. When he'd finished with her, he'd felt the joy of vengeance and nothing more.

Betsy had been slightly different. With her he'd enjoyed the release of his rage. He'd liked the feeling of payback, enjoyed the silencing of the weeping in his head. But it had surprised him to realize he'd liked the actual act of killing another human being.

When he was finished with her, he'd felt a new power surging inside him, the feeling of omnipotence, of complete and total control. There was no remorse inside him. They all deserved to die.

It wouldn't be long and it would be the anniversary date of when his life had fallen apart, the day he'd lost everything he held dear. He was saving that night for Jordan.

And he knew he was going to take particular pleasure in killing her.

When he'd finished cutting out the article, he carried it into the small spare bedroom, where a large bulletin board hung on the wall. The police had their war room and this was his.

The picture of the cheerleaders took center stage, the one that had appeared with Joann's article about her donating a painting to the school. Joann's and Betsy's faces had been carefully marked through with a fine-tip red marker. The others smiled from the photo, unaware of the horror their futures would hold.

On the opposite wall in the room were photos of the life he'd once had before it had all crumbled apart. In here he always heard the weeping, the pitiful sobs that sliced through his heart.

As he tacked up the newest report, he tried to ignore the crying. He stepped back and once again focused on the grainy newspaper photo of the six girls in their light blue and dark blue cheerleading outfits.

Eventually he'd get to them, but first he might have to shake things up a bit. He wasn't worried, even though he knew there were patrolmen unofficially watching the three cheerleaders. Eventually the men watching Jordan and keeping an eye on Jennifer and Pamela would be too busy for that particular duty.

As the holidays approached, the patrolmen would get busier. With the current state of the economy there would be more shoplifters, more purse snatchings and bank robberies.

As people got more and more stressed, the murder squad would get busier. It was a fact of life that Christmas was a deadly time of year. In the meantime, it was time to go to work, where he could plot and plan the next to die.

Chapter 19

"Come on in," Dane said to Jordan late Friday afternoon when she arrived at his house to pick up Mandy. "Want a cup of coffee or something? When I checked a few minutes ago, Mandy was taking a bath, so it might be a little bit before she's ready to go."

"Sure, coffee sounds good," she agreed. It had been a week from hell and they'd hit the wall on Betsy's murder. Mandy was staying with Jordan only for tonight; then Jordan was bringing her home the next afternoon instead of on Sunday. Mandy had a slumber party to attend the next night, which worked out just as well for Jordan, who would go back into the station to work on Sunday.

She followed Dane into the kitchen and sat at the table where they'd once shared meals as a family. He poured two cups of coffee and then joined her. "Where's Claire?" she asked.

"Dinner with friends," he replied. "Any breaks in the cases?"

"Nothing," she replied as she wrapped her fingers around the familiar ceramic mug. She'd bought the set of mugs at an art fair five years ago. Dane had gotten custody of them as well as their daughter. "The killer is smart and he's organized and he hasn't left anything behind at any scene that can help us."

"You taking the necessary precautions? To be honest, I hesitated letting Mandy go with you tonight."

"I hesitated, too. But there are two reasons why I think it will be fine. First of all, he could have gotten to Betsy and her children if he'd wanted, but instead he chose a time when she was alone in the house. Secondly, I've had a patrol car down the street from my house every time I'm home. I'm not sure how long the department can afford it, but for now it looks like they're trying to keep me safe."

"This has all the earmarks of a best seller," Dane said, his eyes glittering with a sparkle that was all too familiar to her. He always got that look when he was about to embark on a new book. When she'd commented on it once, he'd told her it was creative genius, but she'd insisted it looked more like demonic possession. "A madman killing cheerleaders, it has a great angle."

"We aren't even sure it has the cheerleader angle," she replied. "It might just be coincidence that they were both cheerleaders fifteen years ago." There was no way she could tell him about the numbers at the scene, at least not now when it was the only information they'd kept out of the press. "Unfortunately the worst part is we might not know until he kills another woman."

"But there must be some reason that you made the cheerleader connection, something you aren't telling me." He leaned forward, a predatory expression on his face.

"You know I shouldn't talk about the case," she replied. She smiled wryly. "The days of pillow talk between us are long over, Dane."

He took a sip of coffee and leaned back in his chair. "Yeah, I know. But I am going to start researching into this. It's the kind of case I've been hoping for, one I can finally really get my teeth in."

"Personally I'm hoping there won't be any more murders, that this is going to be over very quickly," she replied.

"There's got to be more murders for it to work as a book," he said, then obviously realized how callous his words sounded. "I mean, I hope nobody else gets killed."

"But if they do, you can't wait to capitalize on it," she replied dryly.

"It's a tough job, but somebody has to do it," he said.

At that moment Mandy entered the room, an overnight bag slung over her shoulder. "Hi, Mom. Did Dad tell you I need to be home by five tomorrow?"

Jordan nodded. "He did and that's not a problem." She took a drink of her coffee and stood. "Are you all ready, Freddy?"

Mandy rolled her eyes, but grinned. "Ready. Bye, Dad." She kissed Dane on his cheek and he stood to walk with them to the door.

"If your research turns up anything that might be helpful to us, you'll let me know?" Jordan said to him.

"As long as there's a bit of quid pro quo involved," he replied with that same gleam in his eyes.

Jordan laughed and shook her head. "I'll have her back at five tomorrow."

As they drove home, she was grateful that Mandy didn't notice the patrol car some distance behind them. Since Betsy's murder, Jordan had been accompanied until she got safely into her house.

The team suspected that Betsy had left her front door unlocked. There had been no sign of forced entry and her husband had said she often forgot to lock up before bedtime. She'd made it easy for the killer to get inside her home.

They figured that Joann had made the same kind of mistake. She'd gone to her shed to work and hadn't locked the door behind her. The killer had walked right inside.

Jordan didn't forget to lock her doors and she no longer placed her gun in the nightstand drawer, but instead when she went to bed, she kept it under her pillow. Nobody was going to sneak up on her and find her unarmed and unprepared.

"When are you going to unpack those boxes in the garage so you can park inside?" Mandy asked as they pulled into the driveway. "Jeez, Mom, you should do it before it snows."

"I know, I know," Jordan exclaimed as she shut off the car engine. "I keep telling myself I'll get to it, but there never seems to be enough hours in the day."

They got out of the car as the cruiser drove slowly by. "Is that some of your friends?" Mandy asked, her voice rife with disapproval.

"Maybe, why?" Jordan pulled her house key from her purse.

"That's why you don't have a boyfriend, because all you ever do is work and hang around with other cops."

"Actually, I do sort of have a boyfriend," Jordan replied. Was that what Clint was? Her boyfriend? The term seemed rather tepid for whatever it was they were doing.

"No way," Mandy exclaimed. "You're just saying that to shut me up."

Jordan laughed and unlocked the door and they stepped into the house. "I'm not making it up." She locked the door behind her and then followed Mandy into the living room. Mandy flopped on the sofa and looked at Jordan suspiciously.

"Okay, what's his name?" she asked.

"Clint. Clint Cooper."

Mandy rolled her eyes once again. "That sounds totally made-up."

Jordan laughed again. "It might sound made-up, but it's not. It's a real name and he's a real man."

"Is he a cop?"

"No, actually he's a high school football coach." Jordan sat next to her daughter. "I went to high school with him and then we met again at my reunion."

"And you like him?" Mandy asked.

"Yes, I do."

"Then I want to meet him," Mandy exclaimed. "Call him and see if he'll come over tonight."

"Oh, I'm not sure that's a good idea," Jordan protested. The last thing she wanted was to begin a parade of men through Mandy's life who might or might not stick around for the long haul.

Mandy crossed her arms over her chest and gave Jordan her best mulish expression. "Then I don't believe you. I think you're lying to me and you just made him up."

"I would never lie to you," she protested. Knowing she was being manipulated but unable to resist, Jordan grabbed the cordless phone from the end table and dialed Clint's number. She'd spoken with him late last night from work and knew he had a football game tomorrow night, but he hadn't mentioned any plans for this evening.

He picked up on the second ring. "What a pleasant surprise," he said. "I didn't expect to hear from you tonight."

"I'm sitting here on my sofa with my daughter, who would like to meet you." She figured this was the true test of whether Clint really wanted a part in her life. It was one thing to pop in and out when it was convenient for both of them. It was quite another to meet Mandy.

"I'd like to meet her," he agreed easily.

"How about this evening? You want to come over?"

"Sure." Again there was no hesitation in his voice. "Have you two eaten yet?"

"Not yet. I was just going to head into the kitchen to see what I could whip up," she replied.

"How about I bring a bucket of fried chicken with me?"

"That would be great. And Mandy and I will make a big salad."

"Sounds perfect. I can be there in thirty or forty minutes."

"We'll be here," she said. As she hung up the phone and looked at her daughter, she realized how important it was to her that Mandy like Clint. "He'll be here in about thirty minutes and he's bringing fried chicken."

"Cool," Mandy replied, and got up from the sofa. "I'm gonna go put my stuff in my room, and then I'll help you make the salad."

Minutes later mother and daughter worked side by side chopping peppers and tomatoes for their salad. It was one of those rare moments when Jordan's heart filled with such happiness it was almost frightening.

Mandy was in a terrific mood, and the mood lasted when Clint arrived and they ate dinner. After the meal and cleanup Jordan went out to the garage and dug through the boxes to find a Monopoly game and the three of them settled in at the kitchen table to play.

Clint was good with Mandy. He didn't try too hard like so many adults did when trying to connect with children. He didn't talk down to her or try to be her best buddy. He was just Clint, funny and charming, and as the evening went on, it was obvious that Mandy liked him.

Jordan was surprised and amused when the two of them joined forces to get her out of the game. Their manipulation along with a series of bad dice rolls did her in. Mandy and Clint had an equal number of properties and houses and hotels, so a tie was announced and they all celebrated with big bowls of ice cream smothered in chocolate syrup.

It was almost ten o'clock when Mandy went into the bedroom to get ready for bed and Jordan walked Clint to her front door. "This was fun," he said. "She's a great kid, Jordan."

She laughed dryly. "What you saw this evening was the good Mandy. The head-spinning, soup-spewing, possessed Mandy was apparently in remission."

He smiled. "I guess that just means I bring out the best in both my girls." He sobered and took her chin with his fingers. "How are you doing? You look tired."

"I am," she confessed. "These murders are definitely taking a toll on everyone in the department, but for the most part I'm doing okay."

He leaned forward and kissed her on the cheek, a

soft, sweet kiss that instantly stoked a flicker of flame inside the pit of her stomach. "I know you can't tell me when we can get together again."

"You're right; I can't. Our work hours definitely aren't normal right now. But none of us can work twenty-four/seven. I'm going in Sunday morning and might get Sunday night off."

"You'll call me?" She nodded and he continued. "One of these nights you're going to have to come over and see my place."

"It's been a long time since I've been in a bachelor pad," she said teasingly.

"If you're expecting black leather and a bed that spins, you're going to be disappointed."

She laughed. "Good night, Clint."

He leaned forward and took her mouth with his. Although he didn't touch her in any other way, as always a wildfire blew through Jordan and just that easily she wanted him again. She wanted to be naked with him; she wanted him caressing her and taking possession of her.

She quickly broke off the kiss and took a step back from him. "Don't kiss me like that as you're going out the door."

He grinned. "Then I'll have to remember to kiss you like that as I come through the door. Good night, Jordan."

She stood at the front door and watched as he walked down the driveway and got into his car. There was no question that he stirred a yearning inside her. It wasn't just a desire for sex, although certainly that was there, but it was the desire for something more, for something deeper, and it scared her.

Each time she'd thought she was settled and happy, something bad happened to take it all away. It was as if fate lulled her with happiness and then sprang up with a killing force.

She'd been happy in college. She'd adjusted to dorm life and loved all her dance classes. She'd been making new friends and having fun. Then Julie had been murdered.

She'd been happy in her marriage and then Dane's affairs had snatched that away. And when that had been taken away, she'd devoted all her time and energy and love into Mandy, who had ultimately chosen her father over her.

She was more than a little afraid to embrace Clint and what he had to offer her. She was afraid to reach out and grab the happiness he brought to her life because ultimately she feared it would all be destroyed.

It was what she deserved.

It was her punishment.

Chapter 20

"Della, I need to know where you were on the night that Betsy was murdered," Jordan said wearily late Monday afternoon. The two women were in Della's living room and this was the last thing Jordan had to do before she went home for the night.

"My God, Jordan. You can't honestly believe that I could kill anyone," Della said with obvious outrage. "Just because I said I hated her on the night of the reunion doesn't mean I could ever, would ever, do such a thing." She wrapped her arms around herself and a sheen of tears appeared in her eyes. "I can't believe you're here asking me these questions. God, I thought you were my friend."

The interviews had been assigned to the other detectives, but Jordan had wanted to do this one herself. She knew Della would be upset by the questions, but it was something that had to be done.

"I am your friend. Della, we're talking to everyone who was at the reunion. Even though we're friends, right now I have to get answers from you so I can take your name off our list of potential suspects."

"I'm a suspect?" she squealed in horror.

Jordan winced. "You and about a hundred other people. When you left the football game the night of Betsy's murder, did you go anywhere else after?"

"No, I just came home. I was here by myself. Lately it

seems like I'm always here by myself." The shine of tears grew more pronounced. "Ben is doing so much traveling lately."

"Did you talk to anyone on the phone?"

Della frowned thoughtfully. "I don't think so. I was feeling pouty. You were going out after the game with Clint and I was all alone as usual. Ben called while I was at the game with you, but I didn't even return his call because I was mad that he was gone again." Her eyes widened and she swiped at a tear that ran down her cheek. "Does that make me in trouble?"

"Not necessarily," Jordan replied. She wanted to get through this without Della having one of her major meltdowns. "I'm just getting information. It's part of my job, Della, and since you knew both Joann and Betsy, I have to talk to you and ask you questions."

"Aren't you scared, Jordan? I mean, two cheerleaders have been killed in horrible ways and you were a cheerleader with them."

"I have two things Betsy and Joann didn't have, prewarning of the potential for danger and a big gun. I'm being cautious and that's all I can do."

"But what if you just step outside of your house and he shoots you?" Della said worriedly.

"That's not his style," Jordan replied. "He likes to be up close and personal with his victims."

Della shivered. "This is the first time in my life I'm glad I wasn't a cheerleader."

Jordan closed her notebook and stood, ready to get home and put thoughts of the murders aside for the night. She tugged on her skirt, which had ridden up when she'd sat. She'd been in trial that morning and she usually tried to wear a skirt and hose whenever she was to appear in court.

"Do you have to go?" Della asked. "I could call in some Chinese and we could have a girls' night. Maybe watch a movie or something." There was a plaintive note of loneliness in her voice. Della didn't function well when she had too much time alone.

"Sorry, I can't tonight." Clint was meeting Jordan at her house and she was looking forward to seeing him. "You know how things get when I'm in the middle of a case. When is Ben coming home?"

"Who knows?"

"I'll call you when things calm down and we'll get together then."

Minutes later as Jordan drove to her home, her thoughts whirled around and around in her head. The detectives were working on the assumption that the killer was male, simply because of the force of the rage that each scene had depicted.

But they certainly weren't ruling out the possibility that a woman might be responsible for the murders.

There had been no sexual abuse, which could point to a woman perp or a man who either couldn't or wouldn't rape. Certainly women were capable of rage and any adult could use that kind of rage to plunge a knife into a victim.

As difficult as it was for her to imagine Della being capable of the crimes, she knew the hatred that Della had for those women was deep.

Della had even confessed over drinks one night that she'd hated Jordan when they'd been in high school. But reconnecting as adults, Della had given Jordan a second chance to prove herself different from the impression Della had of her in high school.

What about Ben?

The words jumped into her head unbidden. Ben, who was supposedly out of town when both the murders had occurred. Ben, who would do anything for the woman he loved. Was it possible he was righting wrongs that had happened over a decade ago? Avenging the woman he loved by killing girls who had made her life miserable in the past?

She grabbed her cell phone from her purse and punched in Anthony's number. "What's up?" he asked.

"I want you to check flight records for the week prior and the week after the murders," she said.

"Who are we looking at?"

"Della's husband, Ben. I want to know where he went and when. Once we have that information, I want you to check the hotels and see where he stayed."

"Will do," Anthony replied.

"Let me know what you find out." She clicked off, troubled by this new direction of her thoughts. She'd had dinner with Ben and Della, spent many evenings in their company. Ben had always struck her as a big affable teddy bear.

Still, he had the physical strength it would take to subdue a woman and tie her in a chair. She also knew he had a reputation for being utterly ruthless in his business practices and the only time he seemed to get angry was when somebody snubbed or was mean to his wife. She'd always said that Ben would do anything for the woman he loved. Now she wondered just how far he would go for Della.

Ben hadn't even been on their list of suspects, but suddenly he was at the top of her list. Danny McCall was there as well. The big man who had been everyone's friend in high school hadn't been able to provide a solid alibi for either night of the murders and he confessed that not only had he bought one of Joann's paintings; he'd also sent Betsy one of the dolls that she loved as a birthday present two years ago.

That bothered Jordan. It bothered her a lot. It spoke of obsession, of an inability to let go of the high school girls he'd once loved. She found herself sifting through the past, looking for clues from her high school days in her memories of Danny.

The detectives and a photographer had been at both funerals. Photos of the crowd had been taken at each and then compared to see who had attended both of the solemn ceremonies. Unfortunately, because of the high school connection and the recent reunion, a lot of people had attended both funerals.

She glanced in her rearview mirror, looking for any car that might be following her. It had become a habit in the last couple of days since the patrol car had been pulled off her.

Budget crunches and the usual preholiday crime sprees had made the official tail on Jordan impossible to justify. She'd assured Benny that she'd be fine without it, that she was smart and aware and stayed armed at all times.

She grabbed her cell phone again and punched in Clint's number. "Hi," she said when he answered. "I've got a quick stop at the grocery store and then I'll be home."

"I'll be there," he replied. "And Jordan, I'm kissing you as I come in the door."

She laughed and clicked off, her heart already beginning the race that it always did when she talked to him or he was around. She pulled into the grocery-store parking lot and into an empty space. Before she got out of the car, she unfastened her blazer to allow her quick access to her gun.

What she'd told Della about the killer was what she believed, that a sniper attack wasn't what he wanted, wasn't what he needed. But better safe than sorry, she thought as she headed inside the store. She mentally clicked off the items on her grocery list as she grabbed a basket. Milk and bread, a jar of spaghetti sauce and some of those chocolate cookies that Mandy loved.

She turned into the first aisle and came face-to-face with Parker Sinclair.

His eyes widened in surprise and he quickly gestured to his half-filled basket, then to her empty one. "I was here first. I'm not stalking you," he said quickly. "I've never stalked you, but I'm definitely beginning to wonder if you're stalking me."

"I came in for milk and bread. I'm not looking for trouble, Mr. Sinclair, and I trust that you aren't either."

He scowled. "I've had enough trouble over the past

year to last me a lifetime." He started to move past her, but she stopped him by calling his name.

"That day at your trial when I was on the stand, you kept smiling at me, like you knew me outside the courtroom, like we shared a secret," she said.

He stared at her for a long moment, then released a sigh. "You look a lot like Rebecca. When I first met her, she wore her hair like yours and you have the same eyes. That day as I stared at you, she filled my head and I guess I kind of got lost in the moment."

He tightened his grip on the handle of his shopping cart, holding it so tight his knuckles were white. "Contrary to what you think about me, I didn't murder my wife. I loved her. And the worst part of all of this for me is knowing that you all think you got it right and the case is closed, but somewhere out there her murderer is walking free. Now, if you'll excuse me." He pushed past her and disappeared into the next aisle.

Had they really gotten it wrong? For the first time since Parker Sinclair had been arrested for the murder of his wife, Jordan wondered. Certainly it wouldn't be the first time the police got it wrong in a murder case. Maybe the jury had gotten it right and saved an innocent man from going to jail.

Still, seeing Parker again reminded Jordan of those moments when she'd been certain she was being watched, when she'd felt the shivery sensation of somebody too close for comfort. And again she was left wondering, if it hadn't been Parker, had it been the killer?

She finished her shopping and left the store, eager to get home, tired of her thoughts of killers and death. When she reached her house, Clint was already parked in the driveway. She grabbed her bag of groceries from the passenger seat, then got out of her car.

"Hey you," she said, her spirits rising at the mere sight of him.

"Hey yourself," he replied, and took the bag from her arms. "Bad day?"

"Long day," she replied as she opened the front door. They entered the foyer and he shut and locked the door after them. She'd gone only two steps before he grabbed her by the arm and spun her around to face him.

He placed the bag of groceries on the floor and then pulled her into his arms. "I told you that this time I was going to kiss you coming in," he said, and took possession of her mouth in a kiss that was instantly raw and demanding.

And in an instant Jordan was ready for him. She dropped her purse to the floor as she wrapped her arms around his neck. He backed her against the entry wall and pulled her blazer off her shoulders. It fell into a heap on the floor as she yanked his jacket off.

As the kiss continued, hot and greedy, she fumbled to get her holster off and dropped it on top of her blazer. Immediately his fingers moved to her blouse buttons as she wrapped a leg around the backs of his thighs, pulling him closer, more intimately against her.

He was hard and ready and just that quickly she was ready for him. When he had her blouse unbuttoned, she shrugged out of it, then pulled on the bottom of his sweater to get it off and over his head.

As their mouths found each other once again, he slid his hands up to cup her breasts, his thumbs raking over her taut nipples. Her heart beat frantically and the desire he evoked in her consumed her.

He moved one of his hands down the length of her body and beneath her skirt. His hot touch against her panty hose moved up with a determination that made her want to laugh with giddy excitement. God, this was wild and raw and she loved it.

She fumbled with his belt, wanting him naked and slamming into her. Instead he sank to his knees and reached up to pull down the panty hose, his gasps combined with hers as they reeled further out of control.

He tore down her hose and panties and his breath was hot against her inner thighs. As he grabbed hold of her buttocks and pulled her toward him, she tangled her hands in his hair.

A deep moan escaped her as his mouth found her. Her knees began to buckle as his tongue flicked against her, creating exquisite sensations that rushed through her. He held her upright, plastered against the wall as he made love to her with his mouth.

Her legs began to shake with the stress of standing upright and the white-hot flood of her blood through her veins. The pleasure was so intense she felt as if she were going to shatter apart, as if she were losing her mind.

When she thought she could stand it no longer, she slid down the wall and pulled him down with her, wanting him on top of her, inside her. He stripped off his pants and took her, plunging into her without finesse but with hot, urgent need.

His eyes gleamed at her, filled with a dark desire that drove her out of her mind.

They moved together in a frenzy on the hardwood floor of the entry and when her climax came, it started in her toes and washed over her in waves. She was vaguely aware of him stiffening and whispering her name as he reached his own release.

For a moment they remained locked together on the floor. As Jordan became aware of the cold wood against her bare butt, she started to giggle. It was as if every stress she'd experienced over the past couple of weeks had seeped into the wooden floor beneath her.

"Now, that's the way to say hello to a girl," she exclaimed.

He rose up on one elbow and grinned down at her. "That was hot."

She laughed again. "That was crazy," she replied.

He leaned down and kissed her softly on the lips. "It was crazy hot," he whispered with that sexy grin of his.

He stood and held out a hand to help her up. "Come on, let's go get into the shower and I'll scrub your back."

It was amazing, how natural she felt with him as they got into her shower beneath a hot spray. In all her years of marriage she'd never bathed with Dane. She'd always felt that it was one of the most intimate acts to share, but she had no reservations sharing it with Clint.

They soaped and stroked each other, this time not for sexual release but rather enjoying the sensuality of being together beneath the water. He smoothed the washcloth across her breasts and around to her back, and she mewled with the pleasure.

Then it was her turn to suds him up. As she ran the washcloth down his broad back, she marveled at the fact that he had almost no fat on his body, that his muscles were lean and hard.

When they were finished, she dressed in a pair of old sweats and he pulled his jeans and shirt back on. "I hope you didn't have ice cream in those bags of groceries," he said as they left the bedroom.

"No ice cream," she replied. "But there is a gallon of milk I need to get into the refrigerator."

They went into the kitchen and put the groceries away, then made peanut butter and jelly sandwiches and sat at the table and talked. They didn't speak about the cases she was working on and they didn't mention football. Instead they talked about their favorite food for Thanksgiving dinner and their plans for the upcoming holidays.

"I go a little crazy with the whole Christmas thing," he said. "I decorate the house like it's the North Pole and put up a tree that takes up half my living room, and after Christmas I always hate to have to take it all down." He paused a moment to take a drink of milk, then continued. "When my parents divorced, my mother decided we weren't going to have Christmas anymore."

"That's terrible," Jordan exclaimed.

"Yeah, I thought it was pretty terrible when I was young. She said Christmas was a family holiday, and since we weren't a family anymore, she just couldn't bear the thought of trying to pretend."

"That certainly wasn't fair to you," Jordan replied.

"I didn't think so either. So when I was twelve, I tried to steal a Christmas tree."

"You realize you're confessing a crime to a cop," Jordan said teasingly.

"It's all right. I got caught on the tree lot. By the owner. I was dragging off a little three-foot tree. I'd decided if my mother didn't want Christmas, that was fine, but I was going to put up the tree in my bedroom and have my own celebration. I got it out to the sidewalk when the guy stopped me, scared the hell out of me. I started crying and telling him about the divorce and that we didn't have Christmas anymore and I just wanted a tree for my room. He asked me where I lived and I was sure he was going to tell my mother what I'd tried to do. Then he told me to get home."

"Did he tell your mom?" Jordan asked. Her heart ached for the little boy he'd been. How selfish his mother had been. She should have at least gone through the motions for her son.

"I laid awake all night worrying that when I got up the next morning, I was going to be grounded for the rest of my life, but when I got up and went outside, I found the biggest, most beautiful tree in our driveway with a note that said it had been delivered by Santa."

"And so you had a tree that year?" she asked, a lump rising in her throat.

He grinned ruefully. "My mother sold the tree to the neighbors and that was the end of that."

"Oh, Clint, I had no idea what you'd gone through as a child. You should have told me these things when we were in high school."

"I told you before, tough high school boys don't talk about stuff like that. All I knew then was that I had a pain deep inside me and I found the one thing that at least momentarily took away that pain. I didn't drink. I didn't do drugs. Instead I had sex. It took me out of myself, away from my pain."

"When did you start to figure all that out?"

"In college. I took a couple of psychology classes and realized that my parents' divorce and all the dramas that followed had nothing to do with me. It was all about them, and just realizing that much made me look at myself as a man and decide what I wanted from life. A series of one-night stands and meaningless relationships wasn't what I wanted. I wanted one woman, one marriage that would last forever. Unfortunately that didn't work out."

"That's what I wanted when I married Dane. One man, one marriage. Unfortunately he had other ideas. I think I rushed into marriage with Dane for all the wrong reasons. Julie was gone and my parents were distant. I was feeling terribly alone at the time that he swept into my life."

"But it's admirable the way you two are handling things with Mandy," Clint replied. "At least on the surface it looks like the two of you are putting her needs first, and that's important with divorced parents."

"I want what's best for her." Jordan shoved her empty plate to the side and leaned back in her chair. "I want to force her to live here with me. I think it's in her best interest that she be with her mother instead of with her father. I want to rail against Dane, but I can't do any of those things because at least for now she says she's where she wants to be."

"And that's what makes you a great mother," Clint said.

"I try to be," she replied, his words warming her. But the warmth lasted for only a moment. She couldn't forget that no matter how good a mother she tried to be, it was obvious she wasn't doing or wasn't giving something that Mandy needed. She couldn't ignore the fact that something just wasn't right between herself and her daughter.

Her thoughts brought back all her insecurities and she gazed at Clint across the table. "Are you still working through some sort of inner pain? Am I your latest relapse?"

His eyes narrowed slightly. "Why do I suddenly get the feeling that you're trying to pick a fight?"

"I'm not," she protested. "I just want to know what you're doing here with me. I mean, I'm sure you could find some nice woman who doesn't carry a gun, one who works a normal job with normal hours and would have lots of time to spend with you."

"I'm into quality, not quantity," he replied easily. He reached across the table and captured her hand in his. "Jordan, there's no question that the sex between us is hot, but in case you haven't noticed, I'm falling in love with you all over again."

Everything in the room, including her heartbeat, seemed to still at his words. She wasn't sure whether she was happy or appalled. "Why?" she finally managed to ask.

"Why?" He looked at her in surprise. "Why not? You're beautiful and bright. You make me laugh and we share the same values. I can't explain the chemistry, but it's there. I get excited when I'm going to see you again, and when I'm with you, I never want to leave. And it would definitely make me feel better if you didn't look so horrified by the whole thing."

Jordan released a deep sigh and pulled her hand from his. "I just don't want to get hurt again, Clint. And you scare me more than just a little bit."

"You gave me a hundred chances in high school when I was nothing but a stupid kid. All I'm asking of you now is to give me one chance as a man."

She laughed and shook her head. "I'm not sure which one of us is crazier, but I have a feeling things are only going to get more complicated."

He studied her intently. "Nobody ever said getting it right was easy." He got up from the table. "Now, let's get this mess cleaned up and go into the living room and cuddle on the sofa."

And that was exactly what they did. She lay in his arms on the sofa and they talked until it was time for him to go home. She didn't ask him to spend the night, didn't want to slowly drift into a live-in situation before she was ready.

It was just after ten when she stood on her front porch and waved to him as he backed out of the driveway. A cold wind had whipped up from the north, rustling the last of the leaves on the trees and casting eerie shadows from the nearby streetlights.

The minute Clint's car pulled down the driveway, the respite he'd given her from the crimes immediately fled. Visions of death filled her head. An image of Joann flashed in her brain, followed swiftly by one of Betsy.

Had they known their attacker? Had they not sensed any danger when first approached by the killer? Or had he somehow sneaked up on them to subdue them for the kill?

The wind gusted and her breath caught painfully in her chest as a loud crackle sounded next to her porch. She whirled around and emitted a gasp of relief as she saw the newspaper caught in her bushes.

Suddenly she felt far too alone and vulnerable.

She hurried back into the house and locked the door behind her as goose bumps sprang up on her arms. "Stop being silly," she said aloud, as if the sound of her own voice might chase away her uneasiness. But it didn't help.

Grabbing her gun, she went from room to room, looking out windows and trying to calm the irrational fear that had her in its icy grip. There was nothing amiss, nothing outside that she could see that might be construed as a threat, but she couldn't shake the feeling that danger was getting closer to her and there was no place for her to run, nowhere that she could hide.

Chapter 21

"It's not the same," Ricky said as he stared at the body of Jenny Taylor, who was tied to a chair in her living room. The morning sun drifted into the window, lending sharp light to the horrific scene.

"It looks the same," Anthony replied.

"I'm telling you it's not. Look, the rope is a different kind and the knots are also different from the other two murders," Ricky exclaimed.

"Good eye, Copeland," Jordan said as she fought a wealth of frustration. There were subtle differences, but there were a hell of a lot of similarities. Jennifer Taylor had been tied and stabbed and the sofa had been slashed, the stuffing pulled out and tossed around the room.

"Let's look around and see whether we can find the numbers he left for us at the other two scenes. And remember, at the Baker place they weren't that obvious," Jordan said.

They all began to check the walls, the floors, anywhere that numbers could be drawn. The crime-scene photos had already been taken, but they still tried not to disturb anything too much. The crime-scene techs were waiting to move in, but Jordan wasn't ready to relinquish the area yet.

How had this happened? Dammit, Jenny had been warned to be careful, to keep vigilant. There was no sign of forced entry, which meant either she'd had her door unlocked or she'd invited in her killer.

"No numbers," Ricky said. "I'm telling you, this isn't the work of our boy."

"We'll get the crime-scene guys in here and let them tear the place apart. Maybe whatever they find will let us know for sure if it's our Butcher or a copycat," Jordan said.

A headache pounded at her temples. It was two days before Thanksgiving and she'd been hoping to get through the holidays without any other bodies showing up. There was no question now that the connection was the cheerleader one.

"Has anybody made contact with the husband yet?" Adam asked.

"Jenny's friend said he left two days ago on a hunting trip to southern Missouri, but she didn't know the specific place he was going. We've got the highway patrol on the lookout for his pickup," Anthony said.

Jenny's friend Margie Weller had come to the Taylor house when Jenny hadn't shown up for a lunch date. Jenny's car was in the driveway, and when nobody answered the door, she got worried and called the police. The police had arrived and had found the body. The coroner had estimated time of death sometime the day before.

So here they were with another murder that looked far too similar to the others, with a victim that fit the pattern of the others. As the crime-scene unit moved in, Jordan stepped outside and walked to her car. She leaned against the driver door and drew several deep, cleansing breaths.

Three down.

Three to go.

The words pounded in her brain. She could make the assumption that Sally Kincaid in Chicago would be safe simply by sheer distance from the killing ground. And if that was the case, then it was three down, two to go. She hoped Pamela Albright was being as careful as she was.

She straightened as she saw Sergeant Benny Wendt approaching from the street where he'd parked. His short legs worked overtime as he hurried toward her, his features a study in frustration.

"Is it our guy?" he asked when he reached her.

"Possibly," she replied. "There are a lot of similarities, but there are also a few troubling differences."

"Differences?"

"Different rope, different knots, and so far we haven't found the numbers anywhere," she replied.

He grimaced. "I've arranged for round-the-clock protection for Pamela Albright and for you."

"I really don't need it. If I'm not at home with my doors locked and my gun nearby, I'm in police headquarters, where I should be safe and secure."

"We're still going to keep a patrol car in front of your house until we get a better handle on this. I've called the FBI and they're sending us a couple of agents and a profiler."

"Who is the profiler?" she asked curiously.

"Allison McNight."

Jordan smiled with pleasure at the name. "It will be great to work with Allison again." She'd worked with the FBI agent three years ago on a case where a man was killing prostitutes and cutting off their legs. During that case she and Allison had become close friends. After the case as they each returned to their own work, their own lives, they had eventually lost touch.

"Is John here?" Benny asked, his gaze on the attractive house where the murder had occurred. Jordan nodded. "Is he sober?"

"Completely. In fact, he's more focused than I've seen him in months."

"Good. Maybe the worst is over with him," Benny replied. "Now tell me what we've got here."

Jordan related to him what they knew so far about the case, and as she talked about the details, she remembered the black eye Jenny had sported the day she'd spoken to her. She hadn't believed Jenny's story about rolling over in the night and hitting the nightstand then, and now it seemed even more suspicious than ever.

She turned to look at the house as the body was wheeled out on a gurney. Another autopsy, another murder, and they were no closer to finding the killer now than they had been at the scene of Joann Hathoway's murder.

Who was this person? What had these women done to inspire such hatred? Could this possibly be about mean girls in high school? Did she really believe that somebody had harbored this kind of rage for fifteen years, then decided to kill?

These questions haunted her throughout the morning and into the late afternoon when they finally arrived back at headquarters. She checked the police records to see if there had been any domestic-disturbance calls to the Taylor home as the rest of the team chased down other information about the victim and her husband.

Ray had finally been located when they'd found the number of his cell phone in Jenny's telephone book. He had been three hours away and was being escorted back to Kansas City by a highway patrol car, but hadn't yet arrived yet for questioning.

Jordan hadn't found any records of domestic-abuse calls, but the autopsy, which had been performed almost immediately, had shown many old injuries. A mended broken wrist and two ribs, and her legs had sported several large bruises that hadn't occurred at the time of the murder. Definitely suspicious.

It was almost six o'clock when Allison McNight walked into the conference room. She was a petite woman with delicate features. Large, luminous blue eyes and pale blond hair combined with her small stature gave the illusion of frailty, but it was a false illusion.

At thirty-three years old, Allison was smart as a whip and had the unsettling ability to get into killers' heads to discover their motivations and the passions that drove them.

As she entered the room, Jordan stood up from her desk and the two women hugged. Half the men rose as if wishing they, too, were going to get to hug the sexy little blonde.

"Welcome to the hell room," Jordan said, then introduced her to all the men on the team. When she was finished with the introductions, Allison walked over to the bulletin board and stared at the photos tacked up.

Polaroids of the Taylor scene had been added until the official crime-scene photos were ready. Allison studied each photo as everyone else but Jordan got back to whatever they had been doing before Allison had arrived. Jordan stepped closer to the profiler.

"Looks like a bad piece of work," Allison said. "The field office sent me over here without any details. Is there a connection between the victims?"

At that moment Jordan's stomach rumbled, reminding her that she'd had nothing to eat since a piece of toast that morning. "Have you eaten dinner?"

"Not yet," Allison replied.

"Why don't we go get something to eat and I'll fill you in on everything?"

"Sounds good to me," Allison agreed.

A half hour later the two faced each other across a table in a burger joint three blocks from headquarters. As they waited for their orders, Jordan told Allison about the high school and cheerleader connection. "When we get back to headquarters, I'll see that you have a copy of all the files." At that moment the waitress arrived with their meals, and as they ate, the conversation turned to each other's personal lives.

"I'm not surprised that you decided to divorce Dane," Allison said. "Last time we spoke, you were pretty upset about the state of your marriage. How's Mandy?"

"She seems to be thriving. Dane has actual physical custody although I get to see her whenever her social calendar allows it."

"Sounds like you aren't thrilled with the arrangement," Allison observed.

"I'm not, but she seems happy with the way things are, so I don't want to rock the boat." Jordan picked up a French fry and popped it into her mouth.

"But you miss her."

Jordan nodded. "Desperately. I miss seeing her sleepy face first thing in the mornings. I miss the talks we used to have, about anything and everything. I'm hoping eventually she'll decide to come and live with me full-time."

"Are you seeing anybody?" Allison picked the onion off her burger and laid it on the side of her plate.

"Actually, I'm seeing an old high school boyfriend." A burst of warmth swept through her as she thought of Clint.

Allison grinned. "By the blush on your face you're doing more than just seeing him."

Jordan laughed. Over the last week she and Clint had seen each other several times. He'd met her at the Coffee Shop for a quick sandwich and twice he'd been at her house waiting for her when she'd finally gotten home from work. He'd even met her at Iggy's one night and she'd introduced him to her coworkers.

"It's wild. I refused to have sex with him when we were in high school and now I can't seem to get enough of him both in bed and out. We hooked up again at the reunion and have been seeing each other when we can ever since."

"You've checked his alibis for the times of the murders?"

"Thoroughly," Jordan replied. "It was the first thing I did before agreeing to see him on a social basis."

"Are you in love with him?"

Jordan ate another fry, buying herself a moment before answering. "I don't want to be in love with him," she finally replied. "I don't want to be in love with anyone. What about you? Are you seeing anyone?"

Allison grinned. "Not the smoothest change of topic in a conversation, and no, I'm not seeing anyone. I can't remember the last time I had a date."

"Then you're working too hard," Jordan replied.

"Yeah, what else is new?"

As they finished the meal, they talked about cases they'd worked on and the current ones that had brought them back together.

"I read Dane's latest book," Allison said as they walked back to headquarters. "I think that man might have a bit of a dark soul."

Jordan laughed. "He definitely has a cheating soul." She pulled her collar up against the cold night air as they walked briskly down the sidewalk. "He's thrilled with these latest murders. He'd been bemoaning the fact that lately Kansas City and the surrounding area wasn't providing any book material for him."

"Have you checked his alibis?"

Jordan looked at her sharply. "No, why?" Almost as soon as she asked, she realized where Allison's mind had gone. "You don't really think Dane is killing these women so he will have a new best seller? That's sick."

"Welcome to my world," Allison said dryly.

They thought she was his.

They thought Jenny Taylor was his kill. He'd heard it on the noon news. "The Butcher strikes again," the reporter had said. It was important to him that they knew the difference.

Stupid idiots.

Hadn't they noticed that the numbers were missing? Hadn't they recognized that it had obviously been amateur hour in the Taylor house, a cheap imitation of the real deal?

As he left work at midnight, the air smelled of winter. The forecasters were predicting freezing rain the next day. God, he hated winter. And he hated overtime.

As he walked to his car, his body ached with exhaustion. But he couldn't sleep. His real work awaited him and he had to think things through. With the death of Jenny he knew the police would definitely be all over

Pamela Albright and Jordan. There was no way he could fly to Chicago to get to Sally Kincaid. He couldn't miss work and there would be records of any quick flight he might take to the Windy City.

But he'd come up with a different plan, one that would have them all scratching their heads, unsure who might be the next victim. And if it worked like he thought it would, it would take the attention off Pamela and Jordan and ultimately make them easy targets.

His exhaustion fell away as he anticipated the work that lay ahead of him. He drove too fast home, eager to get to it before finally going to sleep. His blood thrummed in his veins and by the time he arrived at his place, any hint of tiredness had fled beneath the adrenaline burst that consumed him.

He went directly into the room he considered his temple of retribution. Pictures of his victims greeted him and as always he felt a sense of power, of righteousness, as he sat at his computer.

It took him only minutes to access the page he wanted on the Internet. He'd found her MySpace page the night before. It was amazing how much information could be gleaned about a person by reading her profile and following her blog.

She was twenty-five years old and her user name was Cheerleader Girl, and when he'd found her, he'd felt as if she'd been a gift from the gods, a sacrifice to his cause.

Cheerleader Girl lived alone with her cat in an apartment building not far from where he lived. In her blogs she had mentioned so many landmarks it had been relatively easy for him to figure out where she had her apartment. She drove a red Miata and loved hanging out at a bar called Diamond Pete's.

She taught cheerleading classes for community education and had been a cheerleader not only in high school but also in college. Her picture depicted a brunette with long curly hair, a Miss America toothy smile and a slight tilt to her head that read arrogance.

One of them. She was definitely one of them. There was a bitchiness to her blogs that let him know she'd been a mean girl, was probably still a mean girl. Her death would herald a new terror among women. Nobody who had ever picked up a megaphone or waved pom-poms would feel safe.

And maybe, just maybe with her death Pamela Albright and Jordan Sampson would get careless. Eventually he would get to Chicago and take care of Sally. It was important that he complete the extermination of this squad before he moved on to the next.

He smiled as he thought of head-cheerleader-now-detective Jordan Sampson. She was beginning to show not just the strain of the investigation but also the stress of her own personal fear.

So much work.

He had so much work to do. The world was full of mean-girl cheerleaders and nobody except him could champion the unpopular, the misfits they had abused.

He shut off his computer and got ready for bed, knowing he had to be up early the next morning. Before he went to his real job, he wanted to go to the Greystone Apartments and look for a red Miata in the parking lot. Once he found her car, he would easily be able to get her address. And then it was just a matter of time before Cheerleader Girl became Dead Mean Girl.

Chapter 22

"You've all heard it before," Allison said the morning after Jenny's body had been found. They were all gathered in the conference room and Allison stood in front of the bulletin board on the wall. "Eighty-eight percent of serial killers are male. Eighty-five percent are Caucasian and the average age of their first kill is around twenty-eight years old. I'd say our Butcher is a white male between the ages of twenty-five and forty. If these are his first murders, then I'd lean toward the younger of those numbers. Although by the meticulous planning that went into each murder, we might also be looking for somebody thirty or older, somebody who has killed before." She grinned ruefully. "Unfortunately, profiling doesn't give definitive answers."

"What about mental illness?" Adam asked.

Allison shook her head. "I don't think he's mentally ill in the traditional or legal sense of the word. He's organized, and except for the obvious sign of rage that takes place at the scene, I don't think he's nuts, except of course for the fact that he's killing women for a reason we have yet to discover. Unfortunately if he were schizophrenic or psychotic, he'd probably be easier to apprehend."

"But he's smart," Ricky said.

"Yes, probably very intelligent, very organized."

Jordan listened to the conversation. It was obvious

Allison had stayed up the night before to read all the files and to study the cases. Her night of study showed not only in her familiarity with the particulars of the murders but also in the dark smudges of tiredness beneath her eyes.

Jordan could relate to that exhaustion. She'd gotten home just after midnight the night before and fallen into bed hoping sleep would immediately claim her, but that hadn't been the case.

She'd tossed and turned with crazy thoughts, thoughts of Dane murdering women for his next best seller, of Della venting the rage she'd carried with her since her high school days.

The faces of the potential suspects had flashed in her mind. They had a dozen men who had attended the reunion and who couldn't substantiate an alibi for the times of Joann's and Betsy's murders.

The detectives were still working on the assumption that somehow the reunion was the precrime stressor, or trigger for the murders. But exactly what had set things into motion—precisely what had triggered the killing rage—remained elusive.

She'd finally fallen into sleep around four in the morning and suffered two hours of nightmares. She'd dreamed of Julie and she'd felt the bite of the chain that had strangled her. The police had never discerned exactly what kind of chain had been used, although they'd suspected that it had been something that might have held keys.

Julie hadn't been the only dead woman to haunt her dreams. Both Betsy and Joann had been there, too. Whispering to her, warning her that she was next. Finally she'd dreamed of being tied to a chair and stabbed in her stomach over and over again. She'd awakened gasping for air and fighting the blankets as if they were an attacker.

She refocused her attention on Allison. "I think we're looking for a white male in his late twenties, early thirties," Allison said. "He probably lives alone and either works a job with different shifts or is self-employed, or one that gives him the freedom to pick and choose his own hours. Joann was killed on a Saturday night, Betsy on a Friday evening and Jenny on a Monday morning."

"Any thoughts on the background of the killer?" Jordan asked.

"You all know the traditional early signs that most serial killers display—bed-wetting, animal abuse and fire starting." Allison frowned. "I think it's possible our Butcher may not have these traditional markers. I think we're looking for someone whose rage began later than childhood. I think this killer was formed in junior high and high school. He felt powerless in high school, perhaps somebody who was either bullied or ignored by the popular crowd. And who better epitomizes the popular crowd than the cheerleaders?"

Jordan thought about all the "invisible" kids who had walked the halls of her high school. Many of them didn't belong to any of the clubs; they clung to the walls or hid in the shadows, afraid of venturing out for fear of ridicule or rejection.

Occasionally one of those disenchanted kids in a high school would snap and take a rifle to school and garner headlines for a couple of days as the community struggled to make sense of it.

"What took him so long? I mean, if it's somebody from my high school, why has it taken fifteen years for him to act out his anger?" Jordan asked.

"We don't know that for sure," John reminded her as he cracked his knuckles. "We don't know that it's taken fifteen years to set him off. It's possible he's been murdering people all along and we just haven't made the connection."

Adam nodded. "We all have tons of cold cases that might be the work of this guy."

"I'm not so sure," Allison protested. "The signatures of this killer are very distinctive. The victim tied to a chair, the stabbing and of course the numbers that were left behind are pretty specific. If he's killed before, I think we would find at least some of these same kinds of signatures. Which brings me to Jennifer Taylor and the fact that the numbers weren't found at the scene. I understand this piece of evidence has been kept out of the press."

She turned around and looked at the pictures of Jenny. "I'm not convinced that this is the work of our man," she said, then turned back to face the group. "I think you need to be looking at another killer in this case."

"Isn't it possible he's evolving somehow?" Anthony asked. "Or maybe deteriorating?" he added hopefully.

"I'd love to be able to tell you that, but at this stage of the game, I don't think so," Allison replied.

"Or maybe he figured he didn't have to leave the numbers anymore because Jordan figured out it had to do with cheerleading," John added.

"Again, I don't have enough evidence to make a call about that," Allison replied. "But if I were all of you, I'd look closely at the Taylor murder and I wouldn't be too quick to assume it's the same killer involved."

She sat down at the table and for the next hour they coordinated any new information that had been received throughout the night, and planned their next course of action.

"Did we get any information about Ben Broadbent's travel itinerary during the times of the murders?" Jordan asked as she realized she'd never followed up with Anthony about her inquiries.

"Got it," Anthony said as he rifled through the stack of papers in front of him. "He was in Oklahoma City during both murders."

Jordan frowned thoughtfully. Oklahoma City was only about a five-hour drive from Kansas City. It would be possible for somebody to fly into town, then rent a car and drive back, commit a murder, then return. It would be difficult, but it could be done.

"Make arrangements for Ben to come in tomorrow for an interview," she said. Della would be appalled, but Jordan couldn't ignore the fact that Della had hated those women with a passion and Ben was a man who wanted nothing more than his wife's happiness. "And check all the car-rental places, find out if he rented a car while he was in Oklahoma City."

With the official briefing finished, the men all left to continue interviews, interrogate potential suspects and use resources that weren't available in the conference room.

Finally it was just Allison and Jordan remaining in the room. "You didn't tell me yesterday when we had dinner and went over the details of these cases that you were a cheerleader with the victims," Allison said.

"Who told you that?" Jordan asked.

"Sergeant Wendt told me."

"It isn't pertinent to the investigation," Jordan said.

Allison sat back in her chair with a look of disbelief. "Of course it's pertinent. Do you realize that you might be the best piece of evidence we have? That it's probable that you know the killer, that you went to school with him? He might have been on the fringes of your crowd, a wannabe who harbored a secret hatred for you all."

"Don't you think I've thought of that?" Jordan expelled a deep sigh. "Allison, I've racked my brains trying to pinpoint anyone who might be capable of this. I've tried to remember somebody who we were all mean to, or hurt, maybe somebody who was often the butt of jokes. But, honestly, I can't think of anyone."

She reached for her cup and took a sip of her cold, bitter coffee. "Last night you got me thinking about Dane, but I can't imagine him being responsible for anything like this."

"And you know he isn't capable of such a thing because he's a wonderful father, a stand-up guy in the community, and if he has a few issues with women, who doesn't?" Allison raised a pale blond eyebrow.

Jordan knew what she was getting at. Most serial killers were described by neighbors and family members as nice guys; some were good and decent family men. People were always stunned when they learned that the quiet man down the street who went to church on Sundays and kept his lawn neat and tidy also cut the heads off dogs and trapped women in his basement.

"What are you trying to do to me? Make me crazy?" she finally said to Allison.

"No, I'm trying to keep you safe and on your toes. Everyone in your life is suspect. Any deliveryman who comes to your door, a repairman who shows up without an appointment, a mailman bringing you a package, could be the man we're hunting. We don't know how he's gaining access into the homes of the women he's killing. You have to be careful, Jordan."

For the first time since this had all began, true fear clutched Jordan's soul.

Three down, two to go.

The words echoed in her head and her heart began to race. Would she recognize danger if it showed up on her doorstep? Would she unwittingly let the killer into her home, not realizing what she had done until it was too late? Oh God, her heart thundered so painfully fast she felt nauseated, as though she might pass out.

"Jordan?" Allison's voice sliced through the fear and brought Jordan back from the edge. "You okay? You turned pale as a ghost."

"I'm fine. It's just when I really take time to think about it all, I am afraid," Jordan admitted.

"That's good," Allison replied. "Fear will keep you smart. Fear will keep you safe. Now, what are you doing for Thanksgiving?"

"I'll probably be here working on Thanksgiving Day."

"What about Mandy? Don't you have plans with her?"

"She called me and left me a message that she's been

invited to her best friend Megan's house for Thanksgiving and she'd really like to go there, and did I mind if she skipped seeing me for the day?"

Allison smiled sympathetically. "She's twelve. There's nothing more important than your friends when you're that age," Allison said.

"I know, and Megan's family is terrific. I'm thrilled that Mandy has such a good friend." Jordan sighed. "It's probably just as well. With Jenny's murder I was going to have trouble justifying taking off for a holiday. I just hope we tie all this up before Christmas. I want a good Christmas."

"Don't we all?" Allison replied. She looked at her watch, then got up from the table. "I've got to get going. I've got a meeting at the field office in twenty minutes. I'll be back later this afternoon."

"I'll be here," Jordan said.

It was just after three in the afternoon when Ben and Della arrived for Ben's interview. Jordan walked out to greet them and it didn't take a rocket scientist to know that Della was pissed.

"I can't believe you're doing this, bringing us down here like we're criminals," she said to Jordan, her voice sharp and strident and her nostrils flared. "I thought you were my friend, but obviously I was wrong."

"Della, I'm just doing my job." Jordan bit back a sigh and looked at Ben. "Detective Garelli will take it from here." She looked at Anthony, who nodded.

"Mr. Broadbent, if you'll please follow me," he said.

Della started after them, but Jordan grabbed her by the arm. "Sorry, Della, you can't go with them. They need to talk to Ben alone. Why don't you and I go across the street and get a cup of coffee?"

"What makes you think I want to drink a cup of coffee with you?" Della snapped. She pulled the collar of her coat up closer around her neck and lifted her chin with a touch of arrogance.

Jordan looped her arm with Della's. "Because we're

friends and because deep in your heart you know this has to be done. It's the only way to exclude Ben from the list of suspects."

Della sniffed indignantly, but allowed herself to be pulled toward the elevator. The two didn't speak as they left the building and walked across the street to the Coffee Shop.

Once there Della sank into a chair, arms crossed over her chest and her lips thinned in displeasure as Jordan went to the counter and ordered two coffees. She returned to the table and set one of the coffees in front of her friend. "There, just like you like it with two sugars and enough cream for it to be more like a milk shake than coffee."

Della uncrossed her arms and leaned forward. "Please tell me you don't really believe that Ben had anything to do with the deaths of those women. I mean, how could you even think such a thing? You've spent time with him—you've been to our house a thousand times. He didn't go to high school with us. He didn't know those women."

"But he knew them through you," Jordan replied. "He knew they had been cruel to you, that they'd made you cry, made you feel like shit all through high school. And then the night of the reunion it all came crashing back to you, and you told Ben you hated them, that you wished they were all dead."

"And you think Ben killed them for me?" Della wrapped her hands around her coffee cup. "Do you really think he loves me enough to do something like that?"

"I think it's a theory we have to explore."

Della picked up her cup and took a drink of her coffee, her eyes gleaming over the rim of the cup as if she liked the idea that her husband would kill for her. "Be careful, Jordan. If you aren't nice to me, I'll tell Ben," she said. "And who knows what he might do?"

"That's not funny," Jordan replied with a burst of anger.

And it was at that moment that Jordan realized her friendship with Della just might not survive this case. The two had little in common and Jordan recognized that over the years Della had become one of the mean girls she'd professed to hate.

"It was just a joke," Della exclaimed. "Jeez, what happened to your sense of humor?"

"Three dead women stole it right away," Jordan said, not even trying to hide her irritation.

"You're obviously in a foul mood. I want to go back. I want to be with my husband." Della stood, grabbed her coffee cup and headed for the door. Jordan followed behind her, wondering in what other ways this case might change her life . . . if she managed to have a life when this was all over.

Chapter 23

Thanksgiving went by in a blur. Benny had a local diner bring in turkey and all the trimmings for the detectives that worked the holiday. John was there, as was Ricky, but the rest of the team had taken off to spend time with their families.

Jordan had called her parents that morning and she'd spoken to Mandy on the phone; then she had immersed herself in checking and rechecking all the information they'd gained over the last couple of weeks.

Ben's alibi wasn't solid. Even though he'd checked into the hotel in Oklahoma City the morning of each murder, he couldn't give them concrete evidence that he'd actually been in the hotel when the murders had occurred. He'd had a rental car at his disposal, so he wasn't excluded from the list of suspects. They were in the process of checking with the rental-car agency to find out about the mileage he'd put on the car while it had been in his possession.

They also hadn't ruled out that the Butcher hadn't killed Jenny Taylor. Certainly there were anomalies in that particular crime scene, but they simply didn't know enough about their killer to rule him out as Jenny's murderer. Jordan thought it just as likely that Jenny's husband might be her killer, and they were checking him out as well.

It was a day of frustration, just like the day before

and the day before that. At nine that evening she decided to head home. All the facts of the three cases were blurring together and she knew she needed to get away from it. She couldn't think anymore.

Her heels clicked a rapid tattoo against the sidewalk as she hurried to her car. She hadn't gone far from the building when she thought she heard the slap of a footstep behind her.

She whirled around, heart pumping, gun drawn, but saw nobody. She released a shaky breath and tried to tell herself to chill out. But she didn't breathe easily until she was locked in her car and waiting for the heater to warm.

There was no question that with each day that passed, she was more on edge, more aware of her own mortality. The murders had occurred about three weeks apart, and there was no way to know whether their unsub would stick to that time line or escalate.

Three down, two to go.

She'd heard this morning that Pamela Albright and her husband had left town for parts unknown. They didn't intend to return to Kansas City until the killer was caught.

That certainly narrowed the choice of victims for the killer.

She was it.

With the car vents finally blowing warm air, she backed out of the parking space and her cell phone rang. She threw the car in park and fumbled in her purse and withdrew the phone.

"Hello?"

"Good evening, Jordan." The voice was a low, rusty rumble, obviously disguised.

"Who is this?" she asked. There were only a handful of people who had her cell phone number.

"I think you know who I am. Your friends call me the Butcher, but I like to think of myself as Mr. Payback."

The hot air blowing from the heater couldn't begin to

warm the icy chill that clutched Jordan's heart. Before she could say anything, he continued. "Jennifer Taylor wasn't mine. It's important that you know that. I didn't kill her. Don't get me wrong—I would have killed her eventually—but somebody got to her before I did."

There was something about the voice that was familiar, but she couldn't place it. She waited, straining to hear background noise, something that might indicate a clue as to the identity of the caller or where he might be calling from. "Why don't you turn yourself in and we can help you?" she finally said when the silence had stretched too long.

He laughed and the sound of it shot new waves of cold through her. "I don't need help. I'm doing the world a favor and I still have lots of work left to do. I just wanted to tell you that when I kill, you'll know they're mine. There won't be any question about it. Oh, and Jordan, that bush next to your front porch? It really needs to be pulled out."

"Just tell me—"

He hung up.

Jordan checked her caller ID, unsurprised that the call showed up as anonymous. And she knew he was smart enough to have made the call on a throwaway phone. There would be no way of tracing it—or him.

She got out of her car and went back into the station, where she wrote down everything that had occurred during the phone call. Unfortunately she'd heard no background noises, nothing that would help them trace the call. When she'd finished making the appropriate record of the call, she went back outside.

As she pulled away from the parking lot, her blood remained chilled.

He knew her cell phone number.

He knew where she lived.

She didn't want to go home, and wondered whether he was there now, waiting for her. She picked up her phone once again and called Anthony. "Hey, could you direct a patrol car to meet me at my house as quickly as possible?"

"Are you okay?" he asked with concern.

"I'm fine." She quickly told him about the phone call she'd just received. "I want a couple of patrolmen to clear my house before I go inside. Just to be on the safe side."

"It's done."

Jordan clicked off and drove toward her house. She doubted that the killer was in her house waiting for her, but she'd feel better if the patrolmen checked out the entire house before she went inside.

For all she knew, the killer had known for weeks where she lived. There was no real reason to expect to find him there now. When she arrived at her house, a patrol car was already parked at the curb waiting for her. She got out of the car and smiled at the two officers who had responded.

"Sorry to bother you," she said as she found her house key.

"It's no bother, Detective Sampson," one of the officers said. "We'll just get it all cleared for you." He pulled his gun and his partner did the same as Jordan unlocked the front door.

As they disappeared into the house, Jordan remained on the front porch, her heart working overtime as she stared at the bush next to where she stood. It had been half-dead when she'd rented the house, and she'd talked to the landlord about taking it out and replacing it next spring.

She looked around the area, remembering the night she'd seen the figure behind a tree. Had it been him? As head cheerleader of the squad, was she his grand prize?

"Who are you?" she whispered.

She definitely had the feeling that the voice on the phone had been vaguely familiar. Had she interviewed him in the interrogation room? Had he been one of her friends in high school?

"All clear." The two officers stepped out on the porch with her. "We checked every closet and cabinet in every room of the house," the older one said. "There's nobody inside."

"Thank you. I really appreciate it," she replied. As they returned to their patrol car, she went inside the house. She took only three steps into the living room and realized she didn't want to be here tonight.

She picked up the phone and called Clint. "I know it's late, but I was wondering if maybe you'd like some company."

"I'd love to have your company. In fact, I'll put you to work. I'm decorating my Christmas tree."

"On Thanksgiving Day?"

He laughed. "I told you I was a Christmas freak."

He gave her his address and she told him she'd be there in the next twenty minutes or so. When she hung up, she went directly to her bedroom and packed an overnight bag with work clothes for the next morning. Tomorrow she'd probably be fine, but tonight she wanted to be anywhere but here.

Dane had once accused her in one of their many fights of being so strong, so self-contained, that she didn't need anyone else in her life. Perhaps at that time she hadn't needed him anymore, but tonight she needed to be with somebody who cared about her, a man who could handle both her strength and her frailties.

It was almost ten when she pulled into the driveway of Clint's attractive story-and-a-half home in a fairly new neighborhood. The house surprised her. It was bigger, nicer than she'd expected.

As she got out of the car, the front door opened and Clint stepped out to greet her. "You found me," he said.

"What a beautiful home," she replied as she walked toward him. She'd left her bag in the car, not sure how to invite herself to spend the night.

"The minute I saw it, I knew it was exactly what I wanted." He opened the door to allow her into a tiled entry. Directly to her right was a formal dining room with a mahogany table and sideboard. A huge Christmas arrangement graced the center of the table, and greenery was artfully arranged on top of the sideboard.

"Wow, you're quite the decorator," she exclaimed.

He grinned at her sheepishly. "I have a small confession to make. I hired somebody to come in and do the decorations. I'm not really good at that kind of stuff."

She smiled. "Most men aren't."

"There are three bedrooms upstairs and the master is on this floor," he said as they passed the staircase that had been decorated with greenery and twinkling multicolored lights.

"You have been busy," she said as she walked into the living room. The Christmas tree was in one corner of the room and reached to the top of the ten-foot ceiling. It was strung with lights but nothing else.

"You're just in time to help me with the hard part. Stringing lights is easy. It's the rest that could definitely use a woman's touch."

She looked around the rest of the room. He hadn't lied to her when he'd told her he was a traditionalist. The sofa was warm brown leather, well used, and the coffee and end tables were once again mahogany. A flat-screen television hung over the fireplace, which divided the living room from the kitchen.

Nice furnishings, but it was the small items in the room that told her about the man who lived here. A bookcase held football trophies and pictures of various squads from the past. Books about sports were lined up next to history and fishing tomes.

"This is really nice, Clint."

"I'll tell you what's nice." He stepped close to her and wrapped her in his arms. "Having you here with me."

"I just didn't want to be alone tonight."

"What's happened?"

As always it amazed her how quickly he tuned in to her mood. He led her to the sofa and she told him about the phone call she'd received on the way home from work. "It just freaked me out."

"Of course it did," he replied as he pulled her into his arms once again. "I'm glad you came here. I'm glad you know that you're safe here with me."

"I don't always feel quite safe with you." She moved out of his arms and smiled.

"There's a good kind of not feeling safe and a bad kind of not feeling safe." He got up from the sofa and walked over to the stereo and punched a button. The sound of Christmas carols filled the air. "Come on," he said, and held a hand out to her. "We're going to decorate my tree and not think about anything else but good things."

For the next hour they hung ornaments and talked about Christmases past. "Julie used to love Christmas," she said as she hung a football-playing Santa on the tree. "And we always knew what she'd bought us at least a week before Christmas."

"She couldn't keep a secret?" Clint asked.

The simple question caused an unexpected lump to rise in Jordan's throat. "No, I was the one who was good at keeping secrets." She reached for another ornament, surprised by the rising emotion that pressed tight against her chest. "I never get to talk about her."

"I remember her smile. She had a gorgeous smile, like yours," Clint said.

She knew he was opening up the opportunity for her to talk about her sister and she desperately wanted to talk about Julie. "She had such a great sense of humor. No matter what kind of mood I was in, she could always make me laugh. My mom used to call us the giggle twins because whenever we were together, we laughed."

"You were a lot alike, but how were you different?" he asked as he reached into the box for another ornament.

Jordan sat on the edge of the sofa, a glittery candy cane in her hand. "Julie was always way more adventurous than I was. She was the first one to run over the hill without knowing what was on the other side, the first one to try new food or some funky style of clothing. I was always more cautious."

"Funny, that you, being the cautious one, ended up being a homicide detective," he observed. He sat next to her on the sofa. "What do you think Julie would have become?"

"An astronaut or maybe a trapeze performer." Once again emotion welled up inside her. "She was smart enough to be anything she wanted, but I screwed it all up for her." Clint's face began to blur as tears filled her eyes.

"What do you mean, you screwed it up?" Clint took the candy cane from her and placed it on the coffee table as her tears began in earnest.

She shook her head and angrily swiped her cheeks. "Nothing," she said. "It's nothing."

He took her hands in his, his expression so gentle it made her want to cry harder. "Tell me, Jordan. Talk to me. What did you screw up with Julie?"

The guilt that had eaten at her since her sister's murder suddenly seemed too big to contain. It was the reason she knew she'd never really attain true happiness, the one thing she'd done that she felt she should be punished for, the one thing that she wished she could take back.

"Jordan, honey. What is it? You're safe with me, no matter what you have to say, no matter what you think you've done." His blue eyes held her gaze and for the first time she decided to share.

"I could have stopped her that night when she snuck out."

He frowned. "How could you do that? You were at college when she was killed."

Sucking up the tears, she leaned back against the sofa cushion. "She called me that night. It was about eleven o'clock. I'd already been in bed and asleep, so her phone call woke me up."

She closed her eyes and remembered Julie's voice, so filled with life, so wild with excitement, and Jordan's sorrow crashed in on her. She looked at Clint once again. "She was excited. She'd met a new guy, an older guy, and she told me she was sneaking out of the house to meet him that night. I told her it was a really bad idea, but she was determined and nothing I said to her changed her mind. I was tired and cranky, so I hung up the phone, turned over and went back to sleep."

She pulled her hands from his and balled them into fists, her nails biting into her skin. "I could have stopped her. All I had to do was call Mom and Dad and tell them she was planning on sneaking out. But I went back to sleep and she got murdered." Her voice broke and she covered her face with her hands.

"Jordan, look at me." Clint's voice was soft, but held an unmistakable command.

She lowered her hands and stared at him, needing something, but unsure what.

"It wasn't your fault."

The moment the words left his mouth, she knew it was exactly what she'd needed. She'd needed to hear it from her parents fourteen years ago. She'd wanted to hear it from Dane when she'd told him about Julie's murder.

"Honey, it wasn't your fault," he said again, and drew her into his arms. She laid her cheek on his chest and drew a deep, weary sigh.

"I've always felt responsible. I've always believed that if I'd just been a tattletale that one night, then she would still be alive."

"If she wouldn't have snuck out that night, she might have the next night or the one after that. If she wanted to meet the guy, you couldn't have stopped her no matter what you might have done."

His words found the raw, wounded places in her soul. She felt as if a hundred-pound weight had been lifted off her heart. Still, she wasn't ready to absolve herself. "I should have asked more questions that night. I should have insisted she tell me his name, something about him. But I was tired and it was late and I just wanted to go back to sleep."

"You couldn't know what was going to happen. You were nothing but a kid yourself. Have you been beating yourself up over this all these years?" His hand stroked down her back in a soothing fashion.

"I've just always felt responsible. I think my parents blame me and that's why we don't have a relationship now. They can barely stand to look at me and I think it's because they blame me for her death. I've always believed that somehow I didn't deserve to be happy, that I would forever be punished by fate for not stopping Julie from going out that night."

"Wow, I never realized what a big ego you had," he said. She raised her head to look at him. "I mean, think about it. When you didn't stop a murder that you didn't know was going to happen, you figured all the dark forces in the world conspired to steal your happiness. I hate to tell you this, Jordan, but you decide whether you're happy or not. I know it's a terrible cliché, but you're the captain of your own ship."

She gave him a half smile. "That is a terrible cliché." She rose up from him and stood. "Let's finish getting the tree decorated. That's enough drama for one night."

It was midnight by the time they finished, and Jordan was dead on her feet. "You aren't driving home," Clint said.

"I was hoping you'd say that. I have an overnight bag in my car."

"Hang tight. I'll get it for you." As he took her car keys and went out the front door, Jordan looked at the tree with its twinkling lights and thought about everything he'd said to her.

Intellectually, she'd always known that she wasn't responsible for Julie's murder, but emotionally she'd blamed herself for so long. Clint's words had sunk into a place she hadn't been able to access by herself. She'd been looking for absolution and that was what he'd given her.

She turned as he came back into the living room with her bag and hanging clothes in hand. "I was just standing here admiring our handiwork," she said.

"It's pretty, isn't it? But now it's time to call it a night. You look beat and it's getting late."

She followed him into the master bedroom, a huge room decorated in shades of navy and gray. The king-size bed looked inviting and the adjoining master bath was equally large and lush. But this room held the kind of male clutter she'd expected from a bachelor. The nightstand held a coffee cup and a bunch of papers. Clothes littered the floor at the foot of the bed, and the top of the dresser was cluttered with pocket change, a half a bottle of cologne and several energy-bar wrappers.

It was nice to know the man wasn't completely too good to be true, she thought.

"You can have the bathroom first," he said. "I'm just going to go turn off lights and make sure all the doors are locked."

As he left the bedroom, Jordan went into the bathroom to change into her nightgown. She hadn't come here looking for sex. She'd needed something different from Clint and he'd delivered. He was quickly becoming her favorite soft place to fall, the place where she felt safe both physically and emotionally.

She knew she was a strong woman, but there were times when strength was found in being weak, when it was okay to recognize the need for something, for someone other than yourself.

She washed the last of her makeup off and brushed her teeth and by the time she left the bathroom, Clint was back in the bedroom and the bed had been turned down.

"Which side is yours?" she asked.

"Usually right down the middle, but I always start on the left side."

She walked around to the right side of the bed and slid in beneath the sheets as he disappeared into the bathroom. Weariness crashed into her and she closed her eyes, hoping, praying, that at least for tonight she would have no dreams.

She hadn't wanted to fall in love with Clint, but she was precariously close to doing just that. She was reluctant to put her heart on the line again. She thought of her friendship with Della. Della had come into her life at a time when Jordan's marriage had been crumbling and she'd felt isolated and alone. Jordan had a feeling that under different circumstances she might not have gotten so close to the drama queen who was demanding and resentful.

Had she done the same thing with Clint? Had he come along at a time when she was feeling achingly lonely and unsure of where she fit in life? She didn't want to love him for all the wrong reasons.

As he returned to the bedroom, he turned out the light and slid into the bed next to her. Immediately he reached for her, kissed her on the forehead, then moved to his own side of the bed.

"Good night, Jordan."

"Good night, Clint," she replied, and closed her eyes.

She was acutely conscious of him next to her. She could tell he wasn't asleep. There was an energy crackling in the air, a heightened sense of anticipation that cast her drowsiness away.

Did he feel it, too? The crazy need to touch, to do more than just sleep. His body heat scorched her and the mere inches that separated them suddenly seemed too far.

"Did you know that trying to sleep next to a woman you want could cause sudden death?" His voice was deep, husky in the darkness of the room. And his words made a small laugh escape her lips.

She reached out a hand and placed it on the warmth of his taut stomach. "I'd hate to be responsible for your sudden death."

He turned toward her and gathered her in his arms. "I was so hoping you'd say that," he said just before his mouth found hers in a kiss that instantly had her breathless.

It took only moments for her to get out of her nightgown and him to lose his briefs and then they were naked and panting as their desire for each other swept all other emotions away.

They made love slowly, as if the night would last forever. When they were finally finished and she was curled up in his arms, she didn't know if being with him was right or wrong; she knew only that at this moment she was where she needed to be.

John Lindsay sat outside the apartment building where Danny McCall lived. After studying all the evidence and listening to what Allison the profiler had to say, John had become more and more convinced that the big man was the Butcher.

He'd begun surveillance on Danny whenever it was possible, following him to work or to the stores. John was certain that eventually Danny would attempt to claim another victim, and when he did, John would be there.

The man fit the profile. He lived alone, he worked a shift job and John had found out that at the time of all three murders Danny hadn't been at work. According to Jordan, Danny had been one of those on the fringe of the popular crowd. He'd been a friend to everyone, but none of the girls had ever dated him.

He'd obviously had a crush on both Joann and Betsy and maintained some sort of contact with them throughout the years. He was an odd duck, John thought. He'd read the notes from Jordan's interview with the man and the notes from when Anthony had reinterviewed him after Betsy's murder.

He leaned back in his seat and took a sip of the coffee he'd brought with him. Staying sober had been hard, but he kept his eye on the ultimate prize—his own death.

All he had to do was catch the Butcher and then he could kiss this earth good-bye and end the pain of living without Mary.

Chapter 24

The chicken soup Jordan had bought from the deli by police headquarters filled her car with its hearty scent. It was just after noon on Sunday and she'd been at work since six that morning. A little while ago Dane had called and told her Mandy was sick and wanted two things—soup from the deli and her mother.

Jordan hadn't felt guilty about leaving work. There were no new leads and she'd been giving twenty hours a day to the job. Even though it was two days ago that she'd awakened in Clint's arms after spending the night at his place, it felt as if it were a lifetime ago.

She was tired and with just a little push could be downright cranky. But what she wanted more than anything else in the world at the moment was to be with her sick child.

All thoughts of murder disappeared as she marveled at Dane's news that Mandy wanted her, and Jordan couldn't wait to hold Mandy in her arms and rub her back like she had always done when Mandy didn't feel well.

Dane greeted her at the door. "She says she has a sore throat and an earache, but she has no temperature. I suspect she might be milking it a bit."

"She's upstairs in her room?"

Dane nodded. "And waiting for you."

Jordan walked up the wide staircase with the sack

containing the soup in hand. As she hit the landing, she could hear the faint sound of a television coming from Mandy's room. As she drew closer, she realized her daughter was watching *The Little Mermaid* and it brought home to Jordan that even though Mandy tried very hard to act cool and mature, she was still just a little girl at heart.

"Hey, cupcake," she said as she entered the room.

Mandy was huddled beneath her pink bedspread, only the top of her head showing, but at the sound of Jordan's voice she sat halfway up and burst into tears.

"Mandy, honey." Jordan set the sack with the soup on the dresser and hurried over to her daughter's side. She sat on the edge of the bed and pulled Mandy into her arms.

"Mommy, I feel so bad," Mandy exclaimed. She clung to Jordan like a baby monkey and buried her face against Jordan's chest. Jordan held tight and stroked her hand down Mandy's long silky hair.

Dane was right. Mandy didn't feel as though she had a temperature, but a lack of temperature didn't mean she was okay.

"I'm so sorry, honey. Dad said you have a sore throat and an earache?" Jordan would have sat on the bed with her daughter in her arms for the next ten years, but Mandy nodded, then all too quickly pulled away and lay back on the bed.

"My throat feels all scratchy and my ear hurts, but I've also got a bad headache," she said miserably.

"Do you want to try to eat some soup? It's nice and warm." Jordan got up and grabbed the sack from the top of the dresser, then returned to the edge of the bed. As she pulled the container of soup from the bag, Mandy sat up and plumped her pillow behind her.

As Mandy ate her soup, Jordan talked to her about the upcoming Christmas holiday and described Clint's beautiful tree.

"When are you going to put your tree up?" Mandy asked.

"I don't know," Jordan replied. "Maybe next weekend or the one after that. You can come over and help me decorate it."

Whatever ailed Mandy didn't interfere with her appetite. She finished the soup along with three packets of crackers.

"Want me to rub your back?" Jordan asked.

Mandy nodded and turned over.

"You've always loved it when I rubbed your back," Jordan said. "When you were about three years old, you'd back up to me and say, 'Rubadub, Mommy.' "

Mandy smiled. "Tell me something else I did when I was little."

For the next thirty minutes Jordan rubbed her back and told silly stories. As she remembered the moments from Mandy's early childhood, a deep wistfulness welled up inside her.

She wished things had been different. She wished Dane had been different. Everything would have been so much easier if they'd managed to stay married.

Maybe she shouldn't have jumped ship. Maybe she should have stayed and tried to work things out with Dane. Even as these thoughts drifted into her head, she knew they weren't based in any reality. She'd tried hard to make her marriage work, but when Dane kept cheating, she grew more and more angry, more and more bitter.

At the end they were fighting most of the time and the tension in the house had reached epic proportions. It had become an unhealthy atmosphere, not just for Jordan, but for Mandy as well.

She'd decided she'd rather Mandy be the child of a divorce than a child in the middle of a war zone. But when she'd made the decision to leave Dane, she'd never dreamed that this child of her heart, of her soul, wouldn't be with her.

"You can go now, Mom," Mandy said drowsily. "I'm gonna take a nap."

"You'll call me if you need anything else?" Jordan asked. "Even if it's just another back rub?"

"I will," Mandy replied, and snuggled deeper beneath the bedcovers.

Jordan picked up the soup container and trash from the crackers, then stood for a long moment in the doorway of the bedroom and breathed in Mandy's scent.

Was it possible Mandy resented her for leaving Dane? Neither she nor Dane had ever told Mandy the truth of why they were divorcing. Jordan had been no more eager than Dane to let Mandy know that her father was a cheater. She knew how important it was for girls to have a positive relationship with their father.

Little girls needed to believe their fathers were strong and good. But, dammit, little girls should want to be with their mommies, Jordan thought as she went back down the stairs.

She carried the trash into the kitchen, where Dane was seated at the table with a spiral notebook in front of him. It was a familiar sight. Even though he had a fancy office upstairs, he often did his preliminary writing work seated at the kitchen table.

"She'll live to fight another day," Jordan said.

Dane leaned back in his chair and smiled. "I think maybe she's just overly tired. She spent the night with Megan last night and I think they stayed up all night."

"But if she doesn't get better, you'll take her to the doctor?" Jordan asked as she threw the trash into the bin under the sink.

"Definitely." He gestured to the chair across from him.

"Where's Claire?" she asked.

"Gone," he replied.

"As in gone shopping or gone for good?"

"For good," he replied.

Jordan leaned with a hip against the kitchen island. "So, what did you do this time?"

He laughed. "I didn't do anything except get to work on the new project. Claire liked it when I wasn't working, when I could devote most of my time and attention to her. But the last couple of weeks when I've been working again, she decided she really didn't want to be here anymore. She was definitely more high maintenance than I could deal with. By the way, I came up with a great title for the new project."

"What's that?" Jordan moved from the island and sank into the chair across from him at the table.

"'Death Chant: A Cheerleader's Final Cheer.' What do you think?"

"I think it's too early for us to know for sure that this is about cheerleaders," she replied.

"Oh, come on, Jordan. Three cheerleaders dead—what else can you think? You look tired."

"I am tired," Jordan replied. "This case has us all running around like chickens with our heads cut off."

"My sources tell me it's possible Jennifer Taylor's murder wasn't related to the others."

"I don't know who your sources are, but they're right. Our number one person of interest is her husband, Ray, and I think it's just a matter of time before he's arrested for her murder."

"So in reality you have two murders and that doesn't meet the criteria for a serial."

She nodded. Part of the criteria for calling a killer a serial was that there had to be three kills. "True, but none of us think this guy is finished yet. We've brought in a profiler from the FBI. Allison McNight? Remember her? She had dinner with us one evening when I was working that prostitute case."

"Tiny, blond and very attractive," Dane replied, and then smiled. "You know me, Jordan. I never forget a pretty face."

"Don't remind me," she said dryly. "Anyway, she read

your latest book and thinks maybe you have a dark soul. And speaking of that, I've been meaning to ask you where you were on the nights Joann and Betsy were murdered." Even though in her heart she knew it was crazy to even suspect Dane of such a thing, this case had her more than a little crazy.

Dane looked at her in stunned surprise. "You've got to be kidding me," he finally said. "Why on earth would I need alibis for the nights of the murders? I didn't even know those women."

"Maybe you hate me and those women reminded you of me. Maybe crime has been so slow in Kansas City you decided to help make things more exciting. You needed a subject for a new best seller, so you set about making sure it happened. You just told me you have a great title for a book. Maybe all you needed to do was make sure that the case fit the title."

"Jesus," Dane exclaimed, and leaned forward. "Maybe your friend Allison should have a discussion about your dark soul."

"Dane, I don't think you had anything to do with this, but I have to ask. We're grasping at straws here."

He frowned. "I don't even know specifically when those two women were killed."

She told him the dates and he got up from the table and disappeared from the room. Jordan leaned back in her chair and rubbed her forehead, where the threat of a headache was present. Lately she was making friends wherever she went. Della wasn't speaking to her and she knew she'd pissed off Dane.

He returned a few minutes later with his day planner in hand. He flipped to the appropriate page. "On the Saturday night that Joann was murdered, I was here with our daughter. On the Friday night that Betsy was killed, I was speaking to a local chapter of mystery writers." He slammed the book closed. "Satisfied?"

"No, I didn't want to make you angry."

"I'm not angry. I'm hurt that you would even entertain such an idea. If this is where Allison McNight is leading the team, then you're all on a path to nowhere."

"We're on a path to nowhere without Allison," Jordan said with weary resignation. "I don't know if we'll ever find this guy."

"That defeatist attitude doesn't sound like you," Dane replied. "You've always been a tough one, Jordan. You've always been so sure of yourself, so self-contained and yet so cautious. Oh, and I hear you have a boyfriend."

"There's somebody I've been seeing," she replied. She should have known that Mandy would mention it to her father.

"Mandy seems quite impressed with him. Clint—that's his name, isn't it? I hear he's a mean man with a Monopoly board."

She nodded. "I like him. He's a nice man."

"That's good. I want to see you happy, Jordan. If you like him, then I hope you're less cautious with him than you ever were with me."

She narrowed her eyes. "Is that some sort of passive-aggressive way of telling me that you cheated because I didn't give you what you needed in the marriage?"

He laughed. "We both know I cheated on you because I'm a shit. Jordan, you take so many risks in your job. You go forward with guns blazing to accomplish what you want, but in your personal life you've always held back. I'm just saying that if you like this guy, if you want to be with him, then let yourself go."

"I can't believe you're giving me relationship advice," she said with a wry grin, grateful that he wasn't angry because of her previous questions.

"I know how it's supposed to work. I'm just not very good at making it work for me."

Jordan got up. "On that note I'm going home. I have a cleanup date with my garage. You'll let me know how Mandy is doing? And tell her if she needs anything, I'm available."

"Of course," Dane agreed, and got up to walk her

to the door. "Jordan, don't work too hard. Life is about more than murder."

"Tell it to the victims," she replied, and left.

She was determined to spend the afternoon not thinking about murder, or Dane or Clint, but rather getting the boxes in the garage unpacked so she could park in the space through the winter. She didn't want to have to scrape ice from her windshield or dig out snow to get to work.

She needed some distance from everything, from everyone. A couple of hours of physical labor would clear her head and hopefully she'd wear herself out to the point where she could sleep without dreams.

The day was one of those unusually warm ones that Kansas City sometimes saw in early December. The afternoon sun was bright overhead and the temperature hovered around the sixty-degree mark. It was a perfect day to get the job done. There wouldn't be too many days with this kind of warmth left.

She parked at the end of her driveway and went into the house. As she changed into jeans and a sweatshirt, she thought about what Dane had said to her. It was true that she went balls to the walls when it came to her job as a detective. But she didn't bring that same kind of abandonment to her personal life.

Julie'd had that abandon and look where it had gotten her.

Dressed in her grunge wear, she grabbed a bottle of water from the refrigerator and her handgun and then punched the remote on the garage door to open it. She'd arranged for a local charity truck to stop by the next day and pick up whatever boxes she put out. So whatever she didn't unpack and take into the house she was dragging to the curb.

Finding her shoulder holster cumbersome as she lifted and moved items, she took it off and placed it on a stack of boxes nearby, then got to work on another stack. The first box was filled with kitchen gadgets and pots and pans, half of which she'd even forgotten she owned. She carried it into the kitchen, where she could unpack it later, then went back into the garage.

She found a box of old clothes she had no idea why she'd kept, and carried it out to the curb. A patrol car was parked just down the street and she could only assume that Benny had ordered the cops to sit on her for her own safety.

As much as she hated to admit it, the official police presence comforted her, especially as she worked in the open garage. Back and forth she went, taking some boxes into the house and others out by the street.

She stayed focused on the task, refusing to let anything meaningful into her thoughts. It felt good just to work and not think. She'd spent the last four weeks thinking way too much.

It was nearing dusk when she heard the ring of her phone from inside the house. Dammit, she'd meant to bring the cordless out with her the last time she'd gone inside.

Fearing it might be Mandy needing her, she raced inside and grabbed the cordless. It was Clint. "Hey, lady, how are you doing?" he asked.

"At the moment I'm working my way toward complete exhaustion. I decided to spend the afternoon cleaning out the garage." She walked over to the front door and peered outside, surprised to see that the police car was gone. They must have gotten an emergency call and left to respond.

She hurried to the door in the kitchen that led to the garage and stepped back outside. "I've been working for the last three hours and still have piles of boxes. I can't figure out why I brought half this stuff with me."

"You need some help?" he asked.

She knew what would happen if she said yes. He'd come over and they'd finish up in the garage; then they'd have dinner; then they'd fall into bed together. While it sounded very appealing, she knew it wasn't what she needed tonight.

"No, thanks. I'm just about finished for the night. I've made enough room to get my car into one-half of it and now I'm really looking forward to a long bath and then a good night's sleep."

"Jordan, I know you're busy with your cases and your daughter and everything else you have going in your life. But surely you know that I'd like to have more from you than what we've been doing. You know, like maybe time to sit down and have a real dinner together or see a movie. I feel like we're building something here, Jordan, but it's hard to do in the small snatches of time we have together."

"I know; things are just crazy right now," she replied. "Honestly, Clint. I don't know how to give you more." She thought they were building something, too, and it was as frustrating to her as it apparently was to him that there just weren't enough hours in the days for more. "Eventually we're going to tie up this case and hopefully the work will ease up a bit."

"Until the next case comes along," he said.

"Until the next case comes along," she agreed. "This is what I do, Clint." She sank down on the steps that led down to the garage floor. "Clint, if you want to date me, then you have to understand that I'm a cop and my life is never going to be about regular hours and a normal routine."

There was a long moment of silence and she wondered if for the first time he was thinking about what a relationship with her might entail. Broken dates, missed meals and sleepless nights. If he wanted to pursue a serious relationship with her, then he needed to understand that this was her world.

"I figure normal is overrated," he finally replied. "I don't know about you, Jordan, but I'm in this for the long haul."

She smiled into the phone. "So this wasn't just about getting the girl who told you no years ago?"

He laughed. "If that were the case, I wouldn't be talking to you now. It would have been mission accomplished and see ya later. We got it wrong in high school, Jordan. I'm hoping we can get it right this time."

"One day at a time, Clint. That's all I can give you right now."

"And right now, that's enough." He murmured a good-bye and then hung up.

Jordan set the cordless phone on the step next to where she sat, and released a deep sigh as Dane's words replayed in her head. "If you want this guy, then let yourself go," he'd told her.

That was easy for him to say. Jordan didn't think Dane really involved his heart in anything other than his writing and Mandy. He didn't know what it was like to be hurt.

Jordan didn't know if she was willing to put her heart on the line again when it came to a long-term relationship. She'd wanted to keep things light and easy between them, but somehow she'd already allowed him in too far, allowed things to spin slightly out of control.

She stood and at that moment she sensed that she was no longer alone in the garage. All her muscles tensed as a wild fear shot through her. Frantically she looked around, seeking her gun. In the shifting of boxes, she'd lost track of where she'd put it.

The area directly in front of her had been cleared of boxes, but on the other side of the double garage there were still stacks of boxes that might provide a hiding place for somebody who had sneaked in while she'd run inside to grab the phone.

Her first instinct was to push the button to close the garage door, but she was afraid that she might shut somebody inside with her. "Is somebody there?" she asked, grateful that her voice didn't betray the fear that rushed through her.

He stepped around the side of the house and into the open garage door. Danny McCall. She gasped in stunned surprise.

"Danny, what are you doing here?" Once again she gazed at the boxes on the opposite side of the garage and finally spied her gun. Too far away for her to grab. Stupid, stupid, a voice screamed in her head.

"Jordan, I need to talk to you." He seemed to vibrate with energy, making her blood ice in her veins.

"How did you know where I lived?" she asked.

"I got your address from Della. I knew you two were friends and she gave me a card the night of the reunion. I called her and she told me. Jordan, you have to help me." He took two steps toward her and she felt the back of her throat closing up.

"Help you with what?" she asked, frantically looking around for something she could use as a weapon if it became necessary.

"I didn't kill those women. You've got to believe me. You've got to get that cop off me."

She frowned? A cop? "What are you talking about?"

At that moment a car swerved into Jordan's driveway and John Lindsay jumped out of the driver door, his gun drawn. "Everything all right here, Jordan?" he asked.

Jordan looked from Danny to John. "Somebody want to tell me what the hell is going on here?"

"He's been spying on me, parking outside of my apartment and following me wherever I go." Danny kicked one of the boxes near him, his face red with anger. "I didn't kill anyone." He glared at John and then turned to look at Jordan. "I loved all of you in high school. You were like my sisters. I'd never do anything to hurt any of you."

"You want me to take him in for trespassing?" John asked.

Jordan considered her options. She didn't like the fact that he'd come here, but they really had nothing to hold him on. Certainly a charge of trespassing wouldn't hold up in a court.

"No, let him go," she finally said. "Go home, Danny, and don't come here again," she said. "I won't lie to you. You're a suspect in a murder case, along with a dozen other men. I can't do anything to change that. If you're innocent, then go home and keep your nose clean and don't worry about anybody watching you or following you." Her words obviously didn't make Danny happy. He kicked the box one last time, then whirled on his heels and stalked off.

For the first time since he'd appeared, Jordan drew a full breath and looked at John. "You want to come inside and tell me what's going on?"

John holstered his gun as she hit the button to shut the garage door. She walked over and grabbed her gun, then went inside. John followed her into her kitchen, where she gestured him into a chair at the table. "John, what are you doing?" she asked as she sat across from him and placed her gun in front of her on the table.

"Jordan, I think he's our man. I feel it in my gut. He fits the profile and I've been keeping an eye on him in my hours off the job. Did you see the way he kicked those boxes? Rage. The man has a rage issue. This is my last case, Jordan, and I want to get this bastard more than anything else in my life." His eyes were clear and focused with a burn of determination.

"What do you mean, this is your last case?" Jordan asked.

"I'm going to turn in my retirement papers. After we catch this guy, I'm leaving the department."

"Retired?" Jordan looked at him in surprise. She'd just assumed with Mary gone that John would keep working until eventually he was forced to take retirement. "Why would you want to do that? You love this job and you're good at it."

He shrugged. "It's time for me to go. But before I go, I want this bastard."

"We all do, John. But the worst thing we can do for the investigation is to focus all our attention on any one person. When we have time off, you need to take advantage of it—sleep and take care of yourself. I can't have you playing the Lone Ranger with a suspect." She couldn't help but think of how things had gotten out of control when she'd thought Parker Sinclair was stalking her.

"I'll tell you what bothers me most about this whole situation. I thought I was undercover, that I was being careful so that McCall wouldn't know I was there. And I'll tell you what else bothers me and that's that a woman who is supposed to be your friend gave a suspect your home address."

Jordan's jaw tightened as she thought of that particular bit of betrayal. It was one thing for Della to be angry with her, but she'd definitely crossed a line today. It had not only been spiteful; it had been downright dangerous.

"Don't worry, I'll make sure that never happens again," Jordan replied. "Go home, John. And leave Danny alone. If he is our man, we don't want the case to be screwed up by him being able to cry foul. We don't have enough evidence to warrant him being under surveillance, and a defense attorney could take that and run with it."

John frowned. "I just want this guy caught sooner than later. I'm ready to call it quits, Jordan, but I can't do that until this monster is caught."

"I know, John. Even aside from the personal nature of this case, this one has me by the throat, too."

"You okay alone here?" he asked as he got up from the table.

"I don't go anywhere in the house without my gun with me. I'm fine," she replied. "If that bastard tries to get up close and personal with me, he'll find out that I'm not the easiest victim he's ever met."

She got up and walked with John to her front door.

"I'll see you at headquarters bright and early in the morning," she said.

"Stay safe, Jordan."

She smiled and watched as he walked out to his car and a moment later backed out of her driveway. The minute his car disappeared from sight, her smile dropped. She closed and locked the door, then walked over to the sofa and sat.

Danny's appearance had shaken her to the core. In that moment when he'd first stepped into the garage, she'd never known such fear.

It had been the kind of fear that incapacitated a person, one that froze her in her tracks, making rational thought almost impossible. Was that what the victims had felt as they'd been tied into their chairs?

There were easy deaths and hard deaths. Easy was going to sleep and never waking up. Easy was a car accident with instantaneous brain death. Joann, Betsy and Jenny had all suffered hard deaths.

The first slash of the knife hadn't killed them, nor had the second or the third. They had been horrifyingly conscious until mercifully death had finally occurred.

Had the killer paused between each stab of the knife? Had he enjoyed the horror and pain in their eyes, the scent of terror that had hung in the air? Had he laughed as they begged and pleaded for their lives?

Had Danny come here to kill her only to be stymied by the appearance of John? She'd been foolish to be working in the garage with the door open and having lost sight of her gun.

She wouldn't be that foolish again.

Foolish, foolish girl, he thought as he smiled at Cheerleader Girl, who was all tied up at the moment. It had been a risk, taking her in the apartment, where other people were so close, but it had been remarkably easy. She'd opened her door to a stranger and it had taken him about two minutes to knock her down, tape her mouth and subdue her in the chair.

She now stared at him, her blue eyes nearly bulging out of her head as she struggled against the ropes that held her in place. Her cat lay curled up on a pillow on the sofa, licking a paw without a worry in the world.

"You should be careful how much information you put on your Web pages," he said to the frightened young woman. "Don't you know that there's all kinds of nuts out there?"

She moaned against the duct tape that covered her mouth, the air rushing rapidly in and out of her nostrils. With the others he'd pulled the tape off to hear them give their final cheers, but he wouldn't be doing that here in the apartment, where somebody could hear her scream.

"But don't worry, I'm not a nut," he said. "I like to think of myself as an avenger, so to speak. Allow me to introduce myself. I call myself Mr. Payback."

Her eyes filled with confusion and she shook her head. "Ah, I see you're wondering why I'm here with you," he continued. "I've been reading your blogs and your words there have confirmed to me that you're just another mean-girl cheerleader."

As he pulled his knife from his pocket, she screamed into the duct tape and struggled frantically against the binds that held her. Although the apartment was cool, beads of perspiration dotted her forehead.

He took his gloved fingers and ran them across her brow and she shrank back from his touch. "You're sweating, Cheerleader Girl. You mentioned in your blog that you hated fat people because they sweat so much. I'll bet you hated all those fat kids in high school. All those losers who just wanted to be like you, all those kids who just wanted to be your friend."

She was begging. Although she could make nothing more than garbled noises, she was begging for her life with her eyes. But he held the power and as she mewled and sobbed, the power expanded inside him, filling him up with the familiar self-righteous rage.

"I'm afraid I'm going to have to hurt you," he said. "But consider it payback for all the kids you hurt when you were in high school." There would be no mistake that she was his; he'd see to it. This time instead of leaving numbers on the floor or on the wall, he'd put them where nobody would be able to miss them.

She was conscious for the first number that he carved into her arm. She was conscious for the second, but by the time he began working on the third, she'd passed out.

When he was finished, he sat on her sofa and petted the cat and waited for her to regain consciousness.

Chapter 25

"Take a day off and all hell breaks loose," Ricky said from the backseat of the car. It was just after noon on Monday and the team was headed to an apartment building where patrolmen responding to a welfare check indicated that the Butcher had struck again.

Jordan was desperately hoping the patrolmen were wrong. She was supposed to have been the next victim, and if he'd just chosen somebody off the street, then there was no way they could guess what his next move would be.

"Let's just hope the responding officers have it wrong," Jordan said, speaking her thoughts aloud.

"What do we know about the victim?" Ricky asked.

"Name is Tracy Baldwin," Anthony replied. "She works as a receptionist at a dental clinic and when she didn't show up this morning, her coworkers got worried. Apparently she's very responsible and according to them would never just not show up without calling in." Anthony paused to check a street sign, then turned left and continued talking. "Apparently they tried to call her all morning and finally at noon one of her coworkers went to her apartment. Her car was in the parking lot and when nobody answered the knocks on the door, the coworker called the police for a well check."

"And apparently Tracy Baldwin wasn't so well," Ricky said with his usual lack of sensitivity.

Jordan already had a tension headache banging at the base of her skull. All she'd wanted the night before was a good night's sleep, but her conversation with Clint had played and replayed in her head.

He'd been right. After this one, there would always be another case demanding her attention, demanding her time. She couldn't put her personal life on hold in the hope that murder would magically disappear from the Kansas City area.

She'd finally fallen into an exhausted sleep only to dream of being tied to a chair and stabbed over and over again by Danny McCall. She'd awakened more tired than when she'd gone to bed.

Glancing out the window, she realized they were almost to the scene, and her headache increased. John and Adam were in a car behind them and within minutes they would know if their killer had changed all the rules.

The apartment complex was like a hundred others in Kansas City, solid and square two-story buildings arranged around a modest swimming pool. They parked in the lot and then left the cars to search for apartment number 2112.

It was only when they walked around the pool area that they saw a patrolman standing on a balcony and he motioned to them. They entered the building and headed for the stairs that led up to the second floor.

Nobody spoke. It was as if all of them were mentally preparing for what lay ahead. It didn't help that the patrolman standing guard at the door to the apartment appeared pale and shaky.

Adam was the first one inside and he took one step into the living room and his beautiful dark coffee-colored skin took on a gray cast. "Jesus," he said.

The horror in the single word infused Jordan as she looked at the dead young woman tied to the chair, a dead cat splayed across her lap. "She was a dental receptionist, for God's sake," she said with a sudden explosion of anger.

Maybe she'd been wrong about what the numbers meant; maybe it hadn't been about cheerleaders at all. This didn't make sense at all. It didn't fit with the others.

"At least we don't have to look too hard for the numbers," Ricky said, and pointed to her arm where the familiar sequence of digits had been carved into her skin.

"We're looking for a fucking psycho," Anthony exclaimed.

"Agent McNight said he wasn't crazy," Ricky protested.

"He killed a cat. He's killing women." Anthony raised his voice in outrage. "Don't tell me he's not a fucking psycho."

"Everyone calm down," Jordan said, and drew a steadying breath to calm her own emotions. "We have work to do."

As they began processing the scene, a wave of despair swept through Jordan. This changed everything. Tracy Baldwin was a full decade younger than the other victims. She definitely wasn't what the detectives had identified as a target victim.

Dammit, Jordan was supposed to be a target victim. She'd almost hoped he'd come after her, because she wanted to take him out, needed to get him off the streets.

What was driving this killer? And how could they protect the community when they couldn't begin to guess what he might do next, whom he might strike next?

Allison arrived on the scene and watched as the crime-scene unit vacuumed the area and lifted any prints to see if they could find a hair, a fiber, anything that might give them a clue to the identity of the killer.

The other detectives canvassed the building to see if anyone saw anything, heard anything during the time the murder was taking place. The coroner had fixed time of death sometime late afternoon the day before. They were hoping that on a Sunday afternoon people would have been home and somebody in the area had seen something that might be helpful.

Normally there was a lot of banter during the processing of a scene, but today the techs worked silently, speaking only when necessary. Ricky had just gone into Tracy's bedroom to see if there was an address book or something that would give them any information about her personal relationships. Adam and John were still out canvassing the building. Anthony had gone to speak to the building manager to get next-of-kin information and Jordan and Allison stood watching the techs complete their work.

"These are the times I wish I would have become a grade-school teacher or an accountant," Allison said, her voice holding the weariness that Jordan felt through her entire body.

Allison raised a trembling hand and shoved a strand of her long blond hair behind her ear. "I've seen more horrific deaths in the last year than I thought I would see in my entire career. It's really starting to get to me."

"There's no question this is a bad one," Jordan agreed. "We've got to find out if Tracy's life somehow intersected with Joann and Betsy. There's got to be a link."

Allison frowned. "I keep thinking about the scenes. In Joann's case, the slashed paintings, and at Betsy's place all the dolls that were destroyed and now this with the cat. It's like it's not enough to kill the women—he also has to take away something they love as well. I would guess that the paintings, the dolls and the cat were all destroyed while the victims were still alive." Her frown deepened. "I think it's important to him that they see him destroy what they love before he kills them. It's a final bit of emotional terror that he wants to inflict. Maybe our unsub had something he loved taken away from him and that's what's driving that particular element of his signature."

"And that particular element wasn't present at Jenny's scene, unless she loved that sofa more than anything else in her life," Jordan replied.

Allison smiled ruefully. "We both know Jenny wasn't killed by this guy. The killer told you that in his phone call, and the numbers not being at that scene confirms it."

Jordan nodded. "It's just a matter of time before her husband is charged with the crime. His alibi is weak and he has a history as a wife beater." She glanced over to where Tracy's body was being bagged on a gurney. "I thought the numbers related to a cheer, that he was killing cheerleaders, but this one doesn't fit."

"Yes, it does," Ricky said from behind the two women. "I found something in the bedroom you need to see."

"What now?" Jordan muttered as she and Allison followed Ricky down the short hallway. There were two bedrooms. The first was small and obviously a guest room with a bright red futon, a dainty nightstand and a dresser. The bathroom was next, neat and tidy with a shower curtain sporting pink high heels and red lips.

The master bedroom was bigger, with a double bed that hadn't been made, a dresser with a large mirror and a small wooden desk where a laptop computer was open.

"I noticed the computer was on and when I touched the mouse it came up on this page," he said.

Both Allison and Jordan bent closer to look at the colorful screen. "Well, there's our connection," Allison said flatly.

Jordan felt a new sickness well up inside her as she looked at the computer screen that displayed Tracy's MySpace page with her screen name of Cheerleader Girl.

The bio in the left-hand corner indicated that she had been a high school and college cheerleader and still taught cheerleading and pom-pom courses for community education.

Jordan straightened, a new crashing wave of utter despair nearly drowning her. "I thought it was about us," she said softly. "I thought it was about our specific cheerleading squad, somebody from our high school who hated us. But now we have to believe that any young woman who has ever been a cheerleader is a potential victim."

"Do you have any idea how many women that could be in a city the size of Kansas City?" Allison asked. "Thousands. We're talking about thousands of potential victims."

"Stop trying to cheer me up," Jordan said dismally. "Pack it up, Ricky," she said, indicating the laptop. "Maybe we'll get lucky and this creep contacted her via her e-mail."

"Look on the bright side, Jordan," Ricky said. "Maybe this means you aren't a potential victim at all."

"Somehow that doesn't make me feel better," she replied, thinking of all the victims still out there unless they caught the Butcher before he struck again.

It was Wednesday night and Jordan was in bed with Clint. She'd come directly from the job, exhausted and dispirited by the lack of progress on the cases that haunted both her days and her nights.

She and Clint had just made love and even though the lovemaking had been amazing, she still felt tense and on edge, like a simmering teapot about to boil.

The only other case that had ever gotten to her as much as this one had been her sister's murder. She hadn't officially worked it, but it had eaten at her for years. She now felt as if she were being eaten alive and couldn't find the source of the disease. The press had made the cheerleader connection and the mayor was going crazy, pressuring them all for a quick end to this madness.

"You spoke to Della?" he asked as he stroked through her hair.

"I finally broke down and called her this afternoon," she replied. She'd been too angry to call earlier. It had been a difficult conversation. "I told her I didn't think it was a good idea for us to hang out together anymore, that she'd crossed the lines when she gave my address to Danny."

"How did she take it?" he asked.

"Like she takes most things. Badly. She accused me of being a fake friend, told me that I really hadn't changed since high school and she'd just been friendly with me because she felt sorry for me when we reconnected. Dane was cheating on me and my own daughter didn't even like me." She broke off as Clint tightened his arms around her.

"I'm sorry," he said.

"Don't be. She didn't hurt me. All she did was confirm the fact that I don't want to be friends with a woman who has such hate in her heart." Her life would be just fine without Della in it, she told herself.

"I heard Ray Taylor was arrested for the murder of his wife."

"One of the more positive things that have happened in the last couple of days." She snuggled closer against his warm body. "He got drunk and stupid and started running his mouth to his best friend. The friend came to us and said Ray had told him he killed Jenny, then tried to make the scene look like our serial killer. Apparently it had been a volatile relationship. Jenny had been abused for years and had finally contacted a divorce lawyer. Somehow Ray found out about it and he snapped. But I don't want to talk about any of this. Let's talk about something more pleasant."

"Have you done any Christmas shopping yet?"

She laughed. "I hate to admit it, but I'm one of those frantic shoppers who run through the stores on Christmas Eve. Every year I swear I'm going to do things differently, but I guess I like that last-minute mad dash."

"Has Mandy given you a list?"

"Only as long as my arm. I need to get with Dane so we can decide which one of us is going to buy what."

"You know what I want for Christmas?" he asked. "I want you to consider moving in with me."

She tensed and then rolled out of his embrace.

"I just don't know if I'm ready to make that kind of commitment."

He sat up on one elbow, his eyes glittering in the semidarkness of the room. "Don't know if you're ready or unwilling to consider it?"

"What difference does it make? The result is the same," she countered. She sat up. "Clint, I told you at the very beginning that my life was complicated, that I wasn't looking for a relationship in my life."

"Okay, so what are we doing?"

"Having fun?"

"If that's what you need, then that's what we're doing," he replied.

"I've got to go," she said, suddenly needing to get away from him. It was becoming too easy to come to him when she needed to be held, when the world got too confusing and she needed support. He was becoming far too important to her and that scared her.

"You can't stay the night?" he asked, obviously disappointed.

"No, I really need to get back home." She slid out of the bed and grabbed her clothes, then went into the adjoining bathroom. Dammit, she didn't want to fall in love with Clint. She wasn't ready to put her heart on the line again for love. And yet she knew that was exactly what was happening. He'd gotten to her with his sexy grin and easygoing nature. Her life was a mess and being in love felt damned inconvenient and she couldn't trust that Clint was really all in for the long haul.

When she returned to the bedroom, he was out of the bed and had pulled on a pair of jogging pants. "Sure I can't convince you to stay?" he asked.

She shook her head. "Not tonight."

He walked with her out of the bedroom and down the hall to the front door. Once there he took her into his arms and stared intently into her eyes. "Jordan, I've let you set the pace with us, but you have to know by now that I'm in love with you."

Although he'd never said the words before, she'd known it. She'd felt it in his kiss, in his touch, in the way he gazed at her when he thought she wasn't watching. Still, the words created both a spark of joy and a touch of fear inside her.

"You don't have to do anything about it," he added. "It's just something I wanted you to know." He leaned down and kissed her on the cheek. "I'll talk to you tomorrow."

A moment later she was in her car and headed home. He loved her. They were good together, so why couldn't she just let herself go? Embrace the fact that she loved him, too?

It all came back to that faint underlying fear that somehow she didn't deserve to be happy, a feeling she'd suffered since her sister's murder.

Julie had been the victim, but Jordan had taken on the emotional baggage of being a victim. Jordan knew enough about victimology to recognize that often people who have a crime committed against them suffer some irrational thoughts. They believe that somehow it was their fault or that they could have prevented whatever happened to them by being smarter or stronger.

That night that Jordan had told Clint about Julie's death, he'd said that if Julie hadn't sneaked out that night, then she probably would have another night. Julie had always been stubborn, not easily swayed once she got an idea in her head. Even if Jordan had called and told her parents that Julie was planning on sneaking out, that didn't mean they would have stopped her.

It hadn't been her fault, but rationally knowing that couldn't take away the fear of loving Clint, the fear of putting her heart on the line again and risking another heartbreak. She was afraid that fate would rush in and steal whatever happiness she might try to grasp for herself.

She pulled into her driveway and punched the button on her remote to open the garage door.

As she pulled into the enclosure, she thought of the other thing Clint had once said to her. He'd told her that she was the captain of her own ship, and at the moment she felt that the ship was sinking.

He stood in front of Jordan's house and watched as the lights came on. He could have gone inside when she'd pulled into the garage. It would have been easy to hide in the shadows of the night and as the door opened just step into the garage.

He'd spent the evening hours parked just down the street from her ex-husband's house watching the two preteen girls in the front yard. They'd been practicing their cheerleading, waving tissue-paper pom-poms and kicking their skinny legs into the air.

The dark-haired one had kicked higher than Mandy, but it was Mandy who held his attention. Her blond hair had sparkled in the dying gasps of sunset. So like her mother.

And her mother loved her very much.

The cries began in his head. Pitiful and heart-wrenching, they tugged at his very soul. So much pain. Nobody should have to suffer that kind of humiliation, that kind of degradation.

"Shhh," he said, and touched a finger to his forehead in an attempt to quiet the weeping.

He'd driven away from Dane's house with the knowledge that Jordan and the daughter she loved more than anything else on the face of the earth would never live to see this Christmas.

Chapter 26

"Talk to me, people," Sergeant Wendt said as he stood in the conference room where Tracy Baldwin's crime-scene photos had been added to the bulletin board with Joann's and Betsy's. He looked haggard, as if he'd aged twenty years in the last couple of weeks. "Give me something I can take to the captain, who can take it to the mayor."

Jordan knew the kind of pressure he was under, the kind of pressure they were all under. The press was going wild and somebody had leaked the information about the numbers. The mayor was screaming for his police department to get the killer behind bars and the public was demanding action.

The ass chewings began at the top and worked down the chain of command to every cop out on the street, but in particular to Jordan and the detectives working the case.

Although Jordan didn't believe anyone from her team had leaked the information about the numbers, she was also pissed that it had gotten out into the public. At least nobody had made the connection about the childish cheer. Still, the TIPS line had been busy all morning with people calling in about the weird guy down the block who lived at 2468 Oak Street, or somebody who'd dreamed that the number 2468 was the mark of aliens who were murdering women after attempting to impregnate them.

As she sat and tried to listen to what the others were sharing about the cases, which basically added up to a big fat nothing, she thought of the phone call she'd received from Clint just as she'd been about to walk out her door.

"I don't care if you don't love me," he'd said when she answered. "The important thing is that I love you. If you just want to have meals on the run and wild, passionate sex with me whenever it's convenient, I'm definitely good with that."

She'd laughed, and she'd felt optimistic as she'd driven into headquarters, but the minute she stepped off the elevator, the weight of the crimes and their lack of any progress in finding the killer struck her with a weary fist in the stomach.

"I think we need to bring in Danny McCall again," John said. "He was our best suspect for the Hathoway and Baker murders. We need to reinterrogate him for this latest one."

"Then get him in here," Benny said. "I need something to take to the press, something other than the fact that our victim pool now includes every woman who has ever picked up a pom-pom and done the splits for her football team."

"The techs lifted over a dozen prints at the Baldwin scene," Anthony said. "Unfortunately, according to Tracy's friends and coworkers, she liked to entertain often."

"I'm sure our guy is smart enough to wear gloves," Ricky added. "It's doubtful one of those prints will be his."

"We figure she opened the door to him," Adam said. "There was no forced entry and there was a knot on the back of her head. She opened the door, he shoved in and pushed her back, she fell and hit her head and he quickly overpowered her."

"Danny McCall has that kind of physical strength," Anthony said.

"But it wouldn't take somebody too strong to overwhelm her," Jordan protested. "The attacker had the element of surprise on his side."

"Just get me something," Benny exclaimed, then stalked out of the room and slammed the door behind him.

There was a collective sigh.

"I'll get Danny McCall on the phone and tell him we need to speak with him again," Anthony said.

"Ricky, John and I will head back to the apartments to talk to the neighbors we couldn't contact in the last couple of days." Adam stood. "Maybe we'll still find somebody who saw or heard something."

As they all began to rise to head to their particular destinations, Jordan and Allison remained seated at the table. "This guy is like a phantom," Jordan said as she flipped though the reports in front of her. "Nothing left behind at either of the first two murders and there's no reason for me to think he got careless at the Baldwin scene."

"I don't think he's going to get careless anytime soon. Unfortunately there's no indication that he's beginning to disintegrate. He was as organized and in control at Tracy's as he was with the first two."

"But he took a risk at Tracy's. Both Joann and Betsy lived in relatively isolated places. Joann's closest neighbors were miles away and Betsy lived on a three-acre lot. Killing Tracy in her apartment was definitely risky."

"He's growing bolder, more powerful in his own mind. Eventually that will probably get him caught, but I just don't see it happening anytime soon. He apparently knows about forensics. He's extremely careful."

Jordan smiled at her ruefully. "With all the cop shows on television everyone knows about forensic evidence." Her smile dropped. "Initially I was so sure it had to be somebody I went to school with, somebody who had attended the reunion that night. But with Tracy Baldwin's murder I don't know what to think. She just doesn't fit."

"But she was definitely killed by the same person," Allison replied. "The signatures were exactly the same. I've been looking over everything you have in the files and I think our trigger was possibly the article in the paper about Joann and her donation of artwork to the school. I think maybe he saw that picture of all of you as cheerleaders and that somehow set off his rage. This is somebody who has a profound hatred for cheerleaders and it doesn't appear to matter when or at what school they were cheerleaders."

"That sounds so stupid," Jordan said. "I mean, who could hate cheerleaders that much?"

Allison raised a pale blond eyebrow. "Any teenage girl who ever wanted to belong. Any teenage boy who wanted to date a cheerleader and was shot down. There are probably tons of people who look back on their high school days and could confess that they harbored a secret hatred for the girls who got to be cheerleaders."

"But this has to be about more than that," Jordan said as she stared down at the latest crime-scene photos of Tracy Baldwin. "I want it to be for a reason more than just because he didn't get a date with the girl of his dreams."

"I agree," Allison replied. "I think we're looking for somebody who had a tremendous loss in their life, a loss they attribute to cheerleaders. Whatever it is, that loss has built up a rage that has exploded now and he's punishing cheerleaders by killing not just them, but also by taking away what they care about first."

"But his rage, it's a controlled one," Jordan said thoughtfully. "It's vented very specifically."

"What do you know about Danny McCall's family life when you were all in school together?"

"Not much. If he had problems, he didn't talk about them. According to Clint, the last thing teenage boys want to do is tell anyone if they're having any kind of personal problems."

"I'm sure that's true, but we need to start checking the backgrounds of the suspects we have and see if any of them have something in their past that might account for this kind of rage."

"The killer doesn't seem to be working on any kind of timeline." Jordan reached out and grabbed her cup of coffee and took a sip.

"True, but with Jenny's murder off the board, all the others have occurred on the weekend. Maybe I was wrong about him working shift work. Maybe he has a regular job and is off on the weekends." Allison rubbed her forehead.

"Headache?" Jordan asked sympathetically.

"I'm afraid it's burnout." Allison dropped her head to her lap. "I'm thinking once we tie up this case, maybe I need to take some time off, like the rest of my life."

"You don't mean that," Jordan protested. "This is in your blood."

"Maybe too much." Allison stood, as if finding the conversation too personal. "I'm going to head to the lab and see if I can hurry some of the reports along. I'll see you later this afternoon."

As she left the room, Jordan focused once again on the reports, seeking something, anything, that might help them identify the unsub that was killing beautiful, vital women.

During the rest of the morning Jordan spent the time on Tracy's laptop and checked the messages and information her Web site and e-mail contained.

Tracy had been chatty, too chatty about personal information that could lead somebody to her doorstep. The woman had been foolish enough to mention local landmarks, favorite restaurants near her apartment building. She'd mentioned the kind of car she drove and how she could walk to one particular coffee shop when the weather was nice.

Apparently she hadn't recognized the danger of putting so much out there in cyberspace. She'd practically given the killer a map to her front door. That hadn't been all she'd done.

Tracy also loved to blog. She'd blogged almost every day about her life and her thoughts. Her opinions weren't always popular and there were several spirited debates about obesity, body odor and the fine art of being selfish. Although blog-land was notorious for flame wars, surprisingly there were no comments on Tracy's blogs that Jordan felt crossed a civil line.

She would hand the laptop off to the computer geeks who would spend their time identifying the people who had contacted Tracy via her e-mail and whatever other information they could glean, but Jordan wasn't optimistic that they'd find anything useful.

It was just after noon when Anthony stuck his head in the door. "Danny McCall is here and he's saying he won't talk to anyone but you. We've got him in room two and he's not a happy camper."

"Who is?" she asked rhetorically as she got up from the table.

Danny was clearly agitated when Jordan and Anthony entered the small interrogation room. Sweat dotted his broad forehead and he jumped up from the chair at the sight of Jordan.

"Sit," Anthony commanded as he placed a hand on the butt of his gun. Danny glared at him belligerently. "You can either make this easy or you can make it hard, but I gotta tell you I'm not in a good mood and if you give me half a reason, I'll bust you in the head," Anthony warned.

"Danny, please," Jordan said.

Danny eased down in the chair, his eyes blazing with anger as he kept his gaze on Anthony. "You all have some sort of a vendetta against me," he said, and looked at Jordan. "First you had that cop following me everywhere I went and now you've got me back in here for something I didn't do."

"We need to know where you were Sunday," Anthony said.

"I saw the news about that girl who got murdered. You aren't going to pin that on me," Danny exclaimed. "What the hell is wrong with you people? Why are you bothering me with this?"

"Just answer the questions, Danny," Jordan said as she sat across from him at the table.

Danny raked a hand through his hair, his face losing none of its florid color. "I was home. Alone. Like I always am. Are you going to arrest me for being home alone?"

"Did anyone stop by to see you? Did you speak with anyone on the phone?" Anthony asked.

"No and no," Danny replied. "I'd bought a new puzzle the day before and I just wanted peace and quiet to work on it. It's a tough one, 3-D, and with more pieces than I've ever tried to put together. Maybe it's now a crime to sit home and work on a puzzle?" He glared at Anthony once again, but some of the redness had left his face.

"What about your family, Danny? Tell me about them," Jordan said.

He sat back in the chair and frowned at her. "My family? What do they have to do with anything?"

"Let's just say I'm curious," Jordan replied. There was no question that through the years good old Danny had acquired a bit of an edge, but maybe it was just because of the fact that he was seated in a police interrogation room.

Danny shrugged his broad shoulders. "My parents retired a couple of years ago and moved to Florida. My sister lives in Omaha, Nebraska."

"Your sister? I didn't know you had a sister," Jordan said.

"She's four years older than us. She was already out of high school and away at college when we were going to school."

"Was she a cheerleader?" Jordan leaned forward in her chair.

"Nah, she wanted to be. I think she tried out, but she's big like me. Nobody wants to see a fat cheerleader. What does this have to do with me? With the murders?" he asked in frustration.

"Was she upset that she didn't make the cheerleader squad?" Anthony moved closer to Danny.

"Jeez, I don't know. It was a long time ago," Danny replied. "I guess she was probably upset. I don't remember—I was just a kid. Are we done here?"

Anthony motioned to the door and Jordan got up from the table. "We'll be right back. You just sit tight," he said.

They left the room and moved to the pane of glass that allowed them to see Danny without him seeing them. "What do you think?" Jordan asked.

"I'd like to get a warrant and check out his apartment. The murder weapon hasn't been found. Maybe we'll get lucky and find it in Danny's place."

"You think he's the killer?"

Anthony looked at her soberly. "What do you think?"

Jordan stared into the window. Danny had gotten up from the table and paced the room. He stopped in front of his chair and slammed his hands down on the top of the table, as if unable to control himself.

Jordan looked back at Anthony. "To be honest, I don't know what to think."

"The sister thing, that fits with what Allison said. Maybe she was really upset by not making the squad. Maybe she took it out on Danny boy."

"That feels a little forced, but I suppose we could hold him for forty-eight hours without charging him with anything, get our warrant and check out the apartment. But if we don't find anything, we'll have to cut him loose."

"I'm comfortable with that," Anthony replied.

"Let me check it with Benny and I'll be right back."

Benny was thrilled to grasp at anything that might have the appearance of forward motion. Danny was taken to a holding cell and Anthony went to talk to a judge about a warrant.

Jordan cooled her heels in the conference room, waiting for Anthony to return so they could go check out Danny's place. It took an hour for them to receive the search warrant and it was almost four when Anthony and Jordan left headquarters.

"Ricky finally seems to be settling in okay," Anthony said when they were in the car and headed to Danny's apartment.

"I guess. I still think he has a tendency to be a bit arrogant."

"Give it some time and we'll all knock that out of him. John sure has turned over a new leaf."

Jordan nodded. "Has he told you he's planning on retiring as soon as we catch this guy?"

Anthony shot her a look of surprise. "No, I didn't know that. He hasn't put in any papers. Sarge hasn't mentioned it."

"Maybe he hasn't told Sarge yet. All he told me was that when we catch this guy, he's out of here." Jordan gazed unseeing out the window. "I can't imagine what life is going to be like when we do finally catch this guy. This case has consumed me more than any one I've ever worked on before."

"I know what you mean," Anthony replied. "I haven't even had time to think about how much I hate my ex-wife in the last month or so."

Jordan laughed. "Anthony, you really need to get a girlfriend."

"I know, I know. My mom asked me the other day if I was gay. It's not funny," he exclaimed as Jordan laughed once again.

The laughter stopped as they pulled into Danny's apartment complex. "It would be so great if we could just solve this now. Find a knife in a drawer, a lock of Betsy's hair hanging above the bed, a bracelet that belonged to Joann and maybe some fingernail clippings from Tracy," Anthony said as he pulled into a parking space.

"That list sounds more like somebody doing a voodoo curse than taking souvenirs," Jordan replied as they got out of the car.

"John and Adam are supposed to meet us here," Anthony said as they headed toward the building where Danny lived.

"What about Ricky?"

"He was going to continue canvassing Tracy's neighbors before calling it a night. I called ahead—the super is supposed to meet us at the door to let us in." When they got to the door, there was nobody waiting for them.

Anthony leaned against the door with a sigh of frustration and looked at his watch. "Why is it that half of this job involves standing around and waiting on somebody?"

"Let's just hope the wait is worth our while," Jordan replied.

It was thirty minutes later that John and Adam, Sergeant Wendt and the building manager arrived and they finally stepped into Danny's living room. "John, Adam, you two take the bedrooms, and Jordan and I will start in here and the kitchen," Anthony said. Benny was there strictly in a supervisory position.

"We want a thorough search, but let's not get destructive," Jordan said, knowing that there were times when searches could be downright ugly. "I'll take the kitchen," she said to Anthony as he started in the living room.

They hadn't been working for long when Adam came out of the spare bedroom. "Bingo," he said, and showed them a knife case. Using his gloved hands, he opened the case to display a hunting knife with an eight-inch blade.

"The coroner said the wounds were made with a six-to eight-inch blade," Anthony said, his voice holding the thrum of excitement. "Where did you find it?"

"Tucked in the back of a drawer," Adam replied.

"The blade looks clean," Jordan observed.

"Forensics should be able to get something off it," Benny replied.

John came out of the bathroom carrying a box of latex gloves. "Found these in the bathroom sink cabinet."

"Bag it and tag it and see if you turn up anything else," Benny said. "I think we already have enough to charge him, but finish the search and we'll see where we stand."

A thorough search took hours and this one was no different. The only other thing found that could be defined as possibly incriminating was a cutout of the article about Joann along with the picture of the cheerleaders.

It was enough for Benny to take to the district attorney, and as Jordan left to go home, she was cautiously optimistic that they'd gotten their man. It was after eight and she was starving.

She grabbed her cell phone from her purse and called Clint. "Want to meet me at the Burger Shack? I haven't eaten dinner and I'm too tired to go home and cook."

"If you're that tired, why don't you head on home and I'll meet you there and I'll bring Chinese?" he countered.

"That sounds wonderful," she replied.

By the time she got home, she was even more grateful that he'd offered the food and the company. She was exhausted and starving and entertaining some doubts about Danny's guilt despite what they'd turned up at his apartment.

It was just before nine when Clint arrived, carrying bags from the Chinese Wok, one of her favorite places to eat. As he unloaded the food on the table, she got out plates and silverware and told him about what had transpired during the day.

"You don't sound pleased about Danny's imminent arrest," he said.

She scooped another serving of sweet-and-sour chicken onto her plate. "I'm not one hundred percent convinced Danny is our man. I'm not sure Danny has the mental capacity to pull off the murders. Of course, he could have me totally fooled." She shrugged. "The forensics will tell the tale of the knife and we'll see what the district attorney decides to do. I don't know how to explain it, but I just have a gut feeling that it's not over yet."

"There you go again, looking for the world to explode around you," he said with a teasing smile.

"You're right," she agreed. "I need to just enjoy the moment of hoping that we've gotten our man."

"You know, I've been thinking. Maybe the other night I made you the wrong kind of proposition."

She looked at him curiously. "What are you talking about?"

"When I asked you to move in with me, maybe I should have said what I really meant—that I'd like you to marry me." He held up a hand to keep her from replying. "Don't say anything. I'm just putting it out on the table along with the crab rangoons and the egg drop soup. I just figured maybe you didn't realize how serious I was about a commitment to you, to us. I want you to be my wife, Jordan. I want to spend the rest of my life with you."

He leaned back in his chair and smiled at her. "I'm a patient man, Jordan, and I know that you have a lot on your plate right now. You don't have to give me an answer now. I mean, I haven't exactly bought the ring yet and I don't want your answer until you're absolutely sure of what you want."

It was on the tip of her tongue. The words "I love you" tingled in her mouth, wanting to be released, but she bit them back. "A crab rangoon, that's what I want right now," she said, and reached across the table.

He smiled, as if he saw into her heart and knew what she felt for him, and forgave her for not being ready to acknowledge it.

At ten thirty he kissed her good-bye, and she watched as he walked down the path to his car in the driveway. What was holding her back? She didn't question his love for her, nor did she question that she loved him.

She realized Clint wasn't the cheating boyfriend he'd been in high school. He'd become a man she admired, a man she trusted. So what was holding her back? She knew that until she answered that question, she'd never move forward with her life.

Chapter 27

"Have you heard?" Anthony slid into the chair next to Jordan in the conference room. "The knife was clean. They're cutting Danny McCall loose." He smacked his palm down on the table in frustration. "Dammit, I thought we had him. At least we're putting a tail on him. If he is guilty, he's going to have trouble committing another crime."

"At least we have that," Jordan replied. She looked at her watch. It was late, almost ten, and she was exhausted. She'd spent the day catching up on paperwork, waiting for the lab report to come back on the knife.

"You taking off tomorrow?" Anthony asked.

She nodded. "Hopefully no bodies will show up to interfere with the day I have planned. I'm going Christmas shopping in the morning and then Mandy is coming over tomorrow evening and we're going to put my tree up."

"Sounds like a nice day."

"I need it. I need to clear my head and embrace a little spirit of the season," she replied.

"John's convinced that Danny's our man. Maybe with him under surveillance we can all have a Christmas with no new bodies," Anthony replied.

"We could definitely all use a break." She shoved back from the table. "And on that note, I'm out of here."

"I'll walk you out," Anthony said, and together they grabbed their coats and headed out of the conference room and to the elevators. As they left the building and walked out into the cold night air, they talked about their Christmas plans.

"I'm thinking about hiring a date for Christmas dinner so my mom will get off my back," he said jokingly.

"What about Ashley up in accounting? She's cute and I've noticed whenever she's around you, she gives you the eye."

"Really? I've never noticed." Anthony perked up. "You think she'd be interested in me?"

"It's just women's intuition, but I think she could be if you showed a little interest in her," Jordan replied.

"Ah, love is in the air," Anthony exclaimed as they reached Jordan's car. "Drive safe," he said, and gave her hood a playful smack as she slid in behind the steering wheel and started the engine.

As she drove home, Jordan found her thoughts once again going to Danny McCall. Just because the knife had been clean didn't mean he was innocent. It simply meant that particular knife wasn't the murder weapon.

There was also the fact that he'd confessed that his sister had wanted to be a cheerleader and had been denied, that she'd been upset. Although Jordan couldn't imagine that being the motive for these murders, she couldn't imagine anything being a reasonable motive.

A part of her desperately wanted to believe it was Danny and that it was just a matter of time before they got their ducks in a row and could make an arrest that would stick.

She slept without dreams that night and awoke the next morning feeling more refreshed than she'd felt in months. She drank two cups of coffee, then showered and dressed and was at the mall by nine, when it opened.

It was almost impossible to be in a bad mood while shopping to the sounds of "Jingle Bell Rock" and "I Want a Hippopotamus for Christmas." She found herself humming along with the music as she picked out PlayStation games and a pretty pink sweater for Mandy. She bought her father a robe and her mother a new cookbook. She'd drop them off at their house Christmas morning while Mandy was enjoying Christmas with Dane.

Jordan had agreed that Mandy should spend Christmas Eve and Christmas morning in her own home. Dane would bring Mandy over midafternoon on Christmas Day to spend that night with Jordan.

In the meantime she had tonight to look forward to, an entire evening of bonding with Mandy while they put up the tree. They'd drink hot cocoa and maybe bake some cookies. Tonight she would put all thoughts of murder and Julie and the absence of a relationship with her parents out of her head. She intended to focus on giving Mandy a night of sweet memories.

It was just after noon when she got home. She was pleased that her cell phone hadn't rung with a work emergency and there was only one message on her home phone from Clint. He knew she was spending the night with Mandy and had called just to say that he hoped his two favorite women had a good time.

The call warmed her heart, just like he did every time she was with him. What she felt for him was different from what she'd once felt for Dane. Dane had been her first adult love. She'd been starry-eyed with the fact that an older, more sophisticated man wanted her.

She'd been eager to play house, to have babies and build a family to replace the one she'd lost when Julie had been murdered.

She felt no such urgency with Clint, no need to build something to replace what had been taken from her. Her life was full without him. She didn't need him, but she wanted him.

She'd realized today that the decision of whether she had a future with Clint wasn't hers alone to make. Mandy had to have a say, because it was her future, too, that Jordan would be throwing in with Clint.

So tonight they would decorate her tree and have fun

together and decide if Jordan and Mandy had a future with Clint.

John was half-asleep in his chair watching a local cable channel that broadcast mostly infomercials and community-interest stories. He would have liked to be assigned as a tail on Danny McCall, but Sergeant Wendt had warned John off the man.

"We've got it covered, John. Besides, McCall knows your ugly mug and our goal is for him not to know he's being tailed," Benny had said late that afternoon when John had prepared to leave headquarters. "I've got a four-man tag team on him. He's not going to take a crap that we don't know what he's doing."

So John had come home and collapsed in his chair. The last week of putting in his time at headquarters and then keeping an eye on Danny during his time off had taken a toll on him.

He'd thought about shooting himself when he'd first gotten home from work. He was relatively convinced that it was just a matter of time before McCall made a mistake or more evidence came to light and Danny was arrested for the murders. John had done what he could to help solve the cases and there was really no reason for him to continue to draw breath.

Not without his Mary.

Now that he'd napped a bit, his plan to end his life once again played in his mind. He pulled himself up from his chair and got a wooden TV tray and opened it in front of where he'd been sitting. He then walked into the bedroom and grabbed his gun-cleaning kit from the closet.

It had been a while since he'd cleaned his gun, and as an officer of the law he didn't want anyone who found his body to talk about how filthy it had been at the time of his death.

At least they wouldn't remember him as the drunk he'd been becoming at the end of Mary's life. No, he'd managed to clean himself up just fine. It was amazing what you could do when you put your mind to it.

The house was relatively clean and nothing embarrassing would be found when he was gone. Everything he and Mary had owned would go to their favorite charity and that would be that.

When he returned to his chair, he placed his revolver and the items he used to clean it on the tray in front of him. He unloaded the weapon and then broke it apart and squeezed a drop of solvent into the barrel and used a bore brush to scrub inside.

As he worked, a sense of peace he hadn't known since Mary's death filled him. Soon, he thought, soon I'll join her in death and I won't be alone anymore. The silence of the house would no longer matter; the absence of Mary would no longer be felt. When he had the barrel clean, he moved on to the extractor assembly, using an old toothbrush to get into all the small places.

He glanced up at the television, where *The Donna Caldwell Show* had begun. Donna Caldwell was an attractive, blond Oprah wannabe. She had a local talk show that Mary used to like to watch.

John figured the show had a home audience of about ten people, but he supposed everyone had to start somewhere. He reached for his remote control and turned up the volume on the television as Donna stared into the camera, her features somber.

"Today we're going to be talking about bullying and the new threat to our children, cyber-bullying." The camera panned out to show three women seated in chairs behind Donna. "I have three mothers with me today. Their children have all suffered the trauma of being bullied, one of them with tragic results."

As one of the women, a Linda Rivera, began to chronicle the abuse her son had taken at his school, John continued to clean his weapon, half listening to the sad tale of a boy who'd eventually had to undergo therapy to deal with his grade-school torture. He'd gone on to high school and he was graduating with honors this year.

The next mother, Susan Hackley, talked about the abuse her young daughter had suffered at the hands of two boys in her class. She'd been not only verbally abused but also pushed into the boys' bathroom, threatened on the playground and generally terrified to the point she had no longer wanted to go to school.

The third mother, Rita Copeland, had another story to tell. Her daughter had been in high school when the torment began. Her daughter had made the mistake of smiling at one of the cheerleaders' boyfriends, thus beginning a reign of terror from the squad of cheerleaders that had eventually resulted in her daughter slitting her wrists and bleeding to death.

John stopped what he was doing and stared at the television screen as the mother told about her son finding his younger sister dead on the floor in her bedroom. "Those girls killed her," Rita Copeland said. "Later we found a Web page they'd constructed where they called my daughter a crack whore and a dirty slut. They said she had AIDS and all kinds of horrible things."

Rita Copeland.

John's blood thickened and heated in his veins as he stared at the woman on the screen. Rita Copeland. As the women began to talk about the things parents should do if they suspected their child was being bullied, John's thoughts went down a wild path.

Rita Copeland.

Ricky Copeland.

Was it possible they'd gotten it wrong? That Danny wasn't the guilty one? Allison had said they were looking for somebody who'd probably suffered a loss that could be attributed to cheerleaders. Finding your younger sister dead in her bedroom would certainly fit that particular criterion.

Had Ricky been at work during the times of the murders or had he been off work? Was it possible he was paying back cheerleaders for the role they'd apparently played in his sister's death?

Don't jump to conclusions, he warned himself, all thoughts of suicide gone from his head. Everyone knew that Ricky's sister had committed suicide a couple of years ago, but nobody knew the details of the tragedy.

It was possible Rita Copeland wasn't related to Ricky. Copeland was a fairly common name. It was possible this had nothing to do with Ricky. And yet even telling himself this couldn't stop the sickness that twisted his gut.

He hurriedly began to put his gun back together again. He needed to get back into headquarters and check some things. A false charge would destroy Ricky's career and that was the last thing John wanted to do if the man was innocent.

With his revolver once again whole, he grabbed the nearby phone and punched in the number for his partner. Adam answered on the second ring.

"Where are you?" John asked.

"At home. Why? Is something up?"

"Can I stop by later? I have something I want to run by you."

"I plan on being here all evening."

"Then I'll see you sometime in the next hour or two." John hung up, strapped on his holster and then punched the off button on the television. Mary was going to have to wait.

He was parked down the street from Jordan's house, far enough away that if she looked out her window or door, she wouldn't notice him, but close enough that he could see any car that arrived in her driveway.

Soon.

Soon she would know the horror of retribution. Soon she would understand that the pain she'd caused the "little people" in high school had mattered, that the sins of the mean girls weren't magically erased by graduation and adulthood. And hopefully with her death, the cries inside his head would still for just a little while.

Throughout the past week the cries had become nearly intolerable. Centered in the middle of his brain, the incessant noise had grown louder each and every day.

She wept all the time, unremittingly, and the sound of her pain twisted his bowels and made him want to scream. But he'd managed to maintain control. He'd managed to keep it all together.

Until now.

He clenched the steering wheel tightly as he felt the rage starting its build, pressing against his chest, increasing his heartbeat. He felt light-headed with it and wanted to embrace it fully. Easy, he told himself. It wasn't time to let the beast loose. He had to be patient.

This would be his finest hour so far. With her murder and that of what she loved most, her daughter, everyone would know that he was a force to be reckoned with. He wasn't just killing a mean-girl cheerleader; he was killing a homicide detective and her daughter.

Everyone would be talking about his crimes. Women would find it difficult to sleep. They'd walk with one eye over their shoulders, afraid of who might be following them.

And maybe the young cheerleaders would think about the way they treated people. Maybe they would realize that there were consequences for bad behavior. Eventually, when enough cheerleaders had paid, maybe she would be at peace and he'd no longer be haunted by her cries.

He leaned his head back and thought about the night to come. This would be his biggest challenge, two lives in one night. The artwork at Joann's, the dolls at Betsy's and the cat at Tracy's had been only in preparation for tonight. And tonight was only a preparation for whatever came next.

He sat up straighter in the seat as he saw Dane's

car pull into Jordan's driveway. Ah, the guest of honor had arrived. All the pieces of the puzzle had fallen into place.

Dane got out of the car with Mandy, who sported a hot pink overnight bag. Together they walked up to Jordan's front door and a moment later they disappeared into the house.

It took precisely fifteen minutes for Dane to make nice with his ex-wife, tell his daughter good-bye and walk back out the front door. He pulled out of the driveway and disappeared down the block.

Now it was just a matter of waiting until darkness fell. Then there was work to be done.

Chapter 28

"Your tree looks sad," Mandy exclaimed the minute Dane walked out the door.

"That's because it needs some tender loving care," Jordan replied. She opened one of her shopping bags to show Mandy the ornaments and lights she'd purchased that morning. The family Christmas tree with all its trimmings had stayed with Dane. Last year Jordan had been in her tiny apartment and had put up only a table-size tree.

"At least it's a six-footer," Jordan said. "Much nicer than last year's model."

Mandy rolled her eyes. "Anything would have been better than last year's model." She sat down on the floor and pulled one of the bags toward her to start unpacking.

"While you get everything ready to go, how about I make us each a cup of hot cocoa?"

"With little marshmallows?" Mandy asked.

"Wouldn't have it any other way." Jordan headed into the kitchen. This was as good as it got. Christmas carols playing on the radio, hot cocoa warming on the stove and mother and daughter spending the night together—it was almost a perfect night. The only thing that would make it more perfect was if Dane wasn't returning in the morning to pick up Mandy and take her back home.

She'd done three things just before Mandy had arrived to assure that their evening together wouldn't be interrupted. She'd shut off her cell phone, turned the ringer off her landline phone and hidden her revolver underneath the sofa.

She felt no guilt about being unreachable should something happen with the cases. She'd given more than a hundred hours to the job in the last week and they were just going to have to deal with anything that came up without her for the night.

The gun was simply to make her feel secure in her own home. She didn't want it in her bedroom drawer, but she also didn't want Mandy seeing it either. Hiding it under the edge of the sofa seemed reasonable, and after Mandy went to bed, Jordan would move it back to her bedroom with her.

Although she hated to admit it, Tracy's murder had vanquished some of the fear she'd entertained over the last month. She'd been certain she would be the next potential target, but when Tracy had wound up dead, she'd felt as if the target had lifted from her back.

It wasn't just about her squad of cheerleaders. Apparently it was about all cheerleaders. While that fact made it impossible to identify the next potential victim, it had definitely taken some of the edge off Jordan's fear for her personal safety. Still, that certainly didn't mean she was going to stop being vigilant.

"Hey, Mom, these little snowmen ornaments are cool," Mandy called from the living room.

"I thought you might like them. You always loved snowmen." Jordan stirred the cocoa, poured it into mugs and then added a liberal sprinkling of tiny marshmallows to the top. She carried the mugs into the living room and set them on the coffee table.

"Better drink it while it's hot," she said as she sat on the sofa.

Mandy got up from the floor and joined Jordan. "I love Christmas," she said, and then blew on the top of her mug to cool the hot drink.

"Me, too," Jordan replied. "You know who else loves Christmas?"

"Not Daddy. He complains about everything. The music gives him a headache and shopping gives him hives." Mandy giggled. "He's like an old Scrooge." She took a sip of her drink. "So, who else likes Christmas besides you and me?"

"Clint. He has so many Christmas decorations in his house it looks like the North Pole, and his tree is twice as tall as me," Jordan replied.

"Cool, maybe I could go over and see it sometime? I really like him. Maybe we could all play Monopoly again, only this time I'll beat his butt instead of it ending in a tie."

It was the opening Jordan had hoped for. She set her mug of cocoa back on the coffee table and looked at her daughter. "I'm sure he'd really enjoy that. He likes you. He thought you were one cool kid."

Mandy grinned over the rim of her mug, her blue eyes sparkling. "He really likes you. I could tell by the way he was looking at you, all googly eyed like in the movies."

Jordan grinned. "He does like me. In fact, he's asked me to marry him."

Mandy's eyes widened. "For real? Are you going to? Can I be in the wedding? Where are you going to live? If you move in with him, will I have a room?"

"Whoa, one question at a time," Jordan protested with a laugh. "Would you be all right with me marrying him?"

"If he loves you and you love him, then I think you should get married," Mandy replied. "I mean, it would be best if you and Dad were together again, but I know that's never going to happen. Besides, you guys used to fight way too much. I think Clint will make a cool stepdad."

"If I decide to marry him and we have a wedding, then I'd want you to be my maid of honor."

Mandy frowned. "What does a maid of honor do?"

"It's the most important job anyone can have at a wedding and you usually ask your best friend to be your maid of honor."

"Am I your best friend, Mom?"

"You're my very best friend and you're my daughter. That means I get to have fun with you, but it also means I get to yell at you if you do something wrong."

Mandy giggled and the sound filled Jordan's heart. "But I guess if you're my best friend, I still can't yell at you if you do anything wrong," she said.

"That's true. That's the difference between being a mom and being a daughter."

Mandy placed her mug on the table and suddenly threw her arms around Jordan's neck. "I love you, Mom," she said, and buried her face into the crook of Jordan's neck.

"Oh, honey, I love you, too. More than anything on this earth." Jordan hugged tight, breathing in the sweet strawberry scent of her daughter's hair, loving the way her daughter fit so perfectly in her arms. No matter what size Mandy became, Jordan knew Mandy would always fit perfectly in her mother's arms. All too quickly Mandy sat up and reached for her mug of hot cocoa.

"You asked me about the living arrangements if I marry Clint," Jordan began, wishing Mandy would have stayed in her arms longer. "I think if I marry him, I'd move into his house. He has a big home, with a bedroom downstairs and three bedrooms upstairs."

She picked up her mug and took a sip and then continued. "But I want you to know that you wouldn't just have a room at Clint's. You'd have a home, and if you decided you wanted to live there with me full-time, then you could visit your dad whenever you wanted."

Mandy looked at her for a long moment and in the depths of her eyes Jordan saw a yearning, and hope jumped into Jordan's heart. Mandy tipped her mug to finish the last of her drink and then jumped up off the sofa. "Let's decorate the tree."

For a moment Jordan wanted to yank her daughter back to the sofa; she wanted to demand that Mandy tell her everything that was in her heart, confess the reasons why she refused to even consider living with her mother. But she didn't. Instead she swallowed her disappointment and got up from the sofa to help Mandy transform the plain artificial tree into a work of art.

As they strung lights and garlands, Mandy chattered about school and Megan and all things important to a twelve-year-old. "We made up a cheer using some of the moves you taught me and we've been practicing together almost every night after school."

The last thing Jordan wanted to talk about was cheerleading, but she listened as Mandy explained the cheer and then the subject moved to boys.

"There's a boy in my class. His name is Billy Waller. He hates me."

"Why do you think he hates you?" Jordan asked as she grabbed a glittery ornament to hang on one of the boughs.

"He's always giving me a little push or stealing my pencils and he calls me Mandy Candy."

Jordan smiled. "He doesn't hate you. He likes you. That's the way boys your age act when they like a girl."

"He's dumb," Mandy exclaimed, but Jordan could tell she was secretly pleased by the idea that Billy might like her.

"Why don't we go eat some dinner before we turn on the tree?" Jordan suggested when they had finished with the decorating. "It's still too light outside to get the full effect."

"Okay," Mandy agreed. "I'm starving. What are we going to eat?"

"I thought maybe we'd have some tomato soup and grilled cheese." Jordan knew that was a favorite of Mandy's.

Minutes later Mandy stirred the soup and Jordan made the grilled cheese; then they both sat at the table to eat. This time the conversation revolved around a video game Mandy loved to play. As she told Jordan about the different levels and the funny monsters she met at each level, her face was lit with animation.

A sense of pride filled Jordan. Mandy was a pretty girl, but what made Jordan proud was the fact that Mandy was a good girl. Mandy didn't like any kind of confrontation or meanness. She would bend over backward not to hurt anyone's feelings.

Somehow in the muck of their marriage, Jordan and Dane had gotten this right. From the time Mandy was a baby, they had been united and consistent in their parenting of her and the end result showed in everything Mandy did.

"I hear Claire left," Jordan said. "Do you miss her?"

"Not really. She only talked to me when Dad was around. When he wasn't around, most of the time she was on her cell phone with her friends. Don't worry. Dad will get another girlfriend. He always does."

Sometimes it was amazing how astute children could be, Jordan thought.

"What are we going to do now?" Mandy asked as they loaded the dishes into the dishwasher.

"We're going to go in and turn on our tree. Then I thought maybe we'd bake some cookies. If we bake enough, I'll take some to Clint and tell him they're from you."

"Could I wrap them up like a real present?" Mandy asked.

"We can do that," Jordan agreed, pleased that she wanted to make it nice for Clint.

With the dishes taken care of, they walked back into the living room. As they'd eaten, darkness had begun to fall and the room was now cast in the shadows of encroaching night.

As Jordan plugged in the lights on the tree, it came to life with twinkling magic. "It looks beautiful," Mandy exclaimed.

Jordan threw an arm over her daughter's shoulder and squeezed. "We're going to have the best Christmas ever, Mandy."

Mandy leaned against Jordan and in that single shining moment, in the glow from the tree and with the warmth of her daughter next to her, Jordan felt for the first time since her divorce, really for the first time since Julie's murder, as if her life was finally on track.

Adam lived in a neat, attractive ranch house in a middle-class neighborhood where it looked as if his house plan had been repeated over and over again by a builder without a creative flare.

Multicolored Christmas lights outlined the home as John hurried up the front steps. He'd spent the last couple of hours at headquarters, checking facts, reluctant to accuse a fellow officer without some sort of evidence to back up his suspicions.

What he felt now was a sick burn in the pit of his stomach. He hurried up to the front door and knocked. Maybe once he laid out everything, Adam would tell him he was nuts. Adam had always been the first one to talk John down when he got too excitable about some topic or another.

Adam opened the door. "I've been wondering what happened to you," he said as he ushered John into the entry. The air smelled of cinnamon and spice and brought a quick pang of loss to John's heart as it reminded him of his dead wife.

"I got hung up at headquarters," he replied.

"Come on into the kitchen," Adam said. "Louise just finished baking some cookies."

John followed Adam through the neat living room and into the kitchen, where Adam's wife greeted John warmly. "We haven't seen enough of you around here lately," she said as she poured the two men coffee and placed a platter of still-warm cookies in front of them.

John sat at the table and at that moment Adam's father wandered in. Clad in a bathrobe and slippers, he frowned at John. "You come to get me out of this hell-hole?" he asked. "I've never seen an upscale hotel with worse room service."

Louise grabbed the old man by the arm. "Come on, Pop, let's go back to your room. I think room service just delivered a plate of cookies there." She grabbed a small plate of the freshly baked treats and together the two of them left the room.

"How's he doing?" John asked.

Adam shrugged. "He has good days and bad days, lately more bad than good. I'm probably going to have to think about putting him in a nursing home that specializes in Alzheimer patients."

"I'm sorry, man," John offered.

Adam shrugged. "What are you going to do? Life gives you a kick, but you pick yourself up and continue on. So, what's up?"

John wanted to tell him that there were some of life's kicks that were terminal, where you didn't pick yourself up and go on but rather dreamed of death and the release of pain.

"What do you know about the death of Ricky's sister?"

Adam frowned and reached for one of the cookies. "Not much. I just know what he's mentioned, that she committed suicide a couple of years ago. Why?"

John told him about the local cable channel he'd been watching that afternoon. "I think that was Ricky's mother on the show today and according to her, her daughter committed suicide because of a squad of cheerleaders who tormented her."

Adam narrowed his eyes and set his cookie on the side of his saucer. "That doesn't necessarily mean anything," he said slowly, but it was obvious John had definitely gotten his attention.

"Ricky found the body. She slit her wrists and bled

to death in her bedroom. Ricky came home and found her there."

"That's terrible, but it doesn't make him a murderer," Adam replied, but his voice held unspoken doubt.

John understood Adam's reluctance to believe. Hell, John had struggled with the same reluctance since he'd watched that damn show. "I checked the logs at headquarters. Ricky was off work at the times of all of the murders. He fits the profile, Adam. He fits the freaking profile."

Adam leaned back in his chair and swiped his broad, big hand down the lower half of his face. "Have you thought about what you're implying?"

"I've made myself sick thinking about it," John replied. "I think we made a mistake with Danny McCall. Sure, he had a crush on Joann and Betsy and he's a bit weird, but now I don't think he's our killer."

"Have you called the sarge?" Adam asked.

"Not yet. I wanted to get your take on it before I did anything rash."

Adam blew out a deep sigh. "You've got me worried, Johnny boy. Have you called Jordan with this?"

"I tried her on her cell phone and it went right to voice mail. Then I tried her home phone and it went right to the answering machine."

"Maybe she and Mandy are out Christmas shopping or something," Adam said thoughtfully. "Was Ricky at work when you went in?"

"No, he was there this morning but left around noon. One of the guys told me he wasn't feeling well and decided to go home."

"Maybe it would be a good idea if you and I swing by his place, see if he's there and just how sick he really is," Adam suggested, and pushed back from the table. "You can drive and I'll get on my cell and try to reach both Sergeant Wendt and Jordan."

"Sounds like a plan," John agreed as he got up from the table. The thrum of anxiety that had been with him since he'd heard the television show had become an urgent cry in his head.

Bad things happened when Ricky had time off. What they had to figure out was if it was just a matter of coincidence or if he was a vicious killer hiding behind his detective shield.

Chapter 29

The kitchen smelled yummy. The last batch of sugar cookies was in the oven and Mandy was using red cellophane to wrap a plateful of the sweet treats for Clint. "You have to make sure he gets them by tomorrow," she said as she reached for a strand of green ribbon to tie the cellophane. "I don't want him to get old, hard cookies. That wouldn't be cool."

"I promise I'll get them to him tomorrow," Jordan said. "I'll drop them off at his place on my way into work first thing in the morning."

"And tell him I can't wait to play another game of Monopoly with him and this time I'm not giving him any mercy."

"I'll tell him." Jordan leaned back in her chair at the table and took a sip of her hot cocoa. It was the third cup of the evening and she figured she had enough sugar in her to last for at least a week.

"So, if you and Clint get married, then are you going to have a baby with him?"

Jordan sat up straighter in her chair, surprised by the question. "To be honest, we haven't talked about it." Sure, he'd mentioned the idea that he might have liked children if things had worked out differently with his ex-wife, but they certainly hadn't had a real dialogue about children.

"Does he already have some kids?" Mandy finished tying the bow on the cookies and looked up at Jordan.

"No."

"Then wouldn't he want one?"

"I don't know. . . . Maybe he would like to have a baby. How would you feel about it?"

"I'd be happy," Mandy replied without hesitation. "I think it would be cool to have a little brother or sister."

Jordan hadn't thought about having another baby for a very long time, but now as she considered it, she realized it wasn't such a terrible idea. She loved being a mother and she knew Clint would make a wonderful father, but it wasn't something that had to be decided tonight. She hadn't even decided yet if she wanted to accept Clint's marriage proposal. With Mandy's acceptance of the idea, there was really nothing standing in her way except herself.

The timer on the oven dinged, letting her know that the last batch of cookies was finished baking. She got up and grabbed an oven mitt and pulled them out of the oven and set the tray on a cooling rack. "Now, these we get to eat."

As she began to scoop them off the tray and onto a plate, Mandy went to the refrigerator and pulled out the jug of milk. By the time she'd poured herself a glass, Jordan had transferred the cookies to a platter and set them in the center of the table.

Over milk and cookies they talked about the past. Mandy never tired of hearing funny stories about herself, and Jordan had a cache of memories where her daughter was concerned.

As Jordan related tale after tale, she once again felt the burning desire to insist that Mandy move in with her, to demand Mandy tell her why she didn't want to be with her all the time. But she didn't want to ruin the perfect evening they were sharing. She was afraid of alienating her daughter to the point where she would be reluctant to give her anything.

They'd just finished their milk and cookies and cleaned up the kitchen when the doorbell rang. Jordan glanced at the clock and saw that it was just after nine. God, she hoped it wasn't something about work. The night had been perfect so far, and she hated the idea of anything screwing it up.

"Maybe it's Clint," Mandy said hopefully as she reached for another cookie.

"You stay here and I'll see who it is," Jordan replied. She raced to the front door and turned on the porch light and looked out. Her heart sank as she saw Ricky standing on the porch. Something must have happened and they hadn't been able to reach her by phone. Damn. She'd really been hoping for a night away from all the madness.

She opened the door and Ricky offered her an apologetic smile. "Jordan, I'm sorry to bother you at home. I tried to call you, but I only got your voice mail. I was wondering if I could come in and talk to you."

With the cold night air drifting into the open door, she hurriedly motioned him inside the entry and closed the door behind him. "Has something happened?" she asked as they entered the living room.

"No, so far Danny hasn't made a move."

"Look, Ricky, this really isn't a good time unless there's some kind of an emergency. I've got my daughter here with me and I'm off duty. Is this something that can wait until tomorrow?" She had no idea what he wanted to talk to her about, but if it wasn't an emergency, she didn't want to deal with it now.

"Okay, that's cool. Hey, can I meet your daughter? I've heard so much about her from you." At that moment Mandy walked out of the kitchen and into the living room.

Ricky smiled. "You must be Mandy," he said as he walked over to where she stood. He held out a hand. "I'm Ricky. Ricky Copeland."

As Mandy reached out and grabbed his hand to shake it, he pulled her up against him, grabbed his gun and held it to her head.

For a sickening moment Jordan tried to make sense of what had just happened. Was this some kind of a stupid joke? Mandy's eyes were huge, her features frozen in the kind of fear no mother ever wants to see on the face of her child.

"Ricky, what are you doing? Let her go." Jordan's voice seemed to come from some faraway planet as a roar of alarm resounded in her head.

"What am I doing?" The pleasant smile never left Ricky's lips as he yanked Mandy closer against him. The gun remained unwavering, pressed against the temple of Mandy's head. "I'm doing what I do best, Jordan. I'm ridding the world of mean girls like you."

The twinkling lights on the Christmas tree, the scent of the freshly baked cookies and the sound of the carols playing on the radio all disappeared as Jordan fell down a dark tunnel into the horror of realization.

Ricky was the Butcher. And he was here now with her. And worst of all, he held in his arms the thing that Jordan loved more than anything else on the face of the earth.

Chapter 30

Ricky wasn't home.

John and Adam left the small rental house where Ricky lived, and got back into John's car. Adam got on the phone to Benny. "He's not here," he said. "What do you want us to do?"

John thrummed his fingers on the steering wheel, the tension inside him making him want to scream. Something bad was going to happen. He could feel it in his gut, feel it in his bones.

With each passing moment his belief that Ricky was the Butcher hadn't decreased, but rather had grown to sickening proportions. He'd tried to twist and turn what he now knew about Ricky in every way, shape and form to give the kid the benefit of the doubt, but it just wasn't happening.

"Where to?" he asked as Adam got off the phone.

"Benny wants us to check on Jordan. He's tried to reach her on her cell phone and her home phone and he hasn't gotten an answer. Jordan told me yesterday that she was spending tonight with her daughter and they were going to decorate her Christmas tree and bake cookies. She should be home. It worries me that she isn't answering any of her phones."

The bad feeling in the pit of John's stomach burned hotter. "You don't think he killed Tracy Baldwin to take the heat off Jordan?"

Adam raked his hand down his jaw. "Jesus, I don't know what to think. This is a freaking nightmare. He was at each scene. If there was incriminating evidence there, he could have easily cleaned it up when nobody was paying attention. No wonder we didn't find anything worthwhile."

John started the car and backed out of Ricky's driveway. "What I don't understand is, why now? I mean, his sister killed herself two years ago. And Jordan and her squad of cheerleaders weren't even responsible for his sister's death."

"Maybe he knew if he went after the cheerleaders that were responsible, then the trail would lead right back to his doorstep. Maybe that day we all dumped pom-poms on Jordan's desk, something snapped inside him." Adam adjusted the vent to blow more directly on him, as if his thoughts had chilled him. "You know what really makes me sick?"

"What's that?" John asked.

"If you hadn't been sitting in front of the television today watching a channel that probably only a handful of people in the Kansas City area watch, Ricky would still be off our radar and free to continue on his killing spree. If we're right and Ricky is the Butcher, then it was just a matter of dumb luck that we figured it out. That's scary."

"You know what else is scary?" John took a corner so fast Adam slammed his hands against the dashboard.

"Your driving?" he asked dryly.

"McNight's theory was that the killer was destroying what the victims loved before he killed them—Joann's artwork, Betsy's dolls, Tracy's cat. It's like he wanted them to suffer the terrible loss of what they loved before he took their life. What does Jordan love more than anything else?"

"Drive faster, can't you?" Adam replied tersely. "And get on the horn and get some backup to meet us there."

* * *

"Please, Ricky. Let her go," Jordan said fervently. Mandy had begun to silently cry. Tears raced down her cheeks, but she didn't make a sound, and in her silence Jordan knew a grief she'd never known before. "Whatever the issue is, it's with me, not her. For God's sake, let her go."

"There's no God here, just me. Right now I'm God and you're going to do exactly what I tell you to do." There was no hint of stress in his eyes or on his features. He seemed as at ease with the gun against Mandy's temple as he had been having a beer at Iggy's with his coworkers.

There was a place in Jordan's mind that struggled to comprehend the reality of the situation. Ricky? Ricky was the killer they'd been looking for? How was it possible? What had she overlooked? What clues had she not seen? And why? Dear God, why was he doing this?

Her gun was so close, just four steps from where she stood, just beneath the edge of the sofa. But it might as well be a million miles away. She knew that one unexpected or sudden move could result in Mandy's death. There were some risks impossible to take.

Both her heart and her head began galloping races as she recognized the danger they were in. She'd made it clear with Clint and Dane that she wanted to be alone with Mandy this evening, so there wouldn't be an unexpected visit from either of them.

Nobody knew it was Ricky. Nobody would know that there'd been a madman among them all along and that now he was here with her. With Mandy. Oh God, she could take anything he wanted to do to her, but the thought of him hurting Mandy nearly brought her to her knees.

And she'd let him in. She'd opened up her door and invited in the Butcher. She'd welcomed in death.

"Now, we're all going to walk into the kitchen, where you're going to get one of your chairs, Jordan. You know how it goes—you've seen enough of my work. I want the chair in the center of the living room and you planted in it."

Stall. The word swelled in Jordan's head. Stall and see if an opportunity presents itself. There was no question that she would risk her life to save Mandy's. All she needed was an opening.

Mandy was no longer crying. She stood perfectly still with her eyes squeezed closed, and that frightened Jordan more than her tears had done.

"Why? Why, Ricky? I've been working these cases for the last couple of months. Surely I have a right to know why you're doing this," she said. She hoped if she could get him talking, he'd relax his hold on Mandy, and the barrel of the gun would drift away from Mandy's head. Then Jordan could make a move. It was the only thing she could think of doing at the moment.

"Why?" Ricky cocked his head to one side. "Don't you hear her crying? She cries all the time now. She wants vengeance and that's what I deliver for her."

"For who? Who is crying, Ricky?" She took a step sideways, toward the sofa, but he tightened his grip on Mandy, and Jordan froze. Mandy whimpered, and beneath the fear that roared through Jordan, a rage began.

How dare he come into her home and manhandle her daughter? How dare he put terror in Mandy's heart? If she got the chance, she'd kill him for making her baby cry.

"My sister, Elena. She cried a lot, but she wouldn't tell anyone what was making her so sad. We didn't find out until after she was dead. She used a razor blade and sliced her veins and bled to death alone in her bedroom." Ricky's voice grew deeper and Jordan sensed the building rage inside him, a rage she knew when loosened would be the end of her and Mandy. "They tormented her every day for months. They made her life a living hell."

"Who did?" Jordan asked even though she knew the answer.

"The cheerleaders!" he screamed, and Mandy began to cry again, this time deep sobs racking her. "Those bitches made her life hell on earth and you want to know why? Because she was sweet enough to offer a friendly smile to one of their boyfriends. And for that, they crucified her. They made her life so miserable she killed herself. I found her. Blood was everywhere and she was white and still and it was right after that when I started hearing her cries. She's been begging me to do something, to make you all pay, and that's exactly what I've been doing."

How did they all miss this? How had she worked beside him day after day and not seen some hint of the darkness that resided inside him? Somehow, if she was going to get them out of this, she had to tamp down his growing rage and try to connect to the cop inside him who had been on the fast track to success.

The one thing Jordan couldn't do was look in Mandy's eyes. She knew if she saw her daughter's horror, she'd lose her mind. She had to stay focused, had to figure out a way to get them out of this.

"I had a sister, Ricky. She was murdered when I was nineteen. I understand your pain. I know what it's like to lose somebody you love," she said. "Why don't you put your gun down?" Despite her terror, she tried to keep her voice as calm as possible. "Let me help you, Ricky. Let Mandy go and we'll talk, just you and me, and see if we can figure this all out."

For a moment she thought she was getting through to him. He stood perfectly still, as if thinking about her words. Then he smiled and in that chilling expression she knew she'd failed to connect, that he intended to kill them and there was nothing she could say to stop him.

"Let her go!" Jordan screamed as her tenuous control snapped. "She hasn't done anything to you. She's not even a cheerleader. She's just a little girl."

"She's a mean girl in training," Ricky replied. "But she's more than that. She's your artwork, your doll, your favorite pet, and before I punish you for your sins, you're going to watch me punish her." He narrowed his eyes. "Now, let's get that chair and get this party started. If it's any consolation, Jordan, you won't be my last. I'm devoting my life to ridding the world of those girls who think they're above everyone else and do nothing but hurt others."

A million thoughts shot through Jordan's head. Mandy would never have the opportunity to have a first date, to find love and get married and have babies of her own. Clint would never know that she had loved him and wanted to marry him, that the fear that had been holding her back now seemed small and insignificant.

"I don't know what makes you think she's what I love most," Jordan said in a last-ditch effort to save her daughter's life. "Why do you think she doesn't live here with me? It's because I didn't want her here. I force myself to spend time with her when I have to, but I don't love her."

She didn't look at Mandy, hoped and prayed her daughter would understand why she was saying such terrible things. "She'll never be a cheerleader," she continued frantically. "She's too clumsy. She can't move well and she's too stupid to learn any real cheers." Agony ripped through her. "Just let her go. She's nothing to me."

"Touching, but it isn't working," Ricky replied.

Jordan realized she was helpless to stop this and as Mandy began to weep once again, Jordan began to cry as well.

Chapter 31

"Isn't that Ricky's car?" John asked as he drove down the street a block away from Jordan's house.

"Looks like it," Adam replied. John pulled to the curb behind the vehicle. "What are you doing?" Adam asked.

"You stay here and keep an eye out for him. Call for backup, and if he comes back to his car, follow him wherever he goes. I'm going to the house and check things out." He was out of the car before Adam could protest.

One glance into the interior of the car confirmed that it was Ricky's. A package of the Slim Jim sausage sticks that Ricky liked to eat was on the passenger seat along with a New York Yankees ball cap he'd seen Ricky wear occasionally.

As John took off running down the sidewalk, everything felt surreal. He was supposed to be dead now. He'd been cleaning his gun with every intention of using it to shoot himself. If he'd accomplished what he had set out to do before that show had come on, he wouldn't be here now.

Fate had worked to place him here and now and he had no idea what lay ahead, but could only respond to the screaming urgency that drove him. By the time he reached Jordan's house, he was out of breath and had a painful stitch in his side, reminding him that he was no longer twenty years old and was pathetically out of shape.

There was only one reason why Ricky would have parked his car where he had instead of in Jordan's driveway, and that was that he hadn't wanted anyone to know he was there. And there was only one reason why he wouldn't want anyone to know that he was there—he'd come to do something he wasn't supposed to do.

Instead of going to the front door, John ran to the back of the house, hoping to get a glimpse of what might be going on inside through a window. The bedroom windows were dark with curtains, making it impossible for him to see inside.

The kitchen came next and although he could see in, there was nothing to set his heart racing. It was only when he reached a window he could peer into that showed the living room that his heart slammed into his ribs with a force that nearly stole his breath away.

Ricky was there, with Mandy in his arms, a gun held to her head. Jordan stood several feet in front of them, her features twisted in agony. There was no waiting for backup. John knew he needed to get inside now, but he also knew a balls-to-the-wall approach could result in Mandy's instant death.

He went back to one of the bedroom windows, hoping the room was far enough away from the living room that nobody would hear what he was about to do.

When he reached one of the windows, he pulled off the screen, then tried to raise the glass, unsurprised to find it locked. Using the butt of his gun, praying that Ricky didn't hear the noise, he broke the glass just above the window lock, then reached inside and twisted the lock to open the window.

As he slid through the window, he could hear Jordan begging, pleading for her daughter's life. Moving with a stealth John didn't know he possessed, he crept to the door that led into the hallway. If he could get down the hall and through the kitchen without making a sound, then he would be at Ricky's back and could possibly get off a shot before Ricky could hurt the girl.

It was a risk, and once he stepped into the hallway, he second-guessed himself. Maybe he should wait for backup. He wasn't a hero. And what if he made a mistake? What if by his actions he became responsible for Mandy's death?

"Get the chair, Jordan." Ricky's voice drifted down the hallway. "I'm losing patience here."

John knew then that he couldn't wait for backup. He couldn't wait another minute. The rage in Ricky's voice bounced off the walls, and John knew it was just a matter of minutes before it exploded out of control and there would be no chance for him to stop it.

With his gun slick in his sweaty hand, with nerves jangling and bowels clenched, John moved down the hallway. When he reached the kitchen, he had a perfect view of Ricky's back. But he was afraid to take the shot. What if Ricky managed to squeeze off a shot of his own? Mandy would die. The risk was just too high.

He slid his gun back in his holster and realized he had just one chance. He had to physically tackle the man and hope in the melee Mandy would break free. It was the only option he had, he thought as he drew a deep breath and rushed forward.

Someplace in the back of his mind he realized he made a fatal error. He grunted. With that single noise Ricky spun around. John saw several small details—the widening of Ricky's eyes, the slide of Mandy to the floor and the shock on Jordan's face.

The last thing he saw was the flash from the muzzle as Ricky fired. The bullet hit him in the chest with the force of a locomotive and his last conscious thought was that he hadn't had to commit suicide after all.

Everything seemed to happen in slow motion. John appeared from nowhere and Jordan watched in horror as Ricky spun around, releasing his grip on Mandy, who collapsed to the ground.

Ricky fired and in that explosive moment Jordan

knew she had one chance and one chance only to save her daughter, to save herself.

She dived for the sofa, grabbed her gun from beneath it and whirled back around. Jordan had never fired her service revolver off the shooting range, but she didn't hesitate now. She knew she'd get only one shot and she had to make it count. She cried out and pulled the trigger.

The bullet hit him in the chest. Ricky dropped his gun and stared at her in stunned surprise as a red stain began to blossom on his shirt. He took a step backward, then fell to the ground.

Mandy crawled on her hands and knees away from him, sobbing in hysteria as Jordan remained standing with her gun still trained on Ricky. If he twitched, she'd shoot him again . . . and again . . . and again.

The front door burst open and Adam came in, followed by two patrolmen. All of them had their guns drawn. Still Jordan kept her focus on the man on the floor, watching—waiting—for the monster to rise again. As she thought of Mandy's fear, her hand trembled, but she would shoot him again if he so much as twitched.

"Jordan, it's okay," Adam said softly as he approached her. "Lower your weapon, Jordan. We're here now and you're safe." Fear still kept her rigid, afraid to believe that they were okay. "Jordan, for God's sake, your daughter needs you."

These words finally pulled her back to reality. With a sob she dropped her gun and ran to her daughter, who had curled up on the floor. She pulled Mandy up and into her arms on the sofa. Mandy clung to her and hid her face in the hollow of Jordan's throat as Adam called for emergency vehicles to respond to her address.

As the patrolmen stood next to Ricky's body, Adam hurried to John. "He saved our lives," Jordan said as a deep sob welled up inside her. "Is he dead?" Oh God, Jordan had no doubt that if John hadn't done what he had, if he hadn't come in when he had, eventually she and Mandy would have been found dead in the house, more victims of the Butcher.

"There's a pulse, but it's barely there." Adam leaned closer to John. "Hang in there, buddy. We've got help on the way."

Within minutes the ambulance and more officers had arrived. Jordan sat on the sofa with Mandy as John was loaded on a gurney and rushed away. She was still holding tight to Mandy when Benny arrived, looking as haggard as Jordan had ever seen him.

By that time Mandy had fallen asleep in Jordan's arms. It was as if her body had decided that the best way to cope with the stress and trauma she'd just experienced was to drift into oblivion.

Benny sat on the sofa next to her. "You okay?"

"I guess." She stroked Mandy's hair, praying that psychologically Mandy was going to be okay, too.

"I know the timing stinks, but we need to get a statement from you."

At that moment Mandy stirred and raised her head. Sleepy blue eyes gazed up at Jordan and as the drowsiness ebbed, tears began to pool. She yanked her arms from around Jordan's neck and pulled away from her.

"It's okay, honey. We're safe. I'm sorry for everything you've been through." Jordan reached for her, but Mandy batted her away.

"Don't touch me," she cried. "I hate you. I want my dad. I don't want to be with you."

Jordan remembered the horrible things she'd said to Ricky in an effort to get him to let Mandy go. "Mandy, honey, you know I didn't mean any of that stuff I said about you. I just wanted to keep you safe and I thought by saying those things he might let you go."

"I don't care. I don't care about you and I don't want to love you." She curled up and began to sob once again. Jordan tried to reach for her again, but Mandy slapped at her and cried harder.

"You want me to call Dane?" Benny asked softly.

"Please." Jordan didn't take her gaze off her daughter as Benny got up and left them so he could make the call. "Mandy, I know you're upset, but don't shut me out. I love you, Mandy, and everything is going to be okay now."

"Don't talk to me. I don't want to see you anymore. I've just been coming over here and spending time with you because Dad made me. I just want you to leave me alone."

Ricky Copeland couldn't have delivered more killing blows with his knife than these words from her daughter. She tried to tell herself it was just the heat of the moment, the emotional aftermath of what they'd just been through, but what she feared most of all was that finally her daughter had told her what she really felt—and that was that she hated her mother.

Chapter 32

It was almost six in the morning when everything began to wind down. Mandy had been taken away by Dane, John was in the hospital undergoing surgery, Ricky's body had been bagged and tagged and Jordan had told her story of what had happened at least a dozen times.

Anthony sat at the kitchen table with Jordan as the last of the officers said their good-byes. "You going to be okay?" he asked.

She offered him a tired smile. "You know me. I'm a tough broad."

Anthony shook his head. "I still can't believe it was one of our own. I don't understand how we all missed it."

"We missed it because we had no reason to suspect Ricky, because he was smart and didn't make any mistakes. He was supposed to be one of the good guys. If his mother hadn't decided to do that talk show that John saw, then we still wouldn't know it was him, and Mandy and I would be dead."

Adam had explained how they'd come to be at her house, how John had become convinced that Ricky was guilty. It was only because nobody could get hold of her that Adam and John had been ordered to check on her. It was only because John had been sitting in front of his television that he'd suspected Ricky in the first place.

A series of good-luck strokes was all that had saved

her and Mandy. Not good police work, not terrific investigative skills, just plain old luck. Sometimes that's all it came down to, she thought.

Mandy.

Jordan couldn't go there. She couldn't think about how her daughter had run to her father's arms and left without a backward glance or a single word to Jordan. If she thought about it, she would lose it altogether.

"The guys who checked out Ricky's place said he had a regular war room in one of the bedrooms," Anthony said. "Pictures of his sister on one wall and pictures of the women he'd killed on the other."

Jordan nodded. "I heard. Seems he had a picture of me already on the board next to Joann, Betsy and Tracy."

"Adam was going back to headquarters to check into the original incident with Ricky's sister. He was curious to see if anything was done to the squad of cheerleaders who tormented Ricky's sister."

"They probably got a reprimand from the school, maybe got kicked off the squad, but I'm not sure we have any laws in place that would warrant a criminal action against them," Jordan replied. "All I know is that his sister's death put Ricky on a mission. If we hadn't caught him when we did, there would have been a lot of dead women in this city."

"What are you going to do now? You've got to be exhausted."

"I am, but I don't feel like sleeping here." She offered him a small smile. "To be honest, I don't want to be alone."

"I could hang out if you wanted to take a nap," Anthony offered.

She smiled at him again, overwhelmingly grateful for his friendship and support. "Thanks, but I'm sure you're exhausted, too."

He leaned back from the table and stretched with his arms overhead. "I am, but I'm also too wired to sleep. I'm thinking of heading back to headquarters and maybe looking up Ashley and seeing if maybe she wants to catch a movie with me tonight. It's funny; whenever we get to the end of one of these cases, I realize how precious time is and how stupid we are to waste a minute of it."

At that moment the phone rang. Jordan got up from the table to answer. It was Dane telling her that Mandy was insisting she come over, that they needed to talk.

"That was Dane," she said to Anthony as she hung up. "Mandy wants to talk to me."

"Is she going to be all right? I heard she was pretty upset when Dane picked her up."

"She was." Jordan's heart pierced with pain. "But she's strong, and we'll make sure she's okay."

Anthony got up from the table. "I'll get out of here. I'm sure you're eager to get over there and talk to her."

Jordan walked with him to the front door and on impulse gave him a big hug. "Thank you, Anthony."

"For what?"

"For being my partner. For being my friend."

His cheeks grew ruddy. "Yeah, it's a tough job, but somebody had to do it."

She laughed and shoved him toward the door. "Get out of here and good luck with Ashley."

The minute he was gone, she grabbed her coat and purse and left the house. The sun broke over the horizon as she drove to Dane's place, and she tried to find promise in its fiery glow.

She'd like to believe that Mandy wanted to see her to apologize for what she'd said, but she feared Mandy intended to tell her again that she didn't want to spend time with her anymore, that she didn't want to see her anymore.

By the time she pulled into Dane's driveway, she thought she had prepared herself for anything to come. Whatever Mandy needed from her she would give, even if that meant staying away from her for a while. The thought broke her heart, but she would do whatever made Mandy happy.

Dane answered her knock, looking as tired as Jordan felt. "Come in," he said, and to her surprise he pulled her into a tight embrace. There was nothing romantic about the hug, nothing that stirred her on a physical level. It was simply a hug from an old friend.

"I'm so glad you're safe," he said as he released her.

"Ah, you're just grateful to have such a valuable source for your book alive and well," she replied with a forced lightness.

He grinned. "You know me so well."

"Dane, if I'd had any idea that I was in danger, that I was putting Mandy in danger, I never would have had her at my house," she exclaimed. "When Tracy was killed, I thought I was off his radar, that the danger to me was minimal."

"Don't you think I know that? Don't you think Mandy knows that?"

"How's she doing?"

"Surprisingly okay after what she's been through. Once I got her here, we talked for a long time about what happened. She napped for a couple of hours, then woke up and insisted I call you." He smiled. "Don't look so afraid, Jordan. Trust me, you'll want to hear what she has to tell you."

"Is she up in her room?"

He nodded. "Go on, she's waiting for you."

Jordan climbed the stairs with a faint feeling of dread. On the one hand she was grateful that Mandy had asked to see her. On the other hand she was worried about why her daughter had insisted she come over. Dane had told Jordan not to be afraid, but that was easy for him to say. He had nothing to lose.

Mandy was in bed, her back to Jordan as she entered the room. "Hey, girlfriend," Jordan said softly.

Mandy turned over, sat up and opened her arms as she burst into tears. "Mommy," she cried.

Jordan rushed to the bed and embraced Mandy. They clung to each other, both of them crying for several long minutes. "I'm sorry, honey. I'm so sorry," Jordan said over and over again.

Mandy finally stopped weeping and pulled out of her arms. "I'm sorry, Mom. I didn't mean what I said to you." She swiped at her eyes and released a trembling breath and stared down at the bed. "In my heart I want to be with you all the time. I want to live with you instead of here, but I don't want to feel that way. I don't want to love you."

Jordan stared at her daughter in confusion. "Is this because of what happened last night?"

Mandy shook her head. "Not really. I felt this way before last night. I don't want to love you, Mom. It scares me."

"But why?" Jordan asked, her heart breaking all over again.

Mandy looked at her, her blue eyes filled with torment. "Because you're a policeman. Because policemen get hurt or die all the time. I see it on the news and on TV shows. I hate what you do and it makes me afraid to love you."

Jordan frowned at her daughter. Was this what it was all about? Mandy hated her job?

"Oh, honey, my job isn't any more dangerous than anybody else's. I'm well trained to do what I do, and my job is really important. People depend on me." Jordan pulled Mandy back into her arms. "Mandy, honey, life is full of risks, but I'm trained to deal with the kinds of risks I face as a police officer. You probably don't know this, but a lot of my job is sitting at my desk and filling out reports."

"Really?" Mandy looked up at her and there was hope in her eyes along with a need to believe.

"Really. You have to talk to me, Mandy. You have to tell me when you're afraid. I can't fix it if I don't know what you're feeling."

Mandy snuggled closer to Jordan. She wrapped her slim arms tightly around Jordan's neck. "I love you, Mom, and I want to live with you. I already talked to Dad about it and he said it would be okay if that's what makes me happy."

Jordan felt as if her heart were going to explode with happiness. "Why didn't you tell me this before? Why didn't you tell me this when your dad and I first got divorced? We could have talked about your fear. I could have made you understand that I'm good at what I do and I don't take unnecessary chances."

"I was afraid maybe you'd love your work more than you loved me," Mandy said. "But last night you tried everything to save me and then I knew how much you loved me."

"Baby, I love you more than anything else on the face of this earth," Jordan replied.

Mandy yawned. "That's cool, Mom, but could you please not call me baby?"

Jordan laughed. "That's a deal," she replied.

Mandy lay back on the bed. "I think I need to sleep some more now," she said drowsily.

Jordan kissed Mandy on the cheek. "We'll talk more about everything after you've slept. Call me later, okay?"

Mandy nodded and closed her eyes and almost immediately fell asleep. For a long moment Jordan stood in her doorway, watching the rise and fall of her chest, remembering how close she'd come to losing her.

It wouldn't be long and she'd be able to kiss Mandy every night before she went to bed. If anything good had come out of last night's horror, it had been this.

Dane was waiting at the bottom of the stairs for Jordan. "You know what we talked about?" she asked.

"Yeah, she told me. From the minute Mandy decided to live with me, I knew I just had her on loan, that eventually she'd want to be with you. Girls her age need their mothers. I'm assuming I'd get liberal visitation."

"You know I'd never keep her from you."

He smiled. "We might make each other a little crazy, but we always do the right thing when it comes to Mandy. So, what are you doing now? Do you have to go back to work?"

"My immediate plan is to sleep for about forty-eight hours. There's nothing like fighting off a homicidal maniac to exhaust you."

"You know that eventually I'm going to want to interview you about what happened."

Jordan laughed. "It's nice to know some things don't change."

Dane shrugged with a rueful grin. "I am what I am and I've never pretended to be anything else." He walked with her to the door. "Go home, get some sleep and then we'll talk about how to make the transition with Mandy."

Once Jordan was back in her car, she called the hospital to check on John. She was told he was out of surgery and in critical but stable condition. Dane had told her to go home and get some sleep, but as she backed out of the driveway, she knew exactly where she wanted to be and it wasn't her rental house.

It had been fear that had kept Mandy from being with Jordan, the same kind of fear that had kept Jordan from being with Clint. Allison had told Jordan that fear was good, that it was what kept people safe. But that same fear was terrible when it kept love from your life, from your heart.

Somehow in the night that had passed, Jordan had realized that if death wanted you, he would find you, that it was probable that the man who had murdered Julie would have accomplished the horrendous act no matter what Jordan had done.

What had happened to Julie hadn't been Jordan's fault, just like what had happened to Joann, Betsy and Tracy hadn't been her fault. Bad people existed and there would forever be grief and despair for the crimes they committed.

She couldn't fix her relationship with her parents. They were mired in a place of misery and had even become comfortable there. But if Jordan continued to keep Clint at arm's length, if she refused to allow him into her heart, then she was no better than her parents.

She pulled into Clint's driveway and her heart soared. He answered her knock clad in his robe and with the scent of shaving cream clinging to him. "Jordan," he said in surprise as he opened the door to let her in. "What are you doing here so early? Not that I'm complaining," he quickly added.

It was obvious by his words that he had no idea what had happened the night before. He probably hadn't turned on his television yet and so didn't know what she'd been through.

"I've kind of had a rough night and I just wanted to escape from the world and this was the place I wanted to be." She gazed at him, so handsome and strong, so sure of who he was and what he wanted from life. "You're my favorite place to come when I'm sick and tired or when I want to celebrate or when I just need to be held. Some people look for a lifetime for somebody who will make them feel the way you make me feel—so loved, so safe."

"You're really making me nervous because you're either telling me you love me or you're giving me one of the best kiss-offs I've ever heard."

"This definitely isn't a kiss-off," she said as she moved into his arms. "I love you, Clint. I love you and I want to be your wife. I want to spend the rest of my life with you. I want you and Mandy to be my family."

Before she could get another word out, his mouth claimed hers in a kiss that held the heat of desire coupled with an aching tenderness and the promise of love forever. And in the back of her mind she could almost hear her sister whisper, "Way to go, Sis."

Epilogue

It was the week after Christmas, the best Christmas that Jordan had ever had in her life. Over the holidays both Mandy and Jordan had moved in with Clint, and with each day Jordan's love for him grew stronger, brighter. Their wedding was planned for the middle of January, and Jordan couldn't wait to make things official.

Ricky was in jail, waiting for his trial, and it was rumored that his defense attorney was looking for an insanity plea.

But more important, today was the day John was finally being released from the hospital and Jordan had wanted to be here. She now clung to Clint's hand as they walked down the long hospital corridor to John's room.

She'd wanted to come every day to see him, but he'd requested no visitors and she had respected his wishes. This morning when she'd called, he'd answered his phone and said he'd love for her to come and see him before he left.

A batch of cookies from Mandy and a silk tie from Jordan seemed minuscule gifts for the man who had saved their lives, but Jordan knew nothing she could buy could repay John for his bravery.

John was sitting on the edge of his hospital bed when they walked in. He had lost weight, looked a little pale, but offered them a warm smile. "John," Jordan said, and walked over to kiss him on the cheek as Clint hung back by the door. “I’m so happy to see you doing okay. Mandy sent you some cookies and I bought you one of those ties you like.”

“You shouldn’t have done that,” he protested.

“We owe you so much more than that,” Jordan replied.

“You don’t owe me anything. I was just doing my job,” he replied. “Mandy, she’s doing okay?”

Jordan nodded. “She’s fine. She’s moved in with me and we’ve both moved in with Clint. She’s spending today with Dane.”

“Yeah, all it took was a near-death experience for Jordan to realize she loved me,” Clint replied dryly.

John smiled. “Funny thing about those near-death experiences.” His smile faded. He turned his gaze out the nearby window. “I was cleaning my gun, getting it ready to use on myself, when I saw that talk show on television.” He turned back to look at Jordan.

Jordan gasped in stunned surprise. “Oh, John,” she said softly, and sat next to him on the bed.

“I missed Mary so much. I just wanted to be with her and when Ricky’s bullet hit me, my last thought was that he’d done the job for me. You know, it’s true what they say about that white light. I saw it and I was going for it. It was like a doorway and I knew that if I could just get through it, Mary was waiting for me on the other side. I started running, but when I got there, before I could step through, Mary appeared in the door.”

He stood from the bed and shook his head. “She told me to go back, that I still had work to do. She told me she loved me, but she was disappointed in me, that I would honor her memory by living. I regained consciousness and realized what I had to do.”

“And what are you going to do?” Jordan asked.

Again John smiled. “The first thing I’m doing is taking a two-week vacation. I’m heading to Tahiti and renting one of those beachfront grass shacks that Mary and I once talked about. I’m going to walk in the sand and eat fresh coconuts, and as I finish recuperating, I'll remember all the good times I shared with my wife. She'll be with me in Tahiti, in that shack we always talked about sharing. She'll be with me in my heart. Then, when I'm ready, I'll come back to work and do what I'm supposed to do—catch bad guys and drink flat beer at Iggy's."

Jordan's eyes misted with tears. "You're really going to be all right, John?"

He nodded. "For the first time since Mary got sick, I'm really going to be fine."

Minutes later, as Clint and Jordan walked out of the hospital and into the cold late-December air, she clung tight to his hand. "It's sad, isn't it? When people we love die and we're left to carry on without them," she said.

"It is sad," he agreed, "but it's also part of life. The important thing is to grab on to all the happiness you can and to build all the good memories possible."

She smiled at him. "On that note, maybe now's a good time to tell you I'm not wearing any underwear." The look on Clint's face was priceless.

"Quick, get in the car. Just a warning, I intend to break the speed limit to get you home and start making those memories."

She laughed, her love for him buoying up inside her. "In that case, why wait until we get home?"

Read on for an exciting
excerpt from Carla Cassidy's

Last Gasp

Available now from Signet Eclipse

The minute Allison and Sam stepped out on the porch to leave the old farmhouse and return home, she saw it—the ominous rolling black wall of a dust storm. It filled the sky in the distance, like dark billowing smoke driven by a tremendous force beyond the horizon. Allison had seen the natural phenomenon only once before in her life, and that had been on that terrible day fifteen years ago.

"Wow!" Sam exclaimed. "Awesome."

She touched her son's shoulder. "Come on, let's get back inside. We'll have to wait it out inside," she said. The last thing she wanted was for the two of them to be in the car when the storm struck.

They moved off the porch and back into the house, where Sam ran to the window with a southwest view. "It's getting closer," he said, a hint of fear deepening his voice. What had initially appeared awesome to the twelve-year-old obviously no longer seemed so awesome.

Allison moved to stand behind him and placed her hands on his slender shoulders. "I know it looks kind of scary, but it's just wind and dust."

She stared beyond Sam to the approaching maelstrom and, almost hypnotized by the boiling, swirling sight, went back in time, back to when she'd been sixteen years old and on her way home from school.

It had been Ellie Gordon who had seen it first. She'd

squealed in horror as she stared out the window, but nobody paid much attention to her because Ellie squealed about something all the time.

It was only when Jennifer Landers, Ellie's seatmate on the bus, had screamed as well that everyone looked out the window and saw the boiling brown mass descending upon them.

Chaos ensued. The girls screamed and the boys darted from window to window as the bus driver, Mrs. Johnson, yelled for all of them to calm down, to sit down. As the dark cloud approached, the bus began to rock from the force of the wind and the sky darkened, turning the sunny day into night.

Mrs. Johnson pulled the vehicle off the road and parked as the brunt of the storm hit them. Tumbleweeds and other debris struck the side of the bus as the wind screeched like a banshee.

"It's the end of the world," Ellie screamed, tears coursing down her face. "God's wrath is coming down on us all. Oh, sweet Jesus, forgive me for my sins and deliver me from evil."

"Shut up, Ellie," one of the boys shouted.

"Yeah, it's just a dust storm," somebody else added.

Mary Layton, one of Allison's best friends, who was seated next to Allison on the bus, laughed and grabbed Allison's hand. "Everyone knows the last time Ellie prayed was when she thought she was pregnant and prayed for a period."

Allison laughed, too, but she squeezed tight to Mary's hand until the storm passed and the sun once again began to shine.

"Show's over," the bus driver said, and started the engine to finish delivering the students to their bus stops.

There was one stop where Ellie got off; then it was time for Allison's stop. She climbed off the bus and waved to her classmates and noticed that the black cloud of dirt had moved northward.

The first thing she was going to do when she got inside was take a shower. Even though the bus windows had been up, the dust had seeped in through the minute cracks and crevices of the bus and swirled in the air. She felt grimy with it. She smiled as she thought of her little sister and brother in the house with her mom.

She'd bet her mother had spun a story to ease the fears of the two young kids, and the way she knew her mother, it would have been a story about a princess saved from the evil dust monster by a handsome prince. If there was one thing Joleen Donovan loved, it was telling fairy tales where dragons were slain and princesses and princes lived happily ever after.

The porch was covered with a layer of dirt as she climbed the stairs to the front door. She couldn't wait to get inside and tell her mom she'd aced her English test, that Bobby had asked her to go to the prom and that silly Ellie had thought the dust storm was the end of the world.

She'd had no warning of what was to come, no sense of foreboding about the horror that awaited her.

"Mom?" she called as she flung open the door. She took three steps into the room and saw her mother seated on the sofa. Joleen wore her favorite pink-flowered duster and was sitting where she always sat to watch *General Hospital.*

Her head. For a moment Allison couldn't make sense of it. Joleen's head wasn't where it belonged. Rather than being on her neck, on her shoulders, it was in her lap. It was only then that Allison smelled it, the rich copper scent of blood, the raw, ugly scent of death. She opened her mouth to scream, but never released a sound of her horror as she was struck over the head from behind and knew no more.

"Mom! You're hurting me!"

She slammed back to the present with Sam wiggling to escape the biting imprints of her fingernails in the tops of his shoulders. She dropped her hands and backed away from the window. "I'm sorry, honey. Move back. I don't want you standing in front of the glass."

She tasted the tangy flavor of blood and realized she'd bitten the inside of her mouth as she'd remembered that day. What had happened to Mary Layton? Funny. Allison had never seen her again after that day on the bus when they'd held hands and laughed, not knowing the nightmare that Allison would face.

The storm now fell upon the little farmhouse. The room darkened and the house began to creak and groan beneath the onslaught of the wind. A thud sounded against the outside wall. "What was that?" Sam asked, his eyes wide, as they stood in the center of the living room area.

Probably a poor bird, disoriented from the storm, she thought, but she didn't speak the thought aloud. Sam was so softhearted he'd want to go outside and see if the bird could be saved. "Just trash or something picked up by the wind," she replied.

"How long will this last?" Sam asked, and shot a worried glance back toward the window, where it was almost as dark as night.

"Not long." At least that's what she hoped.

"Will we be safe here?" His forehead furrowed with little lines of worry.

She offered him a reassuring smile. "We should be fine. This old place might look a mess, but it was built strong. Why don't you show me some of those karate moves of yours?" she asked. "You have all this space." She gestured around the empty room and then forced a smile. "And you have me as a captive audience."

She needed something, anything, to take her mind off the dust storm. The memories it evoked in her tried to take hold of her once again, to pull her back to that day when her entire world had exploded apart, when a killer had beaten her home and taken from her everything that she loved.

As Sam began his first series of movements, her head was filled with the vision of her mother's milky blue eyes, of that single moment when she'd tried to make sense of what had happened. In a single instant just before she'd been struck unconscious, she'd seen blood everywhere, as if a crazed painter had tried to turn the room red. This room, right where she and Sam stood. Her mother had been murdered here, along with her little brother and sister.

And she should have died as well. The killer had meant for her to die.

She smiled and nodded at her son as her mind filled with the horror, and the wind shrieked around the farmhouse like a loosed wild beast. It will be over in a minute, she thought. The storm will pass and we'll go back to our house, back to our lives, and we won't ever come here again.

"That's great, Sam," she said as he finished up a series of moves. She glanced toward the window, where there was no change in the darkness of the sky. How long could it last? She already felt as if she'd been trapped in this house of death for an eternity.

She and Sam both jumped as the front door flew open and a swirl of thick dust entered like an unwelcomed guest. Allison took two steps toward the door to close it when he appeared in the doorway, a man in jeans and a T-shirt and wearing a ski mask. In his hands he held a hatchet.

For a moment, she thought he was a horrifying phantom from her past, a specter of evil conjured up from her imagination. But as he took a step forward, his boots rang on the wooden floor, and as Sam gasped and ran to her side, she knew he wasn't from her imagination.

He was real.

He was death.

She'd escaped him fifteen years ago and now he was back to claim her.

NATIONAL BESTSELLING AUTHOR

CARLA CASSIDY

Two years ago, Vanessa Abott's husband Jim, an up-and-coming artist, drowned himself in the Missouri River. His body still hasn't been recovered. Now Vanessa has arranged for one last showing of his work. Critics are raving and pieces are selling. She even meets an interesting man.

Then the gallery owner is found dead with a splash of red paint across his body. Vanessa recognizes it as Jim's signature mark. And in her home, Jim's picture somehow finds its way back onto the dresser. Is she going crazy? Or has her husband come back...for her?

Praise for Carla Cassidy:

"An easy, masterful balance that's rare and ambitious for a suspense novel." —*Publishers Weekly*

Be sure to visit the author's website at
carlacassidybooks.com

Available wherever books are sold or at penguin.com

EVERY MOVE
YOU MAKE
Carla Cassidy

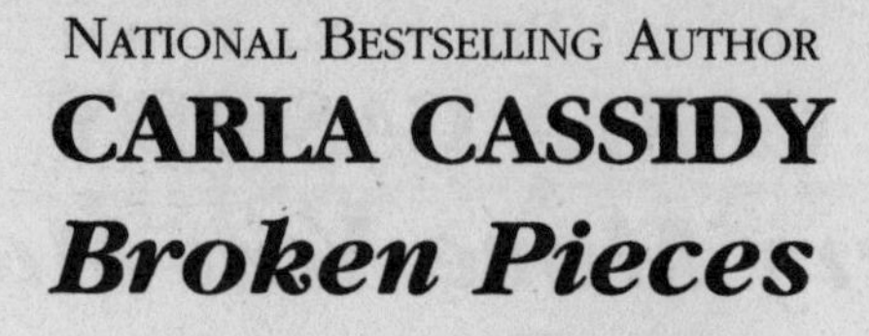

NATIONAL BESTSELLING AUTHOR

CARLA CASSIDY

Broken Pieces

Mariah Sayers survived a brutal attack as a teenager, and ran away out of fear. Sixteen years later she returns with her daughter to make peace with her past. Just as she feels she is rekindling old friendships, she receives some shocking news; a girl has been killed in her town. Now, Mariah will have to confront the unthinkable—and reclaim the broken pieces of her shattered past.

Available wherever books are sold or at penguin.com

NATIONAL BESTSELLING AUTHOR

CARLA CASSIDY

LAST GASP

Ever since she found her mother and siblings murdered, Allison Clemmins has hated her father, Hank, who is imprisoned for the crimes. Then Seth Walker arrives in town, a lawyer determined to exonerate Hank, to unearth the secrets that should have been revealed long ago. He also offers Allison the one thing missing from her life—the ability to trust a man.

But as fate finds them in each other's arms, a psychotic killer—either the original or a copycat—makes himself known...

Available wherever books are sold or at penguin.com